ARROW
—IN—
PARADISE

A NOVEL BY
ROB SORENSEN

Halo
PUBLISHING
INTERNATIONAL

ISBN: 978-1-61244-706-3
Library of Congress Control Number: 2019902046

Printed in the United States of America

Halo Publishing International
1100 NW Loop 410
Suite 700 - 176
San Antonio, Texas 78213
1-877-705-9647
www.halopublishing.com
contact@halopublishing.com

DISCLAIMER

This is a work of fiction. The setting in Yaak, Montana, is real but some landmarks and scene settings have been altered to enhance the narrative. All characters are imaginary and any resemblance to a real person is completely coincidental.

For Alexis.
My muse. My gift. My treasure.

ACKNOWLEDGMENTS

Without the feedback from and inspiration of many, this book would not have been possible. My grateful thanks to the following individuals for their contributions and assistance: Glenna Campbell, Dr. Robert Bond, Bob Lovell, Jack Estes, David Smith, Bobbie Jean Krieder, Dr. Roger Oakes, Dr. Joshua Herbeck, and siblings Drs. Travis and Staci Sorensen. A special thank you to the cover designer Kelsey Redlin.

This group (all of whom are voracious readers and fearless critics!) provided both suggestions and much-needed encouragement, and I cannot thank them enough for their support.

It goes without saying that my wife, Alexis, was my rock throughout the process. Her relentless belief in *Arrow in Paradise* was the force that carried the novel through the highs and lows of the writing process. There are no words to define her contributions.

CONTENTS

INTRODUCTION

In the autumn of 1998, the following article ran in the popular magazine "Our America." The story revealed to the world an undiscovered corner of northwest Montana that had long been considered the most remote area in the continental United States. This was the perfect location to sever ties with civilization and live a simpler life.

AN ESCAPE TO PARADISE

By Anthony Russo

For free spirits seeking a simpler life, Yaak, Montana is the holy grail.

Located in the most remote corner of the state, nestled in the Kootenai National Forest, is the country's ultimate escape destination. The two million-acre national forest is an anomaly in the modern world—a vast wilderness where only five percent of the land is available for private ownership.

How remote is this national treasure? Its northern boundary touches the Canadian border, and the valley is one-hundred fifty miles from the nearest commercial airport, three hours from the nearest freeway, and forty-five miles from the closest town.

The town of Yaak consists of four buildings, The Dirty Shame Saloon, The Yaak Mercantile, and a laundromat with three washing machines, two dryers, and one shower. Rounding out the foursome is an empty log cabin waiting for a new tenant.

The Dirty Shame Saloon is an iconic biker bar: a "must" for dive-bar lovers. Dark and cozy, its patrons sip beer, seated at the battered bar with their dogs curled up underfoot. There are bullet holes in the wall and motorcycle skid marks on the floor.

Bartender Jeremy Barnett remembers the Saturday one year ago when both a Harley Davidson and a horse made separate appearances on the dance floor on the same day. A candidate for the best bar name ever, it is said to have been christened "The Dirty Shame" by unhappy housewives in the 1950s when the bar's construction preceded that of the general store.

So remote is the area that residents claim D.B. Cooper, Jimmy Hoffa, and Ted Kaczynski have all been spotted in the saloon: big talk from locals who will go to any length to discourage visitors from overstaying their welcome in the valley.

Today, there are less than 50 families living in the Yaak. The local school is a two-room log cabin with students from first to eighth grade.

According to Jerry Henderson, a restaurant manager in Libby, Montana, and a regular at the Shame, "Only hippies and movie stars live in the Yaak."

Henderson's pony-tailed drinking partner—who preferred to remain anonymous—retorts that "The truth is the only movie stars in the valley own a 320-acre ranch north of town. A guy named John McIntyre was in a T.V. show called Wagon Train and his wife starred in a few movies in the '70s."

The McIntyre's came to the valley to escape the big city and live a quieter life—the same reason that Flower Children and other free-spirits were drawn to the valley.

There is a trade-off for the laidback lifestyle, however. Snowy winters and icy roads. Short summers. Lack of amenities. Power outages. Road closures. Wildlife so prevalent that residents refer to the whitetail deer population as "hooved rodents." In accordance with nature's food chain, with the deer come predators. Grizzly bears and mountain lions share the territory.

Most folks in the Yaak cope with these inconveniences the old-fashioned way. They live in log houses, cut their own firewood, hunt, fish, and tend gardens to help feed their families.

The local economy is a paradox—there are few jobs, but residents resist any effort to encourage growth or modernization. Every attempt for progressive action is contested, but most of these battles are lost. And with every defeat, a small piece of the character of the Yaak disappears.

"Yaakers are unique," says Stewart Chance, a long-time resident shopping at the mercantile. "We got lots of folks living up here with no electricity or indoor plumbing. You do whatever it takes."

For those who come to visit or to stay, the Yaak is unlike any other place in the continental United States. It is undiscovered, untamed, and unpredictable.

"This place isn't for everyone, and that's what makes it so special," says the self-proclaimed mayor of the Yaak, Lars Thorsen. "We get left alone. We got lots of animals, trees, and rivers. No Walmart. No MacDonald's. Nobody I know wants to live anywhere else."

***

Today, twenty short years later, the flower children of the twentieth century are grandparents, the once-gravel Yaak River Road is paved the full length of the valley and the Dirty Shame Saloon no longer allows dogs. The only movie star is a longtime resident featured in a popular History Channel reality show that now shares the Yaak's once coveted anonymity with over six million viewers each week.

On the surface, the "most remote valley in the lower forty-eight" has been overwhelmed by technological advances.

Despite the relentless progress of the cyber society and the valley's unprecedented exposure to the outside world, the soul of the land remains the same—remote, wild, and lawless. A mysterious wonder of nature where everything changes. . . and everything stays the same.

OREGON

CHAPTER

The graveyard lay still in the damp ocean air, and Clayton Cooper almost missed the entrance.

A metal farm gate, long since rendered useless by coastal winds and a jungle of ferns, devil's clubs and waist-high salal, was trapped open behind the dense vegetation.

Cooper drove through the opening and parked at the back edge of the grounds where he had a clear view of the road bordering the cemetery. Turning off the headlights, he waited for his eyes to adjust to the darkness before surveying his surroundings.

Light from a three-quarter moon filtered through the mist, lighting up an assortment of plastic flowers and broken dream catchers that were strewn about the jumble of graves. Wooden crosses, weather-beaten into twisted gray relics, were scattered about in disarray.

Unlike the set-back entrance, the exterior base of the wire fencing perimeter had been mowed by road crews, but the effect of that maintenance created more of a "prison yard" ambiance than open space. But it was remote. And safe.

A half-hour later, the dank coastal air began to smother the tiny graveyard, and Cooper lowered his window to get some fresh air. Studying the night-sky, he saw a flash of headlights bounce off the low-lying clouds and immediately knew that someone was descending the hill that led to the beachside graveyard.

The flashes grew closer as Cooper tracked the light's progress, hoping that the car would hurry past the cemetery on its way to one of the beach houses along the dead-end road. When the headlights went dark just before reaching the burial site, he swore softly and focused all his attention on the bend in the road just before the burial plot.

Ninety seconds later, a county sheriff's car, with its headlights off, eased out of the mist and crawled alongside the chain-link fence separating the road from the cemetery.

***

Driving down the hill to Gamble Bay, Deputy Clarence Bigelow felt a surge of adrenaline. The cemetery was located on a parcel of Oregon shoreline surrounded by private beach cabins and summer homes. Per a treaty concession ceded to the local Native Americans a century earlier, it was an island of sacred ground owned and operated by the Wapiti tribe, and because it was the only piece of tribal property on this side of the river, it was policed by the Wapiti County Sheriff's Department. The graveyard's separation from the reservation had long been a source of conflict, and the tribe had long neglected it. Only the most traditional Wapiti families still buried their dead there.

Six miles from the town of Skyler, the cemetery occasionally drew privacy-seeking parkers—mostly under-aged drinkers or teenage lovers. It was the first Friday of the new school year and Bigelow thought the isolated parking spot might liven up the remainder of his shift.

Rounding the corner in his darkened cruiser, he slowly drove past the graveyard. Near the back of the grounds, he spotted the outline of a vehicle, noting that the driver had taken care to back into a spot where dark shadows almost concealed his rig from the road.

"Nice try, sucker," he whispered.

Just past the fenced enclosure, he turned into a pull-off behind a clump of windblown spruce trees. Flashlight in hand, he began silently stalking toward the cemetery, a practice he had perfected through the years.

When he had almost reached the open entrance, an engine rumbled to life in the shadows, and a sports utility vehicle, with its headlights off, fish-tailed through the open gate, speeding up the road that Bigelow had just descended.

Stumbling back to his cruiser, Bigelow squeezed behind the wheel, spun a tight U-turn, and raced off in pursuit of the now invisible SUV. Roof lights flashing, it was almost two miles before he spotted the flare of taillights headed back toward town.

The deputy closed the gap between the two cars, and after pulling the driver over, he took his time getting to the vehicle, watching it flicker in the pulsing red and blue strobe of the cruiser's lights and imagining the driver's heart beating in a similar frenetic rhythm.

At the SUV he looked into the open window and was surprised to see that the driver was no frightened adolescent. Well past his teens, he was a grown man, Bigelow guessed in his late twenties, with dark spiky hair, a trendy three-day growth of stubble and an air of confidence seldom present in his usual teenage offenders.

Before Bigelow could speak, the driver said, "Is there a problem, Officer?"

"Yeah. . . there's a problem all right." Shining his flashlight across the front seats of the Ford Explorer, he looked for the driver's date before realizing that the man was alone.

"Can I see your driver's license, please?"

Handing over an Oregon state driver's license, the man remained silent as Bigelow studied the card. When the deputy read the driver's name, he thought it looked familiar. Checking the birth-date, he noted that the man was at least ten years older than he had guessed.

"So, Mr. Cooper. What were you doing at the graveyard this time of the night?"

"Nothing. I was just looking for a quiet spot to do some thinking. When I can't sleep, I go for long drives around the area. I just happened to end up at the beach."

"Uh huh. And when you take these long drives do you always try to sneak away from the law?"

"Sneak away? I didn't try to get away from anyone. I had no idea you were there."

"Yeah, right. Have you been drinking tonight, Mr. Cooper?"

"I had two beers at the coach's party after tonight's football game. . . hours ago. I'm a coach at the high school." Cooper's answer sparked the deputy's memory.

"I know who you are," he said, as if he had known all along, "I think my niece played softball for you a few years ago."

"Really? What's her name?"

After a pause, Bigelow said, "Let's put that on hold for a while, shall we? We can chit-chat after we resolve our little situation here."

"What do you mean? There is no 'situation' here. There's no law against driving around at night. . . or even parking for that matter."

"That's true, Mr. Cooper. It makes me wonder why you left the cemetery in such a big hurry. And, just so you know, there IS a law against trying to evade a police officer."

"I didn't try to evade you," Cooper said. "I had no idea anyone was out there. It was just a coincidence that I left when you arrived."

Rolling his eyes, Bigelow said. "Can you step out of the car, please?"

When he got out of the car, the ocean mist had turned to light rain. Cooper felt the wet chill of the coastal air in his bones, and his knees began to shake.

Bigelow paid no attention to him, intent on checking out the vehicle. Shining his flashlight into the interior, he slid the beam over the vacant passenger's seat, then moved on to the floorboards, probing for the usual six-pack of beer or half-full bottle of cheap whiskey. Coming up empty, he turned the light to the back seat.

On the floor behind the front passenger seat was an odd-shaped pile wedged between the back of the seat and the front edge of the rear passenger bench. It was covered with a faded plaid blanket and to the deputy appeared to be soccer gear and a stack of cone-shaped road pylons that soccer coaches often use as markers during agility drills.

When Bigelow's light stopped on the irregular shape, Cooper quit breathing. He used the suspended moment to say a silent prayer until the flashlight beam moved to the back, where it rested on a collection of more soccer equipment, including two bags of balls, a Skyler Lady Eagles gym bag, and a box of dirty scrimmage vests.

The deputy stayed at the window. Suddenly he swung the light back to the blanket behind the passenger seat.

"What's under the blanket, Mr. Cooper?"

"Nothing. Nothing at all, really. It's just more soccer stuff. You know, cones, nets, things like that. . . nothing really."

"That's good. If it's nothing, then you won't mind if I take a look, will you? Force of habit, you know? Lots of people stash their unmentionables under blankets or tarps. We can just clear the air real quick-like. You don't mind, do you?"

Cooper was silent. When he did answer, his voice caught in his throat. "Actually, I do mind. It's just some personal stuff. Kind of private, you know? C'mon man, I coached your niece. Give me a break here, huh?"

Bigelow sighed.

"Mr. Cooper, your suspicious exit from the cemetery gives me reasonable cause for stopping you. I'm trying to decide whether or not to take you to jail for attempting to evade a police officer," he bluffed. "It might be helpful for you to cooperate. We can do this here and get you on your way, or I can get a search warrant and drag it out for the rest of the night.

Your choice, but either way I don't like that blanket and I need to see what's under it."

Cooper licked his lips, tasting the dampness that clung to his rough whiskers. A bead of sweat slid under one arm, bumping down the outside of his ribcage.

"Okay, I guess. I haven't done anything wrong. Let's get this over with."

The deputy nodded and opened the back door of the rig. Pulling on a corner of the blanket, the cover slid off the top of the bundle and crumpled to the floor. Bigelow's eyes widened in surprise. There was no keg of beer, no stash of illegal drugs or forbidden weapons.

It was a girl. A young girl pressed between the back of the front seat and the stack of orange road cones. She was seated on the floorboards, her knees tucked up against her chest, her hair fanned across her face like she was trying to hide behind her long dark tresses.

2
CHAPTER

Skyler High School Principal Wayne Mason met Deputy Bigelow in the principal's office on Saturday at 2 P.M.

The two had met in the past, and whenever the deputy showed up, there was trouble, usually an underage drinking party or a vandalism incident from outside the city limits. The officer settled into the chair in front of Mason's desk, and with his pinkish cheeks and close-cropped hair, reminded the principal of an overweight crossing-guard from one of the elementary schools.

"Well, Deputy, what have my little angels done today?"

Bigelow snorted. "In this case, sir, it might be one of your BIG angels who's in trouble."

"What do you mean? Are you referring to a school employee?"

"Yeah. We had a little situation with one of your teachers last night. The sheriff thought you should know about it as soon as possible."

"One of our teachers? Are you sure?"

"Well, if I got it right, I think he might be a teacher and a coach. I spotted a suspicious vehicle parked out at the old Indian cemetery on Gamble Bay Road late last night. The car tried to sneak off without being noticed. No headlights, in a big hurry. I caught the rig just before the bridge on the old highway. The driver was Clayton Cooper."

"Clay Cooper!? Really?" Mr. Mason sat straight in his desk chair. "Mr. Cooper isn't a teacher here. He teaches at the middle school, but he does coach several of our high school girl's athletic programs. Are you saying Mr. Cooper tried to escape? Why?"

"I don't know if he was trying to escape or not. I do know he didn't want to be caught. He wasn't alone. There was a young lady hiding in the back of his rig. She's a student here at your school."

Mason's ruddy neck and face colored to a darker red and he cleared his throat before asking, "And who was the girl?"

"Her name is Shawnee McAllister. I know her mother Philomena from the rez. Mr. Cooper claims he was taking her home from a babysitting job at his house. A coach's party after the football game, I guess. He says she was having some personal problems and just needed to talk."

Mr. Mason exhaled a long, slow breath. "Mr. Cooper is very popular in the district. . . although I must say, he does have an annoying tendency at times, to ignore the rules. Even so, I can't imagine him being so careless with a student. This is a very serious matter, Mr. Bigelow. Do you think there was sexual activity involved?"

"Who knows? At the time I stopped him they were both fully dressed. They both say that nothin' happened. He claims he was just trying to help a student. Do you know the girl?"

"I do. She's a freshman here. I think she was in Cooper's eighth-grade class last year. She's on his varsity soccer team. I don't know what to say. This is very disturbing. Is Mr. Cooper in jail?"

"Nope. We're still trying to sort out the details. The sheriff thought you guys would need to be involved. That's why I'm here."

"The sheriff was absolutely right. These types of situations, even if there was no sex involved, are taboo in the school system. This is a most unusual predicament. Shocking, I must say. Mr. Cooper has been at our school system for a long time."

***

Clayton Kennedy Cooper had been teaching eighth-grade homeroom at Cedar Ridge Middle School for over a dozen years. Twice he had been awarded that school's Teacher of the Year Award. Furthermore, Cedar Ridge's student body newsletter conducted an annual Most Popular Teacher Award, an honor that Mr. Cooper had won every year of his tenure at the school.

In addition to his duties as a middle school teacher, Cooper also served as head coach of the Skyler High School girls' soccer team and as assistant head coach for the school's girl's fast-pitch softball team.

Just over six feet tall, he appeared taller because of his slim physique that he maintained by working out throughout the school year with the varsity athletes. His dark hair was short but stylish, a touch more fashionable than his fellow faculty members. In the classroom, he wore a necktie every Monday and a fresh shirt with pressed khakis the rest of the week. During after-school practice sessions, he favored team jerseys, or t-shirts, usually the Portland Timbers or the Seattle Mariners, together with baseball caps and the latest trendy sunglasses.

He had been raised in San Francisco, the youngest child in a single parent family that consisted of his doting mother and three athletic older sisters. His parents divorced when he was four years old, and he had grown up as the only male in a house full of adoring women.

***

Later that afternoon, Mr. Cooper received a phone call.

"Coop, Wayne Mason here. Sorry to bother you, but we need to talk."

"I assume this is about last night?"

"It is. I had a very disturbing meeting with the sheriff's department this afternoon. What in the world is going on?"

"Wayne, it's not what you think. Not what they think. I was with her, but I was just taking her home from babysitting. It was no big deal."

"Are you serious? For God's sake, man, it's a huge deal. It couldn't BE a bigger deal!"

"I'm telling you—it's not what you think. That girl's got some real problems, Wayne. I was only trying to help her talk them through. People know me too well to think there was anything else going on. It was nothing."

"Coop, the coach's party had been over for hours. You know you can't be alone with a student like that. What were you thinking?"

"I don't know. I had a few beers at the party. . . Shawnee and I started talking when I was taking her home. It was obvious she was struggling. We were just driving around and happened to end up at the beach. It was nothing. When I saw the cop drive by I panicked, I guess. I hid her because I knew no one would understand, and the very fact that we're talking about this proves that I was right. Obviously, I would have called you myself if I thought there was an issue here."

"You should have because there is definitely an issue here. This is a potential catastrophe. You know the rules, Coop. Even you have to acknowledge them. Besides, the county is considering a number of very serious charges. The only holdup is Shawnee's denial of any improper behavior between the two of you, and her mother's refusal to agree to a sexual assault test. We're in trouble here. I say we because the school is going to be dragged through this whole thing too."

"A sexual assault test? That's crazy! Everyone's making a mountain out of a molehill here."

"No, we're not, and if you truly believe this is not serious, you are deluding yourself. I talked with Dr. Townsend earlier this morning. As of today, you are officially suspended until we put together an investigation. You'll be paid, of course, but—"

Cooper interrupted, "Suspended? That's bullshit!"

"No. It's not, and you know it. We don't have a choice here. You were with a fifteen-year-old student. That's a potential statutory rape incident. I believe you, but we've got to do this by the book."

"Statutory rape? You can't be serious. We were just talking for Christ's sake."

"I'm sorry to be so blunt. That's a 'worst case' scenario. Look, you need to take some time off until we can get things sorted out. I've called Dave Epperson and Curtis James. Dave's working on a substitute for your class. Curtis said you should call Jason Locker and let him know that he'll have to take the soccer team until we resolve this thing."

"You called them already?"

"I did. As the principal of the middle school, Dave needs to know. And as athletic director, Curtis is in the loop because you're a Skyler High varsity coach. I know you guys are all buddies, but we've got a school to run here."

"Can I talk to my class on Monday? Let them know what's going on?"

"Sorry. No can do."

"How about my soccer team? Can I just meet with them?"

"No. No contact with any students. You can talk with the classroom sub and with your assistant coach. And while we're discussing this, you are not allowed to communicate with Shawnee. No contact. No phone contact, no texting, no e-mails. Zero contact of any kind. Got it?"

"Yeah, I got it. Let me know what's going on with this will you, Wayne? Keep me posted."

"I'll do that. Try not to worry about it."

"Yeah, right. I'll try not to worry about it."

3
CHAPTER

Kelsey Cooper had taken a sleeping pill after the party on Friday night, falling asleep soon after her husband and the babysitter left the house. Awakened by Cooper's early morning phone call from the sheriff's department, she was waiting for him when he arrived home just before daybreak.

"Clayton, what's going on? How could you DO something so incredibly stupid?"

"I didn't do anything, honey! I was just taking Shawnee home, and she started opening up about her life. She's been through hell, Kelse. I mean, some really serious stuff. I was just trying to help her talk things through."

Kelsey's eyes filled with tears. "You just don't get it, do you? You treat these kids like friends instead of students. It makes me crazy. I can't believe you got us into this. How could you do it?"

"I didn't do anything! There's nothing to this whole mess. I didn't do anything wrong."

Kelsey watched him without speaking.

"What?!"

"I hope you're not lying, Clayton. I can't take it right now. I can't."

"I know you're not feeling good, Kelse. I'm sorry. But I'm not lying. We were just talking. I didn't touch her. I need you, baby. You've got to stand behind me on this."

Kelsey was quiet. When she finally spoke, she said, "This is your mess, Clayton, not mine. You created it, and it's up to you to get us out of it. You have to tell the girls. And my parents. And our friends. This could ruin your life and, thanks to your thoughtlessness, the rest of the family's too."

The next day, Cooper summoned his two daughters, Tasha and Mackenzie, into the family office where he explained the situation to them, walking them through what he called a "misunderstanding" and playing down its importance.

The girls were curious but unperturbed. It was inconceivable that their father would misbehave with Shawnee McAllister, who was one of their regular babysitters. Tasha, the eldest, had just entered Cedar Ridge Middle School as a sixth grader, and she was too preoccupied with school's social demands to worry about her father's problems.

Seven-year-old Mac had trouble sitting still through the serious discussion.

Cooper's phone call to Kelsey's parents was another story. He spoke to Kelsey's father and tried to explain the situation with as much tact as possible. A third-generation car dealer who owned Skyler Ford, Jonas Harrington was not pleased with the prospect of a local scandal, and he was incredulous about Clayton's questionable decision making.

Mr. Harrington had always been overprotective when it came to his daughter. The Harrington's only child, Kelsey had survived a frightening bout of rheumatic fever when she was a toddler, and her health had always been delicate. Her parents were terrified by that near-death experience, and Kelsey had never been allowed to participate in athletics or any physical activity.

When she met Cooper at Portland State University, it was an obvious case of "opposites" attracting. Cooper was an upperclassman at the time, and Kelsey was a nineteen-year-old freshman who looked like she was sixteen.

The couple married two years later before teaching junior high school in Hillsboro, Oregon, and then moving to Skyler to raise their family.

Jonas Harrington had never accepted his son-in-law's love of sports, his penchant for the outdoors, or his liberal politics.

"Coop, the family doesn't need this kind of thing. What the hell were you thinking? My advice is to get it resolved as quickly, and as quietly, as possible. This is a small town. If this thing goes public, it'll be the scandal of the decade. You better make damn sure that doesn't happen."

4
CHAPTER

On Sunday morning, Jason Locker answered his front door to his best friend and fellow coach standing on the porch. Locker was a free-spirited English teacher at Skyler High and another favorite of the high school students. He was long and lanky, with a scruffy beard and a tangle of matching red hair tied back into a puffy ponytail. A faint odor of marijuana clung to the dark blue hooded sweatshirt that he had worn to every soccer practice since late August.

"Hey, bro. What's up?" he said.

"Hey, Jase. We need to talk. You got a minute?"

Locker closed the door behind him and stood on the porch with his friend.

"Sure. What's the matter, you worried about Donovan being able to handle the goal against South? She'll be fine. She's a gamer."

"No. It's not about the team. This is a personal thing."

"Okay. What's going on?"

"Um, well, here's the deal. I was taking Shawnee back from babysitting, and the law pulled me over with her in the car."

"Oh no. DUI?"

"No, worse. She needed help with some personal stuff, and we were just driving around. I ended up parking at the old Indian cemetery, by the beach. Some nosey sheriff came by, and I spooked and took off. He found Shawnee under a blanket in the back of my rig. It didn't look too good."

"Are you shitting me? Dude, I told you something like this would bite you in the ass someday!"

"I didn't do anything, Jase. We were just talking, but the school suspended me until they sort things out. You'll have to take the team on your own for a little while. I can't teach or coach. I asked Mason to let me tell you first, but he's going to call you sometime today to make everything official."

"Jesus. What about the law? Is everything okay there?"

"I don't know yet. They haven't decided whether or not to file criminal charges. Shawnee's only fifteen. I mean, if she says the wrong thing, I could be in a world of hurt. I can't believe this is happening, man."

"What about Kelsey? Is she doing okay?"

Cooper said, "If 'berserk' is okay. She's beyond pissed."

There was silence following Cooper's answer. Jason knew that the Coopers were having problems and that Kelsey was not happy.

"Don't worry about it, dude. It'll work out. The school needs you, the soccer team needs you. . . hell, the kids need you. I'm sure everything will be fine."

"I hope you're right, Jase. I don't have a great feeling about this one."

CHAPTER

On Monday morning, the story broke on the front page of the local newspaper.

LOCAL TEACHER INVOLVED WITH STUDENT
By Terry Barlow
Skyler Daily News Skyler, Oregon

The Wapiti Sheriff's Department reported a bizarre incident involving a local school teacher that took place Friday night in an isolated area outside of the Wapiti Indian Reservation. Cedar Ridge Middle School teacher, Clayton Kennedy Cooper, was parked in the tribal cemetery on Gamble Bay Road when Deputy Clarence Bigelow attempted to check his vehicle.

Cooper, a longtime teacher and coach in the Skyler School District, fled the scene and, when stopped by Bigelow, the deputy discovered a 15-year-old girl hidden underneath a blanket in the back of his vehicle.

Charges may be filed, pending further investigation.

It is this paper's usual policy not to use the names of individuals engaged in situations of this nature unless criminal charges have been filed. However, the involvement of a prominent teacher and coach represents a unique "public awareness" situation that obligates us to inform our readers of Mr. Cooper's identity. Naturally, the fifteen-year-old female will not be identified.

By 9 A.M. that morning, the news of Clayton Cooper's incident had electrified the entire Skyler School District. The story ripped through the schools, shocking students and faculty at both the middle school and high school campuses.

Despite the curious circumstances, few believed there was a shred of validity to the implied sexual misconduct accusations. Mr. Cooper was everyone's favorite teacher and coach and a groundswell of denial flooded over the two schools.

***

For the Cooper's as a couple, it was a day from hell. They made and answered a few phone calls, trying to cope with the chaos and mostly attempting to avoid any face-to-face time with one another.

Near the end of the day, Wayne Mason phoned on the family landline.

"Mr. Cooper, I just want you to know that we had nothing to do with that story in the news. They must have picked it up from this past weekend's public records at the sheriff's department. It's a damn shame."

"It's more than a shame, Mason. In one article, I've been tried, prosecuted, and condemned by a bunch of clowns looking for a juicy story. Evidently, the media's approach is 'guilty until proven innocent.'"

"I know. It's tough. I understand how you feel."

"No, you don't. Nobody does. What's going on? Where are we at with this thing? You guys could put a stop to this by letting me go back to work. Make a statement with your actions. This whole thing has been blown way out of proportion."

"You know we can't do that. We've contacted the state and given them what information we have. They will apprise us of a course of action in the next day or so. As you know, these things are 'no tolerance' issues. You've championed that your whole career."

"Are you implying that I'm a sexual predator?" Cooper asked. "That's ridiculous, Wayne, and you know it."

"I'm not implying that at all. I'm just telling you what you already know. We have to do this by the book, and that's what we're going to do. Don't worry. Things will work out eventually."

"Eventually? I have the feeling that eventually will be too late."

***

Jason Locker stopped by Cooper's house shortly after Principal Mason and Cooper had hung up the phone. Grabbing two beers from the fridge, Cooper led Jason into the den.

"Dude, it looks like the shit has hit the fan," the assistant coach said.

Cooper laughed.

"You've got that right. Can you believe that newspaper article?"

"They're just trying to sell more papers. Sue the bastards."

"I wish. It's unbelievable, man."

"Relax, Coop. Nobody trusts that fucking rag. And you wouldn't believe how many people showed up at practice today and asked what they can do. Parents, kids, the whole works. Even the football coaches came over after practice. Things are starting to happen, bro. Your friends are getting ready to go to war."

Locker's assessment of a war campaign proved to be right on target.

As students and their parents finished their evening meals, the Cooper's phone began ringing. Everyone in town had read the article or heard the radio announcements. None of the callers bought into the implied misbehavior. Fellow teachers, coaches, parents, and ex-students offered kind words and encouragement. Close friends stopped by the house to share a hug or a handshake. Every caller had reached the same conclusion: the misconduct charges were preposterous and the newspaper article was a travesty.

The support buoyed the Cooper family.

For the first time in forty-eight hours, Kelsey was civil to her reeling spouse. It was impossible to ignore the community's support of Cooper and their adamant rejection of the possibility of misbehavior on his part. Kelsey wanted to believe, too.

By 10 P.M., the girls were in bed, and the last visitors had gone home to their own families.

Kelsey was exhausted. She said a tight, "Good night, Clayton," and headed for the bedroom.

Cooper sat by himself at the kitchen table, reading the news article for the tenth or eleventh time. He thought about Jason Locker's comment about "going to war" and smiled at the recollection. Jason was right. Fueled by the adrenaline of the positive support, he was already beginning to feel better.

The phone rang, startling him from his reverie. Glancing at his watch, he noted with surprise that it was almost midnight.

"Hello? Cooper residence."

A deep voice, thick and slow, responded, "Clayton-fucking-Cooper?"

Cooper was so stunned that he could only manage a barely audible, "Yes?"

"You shouldn't mess around with little girls," the voice said. "It ain't good for your health. Someone might rip your fuckin' heart out."

Then, the line went dead.

Cooper stared at the phone, shocked by the violent threat.

Apparently, not everyone going to war would be fighting in the same army.

CHAPTER

Shawnee McAllister was the only child of a white father and a full-blooded Sixela Indian mother. She had come to Skyler in the middle of her eighth-grade year, and she was enrolled in Mr. Cooper's class when school administrators determined that she needed the teacher who was most able to help her adjust to a new school and develop her social skills.

At the time, Shawnee was a fourteen-year-old with a sturdy-looking body softened by a hint of pre-adolescent baby fat. She favored her mother's genes, with high cheekbones, brown eyes, and hair that hung down her back almost reaching her waist. Her black hair was her most flattering feature, streaked with auburn highlights—passed down from her Scotch-Irish father—an erotic compliment to her rosy-bronze skin.

She and Mr. Cooper connected on her first day in the new school. After his own personal interview with the new pupil, he introduced her to his class and allowed her to take her seat without the usual introductory speech.

At lunchtime, Cooper walked Shawnee to the cafeteria and guided her to a table where several of her new classmates were seated.

"Hey, guys," he said, "I want you to take care of our new student. I know everyone wants her to feel welcome."

Shawnee stared at her hands, fidgeting with the papers that Mr. Cooper had given her to look through during the lunch break.

"I'm counting on you guys to make her feel welcome!"

The boys and girls at the table exchanged glances, before one of the more outgoing girls said, "Hey, Shawnee, you can sit by me."

Cooper nodded and said, "Thanks, Joanie." Looking around the table he added, "And make sure these guys behave themselves."

Forty minutes later, Cooper was walking through the crowded hallway back to his classroom when he saw several boys from his class talking to the quiet newcomer. As he passed by the group, he heard one of the boys call the girl "Pocahontas."

Mr. Cooper launched himself into the circle of students, young boys scattering in the hallway as they scrambled to the safety of their next class.

When the boys were gone, Cooper rested his hand on his new pupil's shoulder.

"Are you okay, Shawnee? Don't let those yahoos bother you. They don't have enough sense to know that their little comments aren't funny. But I can promise you this. . . it won't happen again if I'm around."

The girl stared at her new teacher and quietly said, "Thank you, Mr. Cooper. That was really nice of you."

"Call me Coop, Shawnee. Just Coop. We're going to be friends here."

From the beginning, Cooper recognized Shawnee's athletic potential as well as an unexpected streak of competitiveness. He made an effort to include her in extracurricular activities, urging her to participate in recess sports, art projects, and other after-class functions.

During the following summer, Mr. Cooper hired her as one of several babysitters the Cooper's employed during school vacation. As they grew to know one another, he even talked her into trying out for the soccer team when she entered high school in the fall.

With her teacher's guidance, Shawnee had slowly adjusted to her new school and friends.

***

A week after his suspension had begun, Cooper slumped behind the steering wheel in his rig, watching the girls' soccer team file off the practice field in small groups of two and three. He knew that Shawnee's mother often picked her up from evening practices under the stadium's lights and that Mrs. McAllister was often late. Cooper never left the girls alone at the field after practice, and on occasion, he had stayed with Shawnee until her mother arrived. Once or twice, he had taken her home. If he was busy, and her mother failed to show, he would drop her off at the bus stop down the street.

Tonight, he parked in the shadows at the far edge of the field. He expected Shawnee would use the side exit closest to the bus stop.

When Shawnee came out of the park, she was alone. She had a school towel draped over her head and her long hair was pulled back into a damp ponytail. When she headed for the bus stop, Cooper knew that her mother would not be picking her up. Checking to make sure that no one else had exited on the same side, he slowly followed her up the street.

Reaching the middle of the block where there was no streetlight, he turned his headlights on, pulled up to the sidewalk and lowered the passenger side window.

"Hey, girl. What's happenin'?" It was the greeting he used for all of his female students—a phrase often mimicked by student impersonators on campus.

Shawnee looked at the rig, smiling for the first time in days and said, "Lo, Mr. Coop. Not much."

"We need to talk, Shawn. Can I drive you up close to your house and drop you off? We're not supposed to—"

Cooper stopped in mid-sentence as a small car rounded the corner on the wet pavement, the driver spotting Cooper's vehicle

39

and the girl standing beside it. The car, a white beat-up Japanese sedan of indistinguishable make with a slash of gray primer paint smeared on the front fender and duct tape securing a headlight, accelerated up the street toward Cooper's SUV.

The car crossed the centerline into the oncoming lane, sliding to a stop, bumper-to-bumper with Cooper's shiny Ford Explorer. The passenger door of the smaller vehicle flew open, and Philomena McAllister stumbled out of the car. The woman's hair was disheveled and her eyes had a wild look of out-of-control rage.

"You son of a bitch!" she screeched, spittle flying from her mouth. "Get the fuck away from my daughter. You're not supposed to be near her. You son of a bitch!"

Cooper stepped out of the SUV, intent on reasoning with the upset woman.

The instant Cooper's feet hit the pavement, the driver's side door of the sedan opened and an enormous man of Native American descent pulled himself out and leaned against the car.

The man was wearing a retro warmup jacket with a white satin body and a green Boston Celtics logo across the chest. Larry Bird's number 33 was on one sleeve. The middle two buttons of the jacket were snapped, the others left undone to allow the garment to stretch across the huge neck and the girth of his midsection. A green baseball cap was perched at an odd angle atop his massive head. It looked as if someone had carelessly placed the cap on the bottom of an inverted rusty bucket.

In a flash of gallows humor, Cooper thought, *they don't make XXXL like they used to*, a thought that quickly disappeared as he looked into the dark eyes squinting through the fat-padded face, noting the long-necked beer bottle that was dwarfed by the man's fist.

Speaking to the woman, Cooper said, "Mrs. McAllister, everything is okay. I just happened to be driving by. I thought I'd get your daughter out of the rain. I swear it was nothing more than that. It's not what it looks like."

Although he was addressing Shawnee's mother, his eyes jumped between her and the silent driver, who was still holding onto the side of the car and who appeared to be very interested in the conversation.

"You're a liar. I'm warning you, mister, stay away from my daughter!"

Before Cooper could respond, the driver of the car spoke for the first time. "Want me to take care of him, Philomena? Want me to?"

The deep, slow voice was hopeful in the night air. Reading the expression on the man's face, Cooper thought he might as well have just said, "Want me to kill him, Philomena? Want me to?"

"No, Duffy. Leave him alone. I'm gonna call the cops. This prick is in big trouble."

She looked at her daughter. "Shawnee, get in the car. Now." As the girl passed her mother on the way to the car, Philomena reached out and cuffed her hard on the back of the neck. "And don't you EVER talk to this asshole again."

Shawnee scrambled into the car without a word.

"Mrs. McAllister, I apologize for the misunderstanding. I haven't done anything with your daughter. Please believe me, this whole thing is a huge mistake."

"You got that right. And you're the one who made it. I hope you go to jail!"

She turned and climbed back into the car with her daughter.

The driver stood alone, staring at Cooper. During the entire exchange, his only contribution to the conversation had been the ominous two-part question addressed to Philomena. Before joining the mother and daughter in the car, he took a long swig of his beer, then focused his hooded eyes on Cooper's face.

"Clayton-fucking-Cooper. Nice to meet-cha, little man."

The hair on the back of Cooper's neck prickled in recognition. There was no mistaking the voice or the scornful greeting. As the man squeezed back into the car, Cooper felt a surge of relief. But even seated inside the vehicle, the big man's presence alarmed him much more than Philomena's threat to go to the police. His words were implanted in Cooper's brain. "Want me to take care of him, Philomena? Want me to?"

The following day, Philomena McAllister filed a restraining order with the sheriff's department at the Wapiti County Court House.

***

By the end of the week, Cooper and his family had accepted the fact that there would be no quick resolution to his situation, no immediate return to the classroom or the soccer field.

Cooper met with Cedar Ridge principal Dave Epperson who confirmed what Cooper himself had discovered from extensive research on the internet. In most states, sexual misconduct investigations carried out by school systems invariably took at least a year to resolve and, in many cases, a good deal longer.

As a management liaison to the local teacher's union, Principal Epperson had spoken with the union's legal advisors, and the feedback indicated that the state was backlogged with sexual misconduct investigations. The department's litigators were stretched to the limit.

"Coop, they weren't particularly encouraging. I'm not suggesting you do this, but lots of folks choose to resign rather than risk putting their families through a nasty hearing process. The experts say you'll need a thick skin to cope with the whole ordeal."

"I appreciate your feedback, Dave. We both know we've lost staff members who left in the middle of the night. But this is different. If I quit, people would take that as an admission of guilt. I'm going to beat this thing."

The fight promised to be a long uphill battle. The school administration was already in their daily routine, dealing with fall sports and the challenges of the day-to-day demands of running the school district. There was research to be done, an investigation to be organized, a ponderous protocol to be addressed.

The state chapter of the union agreed to provide an attorney, but they advised the Skyler contingent that the state's lawyers would not be available until the hearing took place. Cooper was welcome to hire his own attorney if he so chose, an alternative that was quickly dismissed as cost prohibitive.

Once the hearing's groundwork was laid, the waiting began and Cooper was forced to accept life as a suspended schoolteacher. With Epperson's encouragement, he decided he needed to immerse himself in a project.

In his typical fashion, he chose two.

First, he would take this opportunity to hone his interest in outdoor photography. He had minored in graphic arts at Portland State, and he had chosen to attend college there because he loved the mountains and beaches of northwest Oregon as well as the hiking and camping opportunities so appealing to an amateur photographer.

Second, he began to train for the Portland Marathon. The annual race had just been completed, and the area's sports pages were full of marathon hype. A long-time runner, he had never had time to train for longer races. He thought long runs in the country might double as scouting trips for nature photography opportunities.

Whether he ran the race or not was irrelevant. He hoped that the physical release of a rigid training schedule would help him cope with the stress of his on-going ordeal.

CHAPTER

Shawnee and her mother lived in a two-bedroom house with yellow paint peeling from the exterior walls and a faded red roof. One of two dozen identical homes in a low-income complex called "The Project," it was surrounded by a sagging wire fence and littered with discarded pizza boxes and aluminum beer cans.

Philomena worked part-time at the Wapiti Recreation Center on the reservation and often spent evenings in the Thunderbird Tavern with her boyfriend and his friends, so Shawnee was often alone.

The girl was comfortable with her solitary lifestyle, and throughout her childhood, she had learned to fend for herself. She spent hours drawing animals or flowers and sketching caricatures of beautiful people from photos in celebrity magazines.

Philomena was very aware of her daughter's introverted nature, and she knew that the girl might be traumatized by the process of resolving the situation with Clayton Cooper. She also knew that Shawnee's penny-colored skin might not work in her favor—and she was determined to protect her child.

Philomena's Sixela tribe was a small splinter group of Native Americans connected to the Blood tribe located in southern Alberta, Canada. When Philomena had been younger, she had startling black eyes set in an oval face, with skin as smooth and tight as a piece of brain-tanned deer hide. She had worn her hair in long braids, and she was slim and graceful, a featured dancer in ceremonial dance exhibitions at pow-wows throughout the Rocky Mountain area.

It was at one of these pow-wows in Browning, Montana that Philomena had met and fallen in love with a longhaired white man who worked for the Blackfeet tribe. His name was Sean McAllister, and he was an unabashed liberal and an Indian "wanna-be" of mixed-American descent. Philomena had married him before the end of the pow-wow, and nine months later, their daughter was born.

The father, who had begun his career in the northeastern corner of the country, named his daughter Shawnee Little Sparrow McAllister.

Philomena's marriage to Sean was difficult from the beginning. Interracial marriages were not uncommon on the Blackfeet Reservation, but they could be challenging, and Philomena was young and pretty and not ready to accept the lifestyle required with her husband's tribal job status. The marriage fell apart just after Shawnee's second birthday.

The mother and daughter moved in with a boyfriend, this time a full-blooded member of Philomena's own Canadian tribe. The union lasted fifteen violent and miserable months.

Rebounding from the break-up, she and Shawnee lived on several Indian reservations from the Rocky Mountains to the Pacific coast, in both Canada and the United States. Philomena's lifestyle had taken its toll, and the once lithe dancer was now overweight and doughy, her sparkling black eyes dulled by alcohol and cigarette smoke.

When Shawnee was fourteen, Philomena and her daughter moved to Skyler as guests of a distant cousin who had married a Wapiti Indian who owned a fishing boat that he operated off the coasts of Oregon and California. Philomena liked the ocean and decided to stay. She and Shawnee rented a house, enrolled Shawnee in Cedar Ridge Middle School, and tried again to start a new life.

***

At the Thunderbird Tavern in downtown Skyler, Philomena met Jay Dufferin Grayson. Duffy was a local legend, a man of above-average height whose imposing physical presence was amplified by his tremendous girth. He had the strength one developed by lifting great masses, and even his fat was solid, like the body of an eastern European weightlifter.

Duffy was raised on a fishing boat that was often incapacitated in some way, seldom leaving its moorage at the tribe's Gamble Bay boat haven. He had always been big for his age. Unfortunately, his daddy was always bigger, and to ensure that his son would never forget that fact, he was a stern disciplinarian with a short temper and a long leather belt.

When Duffy was eleven, his father drowned in the Bering Sea while fishing on one of the other boats from the reservation. The details were vague, but tribal insiders suspected foul play. His death generated more relief than compassion among the Wapiti.

Duffy loved all sports and excelled at them. As he grew up, he became the unofficial organizer, coach, and manager of the adult softball and basketball teams on the reservation. His teams traveled the Indian Tournament circuit, and Duffy was known throughout the Native American northwest as a once-dominate athlete and a crafty coach.

***

As Cooper's suspension drug on, the whispered rumors and sullen stares of Shawnee's classmates became increasingly unbearable.

She had quit the soccer team shortly after the incident at the practice field. Her eyes were always downcast, her lips pressed together, and her arms often folded across her chest. She spoke only when spoken to and spent even more of her free time in her bedroom with the door closed.

Philomena chafed at her daughter's withdrawal. But underneath it all, she thought she detected a spark of determination burning in Shawnee's spirit. The girl was steadfast in her refusal to bend regarding the incident with Mr. Cooper.

With a mother's optimism, Philomena saw strength of character in the young girl's conviction.

CHAPTER

Months passed, and it was almost springtime before Cooper's internal investigation was addressed by the school district.

Dr. Townsend and Principal Mason met in the superintendent's office.

"Wayne, I think we need to get going on Clayton Cooper's investigation. It's been six months now. Let's get through spring break and then get after this thing."

"I'm ready to go, Lud. I'll do most of the investigation myself, using the secretaries and a Vice Principal to help."

"Good. Why don't you get things organized now, and start your mailings after spring break? You'll probably have to back off a little as we get closer to graduation, but we need to concentrate on this during the summer. Mr. Cooper's been on the dole long enough."

"Yeah. But you know, Lud, I've got to say the guy has a lot of friends. I'm still concerned about the community reaction. It's amazing how many people come to his defense when I'm visiting with them in social situations. Even the faculty's still behind him, although they're definitely a little more cautious than his buddies."

"I wouldn't worry about it too much. If you think about it, does anyone really want a teacher in the system if there's the slightest chance that he's a threat? Cooper's only human. He's a guy, not a God. I'm pretty sure we'll find something."

The school's research began with Clayton Cooper's personnel records. Every paper in Mr. Cooper's file was re-examined in detail, every sentence scrutinized for hidden meaning. Gradually, a pattern emerged that hinted at the evolution of Clayton Cooper's autonomy within the system. All early entries were a testament to school policy and its requirements. As the teacher's popularity began to grow, signs of his independence started to appear; occasional comments on evaluation sheets, entries that noted Cooper's reluctance to follow the letter of the law—his refusal to enforce the district's rule of addressing all teachers as "Mr." or "Ms.", preferring instead the more familiar "Coop" from students and athletes, ignoring the "no touch" policy in favor of a pat or a hug for a student in need, the occasional closed classroom door when a student wanted to visit in private. There were no flagrant violations—only the defiance that comes from someone who believes that he knows a better way.

***

The school's decision to begin an investigation had kick-started the process, and in March, Mr. Cooper met with the attorney assigned by the teacher's union to represent him at his eventual hearing.

Tom Garret was in his early fifties but looked much older, a tight ring of brown-and-white hair encircling his otherwise shiny, bald head. He wore heavy tortoise-shell glasses that slid down his nose, requiring constant repositioning. His clothing was more appropriate for working in the garden than attending a formal meeting and consisted of rumpled khaki trousers with a faded green polo shirt stretched tight across his waist.

"Mr. Cooper," the lawyer began, "I understand that you were hiding one of your students in your car when you were apprehended?"

"It's not really that simple, Mr. Garret. I was taking our babysitter home after a party. She's a mixed-race kid who plays soccer for me and has some emotional issues. I was trying to help her. We got surprised by a cop, I panicked, and tried to. . ." groping for the right words, he said, "um, avoid giving the wrong impression."

"I see. Criminal charges?"

"No. She had no intention of pressing charges, and the county had no grounds." Cooper added, "I assumed you would have access to this information, Mr. Garret. It took place months ago."

"Oh, I've read the file. Sometimes it's helpful to hear things directly from the client."

"Look, I know it was a stupid thing to do Mr. Gar—".

Garret interrupted him.

"Why don't you call me Tom? It might be best if we could be friends here."

"Okay. . . Tom. I know it was a stupid thing to do. I should have handled it a different way. But it is what it is. Now, can I ask you some questions?"

He didn't wait for Garret's answer. "What can you tell me about the hearing procedure? How long will it take? What can I expect? Can they actually fire me? Let's start with those for openers. I need to know what's going on here."

Garret examined his stubby fingers. When he looked up, he met Cooper's eyes and, for the first time, Cooper wondered if he might not have underestimated his appointed defender.

"I think I know most of the details, Clayton. May I call you Clayton?"

"Most of my friends just call me Coop."

"Alright, Coop. Let me see if I can fill in the gaps. For starters, we are still at least six months away from a hearing. When it does begin, the school district will present the results of their investigation, and they will support that information with testimonies from past and current students, parents, and fellow-teachers, whoever. Eventually, you will get to present your side.

"What you need to know is, this process is similar to a courtroom hearing, but without the strict protection of your rights that a true legal trial would offer. 'Hearsay' is not only tolerated, but it can be the entire basis for termination. There will be an arbitrator, who is both judge and jury. His, or her, ultimate conclusion will be presented to Dr. Townsend, who will make his own decision about your future. . . usually based on the arbitrator's recommendation.

"In my opinion, there is no doubt the deck is stacked for the school. If the school district fires someone suspected of sexual misconduct, who can protest? And besides, what the schools are most interested in is covering their own butts—quietly, quickly, and emphatically.

"The good news is that I'm told you are highly thought of by both your students and your peers. That's always a good start."

9
CHAPTER

As the conclusion of the school year drew near, Shawnee looked to its arrival like a prisoner completing a jail sentence. She had not spoken to Mr. Cooper since the meeting on the street after soccer practice the previous September.

On many weekends during those seven months, she would walk to Cooper's neighborhood wearing one of her mother's oversized hooded jackets and a pair of cheap sunglasses. She would amble past his house hoping for a glimpse of her ex-teacher or even some small sign of his presence at the home; a wheelbarrow in the yard or a ladder leaned up against the garage.

Occasionally, she would see a shadow in the kitchen window, and her heart would beat faster even though she couldn't stare long enough to know if it was Mr. Cooper or a family member moving about the room.

If the red SUV wasn't parked at the curb, she would wonder where Mr. Cooper was and what could possibly take him away from his perfect home on Sunrise Heights. Then she would continue along the sidewalk to the end of the block, crossing to the other side and walking past the house again on the other side of the street.

***

The second phase of the school's investigation began with a series of meetings involving Shawnee, Principal Mason, and Vice Principal Diane Lane. During these meetings, the administration probed incessantly for information regarding her relationship with Mr. Cooper. In addition, the school had set up meetings with the district's resident psychologist, Dr. Jonnie Durham. Dr. Durham asked dozens of embarrassing and personal questions to prepare a personality profile.

If Shawnee chose to answer questions at all, she did so in the shortest manner possible, relying on nods, head shakes, and one-word answers. The youngster's refusal to cooperate was especially galling to Principal Mason and Superintendent Townsend. Following a meeting with Dr. Durham, Mason could not contain his frustration.

"Can you believe this?" Mason said, seconds after the psychologist had left the principal's office. "Even the shrinks can barely get a word out of her."

"I know. And the strange thing is that Dr. Durham's suspicion of mental dysfunction lends some credence to Cooper's contention that the girl has problems. It makes one wonder if the man is telling the truth."

"Maybe. But even if there was no sexual interaction involved, he knew he was breaking the rules. Otherwise, why would he hide her?"

"You're right, of course. Still, she's absolutely insistent that nothing happened. It makes one wonder."

When Mason left his office, Dr. Townsend thought about their conversation. He knew that every high school in the country had dealt with sexual misconduct issues. He knew that the great majority of these issues never went public, and individual school districts wanted it that way. Much better to have teachers quietly resign and get out of town.

He looked out the window, checking on groups of students as they walked between classes on the sunny spring day, the girls in short skirts and tank-tops that stretched the school dress code to the outside edge of acceptable skin exposure; warm weather apparel always meant battles with counselors about too much cleavage on top and not enough fabric to cover the strings of thong-style panties riding above low-cut waistbands on the bottom.

He thought about technology's role in accelerating student sexuality: rap music, internet-porn, "sexting," and the ready accessibility of R-rated movies and DVDs. Sometimes he wondered if it was even possible for high school teachers to deal with the temptations they were exposed to on a daily basis.

***

The end of the school year arrived, bringing into focus the reality of a hearing growing closer by the day for Cooper and his family. The family was looking forward to their annual summer retreat to Montana. In normal years, Cooper was involved in organizing summer athletic programs, so the visit had been limited to a single week squeezed into a busy schedule. Cooper's "non-contact" restriction eliminated that constraint. That summer, the family would stay at his uncle's cabin the entire month of July, and all of them were anxious to escape the palpable tension surrounding them.

They arrived at the northwest Montana mountain retreat just before dark. After unpacking the Explorer, they found a phone message from Cedar Ridge principal David Epperson awaiting them. Dave had spoken to Wayne Mason earlier in the day, and the high school administrator had asked him to forward the information to Mr. Cooper.

Dr. Townsend had been in contact with the state, and they had developed a tentative timeline. According to Epperson's information, the hearing would take place sometime during the first quarter of the following school year.

The good news was Cooper's paid suspension would remain intact throughout the projected time frame.

The bad news was that it would be at least three more months before there would be a resolution.

***

Once the Coopers settled in for their vacation, the idyllic mountain valley began to work its magic. Colloquially known as "the Yaak" the valley and its river remained a habitat lost in time. Located west of Glacier National Park, just south of the Canadian border, the Yaak had long been considered one of the most remote areas in the lower forty-eight. Centered in the one-million-acre Kootenai National Forest and inhabited by a smattering of private land owner's, the Yaak was a sanctuary for both wildlife and human life in the wild.

The seclusion, the long northern winters, and the lack of both jobs and modern amenities, all of these factors encouraged an escape to a simpler life. Despite the challenges, a core of loners and free spirits were passionately connected to the river valley and its independent lifestyle.

Cooper's uncle's ranch was located halfway up the Yaak River Road, about a dozen miles south of the town of Yaak. It sat on a piece of private riverside property, two miles from its nearest neighbor.

For a family in crisis, the retreat could not have been more ideal. In the secluded valley, more than seven hundred miles from home, no one knew anything about the Coopers' private life. The valley was a haven of anonymity: the perfect location for potentially healing what had become a slowly disintegrating family.

THE HEARING

CHAPTER

10

The hearing began in early November, fourteen months after the incident at the cemetery. Superintendent Ludlow Townsend's opening remarks left little doubt about the serious nature of the task at hand.

Waving a hand in Cooper's direction, he said, "I think you all know Clayton Cooper, eighth grade homeroom teacher at Cedar Ridge Middle School and head coach of the girls' soccer team here at the high school.

"Although the necessity for this procedure is unfortunate, no one can dispute its value. As educators, we are committed to providing our students with the safest environment possible. The purpose of this hearing is to evaluate Mr. Cooper's behavior within this infrastructure.

"To that end, we are fortunate to have one of the state's most distinguished retired jurists to help us resolve Mr. Cooper's situation. Presiding over this hearing will be Judge Raleigh Halliday. Mr. Halliday is a retired Oregon district court judge who has been appointed by the state to serve as the arbitrator for this hearing.

"At the conclusion of the process, he will make a recommendation regarding Mr. Cooper's actions and, based on that recommendation, we will determine the future of his employment with the school system.

"Mr. Halliday, welcome to the Skyler School District."

Raleigh "Rock" Halliday was a former All-Conference football player from the University of Oregon, whose post-collegiate career included six years in the National Football League, a law degree, two terms as an Oregon state representative, and a long stint as a circuit court judge in Multnomah County.

In spite of his sixty-two years, the man seated at the front of the room looked like he was still ready to suit up for a football game with the Oregon Ducks. He was not tall, but he had long arms and broad, hard shoulders. His once trim waistline had thickened, but there was no evidence of flab or paunch.

Cooper studied the mediator with interest, searching for some clue to his character. His thick gray hair was closely cropped. His most striking features were the incongruous black eyebrows, arching under his mat of silver hair, a stubborn remnant of the once-black hair of his younger years. A pair of steel-rimmed glasses magnified the intense gleam of his eyes, adding a touch of academic credibility to his appearance.

Cooper leaned over and whispered to Tom Garret, "Jesus, why didn't they just get Spencer Tracy or something?"

Garret answered out of the corner of his mouth. "The guy's a freakin' volcano. Don't piss him off."

"Who'd want to?"

The room was arranged in a loose simulation of a traditional courtroom. A half-dozen folding chairs were set up close to the door at the back of the room. Directly in front of these chairs were two cafeteria tables where representatives of the opposing parties were seated.

At one table Clayton Cooper and Tom Garret sat side-by-side. Ten feet away at an identical table was the school district contingent: Wayne Mason, Vice Principal Diane Lane, and school district legal counsel Tyler Cheney. Dr. Townsend had taken a seat in the back row of chairs, where he could come and go with discretion.

Directly behind the tables, Judge Halliday was seated at a 1950's oak desk. Scuffed and worn, it had a huge writing surface, providing a surprisingly accurate impression of a judicial bench. Next to the makeshift bench was an office chair with a worn leather seat and curved armrests. This was the chair where the witnesses would testify.

At the Cooper family's request, the proceedings would not be open to the public or the press. Witnesses would be held in the hallway until their turn to testify, so that they would not be privy to the testimony of others. The only other person in the room was Kelsey Cooper, who sat three seats from Dr. Townsend in the same row of folding chairs.

At exactly 1 P.M. on the boardroom wall clock, Wayne Mason received a nod from Halliday and stood to begin the hearing.

"The school district would like to call its first witness, Your Honor."

Opening the door to the hallway, he said, "Muriel, you can come in now."

A woman of indeterminate age hesitantly walked into the room. With pale skin and a pair of square-framed glasses, she had the bookish look of a member of the school library staff. Tall and round-shouldered, her brown hair was cut short in a style suited to a much older woman. She wore no makeup, and her lips were so tightly pursed that the skin around them was stretched white.

"Ladies and gentlemen, this is Muriel Dunn. Muriel will be the first of a number of Mr. Cooper's ex-students that our investigation found who experienced, or had the opportunity to witness, Mr. Cooper's questionable behavior. We contacted Muriel based on an old complaint found during our research, and she agreed to meet with us about the content of that document. The information that she will share today is the result of that meeting."

Cooper sat at the table with Tom Garret, a look of confusion on his face. He glanced at Garrett, shrugging his shoulders. He recognized the young woman's name, but he had no memory of her classroom presence at all. He studied her as she sat in the chair next to Halliday's desk, her back straight and inflexible, flat chest rising and falling with unnatural speed.

58

Mason said, "Muriel, just relax. This is an informal process, not a trial. We're mostly just sharing information here. Why don't you just tell us about your experience in Mr. Cooper's classroom?"

Muriel looked in Cooper's direction for the first time, careful to avoid eye contact. The furtive look triggered a flicker of recognition. Cooper recalled a shy thirteen-year-old, taller than any boy in the class and painfully self-conscious about it. Cooper could not imagine any improper behavior with the awkward youngster that he had taught over a decade ago.

When Muriel began to speak, everyone in the room leaned toward her to hear her words.

"I had Mr. Cooper in the eighth grade at Cedar Ridge. He was a good teacher, but. . . I don't know, a little overwhelming? He would joke with some of the popular kids about things that seemed to be. . . inappropriate."

"Inappropriate?" Mason asked.

"Yes. Movies, music, boyfriends and girlfriends. Things like that. He was very 'hip.' He liked to banter with the popular girls about teenage things. Dates, dances, sports." She hesitated before adding, "It was almost like he was flirting with them. Anyway, it made me uncomfortable."

"What do you mean, 'flirting'?"

"Well, it's hard to explain. He would tease the girls about their dates, talk about their weekends, things like that. And when he talked to them in class, he would lean close to them and speak very quietly. Sometimes he would put his hand on their shoulder or pat them on the back."

"Really? And did Mr. Cooper ever touch you, Muriel?"

"Oh, yes. He would hold onto my arm above the elbow or pat me on the shoulder."

"And how did that make you feel?"

"Uncomfortable. I didn't like it."

Cooper exploded out of his seat, startling Tom Garret and catching the entire room by surprise. "That's ridiculous! I touch everyone I talk to. That's part of how I communicate. There's nothing sexual in that."

Cooper's outburst was inconsequential in comparison to Rock Halliday's response. The arbiter's face turned bright red, and coupled with the dense black eyebrows and cropped gray hair, the result was a face that more closely resembled a gruesome Halloween mask than the craggy features of Spencer Tracy.

"SIT DOWN, MR. COOPER," he barked. "And keep quiet! I will not tolerate that kind of behavior during this hearing."

Cooper sat down. He looked around the room, whose occupants stared at the floor in embarrassment. He felt his own face growing warm. The room was so quiet that Cooper could hear the rain tapping against the windows. Muriel Dunn looked horrified, trapped beside the incensed mediator.

When Halliday's fury began to subside, he locked eyes with Clayton Cooper. Cooper dropped his eyes to his legal pad and pretended to scribble a note.

"Mr. Cooper. I realize this is a hearing and not a courtroom trial. Despite that distinction, some sense of order and decorum is imperative. Interruptions of that type are not acceptable. Your attorney will respond on your behalf and, at some point in time, you will have every opportunity for rebuttal. Meanwhile, common courtesy will prevail. Do you understand?"

"Yes, sir, I apologize."

"Thank you. See that it doesn't happen again."

Wayne Mason exchanged a glance with Dr. Townsend. Only his fear of Raleigh Halliday kept him from winking.

"Mr. Garret, do you have any questions for Ms. Dunn?"

Garret sat calmly beside Cooper and scribbled a note for his client. When the mediator directed his attention to his own notes, Garret tipped his legal pad for Cooper to read. The page had three words—*I told you.*

When he was sure Cooper had seen his note, he answered, "I do have questions, Your Honor. Just a few."

Rubbing his chin, Garret looked at Ms. Dunn.

"Muriel, how old are you?"

"Twenty-four."

"Twenty-four? So, you were in Mr. Cooper's classroom, what? Eleven, twelve years ago?"

"I guess so. Yes, that would be about right."

"Were you one of those 'popular' girls that you were talking about?"

Muriel's pale cheeks turned a soft red. "No. I was not. I thought that would be obvious from my comments."

Garret ignored the rebuke and continued. "You still go by your maiden name. Are you married, Ms. Dunn?"

The cheeks flushed a shade darker. "No."

"Do you date, Ms. Dunn?"

"I beg your pardon."

"Date. Are you active socially these days?"

"No. I am not."

"I see." He paused. "No more questions, Your Honor."

The school district proceeded to present a string of malcontents, from students who claimed Cooper's "favorites" received preferential treatment to jealous boyfriends who had been threatened by the teacher's popularity. It soon became obvious that the school district's

61

strategy was piling up suspicions in the hope that Raleigh Halliday would assess some of the complaints as credible. In addition, the procession of students gave Mason the opportunity to ask every female student some version of the same question. "Has Mr. Cooper ever touched you? Put his hands on you in any way?"

The answer was always "yes."

Raleigh Halliday finally called a halt. "Mr. Mason, I'm growing weary of this line of questioning. Unless you have witnesses to expand on some kind of 'inappropriate' physical touching, I don't want to hear this again. Spare me the 'Did he ever touch you?' question. We all know the answer to that."

"Certainly, sir. These references were merely to establish a pattern. We have more concrete examples."

"Then use them. I'm not an idiot."

Mason changed tactics the following day.

Her name was Casey Henderson. She had graduated two years earlier. While at Skyler, she had been a football and basketball cheerleader and an outstanding pitcher on the Lady Eagles softball team. Casey was tall and lithe with palomino-colored hair that hung well below her shoulders. Prom queen, Home Coming princess, and star athlete, her picture had graced the cover of the regional "Spring School Sports" insert of the Portland Herald her junior year of high school. She was now in a sorority at Oregon State University, a favored member of a house more famous for beautiful pledges than academic achievements. Casey had eyes that matched the same honeyed hue as her hair, small breasts, and a shapely derriere, carefully maintained during countless hours at the campus fitness center.

She had been one of Cooper's favorites, and in addition to their in-school relationship, she had spent many summer days babysitting his children and attending family barbeques and picnics. Despite her beauty, she was down to earth and uncomplicated, the good-natured target of countless "blond" jokes.

Cooper and Kelsey exchanged looks, surprised that Mason would call her in to support the school district. Casey's was one of the first names that Cooper had provided Tom Garret to use on his own behalf. As soon as she sat down in the chair beside Halliday's desk, every man in the room focused his undivided attention on her. She was wearing a pair of tight jeans and a snug white tee shirt with a Sponge Bob Square Pants cartoon caricature on the front. Her straight blond hair was pulled into a ponytail and stuffed through the cutout back of an OSU baseball cap.

Tyler Cheney, the school district's attorney, had been doodling on his yellow legal pad. Now he was paying attention. He wrote "WOW!" in large letters and circled it several times, before glancing around the room and then hurrying to scribble it out before anyone noticed.

Mason asked Ms. Henderson to explain her relationship with Mr. Cooper.

"Well, Coop was my softball coach for four years. I used to babysit for him and Mrs. Cooper. I'm, like, almost part of the family."

"That's nice, Casey. Now, maybe you can tell us a little about Mr. Cooper, like we talked about in my office last week."

"Sure. He's a great guy. He's funny. He tells great jokes, and he always made us laugh. He didn't really seem like a teacher on the softball field. More like a good friend. He taught me a lot too. Mostly about hitting."

"I see. Casey, did Mr. Cooper ever make you or your team mates uncomfortable in any way?"

"Not really. I mean, for me not at all. One or two of the girls maybe didn't really understand him. He's a tease. If he knows he can zap you he'll do it. It made all of us laugh."

"Can you tell us what you said in our meeting? About what it was that made you laugh?"

"Oh, everything. He'd tell Toni Taylor that he was going to turn her over his knee and spank her if she missed another sign. She'd go beet red every time. It was hilarious. Sometimes he'd zap her in the huddle between innings if we were in a tight situation. It always loosened us up."

"So he threatened to spank Toni?"

"He was just kidding, Mr. Mason. It was no big deal."

With a glance at Halliday, he asked, "Did Mr. Cooper ever spank you? Or hug you? Anything like that?"

"Of course. Well, he never spanked me. But he's hugged me tons of times. It's no fun to be yelled at. I'm the kind of person who responds better to hugs. I think most everyone does."

"Did the team think Mr. Cooper was. . . attractive?"

"Attractive? Heck, yes. He's hot. And funny. For an older guy, he's definitely attractive."

Mason's interview with Casey was a crafty move. Few men could resist such temptation.

Rising for his cross, Garret asked, "Ms. Henderson, have you ever had the opportunity to be alone with Mr. Cooper?"

"Yes, sir. Millions of times. We worked real hard in the off-season to get ready for softball."

"And, Ms. Henderson, did Mr. Cooper ever behave inappropriately when you were alone with him?"

"No, sir, he never has. Coop is a flirt, just like me, but he's never serious. He's the best."

Garret blanched at her choice of words.

"But he's never behaved inappropriately, right?"

"Absolutely not."

"No further questions, Your Honor."

When Halliday excused her, Casey walked slowly out of the room. Tyler Cheney added another small doodle to his legal pad. This one was sketched in the voluptuous shape of an up-side-down valentine heart. He scratched it out as soon as he realized what he had drawn.

***

It was a quiet ride home for the Coopers.

As they neared the house Clayton said, "Can you believe this crap? I've never laid a finger on Casey."

"You have, Coop. You just don't realize you're doing it. I've been telling you that for years," his wife responded.

"Honey, giving a kid a hug is not trying to sleep with her. I can't believe they want us to act like robots when so many kids need someone to care about them. It's ridiculous."

"These are different times. It's not kindergarten, Coop. Girls like Casey get plenty of hugs. And plenty of everything else for that matter."

Cooper shook his head. "I'm sorry. I just don't get it."

***

The hearing was scheduled to conclude by the end of the week, but the school district's tedious approach had slowed the proceedings. It was Friday and the key witnesses— Cooper and Shawnee McAllister —had not yet testified, nor had Thomas Garret been able to bring in a single witness on Cooper's behalf. As a result, the tension level of the hearing was growing with every passing day.

Halliday issued an ultimatum. "I am disappointed with the pace of this hearing, and I want to encourage both sides to use this break to get your acts together. I'm sorry to ruin your weekend, but I can assure you that we all expected to have this thing wrapped up by now."

Glaring at each table, he said, "When we return, I want the key witness to testify. Immediately. And after that, I want to move quickly into Mr. Cooper's defense. Do you understand what I'm saying?"

There were a series of nods from both benches, led by Wayne Mason's eager head bobbing.

***

The weekend provided little relief for Cooper or his family.

For Kelsey, listening to the vague nature of the school district's witnesses had been especially traumatic. She seldom smiled. Her skin was bone pale and accentuated the dark circles under her eyes, circles that never disappeared despite going to bed early and rising long after the rest of the family.

The two days off only exacerbated the tension smothering the Cooper parents. Clayton picked up the slack, driving the girls to their weekend activities, doing the shopping and cooking. He was grateful for even the slightest diversion.

Despite the distractions, no distraction could reduce the couple's most stressful source of anxiety—the pending testimony of the key witness Shawnee McAllister.

CHAPTER

11

On Monday, the meeting room was cool, and there was a faint musty odor as the heating system struggled to warm the open space. When the participants began to arrive, the room grew taut with the anticipation of the final sessions.

Organizing his notes, Raleigh Halliday repeatedly glanced at the clock. For the former football player, it was the fourth quarter of a big game, and his system was already pumping adrenaline through his body. After a brusque greeting, he turned the floor over to Wayne Mason, who began the session by announcing his intent to resume the proceedings by introducing the hearing's key witness, Shawnee McAllister.

There were nods of approval from the school's entourage and an exchange of glances between Cooper and Tom Garret, acknowledging the announcement that did not come as a surprise. The same was not true for Mason's next statement.

"Actually, Mr. Halliday, we intend to introduce two key witnesses today," he paused, knowing that his listeners were expecting only Shawnee's testimony.

"After we talk with Shawnee, we will also interview her mother, Philomena McAllister-Grayson."

Cooper looked at Tom Garret in alarm. He had told the lawyer about his contact with Duffy Grayson in an earlier meeting. Garret shrugged his shoulders, not surprised by any aspect of these investigations but curious about this unusual twist.

Mason went to the door and escorted mother and daughter into the boardroom. He seated Philomena in the row of folding chairs three spaces from Kelsey Cooper and asked Shawnee to take the chair beside Halliday's desk.

"Ladies and gentlemen, this is Shawnee McAllister and her mother Philomena McAllister-Grayson, who asked to accompany her daughter and share her own perspective on Mr. Cooper's relationship with her daughter. This was a special weekend for Shawnee's mother, who got married on Saturday. Congratulations, Mrs. Grayson."

Philomena nodded. She was wearing a business-like dark suit and her only pair of patent leather shoes. Her black hair was neatly combed, the streaks of gray almost concealed behind tidy hair clips. While her makeup had been applied with care, it did little to hide the nicotine lines etched in the corners of her wide-set eyes. She was not tall, but her large bosom and thick arms gave her a statuesque presence, and Cooper knew too well that she would be a daunting opponent. He leaned forward, trying to wrap his mind around her new name and marital status.

Mason started the session by asking Shawnee to take her seat beside Halliday's desk. Except for her obvious Native American heritage, the girl seated in the witness chair bore little resemblance to her newly-wed mother. Shawnee's skin color was a shade lighter, and the smooth texture of the youngster's taut, burnished-copper complexion was a stark contrast to the tired fleshiness of her mother's face.

In the bright meeting room, Cooper noticed that the girl's hair had grown longer since last year and that it now shone with auburn highlights. She was not beautiful but was beginning to outgrow adolescence and, had her expression been less serious, the maturing features would have created an even more flattering impression. She sat stiffly beside Halliday's desk, her arms folded across her chest and her eyes downcast.

"Try to relax, Shawnee." Mason said. "We just want you to answer a few questions. All we're looking for is the truth. Whatever you say will be evaluated along with the input of others. So just relax and answer the questions truthfully. Okay?"

Still staring at her hands folded in her lap, Shawnee nodded.

"Shawnee, can you tell us about your relationship with Mr. Cooper? Where did you meet him? How long have you known him? Things like that."

"In school. Eighth grade." She hesitated, trying to remember the sequence of questions. "Then he was my soccer coach."

"Here at Skyler High?"

She nodded.

"Was he a good teacher?"

She nodded again.

"A good coach?"

Another nod.

Halliday cleared his throat and said, "Perhaps you can ask the young lady questions that require more than a yes or no answer?"

Mason answered, "Sorry, sir. I'm still a rookie here." Then he added, "Do you understand Mr. Halliday's request, Shawnee?"

Shawnee nodded.

The room broke into laughter and even Mr. Mason chuckled. "Touché," he said to the unsmiling witness.

"Shawnee, can you tell us exactly what happened the night of the incident with Mr. Cooper?"

The question appeared to agitate the youngster, who looked at Mason for the first time and squirmed in her chair. She was silent for a moment and then her eyes seemed to glaze over and she began to speak in the near singsong voice of a student who had memorized the first lines of a poem or a speech for an assignment.

"I was babysitting for Mr. Cooper after the game. He gave me a ride home. We stopped to talk." She shrugged her shoulders, and Mason waited for her to continue. But Shawnee was finished and unconcerned about the uncomfortable silence that followed. It was as if she was in her own place, unaware of anyone else's presence in the room.

Finally, Mason said, "And then? What happened when you stopped to talk?"

She shrugged again. "Nothing. We started for home, and then the sheriff pulled us over."

"Where were you when the sheriff stopped you?"

"At the beach."

"No, no. Where were you sitting in the car?"

"The Explorer," she said. "It was a Ford Explorer."

"In the Explorer. Shawnee, where were you in the Explorer?"

Shawnee's eyes had lost their glazed look, and she seemed to be more aware of Mason's role in the conversation.

"In the back seat. I was cold. I put a blanket over me."

The boardroom was rapt with attention now, and even Dr. Townsend and Kelsey Cooper were on the edge of their chairs in the makeshift gallery.

"You were cold? Shawnee, you were hiding under that blanket, weren't you? The deputy said he didn't find you until he removed the blanket. You have to tell us the truth. Everything you say has to be the truth."

Shawnee didn't answer.

"Were you hiding, Shawnee?"

There was a long silence before the girl said softly, "Maybe."

"Maybe? Were you or weren't you hiding under that blanket?"

With a look of defiance, Shawnee stared into Mason's eyes.

"Maybe. The sheriff scared me. It was late. I don't remember. Maybe."

Noting that Shawnee seemed to be recovering from her trance-like state, Halliday called for a ten-minute recess hoping that a break would assist her emotional recovery.

Both sides spent the short recess in furious consultation.

Cooper and Tom Garret huddled in the hallway.

"I don't know what to think, Coop. It's those freaky little losses of focus that scare me. It's bizarre. I get the feeling that she's not telling the truth, but, so far, the words are okay. I'll feel a hell of a lot better when we can get her out of here."

Cooper was a mess. "I know what you're saying. I told you she has some serious problems."

***

When Shawnee's testimony resumed, the school district made an interesting change. Vice principal Diane Lane had exchanged places with Wayne Mason and was standing in front of the stoic witness.

Ms. Lane had worked with Shawnee during the girl's sessions with the school psychologist. Smiling at the teenager, she said, "It's nice to see you again Shawnee. Now, how 'bout a little girl talk?"

The teen shrugged her shoulders.

"Let me ask you a question. Do you find Mr. Cooper attractive?"

"Huh?"

"Attractive. Do you think Mr. Cooper is handsome or charming? You know, is he 'hot,' as you kids would say?"

"No."

"No?" The vice principal raised her eyebrows. The district had asked a variation of this question of every female witness since the first days of the hearing. Until now, everyone had responded in the affirmative, as if the answer was obvious. Some qualified it by substituting "cool," "funny," or "pretty good for an old guy."

Surprised by the girl's answer, Ms. Lane hesitated, not certain how to pursue establishing Cooper's attractiveness to the female students in his classes and teams.

"You don't think Mr. Cooper is attractive?"

"No."

Shawnee's brusque answers gave the vice-principal an idea.

"Do you think he's charming?"

"No."

"How very interesting."

Shawnee was quiet.

"Why did you go to the Gamble Bay cemetery with him if you think he is so. . . boring?"

"We talked. We just talked."

"Really? Is that all you did there? There was no hugging? No touching?"

"No."

"No kissing?"

"No."

"No physical contact of any kind?"

"No."

With every answer, Shawnee's response became less believable. Her answers were too automatic, her body language defensive, her attitude disingenuous. Not one person in the room believed what she was saying.

Ms. Lane pressed forward.

"What about you, Shawnee? How did Mr. Cooper feel about you?"

"I don't know."

"Did Mr. Cooper ever single you out in any special way when you were on his soccer team?"

"No."

"No? What about the rides home, the after-practice training sessions and all the individual encouragement?"

"Mr. Cooper gave lots of the freshmen rides home, and he was nice to everyone on the team."

"What about the babysitting? Why did he choose you?"

"I don't know. He just did."

"Did Mr. Cooper try to help you with personal problems: boyfriends, dating, things like that?"

"No."

"Shawnee, did Mr. Cooper ever touch you or put his hands on you in any way?"

"No. He never did."

Diane Lane left Shawnee's answer suspended in silence for a full five seconds.

"No more questions, Your Honor."

Cooper, Tom Garret, and Mrs. McAllister-Grayson were all horrified.

Rock Halliday called for another short recess before Garret's cross. During the break, the lawyer and Cooper engaged in a tense discussion on how to address Shawnee's testimony and initiate a semblance of damage control.

***

When the hearing resumed, Garret aggressively began questioning Shawnee.

"Ms. McAllister, I understand that you have had several visits with the school psychologist?"

Shawnee nodded.

"Could you tell us a little about what was discussed in those sessions with the doctor?"

"NO! SHE COULDN'T!"

The voice came from the seating section of the room, ringing with outrage. Mrs. McAllister-Grayson stood, glaring at Tom Garret.

"I beg your—"

"I said, no. There's nothing wrong with my daughter, and I won't let you make her out to be crazy."

Halliday jumped into the confrontation.

"Mrs. . . . . Grayson. Please sit down and wait for your opportunity to speak. You are exactly right. I will not allow this line of questioning. Do you understand, Mr. Garret? The young lady's mental competence is not the issue here. Ask another question."

Garret knew the futility of challenging Raleigh Halliday. Besides, he felt he had already made a valid point without having to say anything about the girl's mental state.

"Of course," he said, "My apologies, Mrs. Grayson."

Changing tactics, he said, "Shawnee, I know you must be nervous. No one's trying to trick you this afternoon. It's very important that your answers be truthful." Garret stopped and arranged his face into what he hoped was a mystified expression. "Some of your answers to Ms. Lane were very confusing to me. I find it hard to believe that you don't think Mr. Cooper was trying to help you in the classroom. Are you sure about that?"

Shawnee answered. "Um, he was nice to me but only in school."

Garret ran his hand over the top of his bald head.

"You do understand that Mr. Cooper is being investigated to determine the appropriateness of his conduct with his students and players, right?"

Shawnee nodded.

"Good. Then let's get right to the heart of the matter here. I want to clarify something for Mr. Halliday and set the record straight. Has Mr. Cooper ever touched you in a sexual manner? Ever fondled you? Have you ever had oral or actual sex with Mr. Cooper or been physically involved with him in any way?"

Shawnee, showing a spark of frustration at the necessity of once again answering the embarrassing questions, answered tersely, "No. No sex. No blowjob. No nothing."

Garret blinked several times, caught off guard by the frank response. Not knowing what to say, he settled on, "No further questions" and sat down at the table, not sure as to whether Shawnee's answer had helped his client or hurt him.

***

The hearing continued after lunch when Shawnee's mother took the chair next to Halliday's desk.

Though not an official member of the Wapiti tribe, Philomena was a vocal attendee at meetings on the reservation. She had a keen instinct for the political ramifications of decision-making, honed by hundreds of hours of exposure to the bureaucratic intricacies of the Native American political infrastructure on at least three different tribal reservations.

Philomena knew the exact second that Shawnee's testimony became suspect, and she had no intention of letting her daughter be portrayed as the instigator of the scandal.

Mason started the interview with a simple question, having no idea that he would not ask another during the entire course of Philomena's testimony.

"Mrs. Grayson. Did you ever suspect a physical relationship between your daughter and Mr. Cooper?"

"I suspected a physical relationship from the very beginning. Every girl has a crush on one of her male teachers. This man is a charmer, and these young girls don't have sense enough to get beyond his good looks and nice clothes. They don't know when he's flirting and when he's not. Shawnee wants to be popular. She wants to be accepted. She wants to be white. Cooper's all of those things. He's everything my daughter wants to be.

"I think Cooper brainwashed my daughter. You heard her. Goofy. She won't talk to me, she won't talk to her friends, she won't talk to anybody. She's been mooning about this guy since she was in eighth grade. If you keep him teaching, I will make sure that no girls from the rez are ever in his class. Indian girls don't stand a chance. Even my husband thinks Shawnee will get the blame."

Growing more agitated as she spoke, Philomena continued. "Same old crap. Indians aren't worth nothin'. Well, my daughter is worth something. If she takes the fall for this bullshit, you better line up your lawyers. Because I will sue everyone's ass."

The room sat in stunned silence. Philomena did not wait for any more questions. Her powerful arms propelled her out of her chair toward Shawnee, who was seated in the row of folding chairs and had not looked at her mother once during the passionate rant.

"Get your coat, girl. We're going home."

Halliday rose from his seat and tried to stop the mother and daughter as they moved across the room. "Mrs. Grayson, I can assure you that this situation will be resolved fairly, regardless of race or color. I am a man who has shared locker rooms with black, tan, and yellow. No one can question my respect for the rights of all people. Rest assured that there will be no discrimination in this hearing process."

Philomena looked over her shoulder on her way to the door.

"Yeah, right. We've heard that before. You rest assured that I'm not joking. You hurt my baby, and someone's going to pay!"

***

In the wake of Mrs. Grayson's dramatic exit, Halliday called a halt to the day's proceedings. The school district officials convened in Dr. Townsend's office. Wayne Mason, Diane Lane, and Tyler Cheney gathered around Townsend's desk.

"Okay, people, that was interesting." Townsend looked at Cheney, the school district's legal liaison and advisor. "What do you think, Ty?"

"Well, to start off, if this was an actual jury trial in a courtroom, I'd call today's little exhibition a slam dunk for the prosecution. I've never heard anything like it. All of Shawnee's denials might as well have been affirmations. Sex or no sex, something is definitely weird there.

Second, mama's explosion was perfect. Obviously, even the girl's own mother didn't believe her."

Cheney stopped, scanning the attentive faces around the desk.

"And by the way, Diane's cross with Shawnee was brilliant." He looked at Ms. Lane. "I think you're in the wrong profession. Anytime you want to go to work as a paralegal, just let me know."

Lane blushed at the compliment.

***

Garret and Cooper walked out of the room together and stopped for a discussion in the hallway.

"Was that as bad as I think, Tom? Could it have been any worse?"

"It was. . . pretty bad. But what scares me even more than Shawnee's freaky testimony was her mother's implication that Halliday isn't a god. The old man's got an ego bigger than the state of Oregon, and there's no way he'll let anyone think he's a bigot."

"We can deal with the rest of it. In fact, Shawnee's testimony provides some credibility to your claims that the girl has problems. But to have someone question Rock Halliday's character. . . that is not good."

"Should we let him know that we're concerned about that happening?"

Garret pushed his glasses up on his nose so he could see Cooper clearly enough to determine whether he was serious.

"Yeah," Cooper said, "never mind."

"You know, Coop, after seeing Shawnee on the stand, I'm thinking we have to change our strategy. Why didn't you tell me she was in love with you?"

"I didn't know! I had no idea. I knew she liked me, but not like this."

"Yeah. Well, maybe we can convince Halliday that this is a case of puppy love run amok. That this is a troubled schoolgirl's infatuation that has spiraled out of control. What we have to do is make him believe that there was no reciprocity on your part."

He took a deep breath, slowly exhaling.

"One thing's for certain though. That girl is marching to the beat of a different drummer."

78

CHAPTER 12

When the Coopers arrived home after the hearing, Kelsey had a migraine headache and went to bed without eating or spending any time with Cooper and the girls. The next morning, she was up early, wearing a worn terry cloth robe over her pajamas and a pair of Tasha's stuffed-animal black lab slippers. Her hair was brushed, but without makeup, her skin had a grey pallor, and she looked drawn and tired.

After the girls left for school, Cooper cleared the table and loaded the dishwasher. Kelsey sat in silence at the table until he had finished.

"Clayton, we need to talk."

"Yes, we do," Cooper said. "The kids are worried about you."

"I know. I'm sorry. But Shawnee's interview was awful."

"It was awful. But we need to deal with it."

Tears pooled in Kelsey's eyes.

"I'm not going back until they reach a decision. I can't take it."

"Honey, you have to go. The worst is over now. Tomorrow we start with the people who are on my side. I need you there so you can see I've been telling you the truth. I need you there to show them you believe in me. You have to go."

"I can't. Shawnee said you didn't do anything. No one believed her. No one! I can't stand it. My migraines are getting worse, and I can't eat. I can't risk not being able to take care of the girls."

"Kelsey, we've been through this a hundred times. I didn't do anything. Don't you believe me?"

Kelsey looked at her husband, tears sliding down her cheeks.

"I don't know, Clayton. I just don't know."

***

Kelsey was not in the boardroom that afternoon.

Tom Garret paraded a host of character witnesses before Halliday. Fellow teachers and coaches spoke on Cooper's behalf. All of them shared their admiration for Cooper's character and accomplishments.

Signe Allen, the women's physical education teacher at Cedar Ridge Middle School and a close confidante of Cooper, was especially supportive. A fitness freak, Signe was a huge sports fan, and through the years, she had joined Cooper for early morning runs where they chatted about the potential of the athletes in the girl's programs, all of whom had been students in her phys ed classes.

Garret was hoping to discredit the school district's constant references to Cooper's "hands-on" teaching and coaching style. When he raised the topic with the gym teacher, she testified, "Coop touches everyone when he talks to them. There's nothing sexual about it. And the good thing is he treats the boys and the girls exactly the same way. Especially the kids who need it the most. For some of them, it's the only affectionate reinforcement they ever get."

Principle Mason countered with a question.

"Signe, isn't it possible that some of Mr. Cooper's students might misinterpret his 'hands-on' approach? Might not understand his attention and affection?"

"I don't think so, Wayne. I think Coop's the only one in this district who isn't afraid to show the kids that he cares."

***

Garret brought several students, male and female, to the boardroom, hoping to instill doubts about Shawnee's mental stability and to discredit her reputation. It was a slow process. Prior to the incident with Mr. Cooper, the girl had been almost invisible, one of the many high school students trying to survive at the bottom of the social ladder.

It was the top rung of that ladder that gave Garret the testimony he was looking for.

Jessica Willis was the last interview of the day. She had played soccer for Cooper and, like many of his players, had been a student in his homeroom at Cedar Ridge. Two classes ahead of Shawnee, she was entrenched in the elite social circles of Skyler High School.

Jessica had dark brown shoulder length hair and startlingly blue eyes. She had been the first in her class to develop curves, learning in seventh grade that it attracted boys' attention. Since that time, Jessica was sure to have the tightest dress, exposing the most cleavage at every formal dance. Even as she entered the boardroom, the men at the hearing had trouble ignoring the tight turtleneck and tissue-thin stonewashed designer jeans.

When Garret asked Jessica to share her thoughts about Shawnee McAllister, he was unprepared for her response. Jessica, a master of using sex appeal to get what she wanted, did not appreciate when others used that same skill.

"Every year, the younger girls come in, and all the guys go crazy. They all think they can find some freshman or sophomore who wants to be popular."

Garret asked, "Are you saying Shawnee was popular with the boys?"

"Oh, no. She's way too quiet. But all the new girls are willing to do almost anything to be cool."

"So you're saying that Shawnee is. . . sexually active?"

"I don't know about that. I don't think she dates much. But most of the younger girls are pretty loose. They want to fit in, you know? I think Shawnee was like that. She just wanted to fit in."

13
CHAPTER

As the hearing neared its conclusion, the emotional strain began to increase for Tom Garret. Throughout the process, the attorney had remained detached, resigned to the difficulty of defending clients in a "no tolerance" environment. Over the course of the proceedings, Garret and Cooper had actually forged a friendship. Garret wanted to win this case for his new friend.

They met for lunch before the next session, a daily routine that they had established during the first days of the hearing. "Coop, I really don't like the vibe I'm getting here. The school seems to be working hard for a dismissal, and Halliday is always unpredictable, which, I might add, can be good OR bad. Either way, I think we need a big play here soon."

"What do you mean? They've got an obviously unstable kid and a few ex-students with axes to grind, most of them with issues that are based on pure fantasy. How could Halliday ruin my life with that?"

"Easy. There's no 'three strikes' rule here. It can be one mistake, and you're out. They've got some minor complaints, a record of casual defiance, both issues that we might be able to deal with, but the incident itself is tough to justify. Unfortunately, it's pretty obvious that the school isn't trying to protect you. . . not to mention Shawnee's mother and her threat of a discrimination lawsuit."

"It's bullshit."

"Maybe. But I think our only chance is to convince Halliday that Shawnee's emotional status is so dysfunctional that she can't be trusted, and that you are the victim of a horrible misunderstanding. Even that's a long shot. But maybe we can get some sympathy that way."

"I'll do anything, Tom. Just get me out of this."

***

Curtis James, the athletic director of Skylar High School, was a Native American. Originally from the state of Washington, he was a member of the coastal Sol Duc Tribe located on the Olympic Peninsula.

The James family was highly thought of on the peninsula, respected for their integrity, work ethic, and civic contributions—both to the tribe and to the coastal community adjacent to the reservation. They were admired as role models by many of the Northwestern Native Nations. Curtis and his siblings had excelled academically and athletically in their small high school, and despite the challenges of growing up on a small reservation rife with economic woes, alcoholism, and drug issues, Curtis and his two siblings all had college degrees and successful careers.

The athletic director was popular with students and faculty alike on the Skyler High School campus. A man of solid stature, he had large hands and a crushing handshake that made no indication of his true gentle nature. He wore his hair in a near-shaved buzz cut, accentuating a round face that was seldom without a smile.

Garret began the interview cautiously. "Mr. James, as athletic director of the school, I assume that you have had the opportunity to deal with Mr. Cooper on a regular basis?"

"That's correct. We've coached together and worked hand-in-hand with the girl's athletic programs. But before we go any further, I want everyone to know that I am not comfortable being here today. The conflict of interest is obvious. I want everyone to know that I won't—I can't—choose sides here."

"I understand. And because of that dilemma, I just want your feedback on one issue. . . an issue that I think is neutral. I'm told that you and Mr. Cooper are both active members of the Skylar Teacher's Association, is that correct?"

"It is. We both care about watching out for the little guy."

"Meaning. . . ?"

"Teacher's rights, benefits, wages. Those kinds of things. Even our shared interest in the non-standard sports programs like soccer, wrestling, and of course, girl's athletics. Obviously, we support the majors, but both of us believe the minor sports are for kids too."

Garret nodded, "I can relate to supporting the little guys. I'm wondering, can you tell us what the teachers' union thinks about Mr. Cooper's situation here?"

Curtis looked at Cooper.

"I can't speak for the union. And I don't have a clue what's going on in Coop's situation. But I have heard rumors that some people think Coop might be punished for past pro-union political issues. I hope that isn't true. Sexual misconduct is unacceptable, but standing up for what you believe in is not. Mr. Cooper has never been afraid to fight for what he believes."

"Thank you, Mr. James. No further questions."

Due to the athletic director's connection to both administration and faculty—and his stated discomfort with choosing sides—Mason had no questions for Curtis James.

***

With the next witness, Garret made a final effort to appeal to Raleigh Halliday's judicial background and "beyond a reasonable doubt" mentality.

Because of Shawnee's and her mother's absence from the hearing's proceedings, and the opportunity to schedule her as the hearing's final witness, Garret was able to convince Mr. Halliday that Shawnee's mental state was the most critical aspect of his client's defense and the former judge agreed to allow the school district's psychologist to testify—with the caveat that he himself would closely monitor the content of the interview.

Dr. Jonnie Durham was five foot one-inch tall with her shoes on. She had fine brown hair that she wore short and curly, highlighted with blond accents. Her age was ambivalent; Cooper thought she could be anywhere from her late twenties to her early forties. The impression of youthfulness was exacerbated by her short stature, and when she sat down in the witness chair, Cooper noted that only the toes of her shoes touched the floor.

When Garret asked her about Shawnee McAllister, she replied, "Certainly Shawnee has some deep-seated emotional issues. How could she not? Cultural confusion, a nomadic lifestyle, a broken family. The list goes on and on. There is no doubt that the poor girl is emotionally unstable."

"Can you categorize these instabilities for us, Doctor? How would they manifest themselves?"

"I think it's safe to say that Shawnee is manic depressive and very likely bi-polar, which means she could be delusional and certainly prone to dramatic mood swings."

"Delusional in such a way that she might imagine an affection that didn't exist? Perhaps misinterpret kindness for love?"

"It's possible. Most of these things aren't that black and white. The nature of mental disorders is indistinct at best. The degree of acuteness can vary dramatically."

"Would you say that it's possible for someone like Shawnee to develop an obsession for an individual of the opposite sex?"

Dr. Durham laughed. "Mr. Garret, it's possible for any fifteen-year-old girl to develop an obsession for a member of the opposite sex. Obsession comes with the territory."

"Yes, but abnormal obsession?"

"Abnormal obsessions are possible for a manic depressive. In Shawnee's case, it's difficult to confirm because she refuses to talk about her feelings."

"Do you think Shawnee's mental state allows for her to be a credible witness?"

"I can't answer that, Mr. Garret. Credibility can be an elusive part of my world."

And with that statement, only Clayton Cooper remained to testify.

CHAPTER

When Cooper entered the room the next afternoon, he looked more like a member of the school's executive staff than the administrators themselves and more like a lawyer than either of the two attorneys in attendance. The new suit that he wore was immaculate, a midnight blue worsted wool so dark it was almost black. It was paired with a pin striped blue dress shirt and a solid dove-gray necktie. He was clean-shaven, without a trace of the fashionable three-day stubble on his chin. His hair had been cut and styled by an ex-student who worked at a local salon. She had replaced his usual spiked and gelled style in favor of a more traditional combed and parted haircut that made him look older and more business-like.

Garret opened his interview by asking Cooper questions about his teaching background, his family, and his role in the community. They went through the litany of his awards and accomplishments. After twenty minutes of laudatory reinforcement, the attorney segued into the heart of his defense.

"Mr. Cooper, this entire community seems to be making an unusual effort on your behalf to conserve your association with the Skyler School District. To what do you attribute your popularity?"

Cooper said, "Everyone knows that I love kids. I believe in kids. I try to do everything I can to nurture and mentor them."

"I see. And your recent involvement with Shawnee McAllister? Is that a result of this philosophy?"

"Absolutely. Shawnee has had a very difficult life. She has no real roots. She's surrounded by drugs and alcohol. She needs something. . . solid. . . to provide the stability that has eluded her for her entire life. I tried to fill that void."

"All right, Coop, let's get to the point. That night at the cemetery, did you engage in any improper activities with Ms. McAllister?" Cooper began to shake his head before the question was completed. Garret picked up on the gesture and continued to ask questions, in rhythm with Cooper's physical denials. "Did you hug her? Kiss her? Fondle her? Have sex with her? Behave in any way that might be objectionable?"

Cooper shook his head throughout the entire sequence of questions and then answered when Garret was finished, "No way. I absolutely did not do any of those things."

Spoken with such conviction, the denials were effective. Garret decided to conclude the session, content with his impression that no further explanation was necessary.

***

Wayne Mason stood to begin his cross. "Mr. Cooper, I'm curious. How can you sit there and answer Mr. Garret's questions about your behavior with Shawnee in the cemetery with such forceful denials? Throughout this hearing, you and your attorney have maintained that your 'hands-on' style is part of how you communicate. But in the car, with a girl you say was in dire need of your 'mentoring,' you didn't touch her, you didn't hug her, you didn't lay a finger on her? What are we to believe, Mr. Cooper?"

Cooper's cheeks reddened, the angry blush transparent on his clean-shaven skin.

"The circumstances were different, Mason. It wasn't the time or place to be touching a student."

Mason snorted.

"You're right about that, Mr. Cooper. It was certainly not the time or place to be touching any student."

As Cooper started to rise from the witness chair, Raleigh Halliday reluctantly called a halt to the confrontation.

"Gentlemen, would you mind reining in the hostility here? This is a hearing, not an inquisition. I know it's difficult for all of you, but I'd appreciate it if you'd try to be civil to one another."

Cooper did not answer

Finally, Mason responded without conviction, "Of course, Your Honor."

The principal continued the interview by summarizing the complaints presented by the group of witnesses assembled on the school's behalf. After he had itemized them, he asked Cooper for his response to their allegations.

"I don't recall any of the incidents that your so-called 'investigators' dug up. All of them are either taken out of context or are figments of teenage imaginations. Quite frankly, I don't think they have enough validity to warrant a comment."

"Oh, but you should comment, Mr. Cooper. Obviously, our witnesses remember things that you have chosen to forget."

Cooper shook his head. "No comment."

Mason knew that the interview had deteriorated into a petty squabble. He decided to conclude the questioning as soon as possible. Looking away from Cooper, he directed his comments to Raleigh Halliday.

"Your Honor, I deal with disciplinary issues at the high school on a daily basis. I am all too familiar with tactics invented to avoid telling the truth. Mr. Cooper's refusal to comment would not be acceptable in my office. I consider such immature responses akin to an admission of guilt. Please keep that in mind when you review the content of this particular interview."

He looked at Cooper with disdain, "Besides, all of this rhetoric is irrelevant. The related incidents, in this case, are important indicators of potential sexual misconduct behavior. But even without them, there is no excuse for the late-night incident with Shawnee McAllister."

Halliday nodded that he had heard.

"All right, folks, that concludes the interview phase of this hearing. As I said earlier, we will meet tomorrow to hear closing arguments."

His next comments were directed to Clayton Cooper.

"Mr. Cooper, considering the somewhat 'nonstandard' direction of your session this afternoon and my earlier promise to present your side of this situation, I'm going to give you an opportunity to address the group tomorrow, prior to the closing arguments of both sides. At that time, you may share your thoughts on the incident, the hearing, whatever. I do not want you to look back on this hearing feeling that you were denied the opportunity to say your piece. I assume that you want to take advantage of this arrangement?"

"Yes, sir. I do. And I appreciate your willingness to listen to my side of the story."

* * *

That night Cooper was in a quandary. For almost two weeks he had suffered in silence as the school district's legal team had done its best to malign his reputation. Now that Halliday had offered him an opportunity to present his side of the story, his mind filled with random protests of the unfair treatment, half-truths, and innuendos, all scattered and unorganized, seemingly impossible to remember and implement a defense.

It was well past midnight before he gave in to a persistent headache, heading for the medicine cabinet in the bathroom to search through Kelsey's supply of painkillers, sleeping pills, and over-the-counter medications. He took a single aspirin and washed it down with two glasses of water.

When he returned to the family room, Kelsey was seated in the leather chair next to his makeshift bed on the sofa. Kelsey's feet were tucked under her, and her arms were crossed over her chest.

"Hey, what's up, bro?" She used Jason Locker's standard greeting for her husband, the first friendly greeting she had addressed to Cooper in weeks.

Coop gave a short laugh. "Unfortunately, I'm up. You couldn't sleep either, huh?"

"No. Well, I was sleeping okay. I just woke up and couldn't go back to sleep. Thinking about tomorrow I guess. Are you doing all right?"

"A little headache. No big deal."

She looked at the sofa and said, "Your bed is still made."

"Yeah. So it is. What's up, Kelse? It's not like you to visit me lately."

"I know. I'm sorry." She looked at him and said, "What's going to happen, Coop? Will you really get your chance tomorrow?"

Cooper looked at his watch. It was almost one in the morning. "I should get to talk in a few hours. Now that the moment is here, I don't have a clue what to say."

Kelsey was quiet before asking, "Do you want me to come to the hearing? Will I make you nervous if I do?"

"Honey, you never make me nervous. And yes, I want you to come. I want you to hear me tell everyone else the same things I've been telling you for the past year. Besides, Tom says you should be there. He thinks your absence gives the impression that you're afraid to hear what the witnesses have to say."

"I am afraid. I'm very afraid of what they have to say. But if you want me there, I'll go. I know that it's almost over." She stopped, looking into Cooper's eyes. "I know you need my support. And I think I have to go to try to save this marriage."

Cooper stared at her in disbelief. It was the first time that Kelsey had revealed the true depth of her despair over the ordeal. All the talks, all the arguments, through it all, neither had spoken about the possibility of a failed marriage.

"Kelsey, how the hell could you say that today of all days? I can't believe you would say that now."

"Because I had to. Before the decision. One of us had to bring it up before the decision so that you understand this is not just about Shawnee. I've been thinking about it for a long time now. I won't leave you during the hearing, Coop. It wouldn't be fair to you. But I want you to know that I'm scared. I'm scared for you. I'm scared for us. I had to say something. I'm sorry it had to be tonight."

She used the heel of her hand to wipe the tears from her face. "Get some sleep. I'll get up with the girls tomorrow. And I'll go with you to the hearing. Maybe everything will be okay."

After Kelsey went to bed, Cooper sat alone in the family room, holding his head in his hands. His reputation had already suffered a terrible blow, his career was on the line, and now his family was in jeopardy. He had no idea what to do.

But as he thought about his wife's devastating announcement, an idea began to form, and finally, he knew what he would say at the hearing the next day.

CHAPTER

The next morning, Garret and Cooper met for breakfast to discuss the critical nature of the last day's agenda and how to best capitalize on Halliday's unorthodox opportunity.

"Tom, I've got this. I've never been so ready for anything in my life. I know what I'm going to do and how I'm going to do it!"

Cooper's zeal was palpable, and after listening to his client's plan, Garret knew that an emotional appeal to the judge was probably their only chance for a successful resolution of the hearing. He decided that Coop's plea would serve as the closing statement for the defense.

With Kelsey seated on a chair facing the front, Cooper began, "Ladies and gentleman, I'm going to surprise you all this afternoon and keep my comments short," he said, looking directly at his wife. "As you all know, it's been hard for me to just sit and listen to these testimonies without the chance to defend myself."

He shifted his gaze to the mediator. "I want to thank Mr. Halliday for this opportunity to present my side of the story."

Halliday nodded, and Cooper turned back to Kelsey.

"I think you all know how much I love kids. My two girls are my life. I don't know what I'd do without them. But I do know that I would never do anything to jeopardize their safety or hurt them in any way. And that includes risking my career by intentionally making a student or player uncomfortable with my actions or comments. I am what I am. I touch people when I talk to them. I pat them. I hug them. My students and my athletes. I try to let the kids that need someone to care about them know that someone does.

"It's true that I've spent a lot of time with kids in unsupervised situations. When that occurs, I am the supervisor and, in my mind, that makes it an acceptable situation. It's MY job to supervise my students. As to the incidents that have made kids uncomfortable, I don't remember a single one of those occurrences. If they were uncomfortable, they didn't understand where I was coming from."

He broke eye contact with Kelsey, looking back to Raleigh Halliday.

"I want to apologize to everyone for the situation with Shawnee. I realize that I didn't handle that incident very well. I made a huge mistake by trying to help in the way that I chose. But I think it's obvious that Shawnee needs someone who can help her deal with her life. That's what I tried to do. It was inappropriate, and I apologize for trying to help. It used to be that teachers were supposed to help their students, both in the classroom and out of it.

"Do I know the system well enough to realize that a teacher being out with a student late at night is a huge risk? Yes, I do. I shouldn't have done it. . . and that is the reason Shawnee was hiding.

"But today, I am telling you again that there was no improper behavior between Shawnee McAllister and me at the cemetery. You've heard it from me, and you've heard it from her. We were the only two witnesses. We've both said the same thing. I think you should all remember that fact.

"Teaching and coaching have been my life for as long as I've been here. I want to continue being a part of these schools and this community. I want to teach my own girls in my own classroom at Cedar Ridge. I want to coach my own daughters at Skyler High School. I'm asking you to give me that chance."

His voice broke as he concluded his statement, and lowering his head to hide his tears, he walked back to his seat.

"Mr. Mason, do you have a response before we wrap things up here?" Halliday asked the school's table.

"I do, sir. A very quick one. According to our research, Mr. Cooper's 'hands-on' style can be indicative of 'grooming' his students. Consciously or subconsciously, grooming is not an acceptable activity for our staff. Even the most well-meaning teacher can subject himself to situations that might get out of hand.

"I could list many gray areas regarding Mr. Cooper's behavior. But regardless of the content of student feedback and other questionable actions, it seems almost irrelevant to go there.

"Any teacher parked with a student late at night is in gross violation of the rules of the system. This, and Mr. Cooper's flight and subsequent attempt to hide Shawnee are reason enough for his dismissal.

"The truth is, it makes no difference if Shawnee is emotionally unstable, promiscuous, or obsessed. In fact is, if it is so, taking advantage of such a student becomes even more reprehensible.

"That's all I have to say. Thank you for listening."

***

One week later, the Skyler Daily News broke the following front-page story.

SUPERINTENDENT FINDS CAUSE TO FIRE TEACHER
By Terry Barlow
Skyler Daily News, Skyler, Oregon

There is probable cause for firing Cedar Ridge Middle School teacher and Skyler High School coach Clayton Kennedy Cooper following an investigative hearing on charges of sexual misconduct, Superintendent Dr. Ludlow Townsend said on Thursday.

The district's decision concludes months of controversy following the bizarre early morning discovery of Cooper and a fifteen-year-old former student in a parked car after a Skyler High football game last fall. During a hearing conducted by the state of Oregon, more than a dozen female students told about their own experiences of "inappropriate touching" or witnessing improper behavior.

"Questionable sexual behavior is not acceptable by any teacher toward any student," Townsend stated. He refused to detail any incident of alleged misconduct by complainants.

Cooper, an eighth-grade homeroom teacher at Cedar Ridge Middle School and a varsity coach for both the girls' soccer team and girls' fast-pitch at the high school, has been on paid administrative leave since September of last year.

A district employee for the past thirteen years, Cooper has been involved in the hearing with a state arbitrator for the past two weeks. He can appeal the arbitrator's recommendation for dismissal and request a second formal hearing based on Dr. Townsend's firing. The next hearing would be open to the public only at Cooper's request.

Meanwhile, the district's decision will take effect immediately. Cooper's employment has officially been terminated by the Skyler School District.

According to Townsend, the situation has been difficult for students, faculty, and the administration, creating a heated controversy within the community.

David Epperson, president of the Skyler Education Teachers Association, said, "This has been a very emotional ordeal for Clayton and one that's been very difficult for his colleagues. He is highly thought of in the community as well as by his fellow teachers."

The Wapiti Sheriff's Department checked out the original incident and referred the investigation to the prosecutor's office. No criminal charges were filed when the student involved refused to corroborate any inappropriate behavior.

Cooper could not be reached for comment. His attorney has not returned phone calls to our reporters.

CHAPTER

The Cooper's ordeal did not end with the conclusion of the hearing. As the media barrage became regional, the family's stress level expanded exponentially. Despite Cooper's assurances that the chaos would be short-lived, Kelsey took the girls and moved in with her parents to escape the newsmen, the radio broadcasts, and the phone calls resulting from the statewide reaction to her husband's dismissal.

With the media fervor still raging and his family life unraveling, Cooper decided to relieve some stress by going for a run at the state park bordering the Wapiti Indian Reservation. Because of its isolation, the trail that ran through the park had become his favorite training route during his forced sabbatical. In the winter months, he often had the three-mile loop to himself, especially during the week.

The muddy track discouraged most runners, but it was the difficulty of the terrain that appealed most to Cooper. The treacherous footing demanded concentration and provided no opportunity for his mind to wander. It was a pure escape.

There were no other vehicles in the parking lot when he arrived. He did a few quick stretches, pulled on a knit stocking cap and polypropylene gloves, and began his run.

The sky was the color of wet sand and the shrouded sun barely managed to produce a dull glare on the gray ocean. Cooper could smell the approaching rain, and he ran as hard as he safely could, jumping over exposed roots and high-stepping through the rocky stretches near the shoreline.

The miles passed, and before he knew it, he was straining up the short hill at the end of the circuit. Cresting the hill, he slowed to walk the final hundred yards as a cool-down, stabilizing his pounding heart.

As he entered the parking lot, he was surprised to see a small truck parked beside his own rig near the trailhead entrance. Although the autumn weekends could bring the occasional bird watcher or beachcomber, it was unusual to see another vehicle in the parking lot midweek.

In the cool weather, Cooper's Oakley sunglasses were beginning to fog, and he took them off to clean the lenses and wipe the back of his forearm across his sweaty face. As he reached the Explorer, he stopped to carefully reposition the glasses on his face.

When he looked up, Duffy Grayson stepped around the front of Cooper's rig, blocking his path to the driver-side door of the SUV.

Up close, Duffy was even more formidable than Cooper remembered. His black eyes shone in his fleshy face, and he stared with malice from under the visor of a Seattle Mariners baseball cap that rested on top of his head—a head that melded onto a massive neck, stretching the collar of his faded tee-shirt almost to the breaking point.

"Hey, asshole. Looks like I found you all alone out here in Indian country. How 'bout that? Are ya glad to see me?"

Cooper was not a small man. Six feet tall with his shoes on, he weighed one hundred and eighty-five pounds. In high school, he had been a member of the wrestling team, and his involvement with sports activities kept him in excellent physical condition. He was also three inches shorter and at least a hundred pounds lighter than Duffy Grayson.

"What do you want, Grayson? I've got no time for you today."

"No? According to the news you've got lots of time now. How does it feel to be one of us, man? Not so high and mighty anymore, huh? Tough to be a fuckup, ain't it?"

"What's this all about, Grayson? You didn't follow me out here to call me names. What do you want?"

"You molested my stepdaughter. What do you think I want?"

"I didn't touch Shawnee. She'll tell you that herself. Ask her."

"I don't need to ask her. The school says you did," he paused, and then said, "'The Man' says you're a scumbag. My wife says you're a scumbag. I guess you must be a scumbag."

When Cooper didn't respond, Duffy tried again.

"Maybe I should mess with one of your daughters, huh, scum bag? Let you see what it's like."

When Duffy's words registered in Cooper's brain, the blood rushed from his face and a red fury seared through his body. He screamed as he lunged at the big man, clawing at his thick neck.

Although Cooper's reaction caught Duffy by surprise, the attack was only a momentary inconvenience. The schoolteacher was crawling up the large man's chest when a ham-sized fist delivered a blow with a black hardwood club, landing just below Cooper's left ear and knocking his sunglasses from his face. Duffy dropped the smaller man into the soft mud beside his SUV.

This type of club was an integral part of every fishing boat on the coast. Used to efficiently dispatch netted fish, the dense hardwood weapon was called "a priest"—an apropos title for the tool used to administer last rites to netted salmon.

Cooper writhed in the mud, groaning in pain. Rolling to his stomach, he tried unsuccessfully to rise to his knees.

Duffy Grayson waited over him, holding "the priest" in readiness.

Cooper was hurt too badly to be any trouble. When Duffy was sure he wasn't dead, he snorted in disdain. "Guess you ain't no Little Big Man, huh asshole?"

Duffy walked around the front of the Explorer and sank into the seat of his truck. There was a long-necked beer bottle in the drink holder. As he pulled away from his parking place, he stopped beside the prostrate Cooper who was still struggling to regain his senses.

Coop heard the truck idling and rolled to his side to watch. Duffy held up the beer in a mock toast to his downed opponent. He drained the bottle and steering away from his disabled victim, launched the beer bottle over the top of the cab, in the general direction of the fallen ex-school teacher. Cooper watched as the bottle looped in slow motion through the air, bumping in his direction before bursting into a thousand pieces. Even though the green glass exploded less than two yards from where he lay, Cooper didn't hear it. "The priest" had shattered his eardrum, and his head was filled with rushing noises, like water sloshing around in the bottom of a rocking boat.

***

When he got home, Clayton went into the bathroom and swallowed two prescription painkillers left over from Kelsey's pill stash. He undressed and climbed into the shower to wash off the grime, the dark string of blood, and the unidentified liquid that was seeping from his ear.

When he finished, he dressed and then drove to his in-laws' house to check on his two daughters. The girls were watching a movie in their grandparent's living room. They were both engrossed in the story, and neither bothered to look up when their father greeted them. Cooper was too happy to see them safely watching TV to care about their indifference to his arrival.

His wife was in the kitchen, putting away groceries. When Cooper walked in, she dropped a bag of groceries, and an assortment of canned soups and vegetables clattered across the kitchen floor.

"Oh, my God. What happened? Were you in a wreck? Are you okay?"

100

Cooper stood with his good ear tilted towards his wife. "I'm fine. Listen, honey, we need to talk."

"You're not fine. You look awful. This is serious, Coop. What have you done now?"

"We need to get the girls away for a while. I'm not sure the kids are safe here right now. Shawnee's stepfather jumped me at the beach. He said some things that really bothered me, Kelse. I'm sure he's just trying to scare me. But I don't think we should take any chances."

"What kind of 'things'? Did he threaten you?"

Cooper hesitated, knowing what Kelsey's reaction would be, but he was too concerned to hide it.

"He threatened the girls," he blurted.

Kelsey's face went white. Her hands began to shake. Tears filled her eyes, and she started to sob.

When Cooper tried to comfort her, she jerked away from his outstretched arms.

"Don't touch me!" she shouted. "You've ruined our lives, Clayton. If anything happens to my babies, I'll never forgive you. Never. I should have left you the night you were with that little bitch!"

"Honey, settle down. It's going to be okay."

"No, it's not going to be okay. I will not live my life fearing for my daughters' safety. Just leave. Get out. And call the police. I want that bastard put in jail. Forever!"

She held her head in her hands. "What have you done now, Clayton? What have you done?"

***

Cooper drove to the Wapiti County Sheriff Department and reported Duffy Grayson's threat.

An interested Deputy Clarence Bigelow processed the paperwork. It was an awkward situation for Cooper, who was reluctant to raise any issue that might reopen the Shawnee McAllister case and the potential for criminal charges to be filed against him.

As the officer most responsible for the area around the reservation, Bigelow knew Duffy well, a circumstance that compelled him to empathize with the agitated ex-teacher. Duffy had been trouble for the sheriff's department for years and the deputy never missed a chance to remind Grayson that he was keeping an eye on him.

Bigelow asked about Clayton's swollen face. Cooper insisted that he had not suffered the injuries during Duffy's assault.

"You know what Mr. Cooper? There's a real world out there. And if you don't figure it out soon, it's going to bite you in the ass someday."

CHAPTER 17

Before Cooper awoke the following morning, Kelsey and the girls left for Lake Tahoe to visit Kelsey's ex-roommate from her days at Portland State. Cooper was still staying at the family house alone, unaware that his panicked wife had taken the girls out of school and left town for an unscheduled ski vacation.

Just before breakfast, Kelsey's father called Cooper with the news and asked him to refrain from contacting his daughter until her return. Both girls sent him their love, he said, and he could talk with them when they came back the following week. Meanwhile, Coop's wife had asked him to respect her request for some time to think.

Ten seconds after Mr. Harrington hung up, Cooper called Kelsey's cell phone. There was no answer. For the next several days, he called often, his frustration growing with every unanswered call and every unreturned text message.

While his family was gone, Cooper attended to the details of his departure from Cedar Ridge Middle School. He worked on his retirement package and made arrangements for temporarily extending his family's medical insurance.

He contacted Dave Epperson and had a long talk with the principal, explaining his decision to accept Dr. Townsend's ruling, forgoing any further appeals. The union president understood and accepted his decision with regret.

And then, he waited. Alone in the house on Sunrise Heights, he had lots of time to do some thinking of his own.

***

Like the bruises on his face, the media fervor began to fade, and that occurrence, along with the reduced stress of Kelsey's absence and the relief associated with his decision to get on with his life, dramatically improved Cooper's state of mind.

He wrote a letter to the school district announcing his decision not to exercise his right to appeal. He reiterated his innocence and requested closure from the district. He could not resist placing the blame for his dismissal on an educational system that had "robotized" the role of the modern schoolteacher.

While he waited for his family, he spent hours sitting in the darkness of the empty house. Sometime during his solitary vigil, he yielded to a stirring in his innermost core, admitting to himself that, despite missing his daughters terribly, he was relieved that his ordeal had ended. He was looking forward to the opportunity to start over.

***

When Kelsey returned a week later, she insisted on a trial separation, and Cooper reluctantly agreed to move out of the house, relocating to a small rental unit at the back of Jason Locker's wooded home site on the other side of town. Usually rented to visiting student teachers, it happened to be empty, and Jason made him a deal he couldn't refuse.

To his surprise, Cooper was comfortable there from the day he moved in. Jason's wife Amy was as laid back as her husband. And their two young children, a ten-year-old daughter named Summer and a five-year-old boy Roger called "Bubba," had known and loved "Uncle Coop" for years. It wasn't unusual to find one—or both—of the kids and Cooper in a raucous wrestling match on the floor of the Locker's den or playing a noisy game of tag in the wooded backyard. When the kids were at school, Coop spent most of his free time surfing the web on his laptop or hiking and taking photographs on the Oregon coast.

Physically, he felt good. His head injury was healing, and although he still had trouble hearing out of his left ear, he had adjusted to the inconvenience. He was bicycling now to supplement his running program, and he enjoyed the change of pace.

One day while he was pedaling down a rural road near Gamble Bay, Duffy Grayson's pickup passed him heading the other way. Cooper was wearing his bike helmet, and neither the truck's driver nor his passenger had recognized the cyclist. Duffy, however, was easy to spot, even while driving at 60 miles per hour. It happened unexpectedly, and Cooper had no time to react to the crossing of paths. The passenger was Shawnee McAllister. Cooper's hands tightened on the handlebars, and he didn't relax until he was certain the truck had continued in the opposite direction.

Shawnee and Duffy. One he wouldn't allow himself to think about. The other filled his heart with hate and fear.

CHAPTER

"Shawnee. Get your butt back here. You ain't going nowhere."

Shawnee looked back at her stepfather with the scorn that only a teenage girl can muster. "Why not, Duffy? I've got an art project due next week. I need to go to the library."

"The library? What kind of bullshit is that?"

Philomena stepped in on her daughter's behalf.

"Leave her alone, Duffy. Don't you be bad-mouthing her about her schoolwork, just 'cuz you've killed most of your own brain cells. Leave her be."

"Shut up, woman. As long as I'm paying some of the bills here, she'll do what I say. And so will you. So shut your mouth."

When Philomena was sober, she tried to avoid confrontations with Duffy, instead relying on cunning and guile. When she was drunk, she was more reckless, but even then, her survival instincts often prevailed. Today she chose to remain silent.

Shawnee walked back into the house, but not without a look of disgust directed at Duffy when he wasn't paying attention. She shook off her coat and sat down on the stained gold brocade couch. Shawnee hated this house that reeked of stale beer and endless cigarettes, a combination that made her throat itch and her eyes water. It was a smell that had permeated every house they had ever lived in, always worsened by a procession of bored, unemployed friends and relatives looking for a roof over their heads. Duffy's addition to the family had discouraged many of the visitors, but it had done nothing to change the atmosphere. Shawnee had never grown used to it, and she longed for a home with fresh air and fewer visitors.

She knew that her departure was only on hold, and when Duffy and Philomena left for the bar, she could go wherever she wanted. It was much less stressful when he was gone. Safer too. She could wait.

So far Duffy's abuse had only been verbal, and she had learned to ignore his taunting barbs. But she was still wary of his presence in her house. Every night, she propped a sturdy oak chair underneath the door handle to her bedroom.

***

Duffy and Philomena left the house forty-five minutes later.

The bus that Shawnee caught outside the Project took her straight to the library, where she spent a blissful hour looking through the art section at the top of the stairs. She especially loved artwork that featured animals and nature, and it was usually easy for her to lose herself in its serene beauty.

Tonight, she had trouble staying focused, watching the clock on the wall with nervous expectation. At ten minutes to nine, she put away Audubon's Collected Drawings and walked down the stairs into the night. She was surprised by the cloudless sky, and she reveled in the stars that were so often hidden in the coastal fog and mist. The clear sky meant colder air, and Shawnee shivered as she pulled her jacket collar against her neck and started up the street toward the center of town.

The downtown core of Skyler consisted of a two-block stretch of retail stores and service businesses anchored by the ancient Steelhead Theater at one end and the post office building at the other. Beyond the center of the city, Main Street was lined with blue-collar taverns and cocktail lounges, remnants of a once-thriving logging and fishing community that catered to a hardworking, hard-drinking clientele. The glory days were gone now, and many of the town's drinking establishments had been shuttered and were in decay.

Shawnee walked past the post office and looked down "tavern row" for Duffy's truck on the almost empty street. The little pickup was nowhere to be seen, and she knew that her mother and Grayson must be at the casino on the outskirts of the reservation, seven miles from town.

She turned in the opposite direction and began heading north, walking the route for exactly thirty-three minutes before reaching the Locker's modest ranch-style house built on a wooded lot at the end of a rural cul-de-sac. Behind the house and its Home Depot playground equipment and bright blue trampoline was a small cottage set in a grove of second-growth cedar trees and hemlocks.

Shawnee felt relieved when she saw the light shining through the half-closed slats of mini-blinds. He was home.

She settled herself into her usual spot between two cedars that faced the windows at the front of the cottage. Leaning against one of the trees, she watched for movement through the gaps in the blinds.

When she watched him reading or working on his computer, Shawnee loved to fantasize about the interior of the neat little cottage, especially the imaginary clean, fresh smell of the house. Some nights—tonight was one—she could see a candle burning on the table near the window, and she pretended that it was a scented candle that smelled like cinnamon.

Shortly after 10 P.M., Cooper began to prepare for bed. Shawnee saw the bathroom door open and close. Minutes later, he emerged in the small living room. She followed the dark shadow toward the kitchen, watching as the lights were extinguished. Then, the living room lights disappeared. Still, a warm glow emanated from between the slats of the blinds, and Shawnee closed her eyes and took a long, slow breath, inhaling the imagined aroma of the lone candle, willing it to burn longer and keep emitting its divine fragrance.

Seconds later, the light disappeared, and the cottage went dark.

CHAPTER

14

On the last day of February, Kelsey filed for a divorce. The separation had lasted almost six months, ample time for her to ratchet up the courage to take the final step.

The time apart had resolved Cooper's fears about losing contact with the girls. During the separation, he saw them on a daily basis, driving them to school and taking them to their extra-curricular activities. They stayed with him at the cottage on alternate weekends. He knew that they were worried about the possible dissolution of the marriage, and he tried hard to ease their concerns.

As for himself, he refused to dwell on the consequences of a divorce. He was ready to get on with life, and right now the problem was more fiscal than emotional. He needed to find a job. But even that concern was relative. He was enjoying the first free time he had had in years, making frequent trips with his cameras, working hard on his fitness program.

He had joined a co-ed softball team of thirty-somethings and took pleasure in the late winter practice sessions held at the local community college gym. No one cared that he was the oldest member of the team. Jason and Amy Locker were on the team, and Cooper had been welcomed into their circle of friends and teammates, providing a welcome diversion and support group during the waiting period preceding the conclusion of his marriage.

The divorce was finalized in the third week of May.

***

The slow-pitch team was playing a tournament at the Columbia River Gorge over Memorial Day weekend. To celebrate his new life, Clayton got drunk with Jason and Amy and most of the team at the motel cocktail lounge on Saturday night. The softball players toasted his freedom and made jokes about his love life. As the evening went on, the team's married partners faded into the night. Couple by couple, they returned to their own rooms and their own togetherness.

Cooper and the three single girls on the team partied on. They lost count of the pitchers of draft beer they'd consumed, throwing down an occasional round of tequila shooters. Just before midnight, the two girls who were partners headed upstairs. That left Coop and the team's first baseman Haley Hunter as the last two standing.

Haley was almost as tall as Cooper. Strong and fit, in her mid-thirties, she was divorced and a notorious party girl. Like Cooper, she was a bicyclist, and they had ridden together a time or two since Cooper's initial separation from Kelsey. On the rides, they had joked about the bicycle seat being effective birth control and an effective deterrent for developing any sexual connection between the two of them.

Haley was curious about Cooper, and her flirting had grown bolder as his divorce deadline approached. For weeks now, his teammates had teased him about his refusal to date before the divorce was final, a moral stance seldom taken within their peer groups. The official divorce changed all that. The months of forced abstinence, the release from a teetering marriage and, especially, the beer and tequila, had crushed any remnants of high-road principles.

"Coop, let's go. I think I've had too much to drink." She paused, focused on speaking without slurring her words. "You might have to take advantage of me."

His own voice thick with alcohol, Cooper said, "I always told my wife I would never cheat on her. . . but if someone showed up naked at my door, I couldn't promise that I'd be able to resist."

"Oh, yeah? What's your room number?"

***

Haley knocked on the door of room 314. She was wearing a blue nylon warm-up jacket with a drawstring waist tied loosely over her hips, and nothing else. Her long legs, burnt reddish brown from hours on the softball field and on her bike, were smooth and strong. She was barefoot, and her feet were oddly white as if she had just stepped out of an ankle-deep basin of white paint: a softball player's version of a farmer's tan.

When Cooper opened the door, she unsnapped the Western Oregon All Stars jacket and untied the drawstring that held it together at the bottom. Coop stared at her breasts, now freed from the confinement of the ever-present sports bra. They were larger than he expected and hung low on her chest. The dark aureoles were large, and her nipples were erect in the center of the ample circles.

His eyes slid down her torso, coming to rest on the neat copper-colored hair at the juncture of her body. It was straight and spare and inviting.

"Are you going to ask me in? Or are you just going to enjoy the view?"

Cooper cleared his throat and said in a voice made husky by alcohol and lust, "I'm going to ask you in. . . and then I'm going to enjoy the view."

He pulled her into the room and peeled the windbreaker off her shoulders. She was naked now, and as he drew her close, he nuzzled his face into her neck and inhaled the scent of her body. She had taken a quick shower and applied a moisturizing cream, and she smelled delicious and feminine. His lips moved from her neck to her face, kissing her eyes and her nose, teasing her as he eluded her lips, lifting her chin to kiss the pulsing vein on the inside of her throat once again.

"Kiss me," she whispered.

"Patience, baby. Patience."

Then he retraced the gentle path of his lips from throat to chin, from nose to eyes, before coming back to her mouth and sliding back and forth over her lips, seeking the perfect fit. Only then did he press their lips together.

Haley pulled Cooper onto the queen-sized bed before pushing him onto his back. She reached under his tank top and ran her hands over his sinewy chest and flat stomach. She began to rush now and shoved the tank top over his head, giggling when it got hung up on his chin before she could release it and throw it to the floor. Pushing his upper body flat on the bed she straddled his thighs and untied the drawstring of his baggy shorts. After she fumbled to get the knot undone, she pulled his shorts and boxers off his hips and down his legs, throwing them on the floor at the end of the bed.

Now they were both naked, and the soft light of the wall sconce that Cooper had purposely left on was illuminating their bodies with erotic incandescence. Haley reached down and guided him in, sinking slowly on top of his body, with her eyes closed and her head tilted to one side.

***

Cooper had an epic hangover in the morning. He seldom drank too much, and when he did, his body punished him without mercy. As he put on his softball uniform, he ruefully noted that his discomfort was not limited to a pounding headache.

The team lost their first game of the day, a loss that eliminated them from the losers' bracket, providing a merciful exit from the tournament.

Haley wanted to ride back to Skyler with Cooper, but he discouraged that plan, explaining that he needed time alone to think about what had happened between them.

Even though he had enjoyed the lovemaking, he knew that he wasn't interested in beginning a relationship with his teammate.

The one-night stand with Haley Hunter was Cooper's only sexual encounter of the summer, and his disappointing social life soon became a microcosm of his new life in general.

**

Reflecting on the unstable direction of his life, Cooper noted that the Skyler residents who had petitioned to retain his position with the school system were still cordial, but the decision to terminate his services had introduced an undercurrent of subtle doubt amongst them. Image-conscious businesses sensitive to public backlash weren't hiring. It was the same story everywhere Cooper applied. Even the blue-collar companies were reluctant to take a chance.

Just as surprising for Cooper was his banishment from the youth sports programs to which he had dedicated so many of his summers through the years. He had taken last year off from coaching both of his daughters' fast-pitch teams, knowing that the public incident would put the leagues in a difficult situation, but he had planned to resume coaching during the current season. When he volunteered his services, the parks department politely declined.

In spite of the volunteer community's rejection, his tepid love life, and the frustration of his fruitless job search, Cooper's greatest concern continued to be the constant specter of Duffy Grayson. Deputy Sheriff Clarence Bigelow's talk with Duffy had only been marginally effective. Threatened with a restraining order and Bigelow's personal promise of a diligent surveillance program, Shawnee's stepfather had laughed off Cooper's fears, insisting that his comments about Cooper's daughters were only intended to incite the attack that they had so effectively provoked. Cooper's response had allowed Duffy to react in self-defense and, he told the deputy with fawning remorse, everything had now been resolved between him and the ex-school teacher.

Bigelow did not believe a word of Duffy's explanation. Nor, upon the deputy's report to the concerned victim, did Clayton Cooper. Cooper feared that as long as he and Duffy were in the same location, his children would not be safe, and he would never be able to live a normal life.

ARROW IN PARADISE

20
CHAPTER

The telephone rang, startling Cooper awake. It was Sunday morning, the one day each week that he allowed himself to sleep in, and the clock on the nightstand beside his bed glowed with three red fives. Groping for the phone, Cooper answered with a sleepy, "Hello?"

"Coop? Are ya up yet?"

Cooper sighed as he recognized the unmistakable voice of his only uncle, his mother's younger brother Stanley, who lived in northern Montana and never failed to forget that there was a time zone difference between Montana and coastal Oregon.

"Hey, Uncle Stanley. I'm up. What's going on?"

"Well, I been thinkin' about ya. Ya got a job yet?"

Cooper's sleepy fog was clearing, and he smiled at his Montana-native uncle's tendency to get straight to the point.

"Nope. I'm still trying to figure out what to do when I grow up. Why?"

"Remember you told me you were thinking about doing some writing and taking some pictures the last time we talked?"

"Yeah. I believe I also said I might want to manage the Boston Red Sox. The odds of either one happening are just about the same."

"You know, I think you people get too much rain over there. It makes you so negative. Here in Montana, if we want something we roll up our sleeves and go get it. I got a proposition for you. I'm thinking about taking a trip. A long trip. I don't want to spend the winter up here alone."

Stanley's wife of over forty years, Cooper's Aunt Dodie, had been dead for almost two years now. Cooper knew his uncle missed her and was still struggling with her loss.

"I'm gonna do a road trip with the fifth-wheeler. Might be gone a year or so. . . maybe more. I need someone to care-take the place up here in the valley. You're the only guy I know—at least the only one with no job—who likes this place as much as I do. I thought you might need some time to get your act together. Think about what you want to do. Maybe even take a run at your dream."

The proposal was so unexpected, so foreign to the alternatives that Cooper had been considering, that he didn't know what to say.

His uncle continued, "Free rent. You pay the utilities, and I'll throw in a little caretaker cash to keep you in beer money. You could take pictures, write your articles if you want. I could get the hell out of Dodge. What do you think?"

"I don't know what to say, Uncle Stan. It's not something that had even crossed my mind."

"You got other plans?"

"No. Nothing definite yet, I. . ."

"You still like it up here?"

"Of course I do. It's my favorite place in the world."

"Thought so. Seems like that might be important, huh? You better think hard on it, boy."

"Can I do that? I'm not sure that I want to be that isolated right now. And it's so far from my girls. Can I sleep on it?"

"Sure you can. And don't worry about them girls. They love it here too, 'specially Mac. That girl should have been born in Montana."

It was true. Mac thought the Yaak River valley was heaven. She loved to hike and fish and play in the snow. To Cooper's tomboy

117

daughter, the Yaak was better than Disneyland, and her father loved that she felt that way. Mac would be an easy sell.

"Can I call you back at the end of the week?"

"Yeah, sure," Stanley hesitated, "I'd like to leave right after Labor Day, Coop. I've got a friend with a motorhome who wants to caravan around the country. Glacier, Yellowstone, the Grand Canyon. . . maybe even the Everglades. I might end up heading south for the winter. Who knows?"

"This wouldn't be a lady friend, would it?" Cooper teased. "You're not fooling around, are you?"

"None of your damn business, boy. None of your business."

Cooper laughed. "You got any more Montana girls with motorhomes tooling around up there? If you could throw in a girl, we might have a deal."

It was quiet on the other end of the phone for a brief moment.

"It ain't that easy, son. Take it from me. Sometimes starting a new life ain't all it's cracked up to be."

***

The valley and its river were named by the native people.

Long before the white man came in the early eighteen hundreds, the local tribes had hunted in the valley, and they called the river that created the drainage "Yaak." It was astutely named, since the Yaak waters flowed into the Kootenai River, bisecting the huge river like an arrow notched in the center of a bow. The Native American word for bow was "Kootenai." For arrow, the word was "Yaak."

Even before the white explorers came, the valley had a mystical aura. Impenetrable forests of larch, fir, spruce, and pine surrounded the river. Rugged mountains rose from the sides of the valley, only their raw peaks rising above the tree line. Dark with timber and brushy undergrowth, the primal valley was a wildlife sanctuary,

118

teeming with game and hunting opportunities, but with the abundance of deer, elk, and moose came nature's own hunters— the predators. Tribal legends told of frightening otherworldly experiences with wolves, grizzly bears, and mountain lions, and every hunting expedition to the Yaak required a shaman's presence and protective blessing.

When the white man came, the valley changed. Trapping, hunting, logging, and mining sucked some of the core wildness from its heart. But the spirit of the valley persevered. Its rugged geological make-up, its brutal winters, and the distance from civilization provided protection from the growth and development so common in less isolated wilderness environs. Along with other remote areas near the northern border, it remained a part of the continental United States' last frontier. Eventually, over two million acres surrounding the Yaak became the Kootenai National Forest, and most of the land was reserved for public use.

A fraction of the valley remained private property, and the town of Yaak joined other tiny outposts of anonymity sprinkled below the Canadian border where one could lead a simple life. These solitary outposts were irresistible to loners and nonconformists and to a darker segment of residents seeking to a general escape from society. The local joke was that The Yaak was located halfway between Idaho's white supremacist Randy Weaver's complex and Montana's Unabomber Ted Kazinsky—an apt summation of the areas' power to attract those seeking to live in lawless obscurity.

***

Cooper's aunt and uncle, Dodie and Stanley Kennedy, had acquired their piece of the Yaak a decade earlier, sharing it with Cooper and his family ever since. The Kennedys were native Montanans who grew up in the eastern side of the state, near the town of Glasgow. Childhood sweethearts, they had married young and managed to eke out a living as ranchers on a three hundred and twenty-acre spread halfway between Glasgow and Havre. Throughout their lives together, they had longed to escape the barren plains of Eastern Montana in favor of the more pristine beauty of the Rockies.

In search of their dream, they made frequent trips west, exploring the mountains as well as the grandeur of Glacier National Park and its surrounding country. It was on one of these trips that they discovered the Yaak.

The Kennedys spent the night in a campground on the river and explored the area the following day. They scoured the valley, looking for property or a house to buy. What they did find came as a complete surprise.

The Whiskey Bend Saloon had been built twenty-five years earlier on an oxbow of the Yaak River, a mile or so above where Whiskey Creek emptied into the main stream. The bar was positioned in such a way that the river flowed due south toward the building, rushing to within fifteen feet of its structure where it took a ninety-degree turn and wrapped around the east side of the saloon, creating a spectacular half-moat around this drinking man's wilderness castle.

In its heyday, the saloon's traditional rows of shelved liquor bottles had been replaced in favor of enormous plate-glass windows. The Whiskey Bend Saloon's back-bar wall opened to the river, and customers seated on bar stools had an unobstructed view of the valley and the rum-colored Yaak River that rushed just feet from the building.

The saloon had been owned by a couple struggling to carve out a living in the remote valley with a sparse population and limited road access. When the husband died in a freak hunting accident, the bar sank into disrepair. In survival mode, the wife sold the liquor license to the general store in the town of Yaak, and the store owners added the Yaak River Tavern to their operation. Without the liquor license, the Whiskey Bend property offered prospective buyers a bar without alcohol, and it languished on the market for almost three years.

When the Kennedys spotted the faded FOR SALE sign tacked to the front door, the log porch entryway was in danger of collapsing, and the wood siding had been stripped of its paint and color by the weather. The "Whiskey Bend Saloon" sign painted above the front door was faded and peeling, its once vibrant letters blending into the weathered exterior.

The parking lot in front of the building was littered with crushed beer cans and yellow plastic snowmobile oil containers, and the roadside pull-off smelled like urine and stale beer. Red and green shotgun shell-casings were strewn about like confetti, a colorful reminder of the permanency of contemporary garbage.

Aunt Dodie was not impressed.

"Stanley, this is crazy. We can't run a bar here. This place is a mess."

"Sometimes you gotta see the forest through the trees, ma. I don't want a bar here. I want the land. Maybe we'll bulldoze this down and build something else here someday. We're gonna get a deal on this place, Dode."

"You better!" Aunt Dodie said. "Because it sure as hell isn't worth buying. Besides, it's in the middle of a floodplain. You're crazy."

"I know," Stanley answered.

Later that evening, Stanley offered a surprised realtor forty percent under the asking price. The agent called back in less than an hour and accepted the offer without any attempt to counter.

From the minute they signed the papers and renamed the place Whiskey Bend Ranch, its restoration was a labor of love. Every summer, the two of them would spend a month or so in the Yaak. Stanley rebuilt the porch, repaired the roof, and rewired and insulated the building. The saloon's original bar had disappeared during the years of vacancy, and the couple built a new dry-bar as its replacement. Abutting the wall and four feet closer to the windows, the riverside view was better than ever.

Uncle Stanley kept a salt block across the river, and the Kennedys delighted in the moose, mule deer, and whitetail deer who were frequent visitors to the block. Otters, eagles, ospreys, and ducks provided daily entertainment, and the animals of the valley made the bar feel like the viewing area of a Montana game farm.

After two or three years, Stanley took great satisfaction in having the locals stop by to check on the progress of their "bar-into-a-home" conversion. He was especially pleased when a long-time Yaak resident said, "Goddamn, I knew I should have bought this place. You got the best chunk of river in the valley."

But what gave Stanley the most pleasure was the fact that Aunt Dodie grew to love the place as much as he did himself. They decided to retire and live there together for the remainder of their lives. Time passed, and a short three and a half years later Dodie got sick. She lasted for four months before she died, and Uncle Stanley could not forgive himself for not acting on their dreams sooner.

After Dodie passed, Stanley wanted to live in the Yaak for her, pretending that they could still share their dream together. But he was alone now, and it wasn't the same. It made him sad, and he knew he couldn't bear a winter at the ranch without her. It needed someone who would love the place as much as he and his wife had loved it. It needed a kindred spirit to fill this void.

Stanley Kennedy believed that everything happened for a reason. He believed that Cooper's misfortune had a purpose and that both men's life changes were too connected to ignore. Fate had presented Cooper an opportunity to discover what to do with his life, and his uncle was convinced that the valley should be a part of his future.

21
CHAPTER

Early in August, Cooper moved to the Yaak.

He rented a U-Haul trailer from Sully's Shell Station and hooked it up to the new Toyota pickup truck that he had purchased after his divorce was final. Jason Locker agreed to ride shotgun for the trip to Montana. Their game plan was to drive the almost seven hundred miles in one day, move Cooper in, spend a day showing Jason the area, and then deliver him to the airport in Spokane where he could fly back home.

On the day of their departure, they met in the Locker's kitchen early in the morning, and Jase's wife Amy poured them both a cup of coffee.

"Dude, it's so awesome that you're going to be living in a saloon. Talk about dying and going to heaven!"

Amy rolled her eyes. "Jason, it's not a bar anymore. It's a house. Try to control yourself."

"I know it's not. But think about it, honey. Who's the last person in the entire world that you'd expect to find living in a saloon in bum-fuck Montana? Who's the biggest hipster you know? Could it be Mr. Tight Suit and Skinny Jeans?"

He grinned at his friend. "The Coopster, that's who. Those rednecks will tear him apart."

Cooper winked at Amy and then scratched his nose with his middle finger, making sure that Jason didn't miss the gesture

"Locker, there's more ponytails on guys in the Yaak than there are on that group of potheads that you play soccer with. You'd fit right in up there, so don't give me any shit about not being able to make the cut. Besides, by this winter, I'll look like Grizzly Adams. I'll put that scraggly mess on your chin to shame."

Jason laughed. "Sure you will. Maybe you can gel the sumbitch to make sure it's perfect."

***

They drove nonstop all day, taking turns at the wheel.

When they reached the northern panhandle of Idaho, they turned east on Highway 2, and four miles past the Idaho-Montana border, they took a left on Yaak River Road and headed toward the Canadian border. The road snaked up the valley and before they had traveled even ten miles, Jason had counted five roadside crosses—each stark white marker signifying a traffic fatality. The valley was infamous throughout the area for the treacherous road, too far from civilization to properly maintain or for law enforcers to regulate.

"Dude, it looks like a fuckin' WWII battle cemetery around here. What's the deal?"

Cooper shrugged.

"Lots of drunk drivers. Deer encounters, motorcycle accidents, winter wrecks on icy roads, you name it. They thin out as you go up the road."

"Good. It's kind of spooky."

They rolled into the parking lot of the ranch just before dark.

"Welcome to the Whiskey Bend Saloon, bro. And the beginning of my new life."

"Let's check it out, man."

They climbed out of the truck, and Cooper pointed across the river in front of the house, holding the forefinger of his other hand to his lips. A whitetail doe and two fawns with faded white spots were standing at the salt block staring at them, their ears propped forward, alert to any possible danger. The men leaned back against

124

the truck and watched, enjoying the stare-down in the dusk-blue light. The animals were secure across the water, and soon the doe was busy at the lick while her twins played chase in the small clearing.

"Cool. I'm beginning to see why you like it here."

"You haven't seen anything yet. Uncle Stanley has some wildlife pictures you won't believe. And wait until we get a chance to look around a bit."

"How 'bout we look around for some beer? This place is a bar isn't it?"

"It will be when we get unloaded. There's beer in the cooler. And we can fix a pizza. I'm hungry."

They unloaded the truck, and while Cooper prepared the pizza, Jason looked around the once-notorious Whiskey Bend Saloon, in awe of the setting and still trying to comprehend the novelty of living in a Montana bar.

Cooper's aunt and uncle had done a great job of converting the saloon into a home. The floor plan was open but cozy, the large room decorated in rustic lodge style. Cooper turned on all the lights and lit two scented candles to eliminate the musty odor of the unoccupied house. The candlelight flickered off the tongue-and-groove cedar walls and ceiling, producing a warm patina throughout the open space.

Cooper's uncle had replaced the original wet bar with a custom dry bar, built especially for his wife. It was a long slab of polished pine, so light in color that it appeared white in the evening glow. Beneath the bar, recessed just far enough to avoid the knees protruding from barstools, was a low-slung library. Three shelves high and thirty feet long, it was stuffed with Aunt Dodie's favorite books, haphazardly organized by subject matter.

As much as Cooper loved the books, it was the view above the bar that made the Whiskey Bend Ranch special. The river water skirted around a small island in front of the windows, running toward the center of the bar and then wrapping around the building so close you could see the fish rising in the river from a seat at the bar stool. At the tail of the island, the water pushed through a deep riffle and then slowed, creating trout habitat that was the envy of the valley.

Behind the salt block across the river, the larch forest stretched up the side of Grizzly Peak like an endless army of green-black soldiers blanketing the steep slopes in the pristine wilderness.

Jason was impressed. "Wow, this is incredible. I can't wait to see it in the daylight."

"You should see it in the winter. The tourists go away, and you feel like you're living a hundred years ago. I still can't believe my aunt and uncle were lucky enough to find this place. It'll be a perfect spot to figure out what to do with the rest of my life."

In the morning, they ate breakfast at the bar, watching a young bull moose at the salt block and two ospreys suspended in a lazy holding pattern over the island in the river. They spent the day exploring miles of logging roads on the mountainsides of the valley. Driving up a rutted forest service road, a panicked black bear clattered in front of the truck as they rounded a corner on a tight switchback. Jason laughed at the bear's helter-skelter exit, likening its style to one of the less coordinated girls on the soccer team.

"All hips and ass. No clue about direction. Just like Norton," Jason chuckled.

"I don't know. At least the bear had a game plan."

Jason laughed again. "Yeah. He might be ahead of all of us."

In the afternoon, Cooper took Jason to town.

***

The "city" of Yaak consisted of three businesses: two bars and a mercantile. The merc was part of the building on the east side of the road and shared the space with the Yaak River Tavern. Directly across the road was an iconic biker bar and drinking destination called The Painted Horse Saloon. The "Horse" was a throwback to earlier times, and no visit to the Yaak was complete without at least one beer in its time-capsule interior. They shared the bar with two bearded locals and their mongrel dogs. The animals were curled under the bar stools of the two regulars looking every bit as disreputable and as settled in as their owners.

When they left the bar, Jason was suitably impressed.

"Dude, that place is a friggin' time warp. I felt like I was in the Yukon or something."

Cooper laughed.

"Welcome to the Yaak. I told you you'd love this place."

***

Cooper drove Jason to the airport the next morning.

When he returned to the Whiskey Bend Ranch that afternoon, he grabbed a cold beer, sat on the riverside deck, and contemplated how to proceed with his life. The only noise came from the river, and he realized that he had never been alone in the Kennedys' home. For a moment, he was overwhelmed by a sense of loneliness in the silent mountains.

Just then, a whitetail deer strutted up to the salt block across the river. He had a small set of antlers with three tines on each side but none of the usual wariness typical of young bucks his age.

He approached the salt block like he owned it, confident and unafraid. There was a raw scar running down his right hip, and Cooper thought that his confidence must have gotten him in trouble with a mountain lion or one of the valley's grizzlies. Whatever the deer had encountered had left a nasty mark, but he had survived, and he pranced with the arrogant self-assurance of a rock star.

Cooper smiled and went inside to get his camera. *Okay, buddy,* he thought, *if you can do this, so can I.*

When he came back out on the porch, the little buck was gone, but his confident message remained. Cooper went back indoors and started to organize his new life.

***

The next day, Cooper drove upriver to visit his friend Wing Redmond.

Wing and Cooper had met the first summer that Clayton's family came to the Yaak several years earlier. He was the nearest neighbor to Whiskey Bend, living four miles above the Kennedys' place.

Wing was only five years older than Cooper, but the Montanan's physical appearance suggested a much greater age gap. He was six feet six inches tall and had a mass of unkempt hair streaked with assorted shades of gray, brown, and white with a multi-tone beard to match. The small area of facial skin that was not covered with hair was sunburned and creased from the weather. Driven by a metabolism locked into overdrive, his rangy frame was skeletal, reminding Cooper of the Wizard of Id cartoon prisoner who had spent decades chained to the wall of a medieval castle dungeon.

The reclusive neighbor had built his own log cabin on a wooded parcel at the very end of a remote country road. It was a rustic log building with electricity but no running water and no indoor plumbing. The interior walls of the cabin were lined from floor to ceiling with books, many of a technical nature representing a wide variety of interests, from Chinese warfare to contemporary jazz. Wing had a landline telephone and a newer model woodstove— functional concessions to modern technology.

To Cooper, Wing's most impressive possession was a state-of-the-art music system that the ex-school teacher had coveted on sight. Wing's CD and vinyl collection was as diverse as the rest of his interests, and his taste for classical music suggested a most incongruous type of mountain man.

However, there was little doubt about the wilderness skills of the eccentric hermit. He worked the only legal trap line in the valley, shot the best trophy elk in the Yaak every hunting season, and

128

cherished the road-less backcountry areas as much as any resident of the valley.

When Cooper drove up, Wing was working on his woodpile, stacking firewood into a decaying woodshed twenty feet from his outhouse.

"Welcome back, man. Your uncle told me you were going to be caretaking his place. That should be interesting," he teased.

"Hey. Just because I'm from civilization doesn't mean I can't handle it up here. It's not like I'll be wrestling grizzlies or anything like that."

"God, I hope not. I'm not sure that dinky camera you pack around would help much. Stanley tells me you're thinking about selling some of those snapshots you take. Are you still shooting them from your bar stool?"

During family visits, Cooper had learned to set up his Nikon with a telephoto lens and a tripod at the end of the bookcase bar, facing the salt block across the river. Almost every day of the vacation, he took pictures through the window glass, astonished at the uniqueness of some of the photos.

Wing Redmond teased him without mercy about his "barnyard" wilderness photographs.

"For Christ's sake, man, if you want to take pictures from a bar stool, go to the zoo. At least there you won't have to worry about getting your scrambled eggs in the shot."

Coop took the ribbing in good spirits. He knew some of the pictures were pretty good. Who else had shots of a Clydesdale-sized bull moose exchanging gentle nose sniffs with a four-week-old whitetail fawn? Nevertheless, he also knew that his photographs lacked the wild soul that was the true heart of the Yaak.

"Okay, dog. You're right. Now that I'm here full time maybe you can take me into the backcountry? Somewhere without roads or salt blocks?"

Wing grinned through the sweat-stained beard.

"Hell, I can take you places no one's ever thought about a road. I can get you where you can take pictures of a grizzly's love life if you want. The question is, do you think a city boy can handle it?"

"I can handle it. I'm just not sure I want you to get me lost in the woods for days at a time."

Redmond laughed again. "Little brother, I've never been lost in the woods. I'm just looking for another way out."

"Seriously, man, do you think we could find some of the more secretive animals? You know, mountain lions? Wolves? Grizzlies? I'd love to get some shots of any of those."

"We can find them. You just better hope they can't find us."

Cooper snorted. Fulltime Yaakers were all the same, always trying to scare people with stories of the wildness and danger of the valley.

"I'm pretty sure I can handle it," he said. "If you've lasted this long how hard can it be?"

22
CHAPTER

Back in Skyler, Duffy Grayson was drunk. It was Saturday night, and he and Philomena had been in the Thunderbird Tavern for most of the evening drinking beer and cheap red wine. Duffy's sheer mass allowed him to hold his alcohol better than any of his friends, an advantage that he often surrendered by simply drinking three times as much as anyone else.

Curiously, Duffy had developed a taste for Heineken beer—the status symbol beer of the yuppies that he loved to hate—and he could consume prodigious amounts of the green-bottled brew. He could drink a case of beer and still be affable and cordial; beyond that amount, he could be unpredictable and dangerous. His circle of friends knew this and kept a wary distance at the first signs of change. No one teased him about his favored brand of beer.

Earlier that afternoon, at a local sports bar called the Tip-In Tavern run by a former tribal basketball player, he had run into Skyler Parks and Rec Director Jarred Meyers. After a friendly greeting and some small talk about the past softball season, Meyers turned the conversation to the upcoming fall-winter senior basketball program.

"Duffy, you know we want your guys in the city kick-off hoop tournament. But. . . and don't take this the wrong way, I can't cut you as much slack as I did last year. The tourney fee has to be paid on time, and we have to know that your team will have at least five players for every game. It can't be like it was last season."

Grayson listened impassively, struggling to control the urge to crush the whiney little director with his bare hands.

"Yeah, I know, Jarred. I seen our rec director at the gym last week and already put in a request for the tourney fee," he lied, "I got no problem with that. I'll bring the money to the first meeting."

"That's what you said last year Duff. We've got several teams on a waitlist. The tournament committee thinks everyone should have to stick to the rules. If your guys can't do that, we'll have to make a change."

Duffy forced a smile, nodding his agreement at the director.

"That's what I'm sayin', man. I'm all over it."

***

When Duffy met Philomena in the Thunderbird, it was almost midnight. Duffy was long past the danger point in beer count and still bothered by his conversation with Jarred Meyers. Philomena was seated at a small table with her best friend Francis Luke when Duffy interrupted their conversation.

"Gimme some money."

With one look at his face, Philomena reached into her jacket pocket and took out a twenty-dollar bill. She handed it over without speaking and then slid off the bar stool and moved to a table of three women at the back of the room where the jukebox was playing country music.

An hour later, Duffy turned on his own bar stool and stared at his wife. It was quieter in the bar, the jukebox silent and the few remaining drinkers too drunk to be rowdy.

From across the room, Duffy said, "Philomena. I need some money."

Philomena shook her head to let him know that she was out of cash. Her remaining friend ignored the big man. They both had heard similar orders in the Thunderbird Tav from dozens of drunken husbands, both white and Native American.

When nothing happened, Duffy slid off the bar stool and lurched toward the table of women. Philomena's friend saw him coming, got to her feet, and headed toward the restroom.

Philomena looked up to her husband towering over her chair.

"Give me some fuckin' money."

"It's gone, Duffy. This is all we have left." She waved at some change and three dollar bills in tip money lying on the table near her half empty glass of wine. "Let's go home."

Duffy's response came without warning. He cuffed Philomena across the side of her head with the back of his hand, snapping her head backward with the force of the blow. A dark discoloration began to spread across the bronze skin of her upper cheek. Gritting her teeth, she refused to acknowledge the pain searing through her face.

Loren, the tavern's bartender, hurried to Philomena's table, being careful to stay just outside the range of Duffy's reach.

"C'mon, Duff. Leave her alone. I'll buy you one for the road. I don't need no trouble here. You get the cops here and they'll shut me down. Let me buy you a beer for the road."

Grayson looked from Philomena to Loren and then back at his wife. He raised his arm and faked another slap at Philomena's head. She jerked back to avoid the feigned blow and then rose an inch or two out of her chair and snarled at her husband, "Screw you, asshole." Duffy laughed and followed Loren back to the bar. Loren stayed just ahead of the big man and paid close attention to Duffy's position as he led him across the room.

When the Grayson's got home to the Project, Philomena passed out on the sofa and Duffy left her there to sleep it off. He found a beer in the refrigerator and sat down in his squashed armchair for a smoke before bed. His mind drifted to his conversation earlier with Jarrod Meyers.

If Meyers had been a Native American, their conversation would have lasted only seconds before Duffy swatted him into a corner, the consequences of that action of no concern whatsoever to the powerful Indian. Duffy thought to himself that he had been born a hundred and fifty years too late.

He drained the beer and stubbed out his cigarette. On his way to the bathroom, he stopped in front of the door to Shawnee's bedroom. The door was shut, as it always was when his stepdaughter was home and in bed. He reached for the doorknob, turning it slowly. It rotated a half turn and clicked as the bolt slid out of its receptacle. He pushed the door inward. Nothing happened. He leaned his shoulder against the door and applied steady pressure. It moved a fraction of an inch and then stopped. He laughed out loud. Shawnee must have blocked it with a piece of furniture. He laughed again and walked down the hallway to the bathroom.

Shawnee lay under a thin blanket, the sound of Duffy's laughter still caught in her ears. She stared at the sturdy oak chair jammed underneath the door handle, checking its position with the light of her clock. It was 2:36 in the morning.

She used the chair every night and slept with her clothes on during every weekend, even on warm summer nights. The chair was a deterrent, but in her heart, she knew Duffy could enter the bedroom whenever he really wanted.

Through the years, some of her mother's lovers had been predatory, and as a child, she had learned not to trust the men who spent time at Philomena's house. She had no illusions that a new husband would be any different from the others. As she lay in the bed watching the door with the chair propped under it, her clattering heart began to slow and the chaos within her mind began to take on a semblance of structure. The panic attacks were more frequent now, often brought on by minor stress during the daytime or frightening nightmares at night.

Shawnee didn't understand why just as she neared an age when she could determine her own destiny, her demons were beginning to take control. Her escape mechanism had always been the mental wall that allowed her to withdraw into her own private world. Lately, the wall was weakening, and she would awaken from her nightmares with tears on her face and a cold lump in her chest.

It wasn't just Duffy. She intuitively knew not to trigger the chase mechanism inherent in all predators by attempting to flee her mother's husband. For Shawnee, it was her emotional safety that was most important. The past no longer mattered. She yearned for something to take her away from her miserable life.

23
CHAPTER

As the warm summer days began to shorten, Cooper continued to adjust to his new lifestyle. He was up at daybreak, seated at his aunt's massive roll top desk, organizing and cataloging his photographs as he struggled with the photography software that he was determined to master.

At midday, he ate a light lunch and then did chores around the property. He trimmed the shrubs, split firewood, and filled the bird feeders with sunflower seeds. He watered the raised-bed flower gardens and fussed with the hanging flower baskets that his uncle insisted on keeping in Aunt Dodie's memory.

When the day cooled in the evening hours, he took his camera and drove the valley's network of Forest Service roads searching for wildlife. Sometimes, he would walk the gated roads that led to one of the dozens of clear cuts in various states of regeneration. He soon learned that patience and stealth were the keys to wildlife photography, and his portfolio began to grow. He loved the sense of adventure, and the Yaak's varied habitats made every trip an exciting journey into the unknown. Coop's greatest joy of living in the valley was that he never knew what might appear around the next turn in the trail or road.

Even the wilderness nights were special. When the sun went down, he sat in a rocking chair on the porch and reveled in the brightness of the infinite stars in the night sky, unpolluted by even the faintest hint of civilization.

***

Fall in the Yaak took Cooper by surprise. He knew it would be beautiful, but he had no idea of the magnitude of its splendor. The branches of the green-black larch tree that dominated the landscape began an amazing metamorphosis into a canopy of golden needles. The result was the spectacular conversion of the dark forest into a showy collage of luminous cover that glowed in the sunshine, coloring the valley with its soft autumnal sheen.

Cooper carried his cameras to remote locations where he built crude photo blinds and sat for hours waiting for cautious animals to reward his patience. Occasionally, he set aside his digital cameras and experimented with his older 35mm Nikon using the traditional slide-production or black and white print formats. When he took pictures in these non-digital methods, he had the film processed at a small camera store in downtown Kalispell, Montana, located just west of Glacier National Park.

It was in this shop that he first met Angelina Hailstone.

***

Angelina was five feet five inches tall and had a supple, smooth body that she carried with the grace of a natural athlete. She had short-cropped hair that was dyed dark red—not the auburn shade of a natural redhead or the coppery tones of the Irish but a deep magenta hue resembling a Broadway theater wig—made all the more startling by the contrast with her almost translucent skin. The result was an exotic appearance somewhere between sophisticated and punk.

She was impressed with Cooper's photographs, recognizing the uniqueness of the images: pictures that entailed tenacity and creativity.

"Mr. Cooper, these are really good pictures. Have you thought about marketing them commercially?"

Cooper blushed at the compliment. "I've thought about it. My best pictures are actually digitals. But either way, I don't think I'm ready for a career in photojournalism just yet."

"I disagree. These are really good." She hesitated, then continued. "You know, the community college in town here asked me to keep my eyes open for someone who could teach a photography class

136

for their night school program. I did it myself last year, but I've lined up a job at Big Mountain during ski season, and I can't do both. Would you be interested in talking with them about it? Your pictures are much better than any I've taken."

"Hmm, I don't know. It sounds like it might be interesting. I've done a little teaching in the past." He cleared his throat before continuing, "Any chance you could have lunch with me? You could tell me all about it."

"I've already eaten, but I get off at five. If you're still going to be in town, how about a beer at the brewpub?"

"Why not? What's your name? I like to know who I'm drinking with."

The young lady smiled. "Angelina. Angelina Hailstone. My friends call me Angie." She reached out to shake his hand. "Nice to meet you, Mr. Cooper."

"You too, Angie. You can call me Coop. Mr. Cooper was my father."

They met at the Raven's Nest Brewpub. It was happy hour, and the bar was noisy with a collection of young locals and early fall visitors to the northern Rockies. It was a casual clientele with lots of Patagonia outerwear, baseball caps, goatees, and body piercings. Cooper loved it.

They found a small table at the back of the room and ordered two microbrews. While they waited for the beers, Cooper discreetly checked the girl's hands for a wedding ring, pleased to see only a plain silver watch on one wrist and, on the other, a striking tattoo of red and green hummingbirds with linked wings encircling the wrist like a two-inch wide bracelet.

"Wow. I love your tattoo. Very different. It makes me want to know all about you. Every tat has a story, you know."

"Oh, there's not much of a story to mine. I just like hummingbirds. My family lived in South Africa for a while, and I learned to love nature and beautiful settings. We moved back to the U.S. when I started high school. I'm basically an east coast girl who escaped to a mountain paradise. I like the outdoors, hiking, climbing, and snowboarding. . . things like that."

An excellent athlete, when her family returned to the States, Angelina's physical pursuits had evolved, and her early interests in swimming, tennis, and golf had expanded to include hiking, whitewater kayaking, and snow sports, especially snowboarding. The opportunity to indulge in these activities had drawn her to the Rocky Mountains of northwest Montana. An adventure-sport junkie, she was working at the local camera store, waiting for the ski season to begin at Big Mountain where she had been hired as a chairlift attendant.

Cooper said, "Good for you. How long have you lived here?"

"Almost a year now. I actually live in Whitefish. I got here too late to get hired at the mountain last season, so I spent most of my time snowboarding and getting to know people. I stumbled into the job at Flathead Community College because I was working at the camera store. I told them I'd teach the class on an interim basis. It's been fun. It's a night class, and it's part of the Continuing Education Program. It's more laid back than the academic courses. Most of the students are beginning photographers who live in the area."

"Makes sense. This kind of scenery makes everyone a better photographer."

"I know. It's true. It helps their confidence, too." She sipped her beer. "If you want me to, I can give your name to the college. I'll get you a copy of my course syllabus, and you can get an idea of what the class is all about."

"That would be great. I could study the format, see if it's something I could handle."

"I don't think you'd have any problem." She glanced at her watch. "Listen, I have to run. How about I bring the syllabus to the store and you can pick it up when your slides come back? Then, if you're interested, we can take it from there."

"Oh, I'm interested. I'm definitely interested."

CHAPTER 24

The phone woke Cooper early Saturday morning.

"Hey, Coop. It's Jason. What up, dog?"

"Jason. How are ya?"

"Primo. Hey, I thought I'd call and fill you in on the weekend. Big doings here in Skyler. I thought you might be interested."

"Yeah? What's up? Did you finally win a soccer game without me?"

The girls' soccer team had been phenomenal since Jason took over, winning the league championship a year ago, and this season, they were already off to an undefeated start.

"We did. It's taken me this long to eliminate all the bad habits you taught them. But actually, it's the football team I called about. We beat Chinook 45 to 30 last night. At the post-game coach's party, you were the big topic of conversation. People are still blown away that you moved to Montana to live in a saloon."

Cooper laughed. "Tell them to come on up. We'll take them to the Painted Horse and show them what a real bar looks like."

"No shit, man. That place rocks. And speaking of bars, that's why I called. We had a little excitement last night that makes the Horse look like a daycare center."

"What do you mean?"

"Your friend Duffy Grayson went ape-shit in the Thunderbird Tavern after the game."

"Duffy Grayson?"

"Yeah. Chinook has a little Native American running back—his name is Rodney Greenly—who's just a dandy. His fan club, mostly family and distantly related to Grayson, I guess, went to the T-Bird after the game and apparently, Duffy wasn't too complimentary about the kid's skills. Rodney's old man whacked Duffy over the head with a pool cue. Bad idea. Duffy converted a beer bottle into a pig-sticker and worked him over—plus two of his friends. Nice guy, huh?"

Cooper listened, mesmerized by the story of his nemesis' havoc.

"How bad, Jase? That bastard's crazy."

"You think? One guy lost some teeth and had various 'superficial' wounds. Duffy cold-cocked the other guy, and the kid's daddy is in the hospital in critical condition. The rumor is he's toast. The cops say if he dies it will be manslaughter at the least. I guess the guy was a real mess. That Grayson dude's a piece of work."

"Yeah. I take it he's in jail?"

"Oh, yeah. Word is he wasn't even close to making bail. All I could think of was how lucky you were he didn't use a beer bottle on you."

Cooper was quiet for a second.

"Man, I hope he never gets out of jail. That guy is really scary."

***

Cooper called Kelsey on Sunday morning. He knew the news of Duffy Grayson's brutal encounter would headline the Sunday newspaper and play with her fragile psyche. The caller ID function on Kelsey's phone alerted her to her ex-husband's call.

Before Cooper could say hello, she burst out, "I told you that lunatic was dangerous. He's not just a bully, he's a full-blown psychopath. Clayton, what should we do?"

140

"Hello to you, too, Kelse," he said. "Actually, this might work out okay in a very perverted way. If the man he attacked dies, Grayson will be in jail for a long time. Not that we want anyone to die, but still. . ."

"Today's paper says he's expected to live. He's in critical condition, but he's expected to survive." She sobbed. "I wish he'd die, Coop. I'm sorry, but I really do."

"Don't say that, hon. He'll still get some jail time. Maybe it will teach him a lesson, and he'll leave people alone. Besides, he hasn't bothered you since I left town, has he?"

"No. But just knowing he's out there scares me. We're all alone now, and I worry about the girls. I have nightmares. It's awful."

"You were scared before, Kelsey. You had nightmares before. You've got to be strong for the girls. Nothing's going to happen. That bastard will be in jail for a long time."

"Do you think we should move? Should we go somewhere he can't find us?" Kelsey was crying again.

"Baby, he's not interested in us anymore. You've got to let go of this. The girls don't need any more trauma in their lives. Besides, he's going to jail. Don't let him ruin your life."

***

Philomena Grayson had not touched a drop of alcohol since Friday night's violent explosion at the Thunderbird Tavern. She tried to see Duffy on Saturday, but the sheriff's department refused to admit her, claiming that Duffy was still being "processed." They told her to return on Sunday; she could see him then.

In the morning, an attendant escorted her to the visitor's room where Duffy was awaiting her arrival. The big man was quiet, obviously unsettled by the confinement. He was wearing an orange jumpsuit that was at least two sizes too small.

He growled most of his responses to Philomena's questions and then cut her short with questions of his own.

"Did you get a lawyer?"

"Not yet. I contacted the tribal office, and they're working on it."

"Working on it, my ass. I want out. Now."

"Duffy, I'm not sure what's going to happen. Harvey might die. If he does, we're in real trouble."

"It was self-defense. I've got witnesses."

"I know. But the police say you overreacted. We need to get a lawyer. I'll find someone today. I promise."

"You better. I ain't staying in here, Philomena. Find those jackasses at the center and have them get me a lawyer. And get me the fuck out of here."

***

Twenty days later, Harvey Greenly was back in the town of Chinook. Despite the loss of an eye and a significant portion of his once prominent nose, he was already attending his son's football games.

Duffy would get out of jail. But it wouldn't be any time soon. The judge took a dim view of protecting oneself with a jagged beer bottle, which he determined to be assault with a deadly weapon, and would have jailed Grayson for a long time if the tribal attorneys were not so savvy. The lawyers were able to reduce Duffy's sentence to three months, mostly due to the fact that Harvey Greenly refused to press charges of any kind.

***

For Shawnee, Duffy's stay in the Wapiti County jail meant that one component of her growing angst could settle into remission. She still had bad dreams, and she still put the chair under the doorknob

142

on a regular basis. But the nightmares were less terrifying and for the first time in a long while, she had some good dreams too.

The good dreams were all about Clayton Cooper.

Shortly after Cooper left town, Shawnee had stolen a letter from the mailbox on the porch of her ex-coach's Skyler home. Kelsey was away with the girls, and Shawnee, who had been spying on the family since before the hearing began, walked to the house and, by a timely coincidence, watched the postman deliver a handful of mail. When the mailman left and the street was deserted, she went up on the porch and thumbed through the delivery, where among the bills and junk mail, she found a letter to the family postmarked Troy, Montana. She recognized the neatly printed handwriting and put the letter in her jacket pocket.

Alone in her room, she opened the letter that Cooper had written to his daughters. It was newsy, filled with cheerful gossip about the Yaak and its colorful residents and wild animals: a note about the country that he loved so much.

To the youngster who yearned for a better world, the letter summoned visions of paradise. Shawnee memorized every word. She went straight to the library and did a web search to find out more about the remote area that Cooper called the Yaak.

Although she was born in Browning, Montana, Shawnee had no memory of life in the Rocky Mountains. But Cooper's stolen letter made it easy to imagine all the times near her birthplace as good ones. . . and even the bad times as being better than what she was dealing with now.

During the next few weeks, Shawnee grew increasingly interested in her mother's side of the family. She knew Philomena had been born in the Rockies, and with Duffy away from the house, she was able to ask her mother questions without his abuse. She quizzed Philomena about her birth tribe and any extended family connections, eager to learn whatever she could about the natives of the Rockies and the country of her mother's people.

Philomena assumed that Shawnee's curiosity stemmed from the fact that she was finally beginning to recognize the significance of her Native American heritage. Eager to encourage her daughter's newfound interest, she spoke of the joy of growing up Indian in the Rockies.

Shawnee asked about the Yaak and was disappointed that her mother was unfamiliar with that specific valley in northern Montana.

"What is this about the Yaak River Valley? Where did you hear of such a thing?"

"Oh, I just read about it when I was researching the area. The name Yaak is actually the Indian name for 'Arrow.' It's interesting, that's all."

"I don't know it. But I do know some members of the Kootenai tribe. If I ever see them again, we can ask about this place."

"Would you, Mom? It would really be fun to learn more about your side of the family."

"Hah. I thought all you cared about was the white side of your family. It's about time that you realized you're part Indian, Shawnee. Be proud of it."

"I know. I'm working on it."

"It's strange that you've found a place the natives called Yaak. In my grandmother's tribe, every family lived by the bow and arrow. Your great-grandfather was a famous hunter. His name was White Hawk."

She paused before saying, "I could tell you stories."

When Shawnee didn't answer, her mother rose and walked to her bedroom, returning with a small leather pouch the size of a coin purse, worn smooth and darkened with age to the rich brown of a pair of well-oiled moccasins.

She opened the bag and removed a piece of jewelry attached to a leather thong. When she held it up for her daughter, Shawnee

144

saw that it was an exquisite arrowhead made of white stone, the silhouette of its lines simple and pure. There was a small hole drilled into the center of the flat end, and the soft leather thong that ran through the hole was cut to the length of a necklace.

To Shawnee's artistic eye, it was a thing of beauty.

"Your great-grandfather made this for my mother's mother. It is of the size used for hunting birds and small animals, which he taught my grandmother to do. He gave this to her as a gift to show her how pleased he was about her skill with the bow. It was a gift from the heart. My mother gave it to me before she died. I never thought that you'd be interested in it."

"It's beautiful," Shawnee whispered.

"Yes. It is. I want you to have it. Don't tell Duffy where it came from. It's our family, not his. Let it remind you that being Indian can be a beautiful thing."

CHAPTER

25

In the Yaak, Cooper suffered through his first hunting season, an experience made all the more stressful by his concern for the survival of the whitetail deer that he had seen on his first day in the valley. The buck had become a regular visitor to the riverside salt block on his uncle's property. It was the same animal that had inspired him on his first night alone in the valley. Since that time, the deer had confirmed how unique he was on a regular basis and now served as a frequent subject for Cooper's photographs.

The jagged scar on his hip and his arrogant control of the salt-block area made naming the deer easy. He was nature's version of the Rolling Stone's famous lead singer, and Cooper had called him "Jagger" from the first day he saw him.

***

The opening day of deer season, the hunters descended on the woods like a late October snowstorm. An army of pick-up trucks driven by hunters wearing fluorescent orange jackets and drinking cans of Busch Light beer rolled into the valley and cruised the Forest Service roads in hopes of killing a trophy buck.

The great majority of Cooper's neighbors were avid hunters and joined the visitors in the quest to satisfy their bloodlust. Cooper knew that subsistence hunting could be critical to those living a survivalist lifestyle. With only two game wardens, patrolling the vast Kootenai National Forest was nearly impossible, and the local meat-hunters seldom operated within the seasonal rules and regulations. Deer season was an opportunity to hunt legally for six weeks, and the locals' hunting focus shifted from supplementing their dinner tables to providing bragging rights about killing a trophy buck.

All Cooper really cared about was that Jagger and the other animals who visited his salt block would have a safety zone during the six-week blitz. Although the salt block area was on the other side of the river in a heavily posted "No Hunting" area, it was visible from the road, and Cooper did not trust the hunters who drove past the Whiskey Bend Ranch, looking for careless bucks.

For Cooper, who hunted with his camera almost every day, the official hunting season was a mixed blessing. The animals were at their spectacular best this time of the year, the buck's antlers grown out and honed for battle, their posture alert, and their carriage regal and confident. According to Wing, they would be wily and elusive—so elusive that nine of ten hunters would question their very existence—until the rut began in late November when the urge to mate kicked in and even the most cautious of the mature bucks gave way to lust and conquest. During the few weeks of the rut, even the most inept hunter could be a threat. Without the rut, only the Wing Redmond's of the world would harvest a true trophy.

***

One cold, bright day, early in the hunting season, Cooper had a run-in with three Native American hunters parked in front of the ranch, watching the deer at the salt block surrounded by a picket fence of "No Hunting" signs.

Walking up to the truck, he said "Private property, guys. The public land starts up the river about a hundred yards."

"Says who?" said the spokesman for the trio, a tall, handsome man wearing a blaze orange shirt and carrying a new rifle equipped with a powerful scope.

"Read the signs. Those deer are on private property." Cooper looked at the license plate on the crew cab pickup truck, noting the Idaho designation. "We've got laws here in Montana. Shoot in Idaho if yours are different."

"We're tribal members. We can hunt in the national forest anytime we want."

"I'm sure you can. But this is private property. You can't hunt here."

The spokesman stared at Cooper, trying to decide if the confrontation was worth continuing. Then he said, "It doesn't matter. We can move up the road and shoot as many as we want."

"You do that. Just don't shoot anything on my property. These are practically tame deer."

"That's your problem, man. Maybe you shouldn't feed them."

"You're right. My problem. Good luck up the road."

The man laughed and then got back in the pickup.

Twenty minutes later, Cooper heard two rifle shots echo through the valley.

***

Later, when Cooper recounted the incident to Wing, his friend was far from sympathetic.

"You know what, Coop? The road hunters are good for the area. They chase all the prime animals back into the woods, and then they're too lazy to walk a hundred yards from their trucks to follow the game. They shoot farm deer like those cows you lure to your salt block. If you're going to raise pets near the road, you better get orange jackets on them because some idiot road hunter's going to shoot 'em. Especially that little three-point that hangs out down there. I know you love him, but he's crazy even before his brains move down to his pecker. He won't last a week."

To Cooper's great relief, Jagger fooled the mountain man. Even during the rut, he managed to dodge the carnage. Cooper knew it was only luck that saved him. When the season ended and the buck showed up the next afternoon, Cooper finally relaxed. If he could avoid the predators and the poachers, Jagger would be around for at least another year.

***

As fall turned to winter in the Yaak, the glory of the autumnal foliage began to transition into the harsher beauty of early winter.

The tourists and hunters disappeared, and the valley took on its true identity as it lapsed into quiet isolation. The less adventuresome residents headed south to warmer climes; the hardcore locals settled by the fire with their books and handicrafts, and the animals locked into survival mode, conserving their energy and trying to outlast the winter. For the full-timers, the local bars ratcheted up their role as the epicenter of social life in the valley.

In the valley, there were two types of bar rats—alcoholics and recovering alcoholics. The alcoholics reveled in the confinement of winter when their regular bar stool occupancy was shared by even the non-drinking valley residents. The recovering alcoholics sipped diet colas and non-alcoholic beer as they whiled away the winter. The bars provided the only contact with the world and helped locals deal with long, dark days and the sub-zero cold.

Cooper and Wing were part of a tiny minority that didn't fit the alcoholic or recovering alcoholic role. Both were moderate drinkers whose visits to one of the two bars in the town were of a social nature. In fact, they often bar hopped, drinking one beer each in both of the town's bars, thereby confusing the highly polarized population of the valley whose political alliances were reflected in the bar where they chose to drink.

In the town of Yaak, nothing was the way it seemed it should be. The Painted Horse Saloon, the famous outlaw biker bar and tourist attraction, was actually where the valley's few liberals and conservationists drank, while across the street, the Yaak Tavern was the exclusive safe-house for the local political conservatives and rednecks. Cooper, whose politics tended toward liberal, and Wing, whose politics were staunchly conservative, shared a bond of friendship that was incomprehensible to the locals. However, given the constant nature of the two friends' drinking pattern, the patrons of both bars had come to accept this oddity, content to drink their way through the winter and share the quiet of the off-season with their unusual neighbors.

Cooper, however, was beginning to find the early winter somewhat restrictive.

"Wing, I'm gonna take a trip to Kalispell. I need to talk to my friend there and see what she found out about that job with the college. You want to go?"

"To Kalispell? What for? Too many people. Too many ski bums. Besides," he said, "I'm not interested in getting laid."

Cooper laughed, "I should be so lucky. If I thought that would happen, I would have been there a long time ago."

"Yeah, right. That girl is all you've talked about for weeks."

***

Cooper met Angie at the camera store. She had already given them her notice and expected to start working at Big Mountain any day. Coop was glad to find her there and, once again, was taken with her eclectic beauty.

"Hey, girl. What's happenin'? Can I buy you a drink when you get off? You can fill me in on the college deal."

"Sure. I've been hoping you'd stop in. I've got good news," she paused, thinking for a moment before she continued, "Shall we go to The Raven's Nest again? They've got an excellent bar food menu."

"That sounds perfect. Why don't we meet there? I'll buy you dinner."

"I don't need dinner. Bar food is great. I'm easy."

When Angelina came into The Raven's Nest, Cooper enjoyed watching her walk across the room. He was reminded of the photographs of young people working or playing in the outdoors that gave the Patagonia Sportswear catalogs their uniqueness and personality. He thought he should take his camera to the mountain and photograph the girl with the exotic plum-colored hair running the ski lift or snowboarding. He was pretty sure that any outdoor clothing company would appreciate the subsequent images.

Cooper intercepted her halfway across the room, taking her by the arm and guiding her to the bar where he ordered two house lagers. After the bartender passed him the mugs, he nodded toward a corner booth and said to her, "Let's sit over there. We can talk business in private."

Angie led the way and slid into the booth's bench. Cooper sat down beside her. "Do you mind if I sit here? We won't have to shout at each other."

"Not at all."

When they settled in, Angie started to speak. "So here's the deal, Mr. Cooper. . ."

"Please. Call me Coop. Most of my friends call me Coop."

"Okay, Coop. Here's the scoop." She laughed out loud. "How bad is that? I'm sorry. I couldn't resist."

Cooper liked that she laughed at her own silly joke.

"Anyway, I showed your pictures to Dean Walters at the school, and he was very impressed. They'd like to have you for spring semester if you're interested. That means you'd start after the first of the year. He gave me his card," she dug the battered business card out of her backpack, "and asked me to have you call. Do you think you're interested?"

"Definitely. I'm beyond interested." He hesitated, "I'll tell you what. Why don't we have dinner in the dining area, and you can walk me through what to expect. You brought your syllabus, didn't you?"

Angie looked into Cooper's eyes for a second before she said, "How about a rain check? I've already got plans for tonight. I'll leave all the information that I brought for you. You should probably call Dr. Walters tomorrow if you can."

Cooper's shoulders drooped.

Then she added, "But we can have dinner sometime. I'd really like to see more of your work. Mid-week is usually best for me. If you'd like to call me, I can give you my number. Maybe we could hook up sometime. If not. . ." she shrugged.

"No, no, I'd love to hook up. What's your number?

26
CHAPTER

"Hey bro, welcome back!" Jason Locker wrapped Cooper in a loose man hug.

It was almost Christmas, and it was Clayton's first visit back to Skyler since leaving in late August. The Locker's rental house was still vacant, and Cooper was going to spend a week in the same place that he had occupied after his divorce.

"Thanks, man," he said to Jason, "It's great to be back. I appreciate you guys putting me up."

"No problem. You're welcome to it." Jason grinned. "You can make it up to us this summer when we bring the kids to the Yaak for a visit."

"You got it. Bubba will love it up there. We'll turn him loose on the valley. They won't know what hit them."

Cooper spent Christmas Day with his family. It was odd to feel like a stranger in the familiar house on Sunrise Heights, to knock on the front door that he had opened without thought for so many years, and the nostalgia made the joy of seeing his daughters bittersweet.

The girls were too excited to notice. They buried him in squeals and kisses, and he had to laugh at their exuberant delight in the season. Kelsey watched the greeting with a patient smile before she shooed the girls aside and gave her ex-husband a tentative kiss on the cheek.

Cooper held her at arms-length and said, "Sweetheart, you look great."

Kelsey smiled a thank you. She knew she was still thin and wan, but her appetite was returning and her life had settled into a less stressful routine. Her doctor was treating her for depression, and the regimen of medication and exercise was beginning to pay off as the fog of despair began to dissipate. Only the occasional crisis— Duffy Grayson's fight in the Thunderbird Tavern had been one— shook her confidence and slowed her progress.

The girls were coping well. The timing of the divorce had coincided with their return to school, and their active schedules had allowed little time to dwell on their father's absence. Busy with schoolwork and a myriad of extracurricular activities that ranged from sports to slumber parties, they were happy and busy.

Their father had remained an important part of their lives. He called or e-mailed every day. He sent cards and letters on every occasion, from birthdays to report cards. It was almost like their lifestyle before Cooper's suspension. The long hours of teaching and coaching had forced him to be an almost absentee parent even when he was living at home. Now, at least they communicated with him on a daily basis. Deep down, both girls expected their parents to reconcile. And in the meantime, it was the best of both worlds; each parent was eager to please them. Long shots on the girl's "wish list" appeared under the tree, and the cameras, outdoor gear, music, and designer clothing accumulated in stacks beside each daughter.

Embarrassed by the largess, Coop and Kelsey drank hot buttered rums and quietly visited as the girls sorted through their treasures.

**

In the Project, Philomena and Shawnee slept late. Their gift exchange was quiet and subdued. Philomena gave her daughter a warm jacket and a book on Native American artwork. Shawnee's gift to her mother was a pen and ink drawing of a female Blackfeet jingle dancer, a beautiful, slim girl in full regalia, her face alight with the freedom of the dance. Shawnee had studied a photograph of a young Philomena and then drawn her mother wearing a dance costume that she had designed herself. The result was a charming, if unsophisticated drawing, enhanced by the modern black frame with a wide white border encasing the ink artwork.

Hugging the frame to her bosom Philomena said, "Thank you, Shawnee, for taking me back to that place."

Later in the day, Philomena went to the county jail to visit Duffy and bring him a blackberry pie, made from berries that she had picked in the summer and frozen for a special occasion. Deputy Clarence Bigelow happened to be standing near the front desk when Philomena entered the jail. Bigelow went out of his way to be nice to Philomena, on the off chance that it might irritate Duffy.

"No files in that pie are there, Philomena?" he joked. "I might have to test it to make sure it's okay."

"You start testing them, and I'll fill one with arsenic," Philomena answered.

Bigelow laughed. "You would, too."

When Philomena gave the pie to Duffy, he was quieter than usual.

"Thanks, Philomena. Next summer I'll take you into the Wallowa Mountains. There's a ton of berries over there."

Rubbing his face, he said, "I need to get out of here. I'm going crazy with all these white sons-of-bitches. I need room to breathe. I need a drink."

"Duffy, you were already crazy. Be patient—you're almost done. You're lucky you're not in prison someplace."

"You think I'm crazy? Just wait. I'll show you crazy. That bastard Bigelow's been all over me. He messes with me every day." He nodded to himself. "I'll show them crazy. Nobody messes with Duffy."

***

Cooper stayed at Kelsey's until after supper on Christmas Day. When he returned to Jason and Amy's, the Locker's children were already in bed. Amy, exhausted from dealing with the children, excused herself and went to bed as well. Cooper and Locker opened cold beers and sat in the post-gift wreckage of the family room drinking and talking. When they finished their beers, Cooper yawned and then stood up to let his friend go to bed. He knew the Locker children had been awake before daylight, and for their parents, it had been a long day.

The minute Cooper opened the unlocked door to the rental house, he had the feeling that something was different from the way he had left the place earlier that morning. Looking around to see what had triggered this feeling, he turned to the candles that were the centerpiece of the small table in the corner of the living room.

Leaning against the pewter candleholder that held three red, ball-shaped candles was a small box wrapped in green Christmas paper. There was a handmade card on the package, a square of white paper tucked under the red ribbon. Printed in black ink, his initials were on the square: CKC. There was no signature on the gift card, no indication of who had sent the package.

Cooper was puzzled by its appearance on his table, assuming that it must be from the Lockers, who would be comfortable entering his quarters uninvited. But he had already exchanged gifts with the family and was quite certain that their gift giving had already concluded.

Unwrapping the box, he found another white card, identical to the first, taped to the tissue that enclosed the contents of the box. In cursive, it read, "A gift from the heart." There was no signature.

Inside the package was a leather-thong necklace. Attached to the leather string was the most perfect arrowhead that Cooper had ever seen. Only an inch and a half in length, a skilled craftsman had sculpted the piece of polished white stone. Cooper held it up by the leather lace and admired its beauty, wondering where it came from.

Even though many friends knew that Coop lived in Montana now, there were few people in Skyler who would write such a poignant message and those who might be were all family members or close friends with no reason to give such a gift anonymously.

Studying the card, he noted the lettering lacked the boldness of a confident writer. It seemed feminine, and in fact, it felt somewhat familiar.

A teacher? A coach? A student?

It was an unusual gift to give to a man, but it had an obvious connection to his new home. As he studied the necklace, a thought began taking shape. Oh my God, could this be from Shawnee? He had not seen her since the hearing, over a year ago. He had not thought about her for months.

Throughout his career, he had taught a number of Native American kids and coached a handful more. Shawnee was the only one with whom he had a special relationship. If she knew he was living in the Yaak, this small gift might be just symbolic enough to appeal to her twisted idea of loyalty. With a growing sense of foreboding, he knew that the arrowhead was from the ex-student who had changed his life.

How did she know that he would be in town? How did she know that he was staying with Jason and Amy? How did she know that his door would be unlocked or when he would be gone or how long that he would be away from the house?

Alarmed by his certainty about the gift's source and the bizarre familiarity his former student had with his personal life and routine, Cooper knew that he did not want to deal with his unpredictable former student. Even though he was scheduled to stay one more day, he called Kelsey to say goodnight and goodbye. Something had come up he said. He would explain later.

Early the next morning, he hurried back to the mountains.

***

From the dark woods beside the Locker's rental house, Shawnee had watched the building, waiting for Mr. Cooper to find his Christmas present.

She was there when he made the short walk from the big house. Her heart pounding, she watched as he walked up the crushed rock pathway, his face visible in the glow of the white Christmas lights that the Lockers had strung along the low shrubs lining the walk. Shawnee smiled at the heavy sheepskin jacket that he wore, a garment better suited for the harsh cold of the Rockies than the wet and gloomy coastal weather.

Watching him approach, she studied his appearance. He looked good, she thought. His fashionable stubble had evolved into a full beard, and his whiskers were streaked with gray, especially at the chin. His beard was short and perfectly trimmed, far from the unkempt look of a mountain hermit. Shawnee liked it, although she thought it made him look older, closer to his real age.

It had been almost four months since she had last watched him. That night, like many other nights when he had been living in Jason's house, she had hidden in this very spot, as he was preparing for his move to the mountains. That night, she had been overwhelmed with disappointment.

Shawnee had gifted him the arrowhead without a shred of remorse. She was certain that it had come to her for a purpose and that purpose could not have been any clearer. The timing of her mother's gift was too perfect to be coincidental.

As she watched Cooper open the front door, her body tightened with excitement. She had gone over every possible scenario in her mind and was still unsure what to expect. She knew that he would realize at once that such a gift could only be from one person. She was less certain about how he would follow up after that realization. If he hurried out of the house, heading toward his truck to come looking for her, she intended to surprise him by appearing like a vision on the path in front of the house.

If he remained inside, she would stay hidden until the lights went out and then decide what to do. She thought about tapping on his bedroom window or knocking on the front door. But she was shy, and she knew she was more likely to wait until tomorrow and let him come to her. First, he would try her house, of course, before trying the cemetery where they had once been together.

She herself had spent hours at the Gamble Bay site, visiting the graveyard, and then walking on the beach, thinking about Mr. Coop and the future. They would be together someday. Away from all the people, free from all the confusion. She would be a famous artist, and Cooper would do whatever he wanted to do. It didn't matter what that was. They would be together.

After the lights vanished in the house, Shawnee stayed a long time to see if Cooper was having trouble sleeping. She wanted to go to him to celebrate the spirit of the arrowhead. But with the night slipping away, her courage failed her, and slowly, she walked back to the truck, telling herself that he would come to her in the morning.

***

When Cooper did not show up at the Project by noon the day after Christmas, Shawnee drove Duffy's truck to the old Indian cemetery on Gamble Bay Road. She parked the truck in the same location where she had been with Cooper on the night of the incident. She went to this same spot every time she visited the beach.

She waited in the truck for most of the afternoon. She recognized the few families who came to visit loved ones buried in the graveyard, placing small gifts or holiday flowers on their graves. She listened for approaching vehicles, and she was repeatedly disappointed when each rig turned out to belong to someone else.

Only when the metallic winter sun began to merge with the ocean's horizon did she begin doubting Cooper's arrival. She turned the heater on in the truck and waited for an hour after dark. She finally gave up and drove back to town in tears.

Later that night, Shawnee returned to the Locker's rental house. She stood in the trees that were her regular observation post and waited until all the lights were out in the Locker's main house. A half an hour later, she stole to the porch and tried the front door. As usual, it was unlocked. Opening the door, she entered the front room and stood listening even though she knew the house was unoccupied.

She clicked on the small flashlight that she had used during other visits and went to the table with its red candles to look for her gift to Cooper. Unable to locate the package, she checked the wastebasket beneath the sink where she found the gift-wrap wadded into a ball. Carefully searching through the waste receptacle, she was relieved to find that the arrowhead was not in its contents. He had the necklace.

There was still hope.

***

A day later, when Shawnee realized that Cooper had left town, her euphoria vanished. She had entered the Christmas season on an emotional high. Duffy's absence had eliminated one of her most threatening psychological demons. And with Mr. Coop's arrival, the holidays had promised to bring some light back into her life. Mr. Cooper's failure to acknowledge her gift had cast a pall of darkness over that light.

The crux of her angst centered on the fact that the fate of the arrowhead was unclear. Had he missed the significance of the gift? Could he be so blind that he did not understand its message? Was it possible that he did not recognize that they were meant to be together?

If that was the case, it was up to her to show him the way. She had waited a long time for their destiny to be fulfilled. She could wait a while longer.

CHAPTER

27

At the end of the first week of February, Duffy Grayson was released from the Wapiti County Jail. He had been incarcerated for almost one hundred days.

"Let's go, Philomena," he said to his wife. "I've had enough of these assholes."

Duffy's comment was loud enough for both of the officers at the front desk to hear. One was Deputy Bigelow, who had made a point to be there for Duffy's release. Bigelow looked at his fellow officer, shrugging his shoulders in disgust.

"Duffy, you should have gotten a hundred years instead of a hundred days. Don't worry though. I'll save a cell for you. You'll be back before you know it."

Duffy didn't answer, but his eyes darkened with hatred.

Bigelow looked at the desk sergeant and said, "He's a beauty, ain't he?"

As they walked out of the jail, Philomena said to her husband, "Duffy, let it go. We got no chance against them anyway."

Duffy's head rotated a quarter turn to look at Philomena. "Let's go get a beer. And don't tell me what to do."

Philomena kept quiet, hoping a few beers would loosen him up.

The bar was open, and there were a half-dozen regulars working on their first drink of the day. These were Duffy's people, and here, he was treated like a conquering hero.

"Hey, Duff. Just in time. Harvey's boy is playing basketball for Chinook. Want to make a road trip next Friday?"

The question came from a bleary-eyed Wapiti sitting at the bar, his backpack on the floor underneath the bar stool. The man was in his late forties with silver hair pulled back into a ponytail and a whiskerless, deep-lined face that made him appear to be twenty years older than his actual age.

"Nah, I don't think so, man. I'm gonna stick around the rez for a month or two. I like the home field advantage."

His friend laughed, "Damn right, Duff. We got your back."

Duffy wasn't as worried about getting payback from Harvey Greenly or his friends as he was about being placed in another confrontational situation. He had decided that he would never go back to jail again.

Sneaking his arm around Philomena's waist, Duffy reached down and grabbed a handful of her ample butt cheek. He used his handhold to guide her onto a barstool. Then he pushed onto his own stool, gingerly testing its strength to ensure that it would support his weight as he savored its familiar comfort.

"Two beers, Loren. Me and Philomena got some catchin' up to do."

"Right on, man. These first two are on me. Just don't bust up the bar again, okay Duf? I can't afford no more trouble here."

Duffy grunted.

"Me neither, Loren. Me neither."

***

After their celebration at the Thunderbird Tavern, Duffy and Philomena went home early to find Shawnee seated at the kitchen table, looking at pictures in one of her library books. Shawnee's presence seemed to annoy her stepfather, and he took immediate offense to the pile of books stacked on the table.

"Look at this crap." Duffy scoffed in greeting. "What's the matter, no white boys around this weekend? What a bunch of bullshit. It's Friday night. Why aren't you going out like a normal person?"

When Shawnee ignored him, Duffy tried again.

"You're not a dyke, are you? We don't want no dykes around here. I seen enough of them in jail."

"Leave her alone, Duffy! Don't talk to her. Don't touch her. Just leave her alone."

"What's that supposed to mean? I can't talk to my own stepdaughter? I can't touch her?" His voice rose, "You think I want to mess with the little bitch?"

"No. I don't."

He laughed, "She ain't woman enough for me. I don't do dykes."

"Just leave her be. I swear, if you touch that girl, I'll kill you. I'll cut your balls off in your sleep, and then I'll kill you."

Duffy's deep voice rumbled across the room, a marauding bear oblivious to the angry honeybee. "I love it when you talk dirty to me, Philomena. That's why you're my woman.

***

That very night, Shawnee's nightmare returned.

In the dream, she was dressed in full Blackfeet regalia, wearing a dress not unlike the one she had sketched for her mother's Christmas gift. Her face was painted in contrasting colors: one side dark red, the other bright white. She was at the center of a circle of chanting warriors whose eyes glowed fluorescent green. All of the tormentors held spears with flinted points throbbing with the same intense green color. She could not escape the circle, no matter how hard she tried. With each attempt she made, one of the warriors jabbed at her with a glowing lance.

She jerked awake, her heart revving and the hair at her temples damp with sweat.

She got up and repositioned the chair that was wedged under the doorknob to her bedroom. When she crawled back into bed, she lay awake until morning, afraid to fall back asleep.

As the days passed, the verbal abuse continued, and the bad dreams became a regular occurrence. Every night, she was afraid to go to bed. Shawnee thought constantly about running away and began obsessing about escape. After school, she hung out at the library looking at pictures in art books and savoring the peace and solitude of the quiet environment.

In the privacy of her own bedroom, she read romances. Her mother was addicted to the cheap paperbacks, and they were always strewn around the house, stacked in piles beside the furniture. The books were always about strong men who saved beautiful women from dire circumstances. Shawnee knew her chances of a romantic rescue were rapidly deteriorating. And she knew that somehow, some way, she needed to get to a better place.

CHAPTER 28

Ten days after Duffy Grayson's release from jail, Clayton Cooper walked into his Montana classroom a half hour before class was scheduled to begin. He looked around the room and took a deep breath, reveling in the familiar dry smell of academia. The room was more sophisticated than his former middle school classroom, the walls spare and colorless, adorned only with a map of the world and a few posters about equal opportunity education rights.

His transition back into teaching had been uncomplicated. The community college had not requested any teaching credentials or information about his previous experience. During his interview, he had told Dean Walters that he had been a schoolteacher in Oregon but that he had come to Montana to pursue his dream of a career in photojournalism. He did not mention the scandal or his firing.

The dean was eager to fill a void in the spring schedule, and because it was a night class with a non-academic format, he had no interest in doing a background check or following up on Cooper's resume. Besides, Mr. Cooper's photos were excellent, and he was a pleasant and educated man. That he had teaching experience was an added bonus.

As students began to trickle in, Cooper introduced himself to each one, shaking their hands and welcoming them to the course. It was a small class of fourteen students who represented a diverse age group, from two high school students to an energetic white-haired woman in her early seventies.

"Ladies and gentlemen, since this is going to be an informal class, and we are all adults here," he smiled at the two teenagers, "you can call me Clayton or Coop. Most people just go with Coop. Tonight will be short and sweet. I'd like you to all introduce yourselves to the class and fill out some paperwork. I'll pass out a syllabus that we will review together. We'll finish with questions and answers. On Thursday, we'll get to work in earnest, and hopefully, by the end of the semester, we'll all be selling photos to major magazines."

While his students introduced themselves, Cooper took notes and began putting names to the new faces. The two young girls attended high school in Whitefish and were part of the student yearbook staff. They were interested in journalistic photography and perfecting their artistic photo skills. One of the girls wore an expensive Bogner ski parka and the other a sheepskin leather jacket over a black ribbed turtleneck sweater. The girl in the leather coat was striking, with white-blonde hair and the wholesome skin of a Swedish outdoorswoman. Cooper smiled when she introduced herself as Gun-Marie Erickson. Her friend had medium length brownish hair streaked with blond highlights that hung below a Big Mountain cap. Her name was Zoey Belford.

The remaining students were typical amateur photographers seeking technical direction and assistance with technique and presentation. The age range of the class intrigued Cooper, and although he was most at ease with kids, he thought he could actually teach everyone something of value.

The two girls waited after class and visited with Cooper afterward for half an hour or so. He promised to look at their photography equipment and to make some suggestions for additional lenses, filters, and other accessories.

Cooper enjoyed the evening, and he was looking forward to getting better acquainted with all the members of his class.

***

As the new year settled in, Cooper struggled to adjust to the routine of the winter in the Rockies. "Wintering over" is the litmus test for true acceptance into Montana residency, and those who head south for the winter are always considered part-timers.

In the Yaak, legends are created during the winter. The phenomenon is known as "cabin fever" and those who suffer from it are often called "shack nasty." The deep snows and cold temperatures keep the locals mostly indoors, a togetherness that can weigh heavily on mountain residents.

Cooper's first winter in the Yaak was a classic.

Ten miles below the Whiskey Bend Ranch, an army veteran only known as "Jerome," lived a survivalist's life, squatting in an abandoned log cabin with no running water or electricity. Jerome was a familiar sight on the Yaak River Road, hitchhiking into town on a regular basis to market various houseplants—some legal, some not—always accompanied by his dog, a wiry Chesapeake Retriever that sat on his owner's lap the entire ride into the towns of Troy or Libby when the pair was picked up by a sympathetic driver.

Late one night, Jerome's neighbor, famous for his "clear-cut" mentality of harvesting small logging operations," took offense to something Jerome had said or done and, bursting into the veteran's cabin armed with a double-bit ax, attempted to harvest the terrified occupant. Only the dog's warning barks allowed Jerome time to roll away from the ax-man and avoid decapitation. Bleeding from shoulder wounds, Jerome managed to make it to another neighbor at 3 A.M. to call for help. The county sheriff's department arrested the logger, who was sound asleep when they arrived and took him to jail.

Two weeks later, Cooper picked up the bandaged hitchhiker, who recounted the story of the attack to answer Cooper's innocent inquiry about his bandages.

When Coop told Wing about the incident, his friend laughed with delight.

"Goddamn. That's why we live here, man. That crazy bastard just made himself a permanent part of Yaak history."

"Which crazy bastard?"

"Both of 'em. God, I love this place. It's almost as good as Alaska."

The following week, it wasn't quite as good. Wing and Cooper drove upriver to the bar in Wing's old crew-bus truck. Wing parked the rig in front of the Painted Horse Saloon, and they crossed the road for a beer at the other tavern. When they came out an hour later to have one beer at the Horse, Wing's truck had disappeared, buried beneath an enormous mound of dirty snow. A front-loader sat at the end of the parking strip. The other two pickup trucks parked on each side of Wing were untouched, still sitting in the exact location where they had been when Cooper and Wing arrived.

When it dawned on Wing that his rig was entombed under the pile, he went crazy.

"What the hell's going on? Is this supposed to be funny?"

It was funny to Cooper. Gaping at the eight-foot-tall mini-mountain of snow, he started laughing.

As Wing glowered at Cooper, Rudy Morganroth, the owner of the Horse, came out on the porch and started yelling at Wing.

"If you're gonna drink across the street, park your fuckin' truck over there. Don't be taking up my parking and then doing all your business somewhere else."

Wing looked at Rudy in astonishment and then turned his gaze to the almost empty parking strip in front of Rudy's saloon. "You crazy son of a bitch, there's all kinds of parking here. Get on that machine and dig me out."

"Screw you. There's shovels on the porch." Rudy was not dumb enough to offer Wing the keys to the front-loader. He knew his bar might be leveled. "And don't park here again—unless you're drinkin' here." He stomped back into the bar, leaving the two friends standing beside the buried vehicle.

Trotting to the porch, Cooper returned with two shovels and started a frenzied attack on the pile of snow.

"Grab a shovel, man," Cooper nodded toward the second shovel that he had planted in the snow, "this will only take a few minutes."

Wing stood still, considering the alternatives. Finally, he mumbled, "I'm gonna kill that little prick." Then he picked up a shovel and headed to the other side of the rig. He took a savage shovelful of snow and added, "After I run my fuckin' bar tab out of sight."

***

Cooper had no intention of succumbing to the madness of cabin fever. He called Angelina Hailstone and asked if she would have dinner with him after his class on Thursday night, a date that he had hoped to arrange earlier but had postponed because of his involvement with starting his new position at the college.

Angie accepted on the condition that they not stay out late.

Cooper hurried through his class and turned down an invitation to join the two high school girls for pizza when the class was over.

"I'd love to, Zo," he told Zoey when she asked, "but I have a business meeting at nine. Maybe next week, huh?" He smiled with regret. "My treat, okay?"

He met Angelina at the Raven's Nest Brewery. She was waiting for him, seated at the bar with a glass of red wine. She had not dressed for the date, wearing a North Face anorak and a pair of baggy military trousers. Cooper was wearing a white Hugo Boss shirt with a spread collar and a pair of fitted black jeans. His narrow belt matched his pointy-toed loafers perfectly.

"Look at us," Cooper said with a laugh. "What's wrong with this picture? It looks like I should be the northeast city dude, and you should be the loner from the Yaak."

"Nothing's wrong with this picture. We are who we are. Maybe it's a good thing. They say that opposites attract."

"Hey, we're not so different. I'm actually a radical guy at heart."

Angie laughed and said, "Sure you are. Know what the locals call newcomers to Montana? LL Beaners."

"What? That's not fair; this isn't how I'd dress if we were in the Yaak. I'm just a mountain man trying to fit in when I'm in the city."

Angie laughed again, "Nice try, dude. It's okay. You look pretty cute."

Cooper was mollified by the compliment. And he was quite aware that Angie would fit in perfectly in the Yaak. The thought intrigued him because he knew that such a lifestyle was not for everyone.

"Have you ever been to the Yaak?" he asked her.

"I haven't," she answered, "but I've heard of it. Everyone says it's beautiful."

Cooper ordered Angie another glass of red wine and a microbrew for himself. They settled into easy conversation.

"You'd love it. The valley is beyond beautiful. There's nowhere like it in the lower forty-eight. It's still wild and unpredictable. I'll show it to you someday."

When they finished eating, Cooper offered to drive Angie home, in hopes of being invited in for a drink. She refused the ride, explaining that she had ridden her mountain bike, complete with snow traction tires, to the restaurant, and she wanted to ride it home to settle her meal.

"I've got to get going. I had a great time. Thank you for everything."

"Really? I was hoping we could have a nightcap."

"It's past my bedtime, Coop. Maybe next time."

Driving home after dinner, it began snowing, and the beauty of the snow-dusted valley softened his post-date disappointment as his driving speed slowed to a crawl. It gave him plenty of time to think about his next meeting with the intriguing Ms. Angelina Hailstone.

24
CHAPTER

Back on the Oregon coast, Philomena and Duffy were enjoying a night out on the town.

At the Thunderbird Tavern, they ran into a group of Philomena's friends from the reservation, and the women talked her into joining them for bingo at the casino. Duffy stayed at the bar and spent the night drinking with some of the basketball players from the rez team. Enjoying his freedom, he lost count of the number of beers he had put away as he entertained his buddies with lies about his time in the county jail. Just before midnight, they went outside and smoked some weed. Out of practice, he decided it was time to go home.

Shawnee was in her bedroom brushing her hair when she heard Duffy's truck pull into the carport attached to the little house. She assumed he was still with her mother, so she hadn't bothered to prop the oak chair beneath her doorknob.

When she saw the door to her room open in the reflection of the mirror of her dresser, she froze with her hand in mid-brush stroke. Her stepfather's body filled the open door, blotting out most of the light from the hallway. They stared at one another in the mirror, Duffy's eyes bright with lust, Shawnee's dull with fear. Neither said a word.

When Duffy turned out the light, Shawnee closed her eyes tight and willed herself to fade into the darkness.

***

Afterward, she desperately tried to cope, withdrawing even deeper into her own private world. But the demons were relentless.

170

They pushed her into a dark hole, and the abyss was filled with chaos and confusion. It was boundless, unbearable, inescapable.

On the outside, the only discernable change in Shawnee's behavior was an increase in the dark mood swings that had long disrupted her life. Philomena thought her daughter's depression was a stage that all teenage girls experienced, remembering battles with her own moods when she had been a teenager. But as her daughter's down times began to last longer and grow darker, she began to worry.

She shared her concern with her husband.

"Duffy, I'm worried about Shawnee. She seems. . . different. It's not just the usual moods. Lately, it's almost like she goes into a trance or something. Last night I heard her crying in her room. Something's wrong. You know what I'm saying?"

"She's always been screwed up, Philomena. She's not right in the head."

"Bullshit. She's sensitive and quiet is all. This is different. I'm worried about her."

The big man grunted. "There's nothin' wrong with her. She's always been weird."

"Maybe just a little. But I think we need to do something. I've been thinking that we should visit my family in Alberta. Shawnee's been interested in my side of the family lately. I want to take her home for a visit."

"You might as well take her to the moon. The only family she's interested in is her white old man."

"I don't think so. Maybe her spirit country is calling her. I think we should take her. I think we should do a road trip. C'mon, it would be fun. I'll introduce you to some real Indians."

"Humph," Duffy grunted, "there ain't no real Indians anymore."

But Duffy had noticed the change in Shawnee, and he had also noticed an unfamiliar gnawing at his own conscience. Maybe

Philomena was right. Even the most free-ranging Native American people had a spiritual place that they called home. Maybe a visit to her homeland would bring Shawnee closer to normal.

***

Two days before the beginning of spring vacation, the decision to make the trip was finally confirmed. It wasn't planned; Duffy simply decided that they would go. They would leave on Saturday, driving to Spokane and then to Browning on the Blackfeet Reservation near the border before entering Canada on Monday.

They would have to take two vehicles since Philomena and Duffy filled the front seats of his little pickup truck and the pickup bed would be loaded with luggage and sleeping bags. Shawnee could drive her mother's battered but mechanically sound import, and they would caravan to Lethbridge, Alberta, to see Philomena's family.

Growing more animated by the day, Shawnee was thrilled with the game plan and went to the public library to research their route. Duffy scoffed at her efforts, content to hit the road with a vague idea of the final destination, confident in his ability to get them there. Duffy knew that maps and planned rest stops were futile because something always came up. A new bar, a new friend, a flat tire, or car trouble. Whatever.

Shawnee was well aware of this traveling style, but she tried to create a route more conducive to her own agenda. Using MapQuest on the computer in the library, she prepared an itinerary with pre-planned overnight destinations and approximate arrival times. She even set up reconnection locations in case the two vehicles were ever separated. She monitored Duffy's mood before deciding to share it with him for his approval.

Duffy was semi-impressed with Shawnee's research. Perhaps his uncharacteristic twinge of consciousness contributed to his grudging acceptance. Or maybe it was the logic of the designated "reconnection locations" should they become separated en route. This safety net would keep Philomena off his back if the two vehicles separated, which Duffy felt was inevitable on any road trip.

Duffy grumbled, "Don't go thinking you know everything about road trips just because you know how to work a computer. But we can try it, and see if it's worth a damn."

Shawnee knew better than to expect long days of constant travel. Better to anticipate late starts and occasional bar stops. These interruptions would bode well for her. Plus, Duffy's insistence on two rigs was perfect. Sometime during the road trip, she was going to take a wrong turn, getting lost and ending up miles from her mother and stepfather. The designated meeting areas would keep them from worrying until it was too late.

Shawnee was elated about the trip, and she credited the fortunate occurrence to the magic calling of her grandmother's mystical arrowhead.

***

In the Rockies, Angelina Hailstone was also looking forward to spring vacation. She was scheduled to work during the week at the mountain, followed by an unexpected three days off, when local college kids returned home to work part-time shifts on the ski lifts—an administrative move to negate the management's obligation to pay holiday overtime hours to full-time staff.

Through most of the winter, Cooper had been lobbying for her to spend the spring break with him at the Yaak. So far, she had worked to keep the relationship platonic, careful to ensure that their dates were public, deflecting Cooper's suggestions for nightcaps at her apartment.

Past experience had taught her to be cautious with love affairs, and she was comfortable with her current status, but Cooper's good looks and boyish charm were beginning to grow on her. He had shaved before his first class at the college, and Angie liked the novelty of a clean-shaven Montanan. He dressed well, in a hipster way that she appreciated considering her east coast upbringing.

Cooper had impeccable manners, which was a refreshing change from her current male friends who were oblivious to the old-school courtesy that reminded her of her father.

Cooper's age didn't bother her in the least. She had been with older men before. In fact, she had had an affair with her literature professor during her sophomore year at a small university in Vermont. The man was even older than Cooper, and he had been her first real love.

Cooper's education and artistic creativity appealed to her too. He liked all the activities that had brought her to the west. He was a hiker, a biker, and a fly fisherman. He liked snow sports, and he had even done some snowboarding, although he preferred backcountry skiing if given a choice.

He was persistent but in a compelling way. His efforts were somewhat needy but not so much that they were annoying. Rather, it was just enough to make her feel appreciated and desired.

She knew she was falling in love with him.

***

Shawnee's trip itinerary never stood a chance. Philomena and Duffy closed down the Thunderbird Tavern on Friday night, and their 7:30 A.M. departure time faded into oblivion.

The youngster chafed at the delay and spent the morning trying to control the chaos in her mind and the raucous drumming in her chest. She had memorized the route long ago. Portland. Tri-cities. Spokane. Missoula. Kalispell. The Blackfeet Indian Reservation. Two days of travel. Or maybe three.

When she mentioned their growing delay, Duffy said. "Shut up and make some more coffee. We got time. We'll go when we go."

The man reeked of the tavern, and his bleary eyes were menacing under half-closed lids. His puffy face looked like a post-Halloween pumpkin that was beginning to sag and discolor. He sat at the kitchen table, his head resting in his hands.

"I know, Duffy. It's just that if we're going to get to. . ."

Duffy cut her off in midsentence. "We're gonna get there when we get there," he said, his voice even deeper than usual as his vocal cords strained with the smoke and alcohol of the night before. "Just be quiet and leave me alone," he added.

***

When they finally left, Duffy bought a half case of Heineken for the road, and for the remainder of the day, they made good time. They spent the night in the parking lot of the casino on the Spokane Indian Reservation. Duffy, having honed the skill of extortion, borrowed a little money from a young security officer who he recognized from a basketball tournament in Klamath Falls, Oregon.

Duffy and Philomena headed into the casino, and Shawnee locked herself into her mother's Nissan parked in the far corner of the lot where the young security officer had agreed to let them spend the night. She woke only once when her traveling partners noisily climbed into the bed of Grayson's truck, passing out in sleeping bags on the old mattress that Duffy had unrolled in the back of the pickup.

The next morning was Sunday, and Duffy bummed three meals from the casino's kitchen staff while they prepared the breakfast buffet. Seated on the tailgate of the truck, they ate without speaking, the two adults hung over, Shawnee trying to remain invisible. They planned to drive to the Blackfeet Reservation on the eastern side of Glacier National Park, spending the night in Browning and then crossing the border to meet with Philomena's family the next day.

Duffy, who was now a registered felon, would be unable to cross the border legally, but it was a minor inconvenience for travelers from both countries to circumvent the border stations. The biggest problem was coordinating the crossing with local family members and arranging a pick-up location on the other side.

Somewhere on the route, Shawnee planned to break away. She did not know what would happen after she separated from the others. She expected that once she got to the Yaak, Mr. Cooper would assemble a plan. With a twinge of panic, she realized that she had not considered what would happen if he was not at home. What if he was back in Skyler, visiting his children or looking for her? She had been so consumed with planning this surprise meeting that she had not considered the possibility that Cooper had alternative plans. *He'll be there,* she thought. *The spirit of my grandmother's necklace will make it so.*

"Duffy, can I drive ahead and meet you guys at the planned stop in Browning. Or on the road somewhere? I'll just pull over in the parking lot of a bar or convenience store where you can't miss me, and we can caravan in from there. That way, if you and Mom want to stop for a while, you won't have to worry about me cramping your style."

Duffy snorted. They all knew that cell phone reception in the mountains was dicey. Communication alternatives were limited, which could create problems.

"Or if you know someplace in Browning, we could just meet there. It was supposed to be an official reconnection site. Then you wouldn't have to worry."

Philomena, much more familiar with northern Montana, suggested, "We could meet at the Jackknife Saloon on Highway 2, just the other side of Kalispell. It's pretty much an Indian bar, and it's easy to find. Good people, too."

Duffy said. "Whatever."

Shawnee was elated. Kalispell was even better than Browning, only three or four hours from the Yaak. Whatever happened, she would not be missed for at least twenty-four hours, maybe more. She could find Mr. Coop and then contact her mother's relatives in Alberta by phone. Or she could leave a message at the Jackknife Bar that she was headed into the mountains for some soul searching: like a modern-day vision quest helping her find her way.

"Let's give the girl some room, Duffy. If all else fails, she and I can meet at the border crossing on Highway 89. Shawnee has studied the maps. She can find her way."

Shawnee left as soon as she filled her car with gas and bought coffee for the road. Philomena had slipped her a fifty-dollar bill, and she wanted to leave before her mother changed her mind about the money.

As she began her journey, her spirits soared. She was free. Free at last to pursue the life and love that she had long desired. She knew that Mr. Cooper loved her. She was proud that she had protected him during the hearing and remained dedicated to him throughout the long ordeal.

She couldn't wait to surprise him.

CHAPTER 30

Early Saturday afternoon, Angelina drove into the parking lot of the Whiskey Bend Ranch, parking her twenty-year-old Ford 150 pickup in front of the western-style porch that still reminded people of a bar, even though the neon beer signs had been removed and the painted "Whiskey Bend Saloon" was long gone.

On weekends, Cooper would watch in amusement as travelers pulled into the front yard, stopping halfway through the log arch and freezing with indecision, confused by the domestic look of the once iconic saloon. Closed for well over a decade now, the occasional ex-patron still knocked on his door to ask if the bar was open. The bar was definitely open for Angelina Hailstone. When he heard the truck drive up, Cooper walked onto the porch and met her with a glass of red wine. "Welcome to the Whiskey Bend Saloon," he said. "The home of the baddest bar in northern Montana."

"Well thank you, Mr. Cooper," Angie said with mock formality. She raised her glass in a toast. "Let's hope it lives up to its reputation."

Cooper laughed. "Come on in."

He reached across the seat of the truck to grab her battered backpack.

"I can handle that, Cooper. I do run a chairlift, you know."

"I know, I know. Humor me."

She smiled at him. "Well, I guess I can deal with it. God knows most of the ski rats I hang out with are more than happy to let me do all the work."

He escorted her into the Whiskey Bend Ranch. The house was spotless. The windows had been washed inside, and the snow-covered riverbanks and icy river were so close to the building that they seemed to be a part of the room. There was a fire burning in the woodstove, and the moist heat and aroma of burning larch made the space warm and cozy.

Cooper had candles burning on the bookcase bar and a cheese plate beside the bottle of red wine. His aunt's roll-top desk was placed against the wall opposite the bar, and Cooper's computer sat on this writing surface. A compact Bose stereo rested on top of the desk, softly playing a Bruno Mars ballad.

"Wow. Coop, this is great. I feel like I'm at a five-star bed and breakfast. You didn't tell me this old saloon was so cool."

"I'm full of surprises, girl. I think this will be the perfect place for you to relax and recharge your batteries."

Angie was looking out the windows above the bar.

"People used to actually sit here and drink? This is almost as good as the restaurant on top of the mountain. In fact, without all the people, it might even be better."

"You haven't seen anything yet," he said, toting her backpack through the French doors that led to the master bedroom.

"This place is, excuse the cliché, truly heaven on earth. We can ski, snowshoe, snowmobile, or read by the fire. We've got otters that live across the river, and you can watch them play on their snow slides while you drink your wine. We've got moose, deer, mountain lions, eagles, ospreys, and coyotes that have all been on the property this winter. Up the mountain, there are elk and grizzlies. On top of that, it's quiet and peaceful. Trust me. You're going to love it."

They went to bed in the late afternoon, intoxicated with the wine and the magical beauty of the valley.

So confident and self-assured on the surface, Angelina clutched Cooper's hand as he led her into the house's only bedroom. The room was lined with bookcases that surrounded the polished lodgepole pine bed frame with its tall log headboard. The bed was buried in a thick down comforter.

Cooper put both hands on Angie's chin, tracing the outline of her jaws before kissing her lips. Taking her hands in his own, he removed her wristwatch and set it on the nightstand. Then, he ran his hands down her neck, between her breasts, to her waist and gently pulled her sweater over her head. She was not wearing a bra, and he sat on the bed in front of her, lifting his hands up her body, then using his fingertips to trace the outside of the dark circles on her breasts before he brushed the back of his fingers across her nipples. Her breasts were small and perfectly shaped, immediately responding to his touch, her nipples hardening and rising.

Turning her so that she was facing away from him, he slid her jeans down her hips, excited that she was now completely naked.

He pulled her toward him, surprised to see a tattoo of a red and green hummingbird beside the dimple on the top of her left buttock. It was as if a single hummingbird had escaped the band of interlocked birds on her wrist tattoo, waiting in the darkness to be discovered.

"You're beautiful," he said, "and you have a beautiful body."

She twisted in his arms, facing him now, and pulled his tee-shirt over his head. He stood up, and she unbuckled his belt and pulled his jeans down to his ankles. He kicked them off without finesse, before grabbing his boxer shorts and removing them himself.

She laid her head on his bare chest.

"Don't be disappointed, Cooper," she said. "I'm not always good at this."

"Honey, just relax. Everyone is good at this."

They rolled onto the bed, kicking the comforter to the ground in their haste to get to one another.

***

180

Shawnee's excitement began building as she drove through the afternoon. The spectacular Glacier Country captivated her, and she stopped often on quiet sections of roadway to breathe the crisp, mountain air. She drove well below the speed limit, a new driver on her first road trip, enjoying the experience but afraid of losing her way.

She reveled in the new countryside: the majestic mountains, the juxtaposition of the pristine snowfields and the swollen rivers fighting their way free from tangles of dirty ice. The wilderness was stronger here. It was beautiful but also raw and unpredictable. She felt a strange connection to the area like she had been here before but had been too young to remember the experience. She knew that the Blackfeet were close relatives of the Blood Tribe on the Canadian side of the border. Her mother often claimed to be Blackfeet. Shawnee promised herself that she and Cooper would soon return to explore the reservation country.

As she drew nearer to her destination, she became conscious of the time. It would be dark soon, and she would enter the Yaak after nightfall. She was comfortable in the darkness, but for weeks now, she had imagined arriving at Mr. Cooper's home during the day. She was upset to change her planned arrival time. She had longed for a visual connection to the remote valley, hoping to see and feel what had so completely captured Mr. Cooper's heart.

***

"Wake up, sleeping beauty." Cooper kissed Angie on the forehead and then slid out of the bed. He was still naked and stood comfortably at the bedside in the late afternoon sunlight, smiling at his new lover. "Shall I start prepping dinner?" he asked. "Why don't you just relax? I'll start marinating the steaks. It'll be a while before they're ready."

"Can I help with anything?" Angie asked, trying to stifle a yawn.

"Maybe later," Clayton grinned, "I need a little recovery time. Remember, I'm an old man."

181

"Oh, I don't think so, baby," she teased. "I'm pretty sure that age doesn't matter."

As the late afternoon light began fading, they decided to take a quick walk up the road beside the river. They bundled up with hats, gloves, and scarves, and Cooper held Angie's hand as they savored the solitude of winter in paradise.

"This valley is over forty miles long, and it's almost all National Forest," Cooper explained. "It's perfect animal habitat and has more wildlife than anyplace I've ever seen. It's been called the most remote valley in the lower forty-eight. Unfortunately, I'm not sure that's still true. But I do know it will always be a very special place."

"You love it, don't you?"

"I do. The valley has had a 'Deliverance' type of reputation for years and years. People claim it has the highest per capita murder rate in Montana. Of course, that could be one murder every fifty years considering the population, but strange things do happen here."

"Such as?"

"Well, my uncle bought the saloon after the previous owner died in a mysterious hunting accident. There was something about whether or not the poker game he and his buddies had been involved in earlier might have played a role in the shooting. A year before he died, there was a terrible car wreck right in front of the bar in the spring. A van full of college kids who had come to the valley for a canoe trip rolled their rig into the river after a drinking binge at the old saloon. All of them drowned. Four boys, two girls, all from some school in South Dakota. They say the bar owners never really recovered."

"That's awful."

"I know. Even the Native Americans were afraid of the Yaak. They would hunt here but only in hunting parties, never alone. It's funny; we're in the heart of Indian country, and the only Native Americans that I've seen in the valley came the week before hunting season opened, shot as many deer as they could, and then left. I guess it has something to do with the mystique of the area and the number of carnivorous predators. Weird, huh?"

"Very. Is it still like that?"

"Unfortunately, no. We still have all those animals, but they're getting harder to find. In all the years that I've come to visit, I've never seen a grizzly bear or a mountain lion. They're out there though. It's just a matter of time."

As the sky grew darker, the temperature began to fall. They zipped their parkas tight against their necks and retraced their steps to the house. They could see the old saloon's lights filtering through the heavy dusk, and the prospect of a warm shower and a glass of red wine drew them toward the cozy confines of the ranch.

***

It was dark when Shawnee finally turned up the road that paralleled the river. Her heart began beating rapidly as she recognized the final approach to her dream. She was on the Yaak River Road. She was almost home.

She knew that the Whiskey Bend Ranch was around twenty miles up the road and that there was an increase in elevation as the road wound its way north. Duffy had taught her to monitor the mileage markers on the side of the road, and when her headlights lit up the number "1" on the green milepost stake, she knew there was no turning back tonight.

With the passage of each milepost marker, she could feel her anxiety heighten and her courage wane. The faster her heart beat, the slower she drove the car, and the distance between mileage markers seemed interminable.

She passed the six-mile marker.

Would he even be home when she arrived?

The car's headlights lit up the ten-mile marker, and she watched anxiously as it slid into the night.

With the increase in elevation, the mountain air began cooling down, and pillow-like layers of fog appeared in the low areas of the road. Shawnee lowered her speed another notch, convincing herself that it was safer to drive slowly in the weather.

How would he react? Surprise? Confusion? Joy? It didn't really matter. He would get used to her soon enough.

Passing the fifteen-mile marker, it began to snow. Wet, heavy flakes melted on contact with the windshield. Just beyond the green marker, she saw two deer in her headlights, and she dropped the car's speed yet again. Her heart beat faster.

Would he take her in his arms? Kiss her?

She passed milepost seventeen.

What would he say? I've missed you? I need you? I love you?

Eighteen. Nineteen.

What should she say? *We can be together now? I love you? I want you?*

She didn't know. She only knew that this time there would be no waiting until the next morning. No hesitating. No escape.

She crossed Whiskey Creek Bridge and stopped to get her bearings. She got out of the car to stretch and calm her nerves, knowing that Whiskey Creek must be close to Cooper's ranch. She noticed that there was a road next to the bridge, but it was unmarked and appeared to lead into the dense forest that bordered the river.

Back in the car, she passed milepost twenty, and her headlights lit up a log entry gate on the river side of the road. The two upright logs of the gate were almost invisible in the mountain fog and sporadic snow flurries. She was creeping along now and could just make out a carved sign chain-bolted to the crossbar of the top log. She caught the words ". . . Bend Ranch." Behind the gateway, she could see the dark silhouette of a low building with soft yellow lights shining through the fog, flooding onto the patches of snow that still covered the partially plowed parking lot. The snow that had slid off the roof through the winter surrounded the building like walls of a giant fort built for a snowball fight, and the house looked snug and peaceful in the dim light of the half-moon overhead.

Parked in front of the building were two pickup trucks. She recognized one as the truck Mr. Coop had driven when he was last in Skyler. The other looked like a beater-truck that he must have picked up for work around the ranch.

She stopped the car in the center of the road, the engine idling quietly as she surveyed Cooper's place. She was not surprised at her fear, feeling the same terror that had overwhelmed her at Cooper's rental in Skyler. Her hands shook, and she tightened her grip on the steering wheel; her knuckles shone as white as the bones beneath the skin.

Turning the headlights off, she drove through the log entryway, careful to make her approach as silent as possible. Parking the car in a dark corner of the snowy lot, she decided to use the same tactics that she had developed when Cooper was living at coach Locker's house: she would hide and observe before deciding what to do next.

Spying through the windows of the bar-turned-home was easy. There were no window coverings except for some dark curtains concealing what she assumed was the bedroom. When she stood on the snow that had been plowed to the sides of the parking lot, she was outside the ring of light that flooded outside the house. The darkness provided a safe view into the building.

She saw Cooper's head illuminated from a lamp by the woodstove. He was reading a book. She looked around the room and into the kitchen, trying to resolve the question of the second truck in the parking lot. She did not want to meet Cooper unless he was alone.

And he was obviously alone.

Pushing her hair out of her eyes and smoothing the wrinkles from the clothing that she had driven in all day, she took a deep breath and forced herself to walk to the house.

On the front porch, she stood for a long time, trying to calm herself. Just standing there, she could feel herself moving farther from the abyss that had threatened her for so long.

She took another deep breath and tapped on the door.

31
CHAPTER

The knock on the front door was so gentle that Cooper wasn't certain that someone was there.

The valley's solitude magnified the sound of any mechanical intrusion, and a vehicle arriving at the ranch was usually obvious well before visitors reached his porch. He was absorbed in a new Alan Furst thriller, and Angie's quiet noises in the bedroom had occupied his subconscious, masking the guest's approach.

Setting the novel aside, he rose from the chair. "Coming!" He called out as he hurried to the door. Turning on the porch light, he opened the door.

"Hello, Mr. Coop. It's me."

Cooper stared in shock at the visitor standing in front of him. The glow of the porch light revealed a dark-skinned young woman with long black hair and large brown eyes. She was much slimmer than Cooper remembered, and the once round face had melted away, replaced by defined cheekbones and lips that were fuller in contrast to the sharpness of her chin.

Cooper hadn't seen Shawnee up close since the hearing. He had not spoken to her since the night after practice at the soccer field. The unsettling experience of the strange Christmas gift in Skyler, which had forced him to think about the girl, had taken place four months ago. The only thought that registered in his mind was, *Oh my God. What's going on now?*

"Sh-Shawnee," he stuttered, shielded behind the half-opened door, "what are you doing here? What do you want?"

Shawnee was quiet for a second as if the question was too absurd to require an answer. When she spoke, her voice was as soft as her knock at the door. "I came to you, Mr. Coop. I came to be with you."

It was cold standing on the porch of the mountain ranch, and as she spoke, the look that came over Cooper's face sent an even colder surge through her entire body. "I came to be with you," she repeated as if he hadn't heard her. "So we could be together."

Cooper didn't know what to say. There was a look of panic in his grey eyes. His face tightened as his mind groped for a way to escape.

His reaction terrified Shawnee. It didn't fit any scenario she had rehearsed. Her voice tinged with growing panic, and she said, "Mr. Coop. I've waited for you for two years. You told me you loved me. I love you, too." She was blinking her eyes rapidly in an effort to hold back tears.

Struggling to find the right words, Cooper whispered "Shawnee, of course, I love you. I love all my students. But you have to understand. It's not romantic love. I'm so sorry if you misunderstood. I. . . I thought you knew. I'm sorry. I'm so sorry."

"But that night at the beach. You said you loved me. We. . ."

"It didn't mean anything, Shawn. I was trying to make you feel better."

Shawnee shook her head as he spoke, and before he had finished, the tears began to run down her face. He had never experienced such a heart wrenching emotional reaction.

He reached out and pulled her into the house, bringing her trembling body close to his chest, trying to calm her sobs. She put her arms around his waist, and after a moment's resistance, he surrendered to her fierce embrace, holding her, hoping to end her tears.

"Cooper? What's going on?"

Angie's voice froze both Cooper and Shawnee, who were lost in two separate worlds, locked on different dilemmas, each of their minds searching for the right words.

"Coop?"

Clayton wrenched Shawnee's arms from his waist and stepped away from the girl. Shawnee stared in horror at the young white woman who was only wearing a mesh Skyler soccer shirt. Despite the magenta color hair, she looked fresh and innocent in the high school top, a garment that made her look like a teenager as young as Shawnee herself.

Cooper's mind raced. Angelina knew nothing of his personal background.

"It's nothing, Ang. This is an old student of mine. She has some emotional. . . issues. It's all a misunderstanding. She's a little confused. I'm just trying to help."

"Who is this, Mr. Coop? What is she doing here? What's going on?"

"Shawnee, just relax. This is my friend Angelina Hailstone. She's staying for a few days. We're friends. Just friends, Shawnee."

Shawnee stared at the girl, still uncertain about the young woman's role in Mr. Cooper's life. The girl's sudden appearance, the shock of her colorful hair, the sensual impression of her near nakedness, and her long, white legs terrified the teenager.

Suddenly, Shawnee's eyes opened wide, and she screamed, a sound so tormented, so deeply-rooted that it paralyzed both Cooper and Angelina.

Shawnee's eyes were locked on Angie's neck.

Despite the distance that separated the two girls, Angie's hand instinctively reached to protect her throat. Her fingers closed on a small, white arrowhead, suspended on a string-like piece of black leather.

Shawnee screamed again and threw herself at Cooper, clawing at his face. Three thin lines of blood appeared on his forehead above the left eye, running down his cheek until they disappeared into the shadow of the three-day growth that surrounded his mouth and chin. Cooper fought her off with an intensity that frightened him, a necessary intensity given the fury of Shawnee's attack. When he finally pinned her arms, both he and the girl were bleeding, blood dripping from Shawnee's nose, down her chin, and onto the entryway floor.

Cooper was gasping for breath when Shawnee finally went limp in his arms, her face pressed against his chest and quaking sobs echoing throughout the house.

"Ang, can you get me a towel, please? She'll be all right."

Cooper's houseguest was stunned by the violence of Shawnee's attack and subsequent collapse. "Should I call the sheriff, Cooper? This is horrible. This girl needs help."

"No. She'll be okay. I'm sorry you had to see this. This is part of what I was running away from when I came up here." He wiped the side of his face, noticing his own blood for the first time.

"Goddamn," he sighed, "Why me?"

After Angie returned with a clean towel, Shawnee began a slow recovery. She refused to answer any questions or respond to their attempts to comfort her or get her to communicate. Her eyes were filmed over, and she sucked in air with short gasping breaths. She was lying on the couch in front of the fire, the other two hovering over her trying to help.

When Cooper went to the kitchen to get her a glass of water, she bolted upright and screamed again. It was a howl of primal sorrow. The water glass exploded on the kitchen floor, and Angie shrank back against the wall beside the fireplace.

And then it stopped.

Shawnee fainted and fell backward on the sofa. Cooper and Angelina looked at one another in an expression of relief mixed with distress and uncertainty. The blissful weekend was over, the romantic interlude shattered like the exploding glass punctuated by Shawnee's last scream.

"What do we do now, Cooper? I think we should call the police. . . or an ambulance. Is she drunk? Do you think she's on drugs? Or. . . or. . . just. . . sick?"

"She'll be okay. She'll leave when she wakes up."

"Maybe. I'm going home. This doesn't feel right. She went berserk when she saw the necklace that you gave me. I can't deal with this kind of stuff. I'm going home."

"Don't go, Ang. Everything will be okay."

Shaking her head, Angie went into the bedroom, changed into her own clothes, and threw her things into her backpack. When she returned to the living room, she had her jacket and ball cap on, the pack slung over one shoulder.

The arrowhead necklace was clenched in her hand. She set it on the end table beside the couch where Shawnee lay sleeping. "I can't deal with this, Coop. It doesn't feel right. I'm just. . . too upset to deal with this right now. I need to go home and try to sort this whole thing out."

Cooper said, "Honey, you don't have to go. You've got to trust me. Everything is going to be all right. It'll be just you and me as soon as she wakes up. I promise."

Angelina shook her head. "I've got to go. I'm sorry I can't stay to help you clean up. Call me when you get this thing worked out, okay?"

She hurried to the door and left without another word. Cooper listened to her truck start and then ran to the door. He stood on the porch and yelled, "Be careful on the roads! It's supposed to snow tonight."

Angie nodded through the windshield. Flashing a peace sign, she hurried her truck out of the parking lot. Cooper watched her taillights as they disappeared down the road at the first corner below the ranch.

After cleaning up the broken glass, he went back into the living room and draped a blanket over the comatose Shawnee. Returning to his chair beside the wood stove, he sat and held his damaged face in his hands. He had no idea what to do. It was a horrible dream. He closed his eyes, intent on coming up with a solution.

***

When he woke almost two hours later, Shawnee was gone. There was no note. There was no necklace.

He looked out the front door to check for Shawnee's car. Only his own truck remained in the parking lot. It was colder now and snowing—the flakes the texture of flour, swirling like a dust storm.

Soon, it would cover the dirty snow with a layer of soft whiteness, creating the illusion of an idyllic mountain valley peacefully waiting for spring.

32
CHAPTER

Philomena was worried. Shawnee had missed the designated meeting at the Jackknife Saloon outside of Kalispell and had failed to contact her parents throughout the night. The usually dependable teenager had disappeared.

Philomena wanted to contact the authorities right away, but Duffy was adamant about keeping them out of the picture. He didn't trust white society's legal system, and his recent incarceration had done nothing to change his mind about encouraging any law enforcement agency to have any role in his life.

As the hours passed, the weather continued deteriorating, and Philomena's mental state escalated from concern to alarm. She racked her brain trying to comprehend the situation—and trying to suppress a gnawing suspicion that her daughter might have her own agenda.

Even with the sketchy cell phone service throughout the area, she knew that every town in Glacier country would have some type of tower. If her daughter was in trouble, Shawnee would have called with an explanation.

Worst-case scenarios flooded Philomena's mind, and she forced herself to calm down and think about more logical possibilities. She was surprised that a nagging image of Clayton Cooper forced itself into her mind. She knew from street rumors that the man had relocated to northwestern Montana. And she knew that her daughter had never let go of her schoolgirl crush.

She and Duffy had spent the night in Kalispell, and she decided to make a call to Skyler to find out where Cooper lived.

When Skyler High's athletic director Curtis James told her that Cooper was living in an isolated Montana valley called the Yaak, she knew at once that there might be trouble. She called the Flat Head County Sheriff's Department to report Shawnee's absence and her own concern about her daughter's possible destination. At the mention of the Yaak, the deputy who had answered the phone promised to alert Lincoln County Sheriff Hayes Thompson about the missing girl and see if he could help them out since the valley was located in the other sheriff's county. Sheriff Thompson agreed to check it out.

***

In the Yaak, the snow continued through most of the day, the stubborn remnant of winter's last gasp. Like the mountain version of a rising tide, the flakes were building momentum, slowly covering the valley with a shallow sea of snow.

Cooper, who loved these snowy days of forced idleness, was unable to lose himself in a book or photography project, his usual activities on snowbound days. He tried to call Angie in the afternoon, but the phone rang unanswered in her Whitefish studio apartment. He itched with impatience at each futile ring.

Every vehicle that passed on the isolated road set Cooper's senses on edge, and he peered through the swirling snow trying to track each car, fearful that it might be Shawnee, back for another disastrous confrontation.

Finally, at 7:35 P.M., the phone rang, and Cooper hurried to answer, expecting to hear Angie on the line. Instead, a man's voice asked, "May I speak with Clayton Cooper, please?"

"This is Clay Cooper speaking."

"Mr. Cooper, this is Sheriff Thompson from the Lincoln County Sheriff's Department over here in Libby. I've been on the phone with Deputy Baker from Kalispell. He's trying to track down a young lady who failed to show up for a rendezvous with her parents outside of town there. I'm sure everything is fine, but the mother is quite concerned about the girl's whereabouts.

"Apparently, she thinks her daughter might have taken a side trip to visit you. The mom's name is Philomena Grayson. Sheriff Baker tells me you'll recognize the name. She didn't know exactly where you live, but she knew it was in northern Montana and said something about the Yaak. Honest folks who live in the Yaak aren't hard to find, Mr. Cooper." He chuckled. "Now, the not so honest ones can be a different story.

"Anyway, the missing girl's name is Shawnee. Mrs. Grayson told Deputy Baker that you and her daughter have some history. She thinks the girl might have come looking for you. That's why he called me in on this. Can you help us, sir?"

Cooper remained silent, his mind churning.

"Mr. Cooper? Are you there?"

"Yes. . . yes, of course. Actually, I have seen Shawnee, Sheriff. She stopped by last evening—uninvited—and was here for a few minutes. We talked briefly and she left."

"Well, that's interesting. These shots in the dark are usually dead ends. What time did she leave your place?"

"Umm. . . I'm not certain about the exact time. It was early though. Maybe 8 P.M.? Somewhere around then." Cooper was reluctant to tell the sheriff that he had no idea when the youngster had actually left.

"With this late storm sneaking in, the family is worried about the roads. She's been missing for over thirty-six hours now. We've had no accident reports involving an Oregon car, and we're not sure where she might be. Now that I know she's been up there, we can take a closer look at that area. Did she say anything about where she was headed?"

"No. Nothing. I was shocked to see her. I encouraged her to leave here immediately. She shouldn't have come here, and I wouldn't let her stay," he paused, "I assume you know the details of our history?"

195

"Well, I know what her mother told the deputy. I appreciate your honesty. I'm sure she'll turn up soon, Mr. Cooper. Indian kids take off all the time up here. We'll find her. Can I call again if we have any other questions?"

"Of course. I understand parents worrying about their kids."

"I know." The sheriff paused and as an afterthought said, "How was she when she left? Was she upset or distraught? Anything like that?"

"No. She was fine when she left. Just fine."

"Well, that's good. Thank you for everything, Mr. Cooper. You've been very helpful. And don't worry about her. She'll turn up soon. I'll keep you posted."

When Thompson hung up the phone he sat at his desk thinking about his conversation with Clayton Cooper. Not once had the man expressed concern about the girl's wellbeing. Oh well, he thought, she'll probably roll into Kalispell when she's damn well ready. Meanwhile, I think I'll do a little more research on Mr. Cooper.

***

Early the next morning, Philomena and Duffy drove to Libby, where Sheriff Thompson met them in a small coffee shop on Main Street.

Thompson got right to the point, "Your daughter was in the Yaak last night. Apparently, she drove out in the early evening. That means she should have been back in Kalispell by midnight or maybe a little later with the weather. The snow might have slowed her down a bit. We've checked rollover corners and the most dangerous icy spots. No luck. Which is good.

"We contacted the border crossing people to see if she drove across last night. There was no record of her crossing the border. Don't worry—we'll find her. I'm sure she's fine."

196

Philomena was shaking her head. "This isn't like Shawnee. She's a good girl. Except when she's around that teacher. Then, she starts acting crazy. I knew something like this would happen."

She looked over her shoulder at Duffy who was standing alone by the door to the coffee shop.

"We're going to Cooper's, Sheriff. He knows more than he's telling."

"Mrs. Grayson, you let us handle this now. If Shawnee doesn't turn up today, I'll take you and your husband up to the Yaak myself, and we'll see what we can find out. Meanwhile," he looked from Philomena to Duffy, "you two stay out of this, and let me do my job. Everything's going to be just fine. I'll contact you as soon as we know anything. You need to stay right here so I can find you if I need you."

***

An hour later, the Grayson's left for the Yaak.

Duffy was hung-over, and Philomena drove the little truck. They did not speak, each lost in their own thoughts. Philomena was tired. Shawnee's disappearance and a pounding headache had made for a sleepless night. She wore no makeup, and the puffy circles under her eyes were as dark as bruises. Her hair was lank and uncombed. Her knuckles were white on the steering wheel, and she guided the truck over the slippery roads with grim concentration.

Duffy sat beside her, sipping on a Heineken. He thought about Clayton Cooper and his intense dislike for the former schoolteacher. He thought about the anonymous phone call that he had made, the psychological games that he so enjoyed, and the beating he had administered in the parking lot of the state park in Oregon. He smiled to himself. He was looking forward to dealing with Clayton-fucking-Cooper again.

When they turned onto the Yaak River road, they started to gain elevation, and within a mile, it began to snow again. The Grayson's could feel the untamed mystique of the valley. The mass of dark forest, the animals that they knew thrived in its remoteness, and even the valley's distance from the twenty-first century all contributed to the undercurrent of primal wilderness. As they threaded their way up the road, Duffy sensed a visceral connection to the dark side of the valley called Yaak.

***

The layer of new snow dampened the sound of a vehicle in the parking lot, and Cooper didn't hear the rig that rolled into the Whiskey Bend Ranch. He did hear the porch steps groan and heavy footsteps moving across the covered entryway, followed by two hard knocks that shook the front door.

"Just a second," he called, "I'll be right there."

When he opened the door, his first conscious thoughts were a progressive sequence: recognition, shock, alarm, fear.

Duffy Grayson stood in the doorway, his face contorted in a smile. Behind the man was a disheveled Native American woman whom Cooper barely recognized as Shawnee's mother. Both remained silent and watched Cooper blanch.

"What do you want?" he managed as a greeting.

"Hey, little man. Long time no see. Want some company?"

"No. And if you don't get off my property, I'm going to call the sheriff."

"Too late, little man. This time the sheriffs on our side."

Before Cooper could respond, Philomena pushed her way past Duffy and, leaning toward Cooper, said, "Where's Shawnee, you son of a bitch? Where is she?"

Cooper was alarmed to note the same look of unbalanced desperation that he had seen last night in the eyes of Philomena's daughter. Pulling away from the threatening woman, he said, "What do you mean? How should I know where Shawnee is?"

"Cut the bullshit, Cooper. The sheriff already told us she was here. Where is she?"

As she spoke, Philomena noticed for the first time the three scratch marks running down Cooper's left cheek. This discovery took her breath away, and she stared at Cooper in horror.

Cooper said, "She's not here. She did stop by. . . unexpectedly, last night. I asked her to leave. I don't know where she is."

Philomena's eyes were locked on the scratches.

"Yeah? What the fuck happened to your face? You think I haven't seen scratch marks on a man's face before? Where is she?"

Cooper's hand jerked to his face where his fingertips traced the three tracks that stood out against his pale skin.

"I . . . had a fight with my girlfriend. She got a little carried away. It was an accident. It wasn't from Shawnee."

Duffy had heard enough. He reached past Philomena and grabbed the front of Cooper's flannel shirt, twisting the neckband into a tight garrote just below the smaller man's Adam's apple.

"Listen, you little faggot," he said, "If you laid one finger on Philomena's girl, I'm gonna tear your heart out. You know what I'm sayin'? Now, where. . ." he twisted the neckband tighter "is. . ." He pulled Cooper's face an inch from his own, his beer breath and the strong stench of tobacco further gagging the already choking Cooper. . . "she?"

Cooper, frantic at being unable to breathe, managed to choke out a garbled, "I don't know."

Clayton's need for air triggered his survival instincts. The crushing, eyeball-to-eyeball grasp required Duffy's full attention, and in panicked desperation, Cooper drove his knee between Grayson's legs deep into the man's groin.

Duffy's eyes bulged, and he grunted in agony. Releasing his grip on Cooper's shirt, he transferred his hands to his crotch and sank to the floor of the porch, where he rolled onto his side and curled up in a fetal position.

Philomena had never seen Duffy leveled in a fight. As a result, she was torn between attacking Cooper herself and helping her fallen husband. Both men were incapacitated, Duffy clutching his genitals and Cooper seated on the floor, his back pressed against the wall of the porch with both hands around his throat, as if he could pull the constricted air passages open from the skin on his neck.

At that very moment, a sheriff's car pulled through the log gateway to the Whiskey Bend Ranch and rolled to a stop in front of the house.

33
CHAPTER

Hayes Thompson assessed the scene on the porch with an experienced eye. A quarter-century as a backcountry Montana lawman had taught him to expect the unexpected. This scene could be one of the hundreds that he had witnessed: a bar fight, a domestic dispute or a crime of passion. He had seen dozens of downed combatants in the fetal position and jailed almost as many with scratches on their faces. The anguish on the woman's face reflected the same emotions that he had seen on many of her sisters.

"Afternoon, folks. Looks like I got here just a little too late."

There was no response from the three on the porch.

"Or maybe I got here just in time. I thought I might find you up here when you disappeared from town. Guess you couldn't wait for me to take care of things like we decided earlier."

Glancing at Philomena, Thompson jerked his head toward Duffy, still on his side, moaning in pain. "Looks like you're the spokesperson for the group. At least for a while."

Despite his nonchalant approach, the sheriff was still evaluating the situation. Duffy's prostrate body on the floor of the open porch was startling. In fact, Thompson was surprised that Cooper was still conscious. The sheriff knew that size could be neutralized, but the smaller man in this situation certainly didn't look like the type. He was either deceptively capable or very lucky. Thompson was guessing lucky.

"You must be Clay Cooper, right?"

Cooper nodded. He was beginning to breathe more regularly now, and the look of fear inspired by suffocation was beginning to leave his eyes. Thompson bent low and offered a hand in greeting. Clayton reached up and shook it weakly.

"Hayes Thompson. Pleased to meetcha." He stopped, looking at the three of them and his voice hardened, "When you folks are done foolin' around here, we got a little girl to find."

Thompson leaned down, reaching under Duffy's armpit. "Okay, big fella, let's see what we got here. Let me help you up, and you can walk this thing off. Hurts, don't it?"

Duffy leaned against Thompson's arm and rocked to his knees. His face was contorted, and Hayes couldn't tell if it was pain or rage. He doubted Duffy Grayson would be a problem any time soon. But he had done a background check, and he suspected that Duffy might be a problem before this whole thing ended.

Thompson guided him to a two-person Adirondack style bench pushed against the wall of the porch. Duffy settled his bulk onto the bench, making the wide wooden bench look as if it were a single seat in the economy class of a cheap airline.

"Okay, folks. Since we seem to have some communication problems here, I'm gonna summarize the situation for you. You can ask questions when I'm done, and we can. . ."

"Wait." Cooper interrupted the sheriff. "I want to press assault charges against this man."

Thompson drew in a slow breath.

"Mr. Cooper, we're trying to find a missing child here. I'm not interested in your little personal conflicts. If you want to pursue this after we find Shawnee, go ahead on it. Meanwhile, my priority is to find this girl. Understand? I've had enough here. All of you keep your mouths closed. Understand?"

Not waiting for an answer, Hayes started again.

"We still haven't located Shawnee. We've got the highway patrol, all the sheriff's departments in the area, and the border patrol looking. The good news right now is there's no bad news."

He looked into each face.

"My big concern is the weather and the road conditions for a young driver. Usually, these things turn out to be a kid with a wild hair who shows up at a friend's or relative's somewhere. But," and he stared at Cooper's scratched face, "I'm beginning to wonder. I think we should start from where she was last seen and try to build from there."

"What's that supposed to mean, Sheriff?" asked Cooper.

Before Thompson could answer, Duffy spoke for the first time, surprising them all. "It means you're in deep shit, asshole. And, if you've messed with the girl, you're a dead man."

Thompson stepped in front of Duffy's bench.

"Duffy, I'm gonna say this one time and one time only. You threaten this man or anyone else in my jurisdiction, and this is going to change from a missing-person case to a jailed-Indian case. According to my friends on the coast, you should understand exactly what I'm saying."

Grayson said, "You guys are all alike." He spat off the edge of the porch. "I ain't afraid of you."

"That's good Duffy because I'm not afraid of you either. Don't push me unless you're willing to face the consequences. I win every time. And I'm startin' to run out of patience here."

Duffy could tell who those few people were who he couldn't scare. Thompson stared him down until Duffy looked away in disgust.

"Now," Thompson said, "let's concentrate on finding Mrs. Grayson's little girl."

Thompson called his office on Cooper's landline and requested another car with two deputies. While they waited for the help, he asked Duffy and Philomena to remain on the porch and took Cooper inside to talk with him again about Shawnee's visit.

The sheriff asked Cooper a few questions to verify what he had learned on the phone the night before, and then asked, "What happened to your face, Mr. Cooper? Looks like one of our horned owls mistook you for dinner or something."

Cooper knew the red tracks on his face were going to be difficult to explain. It was hard to claim an innocent student-teacher meeting when his face was tracked with claw marks.

"Sheriff, Shawnee is a very sick girl. She was out of her mind when she was here. I don't know if she was on drugs or drunk or what, but it was really scary. We talked. I tried to get her to leave. She wouldn't go. She. . . she thinks she's in love with me. She finally went crazy and attacked me. She scratched my face and literally tried to kill me with her bare hands."

"Did you fight back, Mr. Cooper?"

"No. I don't fight with women. I just tried to protect myself."

"I see. And this is the same girl that you were involved with in Oregon, right?"

Cooper sighed, the connection to his past as exposed as the scratches on his face.

"Yes, Sheriff. The same girl. The same obsessed, mentally disturbed girl, the same girl I tried to help almost three years ago who won't leave me alone."

Thompson gave Cooper a hard look. "You make it sound like your life might be easier if she did disappear."

Cooper's head jerked up to stare at the sheriff.

"What do you mean? You don't think I would do anything to hurt her, do you?"

"I don't know, Mr. Cooper. You've got some serious scratches on your face. You say that you and Shawnee struggled. I show up, and you and the girl's stepfather are lying half-dead on the front porch. Seems a little unusual, don't you think?"

When Cooper didn't answer, the sheriff continued, "One more question, Mr. Cooper. I assume, since you haven't said anything to the contrary, that you have no witnesses to verify your account of what took place between you and Shawnee?"

Cooper hesitated. He was reluctant to involve Angie in the situation, but Thompson's line of questioning was an obvious reason for concern.

"Actually, I did have a house guest here when Shawnee showed up. She saw everything that happened," he paused, thinking back on the incident. "She'll confirm that everything I've said is true."

"Really? That's good information, Mr. Cooper. I'm surprised you didn't tell me earlier."

Cooper shrugged his shoulders.

"What is your house guest's name, Mr. Cooper? And how can I get in touch with her?"

Thompson called Angelina Hailstone from Cooper's land phone. Angie was upset but cooperative and seemed to be the most normal resource the sheriff had spoken to so far. She corroborated Cooper's version of Shawnee's visit and reiterated his information about the young girl's unstable mental state. She sounded upset by the incident, and Thompson had a good feeling about her obvious compassion for Shawnee.

Angie's distress about Shawnee's mental condition was cause for concern. The sheriff was beginning to think they needed to find the youngster as soon as possible. An emotionally upset new driver on the springtime mountain roads was a dangerous situation. Shawnee's safety was growing more precarious with every passing hour.

Thompson helped Philomena load Duffy into their truck and sent them up to the town of Yaak. This time, he warned them not to leave without contacting him first, and he suggested they drink coffee at the Painted Horse until they heard from him. Philomena nodded her agreement.

Fifty minutes later, a backup cruiser pulled into the parking lot and Thompson met with the two deputies who had arrived.

"I'm not certain what's going down here, guys, but my gut tells me we need to find this girl as soon as possible. This is the last location we can confirm. I want you two to drive up to town and put out the word with the locals that we're looking for the girl or her car. Let them know in the mercantile and both bars. Check all the side roads on the way up and look for slide marks or busted up snow banks on all the corners where someone might go off the road or into the river."

He thought for a second, then added, "Ask the locals to let us know if they've seen an abandoned car. . . or any strange car with Oregon plates parked anywhere in the valley. Check in with me every half hour or sooner if you find anything. I'll drive down-river from here to the highway with the same M.O. I'll radio if I need you. Got it?"

The deputies nodded and headed for their car.

Thompson told Cooper that the search was continuing and that he would keep him posted on any progress. When the sheriff got in his car, he sat for a moment and tried to think like a teenage girl. Hayes had daughters and granddaughters of his own and thought about how difficult this particular role-playing could be—especially if Shawnee was even more troubled than a normal seventeen-year-old girl.

***

The late snow might make the side roads easier to monitor, he thought. Most access roads and driveways had been without snow for a week or so, and the fresh snow was only about a half foot deep. He pulled

206

out of Cooper's parking lot and headed south, checking both sides of the road as he drove toward the highway.

A mile and a half below the ranch there was a bridge where Whiskey Creek ran into the Yaak River at the base of Grizzly Peak. The mouth of the creek dumped into the river, creating a decent fishing hole during the early part of the season. The Forest Service had a small camping area there, with three rustic campsites and an old wooden outhouse. It was unmarked as a campground but familiar to outdoorsmen and locals who liked it because it was free. It was invisible from the road, but local road crews tried to keep it accessible in the springtime so it would be easy to open for the fishing season that began in May.

Thompson almost missed the road himself, since it was half-hidden by the bridge. Only the faintest outline of tire tracks caught his attention as he passed. Stopping in the middle of the road, he turned around and headed back to check out the campground. He wanted to be especially thorough close to the Whiskey Bend Ranch, and he felt disgusted that he had almost missed the little road leading to the campground.

The snow was wet and heavy, but he drove the cruiser under the canopy of dark evergreens that covered the entry without any problem. The dense tree cover enclosed the campground like an underground cavern, and only a skiff of snow had fallen in scattered open spaces on the frozen ground.

Thompson grunted as he rolled into the center of the campground. Parked in the roadway, in direct line with the front of the raft takeout area, was a rough looking Japanese compact. The sheriff pulled behind the car and sat for a moment, studying the vehicle and gathering his thoughts before he got out of his own rig. The car had Oregon plates. Sometimes he hated his job.

Walking to the vehicle he looked through the passenger side window, relaxing a bit when he saw that the car was unoccupied. No body, no blood, no brains splattered across the driver's side window. He let his breath out in a long sigh.

Maybe, he thought. *Just maybe, we'll get lucky.*

He circled the car looking for any sign of tracks or clues. The tight canopy of trees had blocked most of the snow, and the frozen ground was hard, preventing tracks around the parking area. Thompson knew that any tracks leading away from the trees would be covered in snow.

He stood in one place and scanned the brush around the campground for a sleeping bag or an occupied campsite. Surviving a night in the Kootenai National Forest was dicey in the early spring. Exposure and hypothermia were killers in the Rockies, and an unprepared youngster would be in big trouble if she got disoriented and wandered into the woods this time of the year.

And then, there was the river. It was still partly iced over, especially here in this sunless corner, buried beneath the trees. There were stretches of open water where the current was stronger, and the sun shining through the trees had melted some of the ice. But thick slabs of broken ice lined the banks, and the cold night had fused them together in a haphazard jumble.

He walked back to his car and contacted the deputies that he had sent up the road to the town of Yaak.

"Chuck, this is Hayes. I found the car down at Whiskey Creek. You know that little camping spot below the bridge?" He waited for the deputy's response. "Yeah. That's it. The car's empty. I think we should meet back at the old Whiskey Bend Saloon. We can call a few locals and organize a search. The river's pretty rough down this way."

Thompson listened to his deputy's answer. "I know," he said. "But maybe we can catch a break here."

34
CHAPTER

By late afternoon, Hayes Thompson had assembled a colorful group of locals for his search party.

At Cooper's suggestion, he had contacted Wing Redmond, whose outdoor skills were admired by everyone in the valley. Thompson didn't know Wing but was familiar with his reputation as an outdoorsman and pleased that the man had agreed to help. Wing suggested that the sheriff also contact Laura Ballantine to assist with the search.

Thompson knew Laura, a resident of the valley who spent hundreds of hours each year in the woods. Laura and her husband lived on an old homestead that had been in her family for four generations, where she raised Burmese Mountain dogs. The dogs were a labor of love, and her bright red pickup with portable dog kennels was often parked in front of the Painted Horse Saloon or pulled over on one of the Forest Service roads that spider-webbed the valley.

Laura knew the miles of Forest Service roads and the intricate logging roads that radiated from them better than anyone in the valley. Summer or winter, she exercised her dogs on mountain roads, and she was an invaluable resource when it came to the Kootenai National Forest road layout. No local search party would be complete without her.

To round out the group, Thompson added three other locals who knew the country well. They were all hunters and hikers; they were comfortable in the woods and used to inclement weather and rugged mountain conditions.

They met at the Whiskey Creek Campground. Thompson figured they had an hour and a half until dark. Lanterns and flashlights were passed out in case they needed to extend the search past daylight. If she was in the area, Thompson did not believe the girl would be too far away.

He divided the group into two teams, putting Wing in charge of one and Laura in charge of the other. He assigned one of his two deputies to each group as the communications liaison.

"Okay, guys, here's what we've got. You all know that if she's out here, we need to find this youngster as soon as possible. I don't think she would have gone too far. She would have to stay on this side of the river because of the water volume and the ice. It's possible she may have rolled an ankle or had some other accident that laid her up."

The others nodded.

"I'll take one man with me," he said, looking at the volunteer standing closest to him, "and work the river and shoreline going downstream. Wing, you take Mr. Cooper and Deputy Walsh and do the same thing going upstream. Don't worry about going too far back into the woods. Laura, you take the rest of the crew and work all the trails that head out from the campground. Check the game trails and anyplace that looks like someone could hole up in it."

He paused, drawing in a slow breath. "My guess is, if she's still in the area, we'll find her within a half mile of the car. If she's still alive, she won't be in very good shape. Overnight stays up here aren't real healthy this time of the year.

"The other alternative, of course, is she maybe hitched a ride out of the valley. Or she might have met someone up here who took her somewhere else. But those are long shots," he said. "I think we'll find her here. Any questions?"

Wing was standing beside Laura Ballantine. They glanced at one another, and Wing said, "What about an animal attack, Sheriff? Laura says she's seen both mountain lion and grizz sign down here before."

"I thought about that. It's possible, but it doesn't seem very likely to me. It's been years since we've had an attack up here this close to the road. If she were in the backcountry, I'd think maybe. But we all know it could happen. If it did, we'll find some sign. For right now, let's all think positive."

As Sheriff Thompson continued, Cooper watched him direct his final words to Wing. "Let's stay on the radios. If anyone finds anything, let the others know right away." Thompson looked at the tall Yaaker, and it was a look between two veteran soldiers ready for battle. "Let's go," he said.

Like an astute physician, Thompson hadn't talked about the worst-case scenario. One never knew, and it was best to be positive. Even so, he had an idea of what he was looking for, and he knew where he was going to look.

He walked to Cooper's truck and unloaded an eight-foot-long two-by-four that he had found in the ranch's shed to use as a probe in the jumbles of collected ice that lined the side of the river. He and his partner began a methodical search, Thompson wielding the probe, his helper observing and holding the radio. Hayes could hear Laura's crew's muted voices as they searched the brush that encircled the campground.

Twenty minutes into the search, Thompson received the first radio communication from the other crews. He had followed their flashlights as the cloudy day darkened, and he hoped for some good news.

"There's a few animal tracks in the new snow here, boss, but no human sign, so far." The deputy relayed Laura's observations to Thompson. "We talked to Wing's guys, too. He's working the side of the river like you told him, and his guys are searching the woods. Nothing yet."

"Okay. It's getting dark fast. Cold, too. Tell everyone to be careful and that we'll only work this section tonight. If nothing turns up, we'll start again in the morning." Then he added, "There's a log and ice jam below us that I saw this afternoon. I want to check that out before it gets too dark."

"Roger. I'll let everyone know."

As Thompson and his partner worked their way closer to the logjam, Hayes knew that this might be their best chance of finding the girl. The current bottlenecked into a narrow chute, and the flashlight beam picked up a collection of debris and ice churning in front of the snarl of logs.

His partner's flashlight probed the dark waters, and he heard the man grunt like he'd been punched in the stomach. "What the hell is that?" he asked.

Thompson's own stomach tightened as he followed the cone of light into the roiling water, and his heart sank at the prospect of finding what he hoped would not be there.

"Where?" he asked.

"Right there. Where the water funnels into the jam." The man left the light focused on a wide gap in the logs, and both men watched tensely as the river's current surged through the opening.

"There it is! See?"

Thompson saw, hoping that the dark silhouette that appeared when the light and water centered just right was a clump of brush or a root ball, pushing against the snarled logjam like all the other debris that the river swept downstream during the violent ice out.

"Damn. I think we found her."

The sheriff was ten feet from the center of the logs now, and he could see that the dark silhouette was actually a jacket soaked as black as blood by rivers' icy water. The body was wedged below the surface at the vortex of two large slabs of ice that created a strong current as it pushed through the narrow opening. The corpse was face down, legs buried deep in the small opening. The upper body rocked in the strong current, swinging back and forth as if it was still trying to escape the relentless undertow holding it captive beneath the icy water.

Thompson choked back a moan and hoped that the young girl had died before the ice jam had captured her.

Crawling off the slippery logs, he picked up the radio they had left on the bank. He relayed his message to the others without emotion.

"We found her, guys. The body's hung up in an ice jam about two hundred yards below the raft take out. Let's everyone circle up here, and we'll see if we can get her out."

As the message came across the radio, Wing looked at Clayton Cooper and watched his friend's eyes squeeze shut in disbelief. Cooper's legs folded under him, and he sank into a sitting position, holding his head in his hands. Wing hurried over and put a hand on Coop's shoulder.

"Come on, man. We've got work to do. There ain't nothin' we can do now but bring her home."

***

When Philomena and Duffy walked into the Painted Horse Saloon, bar owner Rudy Morganroth grunted a greeting and continued his discussion with a tired-looking bleach-blonde woman seated at the bar.

The Grayson's sat down at a table near the back of the room and waited while Rudy continued bantering with the lady in bursts of filthy language. Finally, Duffy pushed himself up and limped to the bar, standing next to the woman next to the bartender until Rudy was forced to acknowledge his presence.

"Help you?" the proprietor half-heartedly asked.

Duffy asked for two Cokes and then returned to the table.

Rudy continued to visit. When he finished, he shuffled his way to the cooler at the end of the bar, where he picked out two cans of the soft drink and slouched to the Grayson's table. He set the drinks on the table and said, "That's six bucks."

Duffy answered, "Six bucks? Put it on a tab."

"No tabs. Six dollars."

Duffy and Philomena looked at one another.

Philomena said, "Sheriff Thompson sent us up here and told us to wait until he contacted us. He said he called ahead to let you know we were coming."

"You're the Grayson's?"

"Yeah."

"Oh." He paused. "The sheriff never told me you were Indians."

Thompson had not wanted the mother or her unpredictable husband to be a part of the search. He hadn't told the Grayson's that he was organizing a search party but rather that his people had found Shawnee's car, and he would keep them posted.

The two parents had whiled away the time drinking coffee and playing desultory games of cribbage. Their moods matched the coming nightfall, growing darker as the time passed. For most of the afternoon, they had been the only customers of the bar, and it had not been a particularly enjoyable experience.

Rudy disliked Duffy on sight. Twenty years of tending bar in the lawless wilderness had honed his instincts, and he seldom misjudged a potential threat. Rudy kept a length of iron pipe under the bar, and he had used it—with enthusiasm—dozens of times. But his victims were usually too drunk to fight back and nowhere near as intimidating as the sullen man. Indians were a rarity in his bar, and he wanted it to stay that way. He hoped Thompson would find the girl soon.

The regulars were beginning to trickle into the bar, and Rudy's discomfort continued to grow, fueled by shots of Jack Daniel's that he had been drinking since opening at 11 A.M.

He wanted no trouble when Hayes Thompson was so close to town. Even in the isolated valley, the county sheriff was a powerful man. Trouble in the outlying saloons usually resulted in punitive closure of the offending establishment. The length of the closure depended on the offense. Closure meant what the bar owners referred to as "downtime"—and downtime in the bar business was measured by only one barometer—the owner's checkbook.

Rudy hated downtime.

CHAPTER 35

Clayton Cooper had never seen a dead person.

When Wing waded out of the frigid river with Shawnee in his arms, Cooper thought she looked like a cloth doll, bent at the knees, with arms akimbo and her head tipped backward as if it were attached to her torso by a loose hinge.

The search party stood in silence on the river bank, their flashlight beams illuminating the night with the intensity of stage spots in a macabre play, as Wing moved slowly toward the shore. Water sluiced off Shawnee's body and her long hair glistened in the artificial light. Her clothes were black and stuck to her body like dark shadows.

As Wing laid her down on the tarp that Sheriff Thompson had spread on the riverbank, Cooper saw the mottled face and the cloudy, lifeless eyes. He stumbled away from the silent group and began vomiting into the bushes outside the circle of light.

Hayes Thompson watched Cooper leave the group of searchers surrounding Shawnee's body and listened to him empty his insides. Then the sheriff kneeled over the corpse and went to work.

He was careful not to touch the body, knowing that there would be an autopsy to determine the official cause of death. There were no signs of external trauma. No lacerations, no obvious bruises on the face or neck. Her nose appeared to be slightly swollen, but it was difficult to tell with the irregularities of the post-mortem skin.

The icy waters of the river had kept the body in remarkable condition, and Thompson hoped that factor would have some forensic value. There were enough curious circumstances surrounding the death to merit careful handling. Until he found out differently, he intended to address this situation as "unresolved."

He rose from the body and began to issue orders.

"Okay, folks, you get to go home now. Thanks for all your help. We couldn't have done it without you." He looked at Wing. "Wing, go home and get out of those wet clothes. Laura, maybe you can drop Mr. Cooper off at his place on your way home? My guys are going to secure this area, so his rig will be fine here overnight."

Laura nodded her assent, and Thompson addressed the volunteers. "One more thing. I'm going to ask you all a favor and swear you to secrecy for the next hour or two. I've got this girl's parents waiting up at the Horse, and I'd like to tell them myself before the word spreads through the valley. Give me two hours; after that, you're on your own. I'll buy you all a beer the next time I see you. Everyone understand?"

There were nods all around.

Cooper said, "I'm okay, Laura. I can drive back to my place. Why don't you just follow me up there?"

They both looked at Thompson. He nodded his approval, and the group of volunteers started the slow walk upriver to the campground.

***

An hour and twenty minutes later, Hayes Thompson walked into the Painted Horse Saloon, looking for Duffy and Philomena Grayson. The regulars hunched over drinks at the bar and two or three small groups of locals sat at the bar and at small tables, talking in loud voices. A single player sat at the poker machines, and a man and woman were shooting pool on a table famous for the neat grouping of three 9mm bullet holes encircling one of the side pockets.

The Grayson's were at the back table, the furthest away from the bar. Both appeared sober. Duffy had switched to beer and was talking with a heavily bearded man seated at the next table wearing

216

a faded New York Yankee baseball cap, a thick braid of dark ponytail hanging down his back.

Moving toward the table, Thompson politely asked the man in the hat if he could speak to the Grayson's in private. Quickly glancing at the uniform, the man gave a rapid nod and almost knocked the chair he was sitting in over backward in his haste to get away from the area. He left his half-full beer on the table and hurried out the front door without a backward glance.

Thompson sat down at the Grayson's table. Philomena looked into his face, then whispered, "Oh God, no."

Her reaction alerted Duffy who set down his beer and also examined the lawman's face. Thompson looked exhausted, the creases in his face etched deeper than usual, the skin itself sagging with fatigue.

"What's goin' on?" Duffy said.

"I'm afraid I have some bad news. The worst news. I'm sorry to tell you that we found your daughter's body an hour ago. She was in the river, a mile or so below Mr. Cooper's place. It looks like she must have fallen in the river and drowned."

When he stopped talking there was a moment of silence from the Grayson's. Then, as the sheriff's words began to register, an inhuman wail escaped from the depths of Philomena's soul. It was the scream of a mortally wounded animal, and the heads of the woods-savvy bar patrons jerked up in unison, their eyes searching for the dying creature loose in the saloon. In the aftermath of the horrifying sound, the bar was as quiet as a starless mountain night, each person in it hearing only the loud beating of his or her own heart.

Philomena began to sob an incoherent chant in her native Sixela tongue.

Thompson waited for her husband to comfort her, to hug her close, or at least pat her shoulder and offer some words of comfort. When Duffy made no move toward his wife, the sheriff reached across the table and pulled the sobbing woman's hand into both of his own.

"I'm so sorry, Mrs. Grayson. I have children of my own. I know that losing a child is every parent's worst nightmare. There's nothing worse in the entire world."

The woman heard the sound but not the words. She looked with confusion at her hand in the sheriff's and eased it from his grasp.

"My baby," she whispered. "My only baby."

The few remaining customers slid off barstools or pushed away from the small tables and headed for the tavern across the street. The pool players laid down their cues and slouched out of the saloon.

Rudy began a noisy attack on a sink full of glasses in the bar basin, mumbling to himself as he banged the clean glasses back on their shelves. One hard look from Thompson and the mumbling ceased.

The sheriff tried again.

"Mrs. Grayson, I know how difficult this is, and it must be even tougher when you're so far from home. I'm going to get you and your husband a motel room in town, and we can deal with this in the morning."

He looked at Duffy.

"I'll call the Emergency Room at the hospital in Libby. The docs will get her something to help her sleep. Do you want one of my guys to drive you in, or do you want to do it yourself?"

"I got it."

Thompson glanced at the half-empty beer in front of Duffy and wondered how many beers the man had consumed.

"This is my second beer, Sheriff. I said I got it."

"Okay. I'll call ahead and reserve a room at the Tamarack Motel. It's close to the hospital." He hesitated. "I'm going to need you to I.D. the body tomorrow, Mr. Grayson. That's something no mother should have to do. Meet me at the hospital at 11 o'clock. You can do the identification then."

Drawing in a deep breath, he said, "Understand?"

Duffy nodded.

"Are you sure your wife will be okay?"

"Yeah."

"Okay, I'll have one of my deputies escort you to Libby. He'll take you right to the motel and show you where to pick up her medication at the hospital."

Duffy nodded again and gathered up Philomena who was weeping silent tears. As Duffy guided her toward the door, the sheriff said again, "I'm sorry, ma'am. I'm really sorry."

He sat alone at the table after the Grayson's left, listening to Rudy doing bar chores and maintenance. Then he stood, took two twenty-dollar bills out of his wallet, and walked to the empty bar. He set the two bills in front of the sullen bartender.

"Thanks, Rudy," he said, "I owe you one."

* * *

On his way back to the drowning site, Thompson stopped to talk with Clayton Cooper.

Cooper answered the door wearing a full-length terrycloth bathrobe and smelling of hair conditioner. His wet hair was slicked back, and he absently fingered the tender welts streaking his clean-shaven face. The sheriff couldn't remember ever seeing a man wearing a bathrobe in the Yaak.

"This was the worst night of my life, Sheriff, and I've had a few bad ones. I can't get Shawnee out of my mind. The stillness. The nothingness. I don't know how you people do it."

"Frankly, Mr. Cooper, sometimes I don't know either."

219

"What happened? Why would she be in the river this time of the year? Why?"

Thompson had asked himself those very questions.

"I don't know, Mr. Cooper. Maybe it was an accident. She could have been disoriented, slipped on the ice." He spoke slowly, verbalizing his thoughts for his own sake as much as Cooper's. "Maybe she did it on purpose. God knows we've had Indian suicides by drowning before. Or maybe someone pushed her in. Right now, I don't know the answer."

"Pushed her in? How could that be? She doesn't even know anyone from around here. Who would. . ." the words trailed off and Cooper's head snapped toward Sheriff Thompson, his face contorted in disbelief.

"You don't think. . ." he couldn't finish the sentence.

"I don't think anything right now, Mr. Cooper. But I have to look at all the options. That's all I think."

36
CHAPTER

Unaware of the situation unfolding in the Yaak the day after her romantic weekend ended, Angie ran errands and visited with her friends from the Big Mountain workforce. She had a beer with two of her co-workers in the afternoon and listened to some rap CDs at their rental house in the outskirts of Whitefish. It was after 11 P.M. when she returned to her own studio apartment.

There were four calls from Clayton Cooper on her home phone but no messages. She looked at the clock on the wall and decided even though it was late she would call him now.

Cooper picked up on the second ring.

"Hey, Coop. What's going on?"

"Ang, thank God you're finally home!"

"What's wrong?"

"What's wrong? Everything's wrong. You won't believe what's happened up here since you left."

Cooper tried to arrange the day's disastrous events into the proper sequence.

"Shawnee left here that night, sometime after I fell asleep in the chair. I didn't tell you that yesterday because I thought she'd be in Canada by now and that we could get on with our lives. Then, this afternoon her parents showed up here looking for her. I got in a fight with her stepfather—he's a monster—which the sheriff broke up when he rolled into the parking lot. Then. . . this is so unbelievable. They found Shawnee's car, parked in a campground down below the ranch. Three hours later, we found her body in the river. She drowned, Ang. She's dead!"

"Oh my God! Cooper, I'm so sorry. That's terrible. What are you going to do?"

"What CAN I do?" he asked. "Honey, what did you tell Sheriff Thompson when he called you about when Shawnee was here? Did you tell him you left right away?"

Angie thought about her phone conversation with Hayes Thompson.

"No, I don't think so. He was only interested in Shawnee at the time. He did ask me when she left, but I said I didn't know. In fact, I said I thought she left as soon as she woke up. Why?"

"Baby, the sheriff thinks I might have had something to do with Shawnee's death."

"What? You mean he thinks you might have drowned her in the river? That's ridiculous."

"I know. But the scratches on my face are bad. He asked me a bunch of questions about Shawnee's and my fight."

"What did you tell him?"

"The truth. You saw it. She attacked me. I only tried to hold her off. It's scary though. She might have bruises or marks from the struggle we had."

"That doesn't mean you pushed her in the river."

"I know. But you don't understand how screwed up the system can be. I didn't do anything in Skyler either. But," he said, "it cost me my job, my family, everything. I don't trust the bastards."

"They won't think you murdered anyone, for God's sake. It was an accident. She was a very unstable girl. Don't worry, I'll tell them the fight was all her fault. The drowning was an accident. It was an accident."

"You think so?" Cooper hesitated and then said. "I was thinking. . . when the sheriff was here he never did ask if you had stayed or if you went home. He doesn't know you left. Why don't we tell

222

him that you spent the night with me? That would take off all the pressure. We were together, in bed, all night. It's perfect. Should we do that, honey? What do you think?"

When Angie didn't answer, Cooper couldn't tell if she was horrified or considering it.

"Ang? Can we do that?"

Struggling with her emotions, Angie answered, "Cooper, you don't need an alibi. You didn't do anything. They can't prove anything."

Cooper heard the hesitancy in her voice. He pushed harder.

"We've got to tell them we were together, hon. What can it hurt? I can't take another railroad job like Skyler. You know I didn't do it, don't you? You know."

"I know, baby."

"Just think about it, okay. Sleep on it. In fact, come back here and spend the night with me. We need to be together now."

"It's almost midnight, Coop. I'm going to sleep here." Then she added, "I'll try to come up in the morning, though. We can talk things over then. There's a lot we need to talk about."

"That's great, sweetie. I'll see you in the morning. I love you."

"You MIGHT see me in the morning," she added, "I love you, too."

When Cooper hung up the phone, his hands were shaking.

***

Sheriff Thompson used the coroner from neighboring Flat Head County to examine the body the next morning. The pathologist was an old friend of Hayes Thompson. The two of them had done a number of traumatic death investigations through the years and more than a few accidental drowning examinations. In those cases, any autopsies had been optional, the cause of death obvious and a full autopsy merely an elective routine. This one was different.

All the indicators were consistent with death by drowning. The coroner noted some unusual, but pre-existing, markings. There were small oval shaped bruises inside both elbows where someone had gripped her arms tightly. Her nose was swollen and showed signs of pre-mortem bleeding. There were dark stains on the red parka and the coroner confirmed that those stains were blood. Thompson had no reason to suspect foul play of any kind. A troubled teenager with a history of psychological problems and dysfunctional behavior was always unpredictable.

However, the odd circumstances surrounding the girl's death gave the case a whole new meaning. The previous relationship between Cooper and the youngster, the violent hostility of the adults involved, and the murky details of Shawnee's visit: all of these things needed to be considered in a new light.

Something about Cooper didn't feel right. Despite the man's devastated reaction following the recovery of Shawnee's body, deep in the sheriff's own subconscious, he felt a twinge of uneasiness about the situation. And his instincts told him he needed to handle this case with special care.

***

Duffy identified the body the next day. When the coroner pulled the sheet off Shawnee's face, he stared at her waxen features. Her eyes were closed and she looked peaceful, at rest, her dark hair a dramatic contrast to the stainless steel body tray.

"It's her," he said. He turned and walked toward the door.

Hayes Thompson followed him out and stopped him in the hallway.

"Can you and your wife be at my office at five this afternoon? We need to talk as soon as possible so that I can proceed with the investigation. I can have someone pick you up if you like."

"I can drive, man. We'll be there."

When Duffy and Philomena entered the sheriff's office, Thompson rose and held out his hand to welcome them. Duffy accepted the extended hand with reluctance, his own grip loose and unenthusiastic. Philomena ignored the gesture and collapsed into the chair in front of the sheriff's desk.

Despite the prescribed sedatives, she looked as though she hadn't slept at all. The bags below her eyes were reddish-purple and without makeup, it looked like cordovan shoe polish smeared on her tired face. Her hair was matted and unwashed, and she was wearing the same clothing that she had on yesterday in the Painted Horse.

"Mrs. Grayson," Thompson said, "I know this is the worst time of your entire life. I wanted to meet with you and your husband so we can get you back to your home as soon as possible."

Philomena responded with a vacant nod.

"I want to tell you what happens next. We're going to do a comprehensive forensic analysis on Shawnee. That means a full autopsy, DNA testing, sexual activity research, things like that. I know it sounds awful. We want to be as thorough as possible and make certain your daughter's death was an accident."

Duffy snorted.

Thompson looked at him and asked through tight lips, "You got something to say, Mr. Grayson?"

"Yeah. I do."

Thompson raised his eyebrows, nodding for him to go ahead.

"What happens to that bastard Cooper?"

"What do you mean?"

"He killed her. What happens to him?"

"Mr. Grayson, let's get something straight here. We don't know that Clayton Cooper killed your stepdaughter. In fact, all the preliminary information indicates her death was an accidental drowning. However, to make certain that is the case, we're going to check into every possibility during our investigation. That's why we're doing a more comprehensive autopsy and all possible forensic work. If there is any reason to expect foul play, we will pursue it to the fullest extent of the law."

"It's bullshit. She wouldn't be dead if it wasn't for him. It don't make no difference if he drowned her or she drowned herself. He did it." He looked at the sheriff. "And he'll pay."

"Duffy, I already warned you about making threats in my territory. Shawnee's death lets you get away with that one. No more. You stay away from Clayton Cooper. If he's done something outside the law, we'll get him. If he hasn't, we won't. It would work the same way if you were in his shoes."

Duffy made another noise, half snort, half laugh.

"Yeah, right. I'd be treated just the same." He looked at Thompson through hooded eyes. "I'm not threaten' nobody. Sometimes the old ways are the best ways. White people's justice is different from Indian justice. That's all I'm sayin'."

Thompson sighed and shook his head.

"Don't mess with me, Grayson. Like I said before, you can't win."

***

Thompson considered filing a restraining order on Duffy Grayson but decided against it because the Grayson's were leaving town the next day. He did make a point of visiting their motel in the morning, where Duffy and Philomena were packing Duffy's truck.

"Let me handle this, Duffy. You have my word that if there's been foul play, I'll get him." He looked hard at the big man. "Let the law handle this, understand?"

226

Duffy, who had not spoken to the sheriff yet, broke his silence with two sentences.

"The law don't mean shit. He killed our girl a long time ago."

**

Angelina was called into work that afternoon and was unable to return to the Yaak to talk with her lover about his proposal.

Cooper decided to take matters into his own hands. He left a message with dispatch at the sheriff's office and requested that Sheriff Thompson call him as soon as possible.

It was almost dinnertime before Thompson could return the call.

"Mr. Cooper, this is Hayes Thompson, what can I do for you?"

"Hello, Sheriff. I just wanted to touch base, see what was going on." When the taciturn sheriff remained silent, he continued. "Also, there's something I haven't told you about the night Shawnee stopped at my house. Under the circumstances, it might be important, and I'm embarrassed that I didn't tell you earlier."

Cooper paused.

"Go on, Mr. Cooper. I'm listening."

"Well, the night Shawnee was here, my house guest, Angelina Hailstone, the one you called who witnessed Shawnee and my confrontation? Ang didn't go home that night. She stayed here with me. In my bed. I didn't want to say anything before because Shawnee was only missing, and I didn't think I needed to embarrass Ms. Hailstone. But now it seems like something you should know."

"Why's that, Mr. Cooper?"

"Sheriff, can we stop playing games here? You've made it obvious that I'm some kind of a person of interest. Forgive me if I'm a little gun shy. I've got scratches on my face and my skin's probably under Shawnee's fingernails. But I didn't do anything. I want you to know the truth. Angie can clear up any confusion."

"This information is a surprise, Mr. Cooper. It might have been better for you if you'd told me before we knew the girl was dead."

"Discretion seemed like the way to go, Sheriff. Our sex life is kind of personal."

"I guess I can understand that. Is there anything else you've forgotten?"

"No, sir. That's all I left out. I was just trying to protect Angie, is all. I apologize if I misled you. . . it didn't seem important when Shawnee was alive."

"Everything's important, Mr. Cooper. I'll check it out. Call me if you remember anything else."

Thompson called Ms. Hailstone as soon as he got off the phone with Cooper. There was no answer, so he left a message and number on her machine. The sheriff didn't know that his was the second message on her machine that day. The first was from Clayton Cooper. Cooper's message was: "Hey honey, it's me. Can you call me as soon as possible? Before you call anyone else? I may be in trouble here. I need your help. Oh yeah, and can you delete this message from your machine right after you listen to it? Thanks, baby. I love you."

***

When Angie got home, she checked her messages first thing, hoping that Cooper had called. She listened to his message twice, paying close attention during the second playback. His voice was shaky, the fear and tension palpable.

When she listened to the sheriff's message, she frowned at the tone of the request for a return call. She suspected that the two messages were connected and that suspicion made her uneasy. She deleted Cooper's message and dialed his number at the Yaak.

"Coop, it's me. What's going on?"

"Hey, baby. Good question. I talked with Sheriff Thompson today, and it didn't go too well. I need to ask you a huge favor."

228

"What do you mean? What didn't go too well?"

"He was really negative. He started asking me questions, almost grilling me. I got scared and kind of panicked. I just couldn't deal with all the bullshit. I had to tell him that you spent the night here."

"What?!?

"I had to, Ang. It's okay. He stopped leaning on me right away. Honey, you know that I wouldn't—couldn't—do anything to Shawnee. This is just a little white lie that will make this whole thing go away. It forces the truth on them. You've got to back me up on this. It's just a matter of a few hours difference. What can it hurt? Let's get this thing over with and then go live somewhere with a beach and a lot of sunshine. I need you, Ang. You know you would have stayed with me if Shawnee hadn't come. You've got to back me up."

"Cooper, I don't know. It seems so. . ."

"It's not. Listen, I can't change my story again. Thompson was upset I hadn't told him during the first interview that we were together. If you back me up on this, it's over. No investigation. No hearing. No nothing. Now they have to focus on the truth. She fell. Or she jumped. You saw her. She was crazy as a loon. I think she did it herself. She was crazy, honey."

Angelina knew in her heart Cooper was innocent, and the little lie did seem like it might be a good way to resolve any issues.

"Okay, Coop, I'll do it. I don't know if I should, but I'll do it."

"I know what you're saying, honey. I'm not sure I'm comfortable with it either. But we don't have any choice here. Thank you. I love you."

"You better. And I won't forget about that beach you talked about."

***

Angelina returned Sheriff Thompson's call first thing in the morning.

Their conversation was brief and to the point. Her voice was tight with the hint of a quiver. Thompson suspected that she feared he would question her about intimate details involving her romantic relationship with Clayton Cooper. She seemed embarrassed by the situation and told the sheriff, "I slept with Mr. Cooper, Sheriff. We did what people do when they sleep together. I hope you won't need more detail than that."

Thompson didn't.

But the convenience of the new-found alibi, coupled with Angelina's alleged modesty, continued to bother him. Most of the operations crew who worked on the ski mountain were far from prudes. There was a "mountain work-force" culture that was notorious for its party antics. Alcohol, drugs, and sex were a part of the ski bum lifestyle. He knew that more than a few members of the ski area's employee-base had spent a night or two in the Kalispell jail.

When he hung up, Thompson was more determined than ever to conduct a thorough investigation into the death of Shawnee McAllister. Cooper's newly found alibi aside, the sheriff was reluctant to close any doors. And yet, there was still no evidence to support anything but an accidental drowning. Externally, the only suspicious markings were the bruises on the body's arms, and evidence of a bloody nose—and both of those factors were consistent with Cooper's explanation of his spat with the girl. Thompson himself had looked carefully for the ligature marks or soft tissue neck hemorrhages that might accompany a homicidal drowning. He found nothing.

The sheriff had no choice but to wait for the crime lab's information before proceeding. If it weren't for the unusual circumstances surrounding the girl's death, he thought this case would already be closed.

37
CHAPTER

Three days after the drowning, an article appeared in the Skyler Daily News:

SKYLER HIGH SCHOOL STUDENT DROWNS ON SPRING BREAK
By Terry Barlow
Skyler Daily News Skyler, Oregon

A local high school student drowned in the Yaak River of northwest Montana while on vacation over Spring Break. Shawnee McAllister, eighteen, had been missing for two days when her body was discovered in the Yaak River, a stream located in a remote Montana valley close to the Canadian border between Montana and British Columbia.

The daughter of Philomena Grayson and Conrad McAllister, Shawnee was a senior at Skyler High School and had been a part of the local school system program since the eighth grade.

She played on the Lady Eagles soccer team and was also interested in art.

Shawnee and her family were en route to visit relatives in Alberta when the accident occurred.

A date for services has yet to be determined. Shawnee's full obituary will be published in a later edition of the Skyler Daily News.

***

Back in Montana, the forensic investigation continued. Crime lab analysis reports were notorious for their tardiness and the drowning of a youngster in a remote corner of the state turned out to be a low priority.

In the Yaak River valley, debate raged about the drowning. It was a dominant subject of conversation in both bars, and speculation ran rampant as the locals voiced theories about potential motives. Those who had known Cooper throughout the years insisted that the drowning was accidental. Those enamored of the mystique of the valley and its reputation as a melting pot for outlaws and fugitives—having been fooled by "normal" neighbors in the past—preferred an "I told you so" approach.

For the old-timers, it was just another chapter in a colorful book. It was early springtime in the Yaak and anything abnormal was normal.

***

Cooper continued his regular routine and tried to ignore the critical nature of the impending results of the crime lab analysis. He taught his class two nights a week. Now, he usually spent the night at Angie's apartment rather than driving back to the Yaak. The days grew longer and the spring runoff proceeded at a normal pace.

Cooper asked Angie to move in with him at the ranch, and although she was tempted, she thought it was too soon to commit. Even so, she fantasized about the romantic prospect of living with her man in the idyllic valley, just the two of them. She envisioned them cross-country skiing, fly fishing, and exploring the northern Rockies with their cameras, making a living photographing the country and the animals that they both loved so much.

Ironically, her dreams were similar to the fantasies of the late Shawnee McAllister. But unlike Shawnee, she recognized that a relationship with the ex-teacher might be fraught with uncertainty—and it was that very potential that she found irresistible.

Although she had always preferred older men, when dating men of any age, her preference had always tended toward outlaws. She was drawn to older skateboarders and musicians. Occasionally, she had been intrigued by married men. Except for the college professor in Vermont, these attractions had never evolved into a serious long-term relationship.

Cooper was mature and comfortable, but his troubled past and the circumstances of the last few months provided an edgy hint of the unknown. It was a titillating attraction for an adventure junkie, a twisted combination of the best of both worlds that seemed to fit well with her eccentric life view.

Still, she wasn't ready to move in with him. Yet.

***

It was Cooper's habit, since relocating to the Yaak, to call his ex-wife and the girls at least three times a week.

He had told Kelsey about Shawnee's tragic accident the day after her body was discovered, knowing that all of Skyler would soon be aware of the tragedy. He made a point of presenting the incident as the final episode in the whole sordid affair. He did not mention that the case was unresolved or that there was any question about the cause of Shawnee's death.

Kelsey listened to her ex-husband's explanation. She was still haunted by Shawnee's shocking display of obsession from her testimony at the hearing, and she was not surprised that the girl had stalked Cooper. For the first time, she felt like she had done the right thing by filing for a divorce. She knew she would not have been able to handle the tragedy of the death of one of his students: it was only the geographical separation from the drowning that had protected her own vulnerable psyche. Even the article in the Skyler News had shaken her to the core. Shawnee was only four years older than her own oldest daughter.

Shawnee's was buried in a traditional Wapiti ceremony, and her remains—along with a simple arrowhead necklace that had been returned to the Grayson's with Shawnee's private effects following the drowning—were buried in the Wapiti tribal cemetery at Gamble Bay.

It was the same cemetery where Deputy Sheriff Clarence Bigelow had surprised Shawnee and Clayton Cooper almost three years earlier.

3♀
CHAPTER

That June, Sheriff Thompson and the Lincoln County Prosecutors Office received the crime lab's forensic evaluation of Shawnee McAllister's death.

When Thompson reviewed the data related to the drowning, everything seemed to confirm Cooper's version of what had taken place the evening of Shawnee's visit to his house. The local coroner's report cited "asphyxia associated with drowning" as the cause of death. Aside from the pre-existing inconsistencies caused by the altercation at Cooper's home, there were no other external wounds, no abrasions, no cranial trauma. Although there were indications of some prior sexual experience, there was no evidence of recent intercourse. No semen deposits, no vaginal trauma, no indicators of a sexual assault.

Mr. Cooper had provided a DNA sample, and the skin and blood collected from underneath the fingernails of Shawnee's right hand matched his DNA, just as Cooper had known it would.

The analysis of the clothing that the girl had been wearing was equally benign. The stains on the front of the red parka were Shawnee's own blood, and they were the result of a pre-drowning injury, most likely a bloody nose.

Everything was consistent with Cooper's description of Shawnee's fateful visit.

Once Thompson had completed his analysis of the two reports, he decided to interrogate Cooper one more time. Throughout the questioning, Cooper recited the details of the confrontation exactly as he had during his initial interviews. The sheriff could find no inconsistencies in Cooper's story of the incident preceding Shawnee's death.

***

During the long wait for crime lab results, Thompson had taken advantage of the delay to learn as much as he could about Clayton Cooper and Shawnee McAllister.

He called the Skyler Sheriff's Department and talked with Deputy Clarence Bigelow, in an attempt to get background information that might be helpful. Bigelow was skeptical about the ex-school teacher.

"Cooper had a great reputation here. He's got lots of friends, and they say he did some good things. But I think something was strange about that deal. I've got a nose for things like that."

Thompson appreciated the input, but he knew that a cop's instincts meant little in a court of law. Without supporting evidence, Bigelow's "nose" was useless. He also called Dr. Ludlow Townsend, the Skyler Superintendent of Schools. Mostly, he wanted the school's take on Shawnee's mental stability to verify Cooper's contention that the girl was mentally unbalanced.

Dr. Townsend concurred. "Our school psychologist suggested that Shawnee is—was—bipolar and manic-depressive. She had all the classic symptoms. Mood swings, self-destructive behaviors, a romantic obsession. Not that those things make a difference in student-teacher relationships. We don't tolerate any violation of teacher ethics here, Sheriff. But, for what it's worth, I don't believe Clay Cooper would murder someone. We thought it was his lower brain that got him in trouble. It happens. But I can't imagine him being a killer."

The more he learned about Cooper, the more uncertain he was about the man's role in Shawnee's drowning. He didn't trust Cooper. However, he wasn't sure the man had drowned the girl either.

But if Cooper didn't drown her, was it an accident or a suicide?

Thompson had two teenage granddaughters of his own, which was one of the reasons he empathized so strongly with the parents. He wanted to believe that Shawnee's death was an accident. He could not conceive of his own family's girls, granddaughters or daughters, experiencing an obsession so intense that they would take their own life because of it.

Maybe, he reasoned, *Shawnee parked the car and then waded into the river with thoughts of drowning herself.* In April, the Yaak River was cold as death and just as dangerous. Exposure and subsequent incapacitation and hypothermia would be almost instantaneous, five to seven minutes at the most. If she got too far into the powerful river, she would have died even if she changed her mind. Every spring, the locals found deer or moose that had fallen through the ice and drowned in the river.

The sheriff knew that suicide was a very real possibility. He had lived in Montana his entire life, delivering the news of too many dead sons and daughters to discount that alternative. He knew the high rate of suicide among Native American teens. If one more tortured soul chose to leave this earth, it would not come as a surprise, but as a parent, he wanted to believe that it wasn't so.

The prosecutor's office, in what amounted to a gesture of sympathy for the girl's family, decided that Shawnee McAllister's drowning was most likely an accidental death. The DNA confirmation and forensic analysis verified that the incident at the Whiskey Bend Ranch took place exactly as claimed by the two witnesses and that there were no other signs of foul play.

The county officially classified the drowning an accidental death and closed the file on Shawnee McAllister.

***

A half hour after the sheriff received the county's decision, Thompson phoned Cooper with the news, the first of two phone calls that he needed to make.

Cooper tried to control his relief.

"I wasn't worried about you, Sheriff. I was worried about the system. My experience in Skyler was not a positive one. I'm not certain I could have handled another ordeal like that."

"I understand, Mr. Cooper. Going to court isn't fun for anyone. I wanted you to know as soon as possible so that you could get on with your life."

"I appreciate it. Thanks for your support."

Thompson was silent for a moment, and then said, "It wasn't support, Mr. Cooper. There just wasn't enough evidence to conclude otherwise."

"I see. Well, thanks anyway. If it makes you feel any better, I can tell you there was no evidence that I caused her death because I didn't."

The instant Cooper got off the phone with the sheriff, he tried to contact Angie Hailstone. As he dialed, he looked through the windows above the bar and watched Jagger, his pet deer, walk to the salt block and chase off two younger whitetails with spiked horns. The deer stared at the windows of the house, twitching his ears—as if to let Cooper know who controlled the area. Jagger had grown and matured into a handsome four-point, his antlers thick at the base, showing promise of growing even larger if he could survive another year or two.

Listening to the ring of Angie's phone, Cooper stared back at the buck, smiling at the animal's confidence. He loved the deer's cockiness, and at this moment, his own exuberance mirrored the buck's attitude. *We're just the same,* he thought. *Survivors.*

When Angelina didn't answer, Cooper left a message on her phone and asked her to call him back as soon as possible. Then he went to get his camera to take some more pictures of his pet deer.

***

Sheriff Thompson called the Grayson's right after he spoke to Clayton Cooper.

"Mrs. Grayson? Hayes Thompson with the Lincoln County Sheriff's Department in Montana here. How are you?"

"I'm okay. What can I do for you, Sheriff?"

"I just wanted to keep you and your husband in the loop regarding the investigation into your daughter's passing. I know how difficult this has all been for you, Mrs. Grayson. We've recently received all the forensic reports, and I met with the prosecutor's office a few minutes ago. The county has determined that Shawnee's death was an accident. We think she may have gotten into the water, miscalculated the current and the cold, and couldn't get back out."

When there was no answer, he tried again. "I'm sorry, you know. It was an accident."

Philomena asked, "And what about Cooper?"

"The crime lab verified that Clayton Cooper's DNA and blood were under Shawnee's fingernails. Mr. Cooper told us it would be there. There were no external signs of further trauma. No ligature marks, no soft tissue damage, nothing that didn't coincide with the two witnessed versions of what happened. And there was no evidence of recent sexual activity or forced penetration. It was an accident, Mrs. Grayson. A terrible, tragic accident. We all need to move forward now. I know it's hard, but please, try to move forward."

There was another silence on Philomena's end of the phone.

"No, Sheriff. I can't. Cooper ruined my daughter's life. He had scratches on his face from my daughter's fingernails. How can you let him go? If Shawnee was a white girl, would you ask her mother to go on with her life?"

"Yes. I would. What you say is true. But there are explanations for all of those truths. We can't proceed without evidence that will prove that Mr. Cooper physically took Shawnee's life. No one knows what really happened. But what we do know is that no jury would convict a man on what we've got. Shawnee's ancestry has no bearing on this decision. It's over. It was an accident. It's time to move on."

Philomena didn't answer.

"Are you still there, Mrs. Grayson?"

"I'm still here. But Shawnee isn't. Duffy was right. Cooper may not have drowned my daughter, but he killed her just the same."

"No, Philomena. I don't think he did. He's probably no saint. But he's not a murderer either. I don't think he wanted her to die. I know you don't believe that. But I believe that it's true. Don't let this tragedy get any worse. It was an accident. Let it go."

***

Philomena found Duffy in the Thunderbird Tavern. It was just past noon on the west coast, and today, Duffy was the only one seated at the bar, visiting with Loren the bartender. He greeted his wife with a semblance of good cheer.

"Hey," he said, "want a beer?"

"No. I've got news. I just got off the phone with the sheriff in Montana."

"Yeah?"

"They have all the tests back from the crime lab. They say it was an accidental drowning."

Duffy turned his head so he could see Philomena's face. He stared at her for a moment, then picked up the half-empty beer bottle in front of him and drained it in one swig. He set the bottle back on the bar and ran the back of his thick wrist across his mouth.

"Accidental drowning, my ass. I told you. They don't give a fuck about a half-breed teenage girl."

"I know."

"The old ways was better. If they took one of ours, we took one of theirs. That chicken-shit little bastard kneed me in the nuts. I owe him one."

"You need to get him, Duffy," she said. "He kicked your ass."

Duffy reached out with one hand and grabbed Philomena by the front of her sweatshirt, pulling her into his face as if she were as light as paper.

"Don't ever say that again," he said. "Nobody kicks my ass."

Then he pushed her back toward her barstool.

Philomena turned away and smiled.

"Gimme a beer, Loren. Me and Duffy need to talk."

BROKEN ARROW

34
CHAPTER

Cooper's daughters arrived at the airport in Spokane on Friday afternoon, looking forward to spending the long Labor Day weekend with their father. The weather was warm and sunny, and only the highest mountains showed a touch of stubborn snow still covering their peaks. The birch and aspen trees were just beginning to turn colors, grouped on riverbanks and mountainsides in calendar-cover perfect clusters of orange and gold.

The girls' busy summer schedules of camps, sports, and social events had prevented any earlier visits, and their reunion with their father was filled with hugs and tears. The long separation had been difficult for the family, and Cooper marveled at the changes in his two daughters.

At fourteen years old, Tasha was well on her way to becoming a young woman. She was taller than her mother, and she stood with her shoulders back and her head held high. Her long, honey-colored hair was worn loose and hung down her back to the middle of her shoulders. Her features were delicate, and her flawless skin had a translucent glow. Cooper was surprised to see a touch of mascara around her eyes and her lips highlighted a subtle shade of pink.

Mac, the twelve-year-old, was much shorter than her sister, with a solid body and her father's dark hair that she wore cropped in a short, no-nonsense style. The only girl in Skyler drafted to play in the boys' junior league baseball program, she had surprised even her own family by earning a spot on the all-star team at the end of the regular season. She was as darkly tanned as dark as the leather outfielder's glove that accompanied her as she left the plane.

Despite their differences in both body-type and interests, the girls had always gotten along well. Neither was threatened by the other's success because neither cared in the least about the other's passions. It made for a special relationship between the two, without a trace of sibling rivalry or jealousy.

***

Arriving at the ranch, the girls settled in quickly. Seconds after entering the house, Mac had turned the television on, searching in vain for a baseball game and settling for Sports Center on ESPN. Tasha made a tour of her father's house. She examined the artwork, checked out new photographs, and turned on Cooper's computer to inspect the screen saver that always produced an image of her and her sister in some silly pose—a measure, for her, of their presence in their father's life. She made a mental note to suggest a newer photo than the current picture of her and Mac clowning in their pajamas— one that might better represent her budding sophistication.

Cooper built a fire in the fire pit just off the deck, and the three of them roasted hot dogs and marshmallows, savoring the setting and breathing in the fresh mountain air. After watching Jagger lord over the salt-block, they went to bed early, the girls on couches in the living room and their father in the master bedroom.

Cooper had planned the girls' visit with care, and the next day, the three of them spent as much time together as possible.

Breakfast in the living room, followed by an easy hike and some huckleberry picking was the order of the day. They would drive to town for lunch—he knew the girls loved being able to legally enter the bars in Montana. Then, they would return to the ranch, prepare a barbeque together, and end the day fly-fishing the evening hatch on the river.

Ever since the family had escaped to the Yaak during the difficult times surrounding the incident in Oregon, the ranch had felt like neutral ground for the Cooper family. Cooper hoped that this comfortable neutrality would be the perfect environment to introduce his girls to Angelina Hailstone.

***

The early part of the day went exactly as planned. When they returned from town, Cooper put the girls to work in the kitchen, preparing the salad, creating a cheese platter, and cleaning the berries they had picked earlier in the day. They puttered about, enjoying each other's company as they shared the kitchen.

Cooper headed for the backyard patio to fire up the barbeque and get ready to impress his daughters with his grilling skills. He was pleased with the day so far and happy about the progress of the family's smooth reconnection.

Stepping through the glass door that led to the outdoor cooking area, any sense of satisfaction was immediately wrenched away from him. What he saw took the breath from his lungs.

Sitting on the round outdoor table was an empty beer bottle. The bottle was green glass, and its label was turned to face the door that separated the house from the patio and deck. It was in front of one of the chairs that was pulled away from the table as if someone had enjoyed a leisurely beer on the deck before leaving the bottle as a calling card. Cooper recognized the label. Heineken Beer was as rare as a Mercedes Benz in the valley, and Cooper knew that neither of the two local bars nor the mercantile in the town of Yaak sold the brand.

When he could breathe again, he forced himself to think rationally. He realized that he was overreacting. Anyone could have brought a cooler of beer into the valley, and Heineken was a generic brand. But who would visit, bring his own beer, and not leave a note? He shook his head, frightened by the memory of an insolently launched green bottle that had exploded beside him as he lay in the gravel parking area of the state park on the Oregon coast.

He couldn't resist going back into the house for a quick inspection. He looked in every room, checking the closets and going from window to window, closing them tight, and latching each of the locks. He couldn't imagine his nemesis crawling through anything smaller than a garage door, but the activity gave him a small measure of comfort.

Once he was certain the house was unoccupied, he went to the roll-top desk and, checking to make sure that the girls did not see him, pulled his uncle's ancient handgun from the top drawer. A snub nose .38 caliber Smith and Wesson, it was sheathed in a worn holster and—even though it was always loaded—had not been fired in at least fifteen years. Sneaking it into the bedroom, he tucked it underneath his pillow. He felt better after that and forced himself to relax. He didn't want to frighten his daughters with his silly paranoia.

When the girls finished in the kitchen, they came to visit with their father as he completed preparing to grill.

"Can we go fish for a few minutes while you're fixing dinner, Daddy?" asked Mac.

"No!" Cooper said. "Just wait for me, okay? I don't want you guys out there on your own this weekend."

"Why not, Dad? We'll just be in the backyard, for heaven's sake."

"Because, Tasha." Cooper's brain raced. "If you must know, there's been some bear activity in the valley the past few days. It's no big deal, but I know how you feel about bears. Let's just wait, and we'll all go together, okay?"

"Cool. I hope we see one, Daddy. Maybe we'll spot a grizz."

"Be quiet, Mac," her sister said. "You don't know what you're talking about."

"All right, Tosh, that's enough. Maybe neither one of you knows what you're talking about. We'll all go after we eat."

Tasha rolled her eyes at the television as if she hadn't heard a word her father had said.

***

Across the river, hidden in the dense brush, Duffy Grayson watched the small family as they circled around the grill on the open deck. He grunted at the ignorance of city folks, whose home-sites prioritized spectacular views and sun exposure. Cooper's house had been built ten feet from the river, clearly in the floodplain, where no self-respecting Indian would be foolish enough to position even a temporary sweat lodge.

Philomena had encouraged Duffy's visit, and Duffy, trusting her intuition, was eager to even the score with Clayton Cooper. He had been in the Yaak for a week now, learning the country, familiarizing himself with the terrain, and trying to come up with a plan.

After his own visit to the valley in the springtime, its mystique had drawn him as if he were one of the wild predators that early Native Americans had so respected. It was a place where strength and power ruled. In the Yaak, there were hunters and hunted. Duffy Grayson had looked for such a place all his life.

Getting into Cooper's home had been as easy as getting into Cooper's head. He had hidden his truck upriver in an abandoned gravel pit, waded across the thin summertime river, and worked his way downstream, traveling just inside the tree line on the riverbank—invisible from three yards away. When he could see the house on the opposite side of the river, he found his way to the salt block area with a perfect view of the one-time saloon.

He built a small brush cave at the edge of the clearing, making certain that his hunting blind was well hidden. He wove fir branches and leafy brush into a small wall to cover the front of the blind. When he was finished, he went back to town and spent the night in a cheap motel.

The morning the girls arrived, he was back before dawn, already in his hiding spot when Cooper began to stir. When the man closed the gate on his way to the airport, Duffy had waited an hour, then waded across the river and entered the house through the unlocked slider on the back deck. He searched the house, checking the layout and sight lines to his hidden lair, then returned to town to rest and plan.

The following morning, he watched as the Coopers loaded their truck with berry buckets and backpacks and drove out of the parking lot. Crossing the river, he sat on the deck shielded from the road, studying the bronze sunlit waters of the river. He took a bottle of beer out of his daypack and drank it while he sat on the patio. When he was finished, he set the bottle on the table, turning it so that the label faced the doorway, hoping that Cooper would recognize his brand.

Now, he watched from his hiding spot across the river as the Coopers came out to fish the evening hatch. Fly fishermen he thought. . . six hundred dollars of fancy gear to catch and release tiny fish. Why bother to catch something that you didn't intend to eat?

He smiled as he watched Cooper hover over the two girls. The man kept his daughters close to him and did little fishing himself, watching the river like a focused osprey, studying both sides of the stream with care. Neither Philomena nor Duffy had anticipated the girls' visit, and all their options would have to be altered.

Duffy sat motionless, studying his quarry as hunting instincts ran through his brain. As he thought about the river and the little family fishing it, he had a sudden inspiration. When the thought crystallized in his mind, the corners of his mouth twitched with the hint of another smile. He had been seeking the perfect payback. Now, he knew what he wanted to do.

From across the river, Cooper looked at the vacant salt block area and then glanced at his watch. It was getting late. He hadn't seen any animals at the salt lick for two days now.

It wasn't unusual for activity around the salt to disappear for a day or two if there was a predator in the area or a recent kill in the vicinity. Usually, the deer and moose would avoid a kill zone until the smell of death dissipated. But the lure of the salt seemed to accelerate this time frame.

Jagger was always the first animal to return. He was an incurable salt junkie who seldom missed his regular fix. Cooper knew the area should be safe when the buck showed up.

***

The next day Cooper was up early. His night had been as restless as the weather. An unstable southeast front had blown through, and the house had been a jarring collection of discordant groans and rustles. The wind splattered raindrops against the glass wall of his bedroom in staccato bursts, the usual comforting drum of falling rain distorted by violent flurries that disrupted the normal mountain rhythms, making for an almost sleepless night.

In the morning light, Cooper was able to ignore the sense of foreboding that the weather had brought with it. Though the night had been wakeful, it had passed without incident, and his anxiety began to fade with the rising sun.

Today was the day that Angie Hailstone would meet his daughters. He had planned their first meeting with care, letting the girls settle into the routine of the ranch and see that their father was the same person he had always been. He had avoided bringing Angie to the airport or inviting her to the valley earlier during the girl's visit. He had hidden every sign of her weekend stays at the Whiskey Bend Ranch. Toiletries, extra clothing, even books and CD's were all boxed and pushed into the back of the closets.

The night before, Cooper told the girls that he had invited a "friend" for breakfast. Tasha and Mac, who were used to a procession of students and athletes at their own house during Cooper's school-teaching years, were neither surprised nor curious.

As Cooper prepared his coffee in the open kitchen attached to the living room, he was pleased to see that both girls were still sound asleep on their couches. Angelina wasn't due to arrive until ten o'clock. Cooper knew his daughters would still be on west coast time, and he would have to wake them before Angie's arrival.

The weather had changed again. The wind was quieter now, and the sky was a bluish gray. A bank of low-lying fog drifted around the dark barrier of trees up the river, and the tallest treetops were silhouetted like neat rows of farmed Christmas trees growing in a blanket of pillow-like white smoke. Cooper sighed with satisfaction and made a mental note to program his camera to black and white mode and photograph the surreal scene when there was a little more light available.

Cooper's routine seldom varied in the morning. He brewed his coffee and then sat at the bar that looked out on the river. Most days he read a book or a magazine while he drank his two cups of coffee. Then, he checked the salt block for early morning activity. This was the part of his morning ritual that he enjoyed the most, and he always saved it for last.

As was his habit, he tested the extent of his near-sightedness by squinting across the river without his glasses. As usual, he knew something was there but had no idea what it was. He pulled the powerful spotting scope that rested on the bar into position, twisting the focus ring to dial in the enlarged image. It took a second for his mind to comprehend what he was seeing.

"What the hell?" he said.

What Cooper was trying to understand was a sinister juxtaposition of the familiar and the unimaginable.

It was Jagger who stared back at him from the salt block as he had done so many mornings before. But this time, there was no body attached to the buck's head.

Just below the animal's chin was a bloody stump of the neck that had once held the proud head of Cooper's favorite whitetail deer. Now, the disembodied head rested on the end of a thick willow branch, the other end of which was anchored into the soft ground that surrounded the salt block. The dirt below the branch was soaked in blood. Through the spotting scope, Cooper could see a cloud of black flies floating around the buck's head and antlers.

The head looked as if it had been ripped from the animal's body by sheer force. He knew that was impossible, but he also knew the bone and muscle had been hacked through with a crude cutting instrument.

Cooper choked back the bile rising in his throat.

249

Hurrying to check on his daughters, he was relieved to see they were still sleeping hard, their chests rising and falling, wrapped inside their down comforters. He headed for the bedroom as quietly as possible so as not to wake them.

In the bedroom, he pulled the pistol from under his pillow. His hands shook as he snapped the barrel down and rotated the cylinder to re-check that the gun was loaded. The pistol was not designed for the backcountry, and he thought about Wing Redmond's disdain for the out-of-date .38 caliber. He wished that he had replaced it with a more lethal weapon. Fumbling the holster onto his belt, he slipped out the front door, careful to lock it behind him.

In the backyard, he dragged his uncle's canoe down the bank, slid it into the river, and stroked across the stream to the opposite side, driving the bow of the canoe into the opening in the brush where the moose had worn a path from the salt block to the river. He pulled the canoe onto the bank and, un-holstering the gun, walked cautiously to the site of the slaughter. He was mesmerized by the deer head, a sight made all the more repulsive by the hundreds of frenzied flies attracted to the smell of blood.

He stood searching the wall of the forest, seeking any slight movement or clues about a hiding place. Listing carefully, he was aware of every nuance of the forest. There was no sound. No squirrel chastising an uninvited intruder. No birds protesting a stranger in their midst. Nothing. Only the maddening thrum of the relentless black flies.

He forced himself to step up to the staked head, looking for a clue about the savage decapitation. He made himself examine the turf, soaked with jellied black blood and fragments of meat and hair. He looked carefully for a track or a sign. Again, he saw nothing.

Tears in his eyes, he reached for one of Jagger's antlers, grasping the base of the horn in front of the left ear. The cloud of flies swarmed in protest as he dislodged the severed head from its humiliating display. To his disgust, the stake pulled out of the ground but did not separate from the head.

"Fuck!"

Unable to remove the branch, he headed back to the canoe, the stake gouging a snakelike line in the soft ground at the river's edge.

Back on his own side of the river, he hurried to the shed for a shovel, went behind the building, and dug a shallow hole. Using an ax, he cut the stake near the ragged edge of Jagger's neck and stuffed the deer's head in the hole, covering it with dirt and rolling a rusty burning barrel on top of the hole to hide its location.

When he finished, he went back into the house, undressed, and took a hot shower, trying to wash the stench of horror from his body and his mind.

CHAPTER 40

Angie drove into the ranch parking lot at exactly 10 A.M.

Cooper had woken the girls twenty minutes earlier, and both were still in their pajamas, Tasha seated cross-legged on the hide-a-bed sofa and Mac in the leather chair, her feet tucked beneath her.

"Hey, ladies. We've got company."

Cooper had composed himself somewhat, determined to keep the horrors of the morning hidden from his daughters. He hoped the arrival of a visitor might help conceal his anguish.

Meeting her truck in front of the porch, Cooper held the door open for Angie.

"Ms. Hailstone. Welcome to the Whiskey Bend Saloon."

Angie raised her eyebrows.

"Mr. Cooper. Thank you so much. I'm anxious to see your. . . place." She stuck her tongue out in a lewd waggle.

Cooper took her hand, and with a slight shake of his head, discouraged any further playful exchanges.

"Tasha, Mac, I want you to meet a friend of mine from the school where I work. She used to be an instructor at the college, and now she runs a ski lift at Big Mountain. This is Angelina Hailstone. I invited her to have breakfast and to hang out a little bit today. Angie, meet my daughters, Tasha and MacKenzie. We call the little one, 'Mac'."

"Hi, guys. Wazzup?"

The girls checked her out, first examining the startling shock of magenta-colored hair, then the baggy pants and nylon anorak, topped by a Burton Snowboarder baseball cap. A pair of wrap-around sunglasses sat at the front of the cap where the bill attached to the crown.

"Okay, you two," she said, "I brought some DVD's in case it rains. Mostly action flicks, but there are a couple of Johnny Depp movies in here. One of them might be R-rated though."

"Cool." Both girls were impressed. Their mother was so strict about movies that she did not allow them to even sleep at their friends' unless their parents promised parental guidance or lower.

"Nice try, ladies. You know we don't allow R movies at the ranch," Cooper said, separating the offending options. "Pick one of these," he said of the remaining movies. "You can watch it after breakfast."

After the exchange, Angie stepped back and began making herself comfortable. Turning her back to the girls, she removed her cap and pulled the anorak over her head. The tee shirt under the jacket rode up to the center of her back, and the baggy trousers slid down on her narrow hips, revealing the top portion of a red and green tattoo peeking above the waistband. It looked like the top section of a hummingbird in flight, and it had the authentic permanency of an ink-inject tattoo. The girls noticed that it matched a similar cluster of tattooed hummingbirds more conspicuously banded around one wrist.

The girls exchanged glances. This was cutting-edge stuff, an act so rebellious that it would be inconceivable at home, and they admired it as a bold symbol of teen independence.

Cooper had no idea what invisible message had been communicated to his daughters. He himself had been face-to-face with the derriere tattoo many times, and he was blind to its significance for the girls. But it was apparent that Angelina Hailstone had passed some sort of test. The girls chatted with Angie and seemed oblivious to any romantic connection between the hip snowboarder and their ancient father.

After they ate, Cooper started the movie and then announced he was going to give Angie a tour of the property while they watched the film. The girls hardly noticed and began to debate who was the hottest actor, Johnny Depp or the sexy Robert Pattison.

***

By the time Cooper and Angie were finally alone, Cooper's nerves were shot.

"Coop, what in the world is wrong with you? I've never seen you so fidgety. If I didn't know better, I'd think you were on speed."

"Honey, you won't believe what's going on up here. You remember when I told you about Shawnee's stepfather?"

"You mean that big Indian guy? Of course, I remember."

"He's here. Yesterday he broke into the house. He left me a little calling card. This morning. . ." he stopped, choking up at the loss. "This morning, he killed Jagger."

"What!"

"Yeah. He killed Jagger. He cut his head off and staked it up at the salt block."

Angelina was horrified, uncertain whether or not to believe Cooper while trying to understand the inconceivable. "That's insane."

"Yeah, the son-of-a-bitch is crazy. I don't know what to do. I think he's capable of really, really hurting somebody."

"Obviously, you've got to call Sheriff Thompson. Right now. The man's a psychopath. He could kill someone. He almost killed you twice before."

"I know. But what do I say? I can't even prove it's him."

"What difference does it make who it is? I can't believe you haven't called already. What's wrong with you, Cooper?"

"Nothing's wrong with me. I promised you this whole thing would go away. I don't want everything to start over again because some lunatic is trying to scare me."

"I think you're the lunatic here. Who knows what this monster might do to you? Or your family. Or me. Call the friggin' sheriff, Coop. Get him away from your family."

"You're right. It's just, I don't like letting a bully like Duffy Grayson ruin my life. And . . . and . . . I'm not sure I want the sheriff involved in this whole thing."

"You already tried fighting back. It didn't work. You've got to call. Someone's going to get hurt."

"I know. But I don't want to scare the girls. They don't know anything about this. I'll call first chance I get when they can't hear me."

***

Hidden in the brush blind at the back of the salt block area, Duffy had watched Cooper stroke the canoe across the river. As Cooper guided the canoe onto the bank, the big man sank deeper into the bushes, pulling the camouflage jacket up tight to his neck, then tugging the matching hunting cap as low on his head as it would go.

He saw the revulsion on the man's face as the flies lifted in protest, and he smiled when Cooper recoiled from the stake protruding from the bloody stump of the neck.

Duffy had killed the deer from fifteen feet away on one of the game trails leading to the salt block, using a large bore pistol with a black-market silencer on the barrel. One shot, right through the lungs. He had used a hatchet to decapitate the animal with no more concern than a butcher working on cheap cuts of a pig with a meat cleaver.

Then, he dragged the carcass back into the woods for the coyotes. Never was a kill easier than shooting the careless buck. He knew it would be just as easy to kill the jumpy white man. But Duffy had other plans.

Years of hunting and fishing in the Pacific Northwest had prepared him well for the Rocky Mountain outdoors. Duffy was just as comfortable in the woods as he was on a fishing boat. He knew he could disappear in the thick forests if he needed to. In addition to the nearness of the Canadian border, the presence of Philomena's family in Alberta was a huge advantage. Once he got into Canada, there was a vast wasteland all the way to Alaska where he could hide and take his chances.

Clayton Cooper was going to pay for his role in Shawnee's death and his cheap shot in the fight earlier in the spring, and Duffy was going to be the collection agency.

Whatever happened, he knew he wasn't going back to jail.

Sensing that Cooper shared a fear of the law not dissimilar from his own feelings about the system, Duffy thought the man would contact the local sheriff's department only as a last resort. The ex-teacher's caution—and the distance from the closest law enforcement—would give him ample time to disappear.

But first, he needed to even the score.

***

Mac was getting bored watching movies in the house. Tasha was snuggled down in the covers of her hide-a-bed, lost in the movie. Mac could see the sky through the windows leading to the deck. Outside, it was gray and overcast, with a soft patina of steely light beginning to filter through the valley. Her father and Angie were washing dishes in the kitchen.

Wandering into the back bedroom where the girls kept their travel packs, she changed into jeans and a long-sleeve tee shirt and pulled a fleece Gap top over her head. She walked into the attached mudroom and found her fly fishing vest and a pair of knee-high rubber boots. Her fly rod was already outside, and as she moved toward the deck at the back of the house, she stuck her head into the living room to tell her father that she would be on the river. The television was blasting, and Cooper and Angie were deep in a half-whispered conversation in the kitchen. Rather than interrupting the adults, Mac said to her sister, "Tosh, I'm going to the river to practice my casting. Tell Daddy I'll be right behind the house and that I won't go in over my knees."

"Whatever."

Without a second thought, Mac walked to the river and positioned herself at the boat take-out, a low bank opening hidden from sight from the house by the chest-high grass. There was a good riffle there and, despite the late-season reduced flow, it was just deep enough to serve as holding water for the native rainbow trout that thrived in the river. They had caught several of the coveted "red side" rainbow trout in the pool last night and released them after bringing them to the net.

It was almost midday, and the youngster didn't bother to replace the battered dry fly that she had used to fish yesterday's evening hatch. She didn't expect to catch anything anyway. Three casts into her practice session, a big trout rolled under the fly and changed its mind at the last second about swallowing it for lunch. Mac saw the large fish swirl away and went to work trying to entice a strike. After fifteen minutes of patient casting, she decided to change flies, determined to fool the suspicious fish.

She replaced her fly with a Royal Coachman Wulff and waded out to within an inch of the top of her boots where she could get another few feet of drag-free drift for the new fly. She false cast twice, and on the next cast, the fly settled ten feet above where the fish had risen. The fly began its dance down the foam line of the current. As it bobbed along without drag, Mac knew that if the big fish was still there, it would be unable to resist the temptation.

***

Duffy had watched the little girl miss the big fish and leaned forward, his predatory instincts sensing an opportunity. He had studied both girls for two days now and had been impressed with the little one's patience. The girl was focused. Very focused. After she missed the fish, he knew she would stay on the hunt. He slid out of the blind and pushed through the brush on his side of the river, careful to stay hidden in the woods and out of sight from the house. Sheltered by the willows growing on the small island above the fishing hole, he scrambled into the river, trusting the noise of the running water to hide the sound of his crossing. Reaching the other side, he entered the meadow behind Cooper's house.

Once he reached the corner of the house, he watched the girl change her fly and study the river. When she waded into the water, he began his stalk. Reaching the shoreline undetected, he crashed into the river like a charging bear. The startled girl turned her head just as the trout sucked the fly under the surface. One blow knocked her senseless. He scooped her into his arms and forged across the narrow riffle toward the salt block.

Fording the waist-deep water with ease, Duffy went huffing up the moose trail, past the blood-soaked salt patch and disappeared into the woods.

***

When Cooper and Angie finished talking in the kitchen, Clayton looked up to check on the girls. Angie had convinced him to tell them what was happening so that they would not be alarmed by his planned call to the sheriff. Cooper was uncertain about how much information to share. He knew both girls would be devastated by Jagger's death, and he did not want to frighten them with the details of the sadistic beheading. He decided to give the girls just enough information to let them know that this was serious and that they needed to stay inside the house, at least until the sheriff's department arrived. Then, the family could determine if they wanted to move to a motel for the rest of the visit. Cooper was leaning toward that alternative. He would present it as an adventure, and he thought the girls would be okay with it. At least Tasha would be—he wasn't so sure about her sister.

"Where's Mac, Tosh?" he asked the teenager. "In the shower?"

"Nope. She's on the river. Practicing her casting."

"What!" He rushed to the window to check on his youngest daughter.

"It's no big deal, Dad. She said she'd stay right in front and wouldn't get in over her knees."

Cooper was at the window, looking frantically up and down the river, trying to locate Mac.

"Where is she, Tasha? Where is she?"

"She must be right there, Daddy. Relax."

He ran through the master bedroom and threw open the slider to the deck. He hit the back lawn on the run, sprinting to the river. Mac's landing net was on the riverbank beside the boat take-out and casting area. There was no sign of the girl. The river seemed soft and innocent in its low-water state. The only sound was the copper-black water as it slid by the house on its journey to the Kootenai River, flowing with a monotonous hum that was only broken by the occasional gurgle of the water bumping into submerged rocks or logs. The sound reminded Cooper of a more musical version of the buzzing flies at the salt block earlier that morning, and the connection filled him with terror.

"Mac! Mac, where are you!"

He searched the riverside below the ranch, panic surging through his body. "Mac! Mac!"

Angie and Tasha rushed to join him, Tasha still clad in flannel pajamas, her bare feet and ankles shining white in the gray overcast of the day.

"What's wrong, Daddy? What's going on? What are you doing?"

Cooper ignored her questions and said, "Tasha, look in the shed and the pump house. Then check out front in case your sister wandered over that way. Hurry! Let me know right away if you find her. And be careful. Don't go near any strangers or anything."

"Strangers? What are you talking about? There aren't any strangers up here. What's happening?"

"Tasha, just do what you're told. Now!"

"Okay, okay. I'm going."

As the barefoot girl jogged back toward the buildings, Angie moved close to Cooper and said, "It's him, isn't it? I know it's him."

"Don't say that. We don't know anything yet." He looked at Angie, his eyes beginning to tear up. "But it might be him. If he hurts my daughter, I swear I'll track him to the end of the earth. She hasn't done anything to deserve this." He sank to his knees on the rocky shoreline cradling Mac's landing net. "Oh, God. This can't be happening."

Angie, who had once been a lifeguard in South and was also trained in search and rescue techniques involving missing skiers at Big Mountain, had dealt with panicked fathers on several occasions. "Coop, we need to stay calm. Get up, and let's do something. We need to find her. Call the sheriff. Now!"

Cooper struggled to his feet and stumbled up the riverbank, brushing away the hand she offered to help him up. She stepped aside and followed him onto the deck and into the house.

Just as he was picking up the phone, he looked out the window and saw Wing Redmond's rig drive into the parking lot. Cooper reached Wing's battered crew bus before it rolled to a complete stop and was talking to his friend before Wing's feet had hit the ground. "Thank God you're here! Wing, I need some help right now. That deranged bastard's kidnapped Mac, and I think he might hurt her if we don't find them right away."

Redmond, who had just dropped in to see the girls, tried to calm his neighbor. "Take it easy, man. Slow down. What the hell are you talking about? A kidnapping? Are you serious?"

"This is for real. This is the most fucking serious moment of my entire life." Coop's voice cracked as he spoke. "That bastard has my little girl."

At that moment, Tasha rushed up to the porch. "Dad, she's not here! She's not anywhere. What's going on? Mac can swim; she wouldn't drown. What's happening?"

Cooper's heart went out to his frightened daughter. "Honey," he said, hugging her close. "We think someone has taken your sister. You remember the guy who attacked me in the park back home? He's here. He's trying to hurt me again. Mac is his way of hurting me."

"You mean Shawnee's stepfather? That's who has Mac?"

"We don't know, Tosh. We think so."

"But he's crazy. Isn't he the one who cut up that man in a bar fight? Is he even out of jail?"

As the reality of the situation set in, Tasha's voice began wavering, the thought of her sister as Duffy Grayson's captive too appalling to accept.

"He's out of jail. Now, get ahold of yourself, sweetheart. We'll find her. Wing's going to help."

***

Like so many residents in the valley, Wing Redmond was a man who kept to himself, asking no questions of anyone else and answering even fewer if they related to his own background. Except for Cooper, Wing had no close friends in the valley, and the locals knew nothing of his history. What people did know about Wing Redmond was that he was a skilled woodsman.

When Cooper finished his story, glossing over the details of Jagger's gruesome beheading, Wing reached behind the front seat of his truck and pulled out the hunting rifle he always carried. The gun was a Winchester carbine, a lever-action .30-.30 caliber rifle, ubiquitous in the valley and most of Montana.

He nodded at Cooper and said, "Let's go inside and get ready to roll."

When Cooper came out of the bedroom, Wing was checking the Smith and Wesson pistol, ensuring that the gun was loaded and stuffing a handful of extra bullets in the pocket of his trousers.

"You sure you want that BB gun? It ain't gonna be much good if we run into a grizz."

Cooper grimaced at the irony. "This guy makes a bear look like a fuckin' bunny rabbit. I wish I had a machine gun."

"Yeah, those are handy. Show me what happened, man. And we best be quick about it."

Cooper took Wing out the back way and showed him where Mac had been fishing. He waved at her landing net, unable to speak as he stared at his daughter's prized possession.

Wing studied the ground on the riverbank. He squatted down and touched some loose stones. Then he stood, looking up the river, down the river, and across to the moose path leading to the salt block.

"Grab the canoe," he said. "Let's check by the salt block."

Cooper slid the canoe off the shoreline and into the water. A dozen hard strokes pushed them across the current and onto the soft bank in front of the moose trail.

"Don't step on any tracks. Pull the canoe upstream, and let me take a look."

The bank was soft next to the shrunken river. Wing grunted. "Hell, Tasha could read these tracks. The sumbitch must weigh 300 pounds."

Wing walked to the salt block. He saw swaths of bloodstained dirt mixed with twigs and debris and hair and bone. He looked at Cooper, raising his eyebrows.

"Like I told you, Grayson was here earlier. All that blood and shit is from Jagger. I came over, took the head down, and buried it."

Wing did not seem to be as shocked or horrified as Cooper expected. Instead, he started working his way out from the salt block in concentric arcs, looking for the route Duffy had chosen after he took Mac. There were several game trails radiating out from the salt block, and Wing had to sort through them.

Cooper could almost see the thoughts taking place inside Wing Redmond's head, and he knew his friend was considering their options. When Wing spoke, Cooper's blood ran cold.

"Coop, yell at the girls. Have them call the sheriff. Tell him he should get up here right away."

CHAPTER 41

The little girl was still unconscious.

Duffy was not surprised that she was still out. Grown men had been knocked cold by similar punches.

Entering the woods undetected, he followed a game trail to where he had spent the previous night. There was an open area with a crude shelter, a bed of fallen needles on the ground, and a lightning-seared larch tree stump to shield the wind.

A backpack was leaned against the charred tree, its contents as sparse as the campsite itself: a sleeping bag, flashlight, matches, compass, hatchet, a roll of duct tape, the pistol, and a box of bullets for the .44 magnum. Lying beside the pack were a half a dozen store-bought packages of beef jerky and a three-quarters empty bottle of whiskey.

He dug through the backpack and found the roll of duct tape. Tearing off two long strips, he secured the girl's hands and feet. He ripped another shorter piece off the roll and placed it over her mouth, careful not to restrict her breathing.

Finished with the taping, he leaned back against the stump, thinking about the best way to execute his plan.

***

Wing was an excellent tracker. His skill had less to do with his skill for reading signs than it did with his ability to understand the mindset of his quarry. He simply thought like the animal that he was pursuing. He knew which species were sly and devious, which were practical and purposeful, which were cautious, and which were dangerous.

Looking at the game trails that surrounded the salt block area, he decided that only two paths would allow a man of Duffy Grayson's size to carry a youngster through the woods unhindered. He did not think Duffy would be playing games now. Duffy had no idea that Cooper had help, and consequently, he wouldn't be in any big hurry. Besides, predators like Duffy were over-confident and arrogant, more reliant on power and strength than on cunning and guile.

"Coop," he said over his shoulder. "Take a look over here. If you were a big man, carrying a load, which way would you go?"

Cooper looked at the game trails in the jumble of trees. "Right there," he pointed. "It's open and well worn."

"Yeah. Maybe a little too obvious though. How 'bout here? It's almost as open, and it leads back to a dry creek bed on the other side of the ridge. It's pretty clear down there, and there's some tree cover. It's a holding area for your zoo pets. I think that's our best bet."

"Whatever you say. But we've got to hurry. We need to find Mac as soon as possible."

"I know." Wing paused, "Coop, um, we need to be careful here. We know this psycho is armed. He could ambush us anywhere if he wanted to. Maybe Mac is just the bait. We need a game plan."

"Let me go first," Cooper said. "If Mac's the bait, I'm taking it. It's my fault she's in this mess, and believe me—there's no telling what this maniac will do to her. If he shoots me, he shoots me. Just make sure you don't miss the son-of-a-bitch."

Wing stared at Cooper, then stepped into the lead and walked down the chosen trail. Cooper followed close behind, his hand resting on the pistol holstered on his hip.

Wing saw the makeshift camp well before they reached it. It was the place he would have chosen himself: well concealed but with a good view of the open trail where they stood. He knew if he looked around, he would find the very spot where Duffy had killed

Jagger. Signaling Cooper to stay behind the trees, he worked his way toward the charred tree stump.

The campsite was empty. Wing felt the ground around the base of the tree where the larch needles were still pressed into a slight depression. He noted the faint smell of whiskey soiling the mountain air. Before Cooper could see it, he pocketed a short piece of duct tape lying beside the bed site, then signaled for his friend to join him.

"They were here and not too long ago."

Cooper's eyes darted around the campsite. "Is she okay?"

"I don't know. There's no blood. I think she's still alive. At least, she wasn't bleeding when she was here."

"We've got to find them, Wing. That sick bastard's going to do something crazy."

"I know." Wing looked around the campsite, puzzled by the absence of an exit trail heading upriver. A quick circle around the area showed evidence of a hasty departure. Strangely, the trail doubled back down river on a path parallel to the trail leading into the camp.

"It looks like he circled back into the woods and headed downstream. See how the ground is scuffed up here headed south?" Thinking out loud, he said, "Why would he do that? Downriver takes him back toward the highway. He must know that you'd have called the law by now. Even if someone's coming to pick him up. . . which seems unlikely. . . that direction's heading back to civilization. It doesn't make any sense."

Cooper thought about what Wing was saying. He thought about Duffy's twisted nature and his penchant for psychological torture.

Suddenly, and with dreadful clarity, Duffy's game plan became apparent. Cooper was horrified that his own mind could assimilate Duffy's sick reasoning, but as soon as the idea entered his head, he knew without a doubt what the man intended to do. The horror of

266

Duffy's plan made indisputable sense to the terrified father, and he was beside himself with fear.

"Wing, he's headed for Whiskey Creek! Where you guys found Shawnee in the river. He's going to use the same spot. The same spot where Shawnee died. I know it! I can feel it in my bones."

Whiskey Creek was almost a mile below the ranch. The logjam where Wing had retrieved Shawnee's body was another two hundred yards below the raft take out. The ice was gone now, but even in autumn, the river ran strong through the canyon above the campground. If they were too late, Cooper knew he would find his daughter's body in the same location.

Wing didn't question his friend's intuition. He headed toward the river at a fast trot, calling to his friend, "We can make better time on the river bank. He'll have to stay in the woods to stay hidden from the road, and it gets pretty nasty in there. Carrying Mac's going to slow him down, too. Come on, let's go."

When they reached the river, Wing started to run, covering large chunks of riverbank with his long, loping stride. Cooper was right behind him, driven by panic and fear. They ran until the brush line of the dense willows crowded them off the high bank of the river. They slid down the bank and into the river, careful to keep their weapons dry as they splashed through the thigh-deep water, struggling to stay upright on the slippery rocks.

***

Deep in the woods, Duffy Grayson found the going more and more difficult as he forced his way through the blow-down and brush. The girl was not heavy, but she was awkward to carry, preventing him from using his hands to deflect the branches that caught and held his clothing or slapped across his unprotected face.

The big man was not used to running. He much preferred to stand and fight. He knew he could have shot Cooper back in the woods near his campsite, and then he could have taken his time. But if he had done that, Cooper wouldn't have been around to appreciate the act of revenge.

He could have thrown the girl in the river anywhere. She wouldn't last long, bound hand and foot. But he had decided against it. After he drowned the girl in the proper spot, he would go back upriver, heading for the mountains along the Canadian border. He wanted to get into the backcountry before the law showed up. It wouldn't be long before the place would be crawling with cops.

***

Fifteen minutes later, Wing and Cooper completed their frenzied charge to the Whiskey Creek Campground. As soon as they arrived, Cooper raced downstream to the logjam, searching frantically for some sign of Mac. The shady riverside was silent, the campground deserted this late in the season. There was no sign of Mac or her abductor, no indication that anyone had been there.

Wing whistled at Cooper and held a finger to his lips. Assuming Cooper's intuition was accurate, they had beaten Duffy to the area.

Wing looked across the river and tried to determine where Duffy might come out of the woods. There was only one place where someone could wade across the river, and even with the low water, it would take a heavy man to do so. Only a strong wader could negotiate the swift chute above the boat take out. In order to guarantee that a body would sink in the water above the logjam, it would have to be deposited from the west side of the river—the side that Wing and Cooper now occupied. Duffy had to cross the river, and he had to cross it here.

He positioned Cooper directly across from the narrowest crossing point and hid him behind a protective boulder.

"Coop, he's going to cross here. He'll be coming right at you. Once he gets into the water, your job is to keep him focused on you. Do not shoot the man. If he still has Mac, he'll probably use her as a shield. You could hit her, and then we've lost her. If he doesn't have her, we want him alive so we can find out where she is. I'm going to be downstream, at an angle. I'll do the talking. And if there must be a shot, let me take it. Understand?"

Cooper nodded, his eyes vacant and unseeing.

Grabbing Cooper by the front of his shirt, Wing shook him hard. "Snap out of it, Coop. I said, do you understand?"

Cooper's eyes came back into focus. He nodded again and was able to answer, "I understand. I won't shoot."

"Good. We're gonna use YOU as bait, bro. Take that BB gun out of your holster, and put it where you can reach it if something goes wrong. I don't think this guy's afraid of you. Let's get him over here, get Mac, and see what happens. Stay low, since we know he's got a gun." Wing stopped, looking at his friend. "Remember, no shooting. Let me do the dirty work if we need to, okay?"

"Yeah. Okay."

***

They heard him before they saw him. He was in the woods, pushing through the underbrush as he moved toward the river. There was no finesse, no stealth involved in his approach. Even across the river, they could hear branches snapping and brush rattling as the man bulled forward.

Cooper felt the hair on the back of his neck rise. He stared at the opposite river bank and awaited his nemesis' arrival, praying that his daughter was still alive.

Duffy burst out of the underbrush and onto the bank of the river with Mac still cradled in his arms. His cap had disappeared in the woods, and his heavy black hair was soaked in sweat. Cooper could see Mac rise and fall in front of Duffy as his chest heaved. He saw the duct tape wrapped around her wrists and ankles, covering her mouth and around her head.

Duffy's run for the campground had jostled Mac into consciousness, and Cooper could see her eyes opened wide, a fawn in the grasp of a savage bear. He forgot everything Wing had told him.

Stifling a cry of anguish, Cooper rose from behind the boulder. He stood defiantly in the open, ready to sacrifice himself for his daughter's release.

Duffy swore as Cooper stood up behind the rock, and they stared at each other across the waters of the Yaak River.

"Grayson, let her go. Just set her down, and let her go. Don't hurt her."

Duffy laughed.

"Is that what you did with Shawnee, asshole? Set her down? Didn't hurt her?"

"I didn't do anything to Shawnee. You have to believe me. You've got this whole thing wrong. I have never hurt anyone!"

"Too late, little man. I owe you one. This one's gonna die where Shawnee died. Now."

Wing's voice rang out from twenty yards downstream. "Put the girl down, Geronimo. Unless you want your brains blown all over this mountain."

Duffy looked with surprise toward the strong voice, so different from Clayton Cooper's desperate pleading. He saw the rifle leveled at his face and, for the first time, felt a touch of fear pulse through his body. There was no quaver in this voice, no hint of panic.

"This is between me and him," he nodded toward Cooper. "It's payback time.

"Not anymore. Now it's between you and me. And there's no payback time. I'm going to give you one chance to put that girl down. Slowly, or I'll put a round right between your eyes and pick her up myself. Your choice. You've got five seconds to make it happen."

Duffy knew with certainty that the man would shoot him.

"Okay. Don't shoot. I'll put her down." He knelt toward the ground to set the little body on the beach. The rifle moved with him, never wavering from its mark. When Mac was inches from the beach, Duffy suddenly lurched to the right and threw the girl into the river at the exact moment that he initiated an awkward shoulder roll.

Cooper heard a shot thunder through the canyon, and he screamed his daughter's name, watching in horror as her body hit the water, submerging into the powerful current.

"I'll get Mac!" Wing yelled as the current swept the girl downstream. He had positioned himself where the canyon widened, and he leaped to intercept the girl. Since Duffy had been forced to launch her into the water from the far side of the river, she would not be swept into the treacherous logjam.

Cooper was riveted by Wing's rescue efforts when something crashed into the river in front of him. The force of the entry was explosive. He jerked toward the sound.

Duffy Grayson, blood pumping from a wound in his neck, splashed toward him at full charge. He crossed the waist-deep water with amazing speed, growling and snarling like a rabid animal. When he hit Cooper's side of the river, the water and blood sluiced off his body, and he gained momentum as his rage propelled the charge. Duffy had no time to get his weapon out of the backpack, and his fear of Wing's next shot had forced him to action.

Cooper remembered his own gun as Duffy cleared the water just to the side of the rock where he was standing. Grabbing the pistol off the top of the boulder, he pointed it at the charging madman and pulled the trigger. Locked onto the rushing Duffy, Cooper didn't hear the sound of the gun going off: he only heard the bullet as it thudded into the body just below the collarbone of the other man's huge chest. He pulled the trigger two more times, and he heard neither the blast from the handgun nor his own screams each time he squeezed the trigger.

Duffy charged into him unabated and swung a massive fist from his one good arm. Cooper felt his nose flatten as his vision blurred. He pressed the barrel of the pistol against the body that was crushing him, pulling the trigger again and again and again, without realizing that only three bullets remained in the gun and that the reflexive trigger pulls were not pumping additional rounds into the body that was crushing him. He was still squeezing the trigger over and over when Wing rolled the heavy weight off of him.

271

"Coop. Coop! He's dead! Stop shooting! It's over. Stop."

Cooper looked at him, still half-blind with shock. He watched dully as Wing unwrapped his fingers from the empty handgun. Only when the weapon was separated from his hand did he begin to focus.

"Mac? Where's Mac?"

"She's here, Coop. I got her. She's gonna be okay. She's still scared. You've got to settle down so you can take care of her. She needs you, man. She needs you!"

Pushing himself up on a trembling elbow, Cooper looked for his daughter. He saw her inert form lying on the rocky shore, and he could hear her coughing and crying.

"Mac," he called. "I'm coming."

"Uh, Coop? You're covered in blood. Let's at least get the blood off your face before you scare her to death. You don't look very comforting right now."

"Is she all right, Wing? Are you sure she's all right?"

"She's good. Just scared. She was awesome: held her breath, got her head above water. But we need to get her to a doctor."

Soaking a bandana in the river, Wing helped Cooper wipe his face, checking the smashed nose as he did the cleanup. It wasn't pretty, but it certainly wouldn't be fatal. As he helped Cooper, he talked to Mac in a steady voice and assured her that her father was fine and that he would be at her side at any minute. He rinsed the bandana in the river and gave Cooper the cold compress to staunch the bleeding from his nose. Then, he guided the father to his daughter's side.

"I'm here, baby. I'm here. Everything's going to be okay."

He lay down beside Mac and wrapped her in his arms. "How are you, honey? Are you okay?"

"I'm okay, Daddy. You should have seen the size of the rainbow that I missed."

Cooper squeezed his daughter tight and felt a sting of the tears running into the cuts near the sides of his nose.

***

While Cooper held Mac's shaking body, Wing took a moment to survey the damage. He bent down to examine the body. There was a deep crease in the thick muscle of Duffy's neck where his own shot had come inches from severing the man's jugular. Four of the six rounds in Cooper's .38 caliber pistol had found their target: the bullet that had struck the right shoulder, another above the hip on the same side, and two in the thorax area. Only the final bullet had stopped the man, and Wing knew it was the luckiest of circumstances that it had entered his heart.

Wing looked at Cooper's gun. "Worthless piece of shit," he muttered. Then he said to Cooper, "I told you to get yourself a real gun, man. You're lucky to be alive."

He didn't mention the long-barreled pistol that he had found in Duffy's backpack or the fortunate circumstances that had prevented the man from accessing his pack.

"I don't know if I'm lucky or not. A man's dead, Wing. Dead!"

"Hey, shit happens. None of this was your fault. You did what anyone would do to protect his family."

Cooper said without conviction, "Yeah, what do we do now?"

"I dunno. Wait for Sheriff Thompson, I guess. You seem to be a full-time job for him. I don't think we have too many choices here, bro."

Cooper was silent for a few seconds. "I'm not sure what to do Wing. Let's just go slow, okay? Let's get Mac home and check on the girls. I need to think about this."

"There ain't nothing to think about. Mac needs to go to the hospital. And we can't leave a body full of bullet holes here on the riverbank. Someone might roll into the campground. It looks like Nam with all the blood and shit."

Cooper said, "Let's just cover him up with a tarp. The sheriff's department won't want us to move him anyway. Let's do that and then decide what happens from there."

"Cooper, listen to me. You haven't done anything wrong. If you screw around here, you'll only make things worse. You've got to be here to take the credit. This is Montana. You'll be a hero for what went down."

"Not with Hayes Thompson, I won't. He's not going to be happy."

***

Wing walked back up the road to the Whiskey Bend Ranch while Cooper remained with Mac.

Angie was tending to Cooper's almost hysterical older daughter when Wing arrived at the house. Both girls were scared, relieved to see Cooper's friend, and elated with the news of everyone's safety.

Wing wasn't certain what to tell them about Duffy's death.

"Well, uh, there's been an accident. Your dad and Mac are just fine. I need to get some stuff from the shed. Angie, can you call the sheriff again and tell them to meet us at the Whiskey Creek Campground? Ask for an ambulance too, and send it to the same place. Tell them it's a near drowning and that Mac's in shock. We need them right away."

He stopped, lowered his voice so that Tasha could not hear. "And tell them they'll need a coroner too. We've got a body down there."

***

When Wing left to get help, Cooper laid back down with his daughter and pulled her close, hoping that his body heat would quell the tremors that continued to wrack her body. Her eyes were vacant

274

and unfocused, and she struggled to answer his questions. The side of her face was swollen, and he suspected she was suffering from some type of head injury.

Coupled with her shock, he feared his little girl was in dangerous territory. Afraid that she would lapse into a coma, he rambled on, bombarding her with questions that forced her to pay attention and drew an occasional head nod in affirmation.

At the same time, his thoughts wandered, and the horror of the day's events began to take shape in his mind. The bloody corpse lying on the riverbank was real. Despite his horror, he felt no remorse. He had a frightening thought that the valley must have touched his soul and seduced him with its darkness. He fingered his battered nose and looked at the blood covering his jacket and trousers. There was a pungent odor surrounding him, and he didn't know if it was the smell of blood or his own fear.

He tore his jacket off and threw it into the brush in an effort to cleanse the stench from his body and his spirit.

CHAPTER

42

Twenty-five minutes later, Wing, Angie, and Tasha drove into the campground.

Tasha rushed to her father and hugged him close, while Angie forced herself to concentrate on Mac.

"Tasha, get the blankets from the truck. Hurry! We need to keep her warm. Bring me the first aid kit and anything from Wing's rig that we can use to get something between her and the ground. She might be hypothermic."

Tasha let go of her father and ran to the truck.

Watching Angie take charge, Wing nodded with satisfaction. He began to work on Duffy's body, positioning it as unobtrusively as possible as he rigged out a nylon tarp to use as a makeshift shroud, trying to shield the girls from the grisly scene. He checked the bullet holes one more time, noting the powder-burned edges of the entry punctures on Duffy's jacket where Cooper had pressed the barrel of the gun as he fired the fatal shot into his massive chest.

Wing had seen some bullet holes in his lifetime. The close-range killing concerned him. He knew that four rounds in one body, three of them fired with the barrel of the gun pressed against the victim, would be a red flag for law enforcement investigators and coroners.

Not to mention his own shot that hit the man in the neck. But he also knew that smaller men than Duffy had soaked up a pistol's full cylinder and still kept on coming—and attacking—until they bled out a full 30 seconds later.

***

The sheriff's department, in tandem with an ambulance, pulled into the campground just under an hour later. Sheriff Thompson had been detained on an accident site, and a young deputy named Chuck Walsh had been assigned to handle the scene. Walsh was one of two deputies who had assisted in the search for Shawnee and was familiar with the original case. He was uneasy about another near-drowning in the same location and incredulous when Wing showed him the body underneath the blue tarp.

"Jesus. It looks like Bonnie and Clyde. Don't touch anything. I've got to call Hayes and get him up here for this. He won't believe it. Goddamn. Only in the Yaak."

"Yeah. Only here. Listen, this has been a God-awful day. My daughter—"

"I know. The EMTs will take care of her. What about you? You don't look too good either."

"I'm okay. Just beat up, I guess."

"Let me see if I can get a hold of Hayes. He'll let us know how to proceed from here."

***

Hayes Thompson was at the scene of a traffic fatality near the Canadian border. The site was a mess, and he was still working with the Montana Highway Patrol. The sheriff asked his deputy to take brief statements from the adults, secure the crime scene, and then stand by until he could get there. The witnesses could go home but could not leave the area. He would send another deputy as soon as possible.

Angelina's first aid skills paid precious dividends. By the time the ambulance arrived, Mac's condition had stabilized. The shock of the traumatic kidnapping and the near drowning was beginning to wear off as her body temperature warmed back to a normal range. The ambulance crew loaded her into the vehicle and, much to

Cooper's relief, agreed to let Angie ride with her to the hospital in Libby. Cooper and Tasha would follow as soon as possible.

Deputy Walsh took short statements from Cooper and Wing Redmond. He asked both men to remain close to a phone until they spoke with Sheriff Thompson. Then he sent them home to clean up and rest until the sheriff's arrival.

***

When they got back to the ranch, Tasha's adrenaline began to ebb, and she took a closer look at her father. There was little resemblance to the fashionable man that she was used to seeing. The broken nose sat oddly off-center on his face and his eyes were almost swollen shut. He had a small cut at the side of his nose, and the skin on his upper cheeks was shiny and tight. His unshaven face showed traces of dried blood and grime despite Wing's cleanup efforts.

Noting her concern, Cooper said, "How are you doing, honey."

Tasha answered, "I'm okay, Daddy. How about you?"

"I'm fine. A little shaky, I think." He touched his face with the tips of his fingers. "And a little sore. Wing tells me I'm not too pretty, either. I'm sorry you had to be a part of this, sweetheart. I'm sorry that any of us did. I can't believe that it really happened. I keep thinking it's just a nightmare."

"I know, Daddy. I was so scared." She started to cry, and Cooper took her into his arms.

"It's okay, Tosh. It's okay. Everything is fine. We'll call your mother right away and tell her what happened. Now that we know Mac is fine, nothing else matters. We're all okay. . . and that maniac will never hurt anyone again."

Tasha sobbed against his chest, her thin arms locked around his back.

"Can we all be together again, Daddy? Can we?"

"I don't know, baby. Maybe. Right now, let's just call your mom."

* * *

It was nearly dark when Hayes Thompson arrived at the Whiskey Bend Ranch. The sheriff looked exhausted, the skin on his face sagging and rough with blotchy tatters of white whiskers on his cheeks and chin.

But one look at Cooper and the sheriff forgot about his own fatigue.

"Jesus, Mr. Cooper, are you all right? Looks like you need medical attention."

"I'm fine. I've been icing my face. It's getting better."

"That's good. You still look a little pale." He got right to the point. "I just left the team down at the river. Looks like we've got ourselves another situation, huh? Things seem to be somewhat unsettled up here, don't you think? Two deaths in the same spot in five months are a little unusual. Even for the Yaak."

Cooper nodded, unable to disagree.

Thumbing through his notes, the sheriff tried to reconstruct the bizarre events of the day.

"Why didn't you call us the minute you realized that your daughter had been abducted, Mr. Cooper? It seems like that would have been the logical thing to do."

Drawing a breath through a nose clogged with dried blood, Cooper tried to clear his muddled thoughts. "Because I knew Duffy Grayson had her, and I knew there wouldn't be time. You don't fool around when a madman has one of your children, Sheriff."

"Fool around? If you'd called us when you first knew Grayson was here, there might not be another body downriver. We try not to kill our perps if it's at all possible."

279

"I know Sheriff, but you have to put yourself in my shoes. What would you do if someone took your daughter? Would you sit back and wait for help before you tried to get her back? Would you let her die while you waited for help? Could you do that, Sheriff? Honestly? I don't mean any disrespect, but there's an old saying that goes, 'When seconds count, the police will be here in minutes.' And when you talk to Wing, you'll find out that my daughter was as good as dead the minute Duffy dropped her, all tied-up and duct-taped, into the river. If we had been 30 seconds later, you'd be looking at two corpses right now instead of just one!"

The sheriff studied Cooper for a long time.

"No," he said finally. "I wouldn't wait for anything. You've got that in your favor. But I'll tell you what. You better be able to walk me through this whole thing in a satisfactory manner. Even in Montana, we're accountable for our actions. And even here, four bullet holes in one man requires an explanation."

Cooper didn't answer.

"Listen, we're all tired right now. Why don't you get some rest? I'll do the same. Let's meet in town tomorrow morning, and we'll go over this whole situation. I know you'll want to be with your daughter as much as possible. Is that clear?"

Cooper nodded his agreement.

I'll contact Wing and get his statement sometime tomorrow. We'll need to handle this one by the book."

***

After the sheriff left, Cooper and Tasha called to check on Mac. Angie answered the phone in Mac's hospital room and assured them that the little girl was doing well. She was sound asleep and would be for the rest of the night. Angie was headed home and would see them in the morning.

Cooper tucked Tasha into bed and then laid down on the couch in front of the wood stove with an ice pack on his throbbing face.

He struggled with his thoughts, too exhausted to think about them, too traumatized to make them go away. Fragments of the day's events ran through his mind.

His daughter had been kidnapped by a monster who had tried to take her life. He had killed the man, shooting him through the heart. It was incomprehensible to him that such events could be a part of his life. Finally, his mind still struggling to accept the futility of what had happened, he lapsed into unconsciousness. It was an uneasy sleep marked by red visions of deer and death and drowning.

43
CHAPTER

Cooper and Tasha met the girls' mother at the Spokane airport early the next morning. Kelsey had flown from Portland to Seattle on a commuter flight and then boarded the first plane to Spokane. After an emotional greeting at the airport, made even more awkward by Cooper's disfigured face, they left at once for the hospital in Libby.

Kelsey insisted that she and Tasha ride together in the back seat of Cooper's truck for the three-hour drive. She wrapped her daughter in her arms and would not release the girl from her grasp. She sniffled softly, refusing to speak to her ex-husband.

"Mom, it wasn't dad's fault. He saved Mac's life."

Tasha felt her mother's body stiffen. "I know, honey," she said. "I just want to get you girls away from this awful place as soon as possible. Your father's responsible for your safety when you're with him, you know. We're going home as soon as your sister can leave."

When they arrived at Mac's hospital room, she was sitting up in bed focused on Angie's iPad. She was so absorbed in her game that she failed to notice her visitors at the door. Kelsey rushed to her bedside, encircling her daughter in a fierce hug accompanied by another deluge of tears.

Mac managed to squeeze out a: "Hi, Mom. When can I get out of here?"

Kelsey said, "Soon, baby. Very soon."

After conducting a full-body examination of her daughter, she concluded that, except for some facial swelling and a minor skin rash from the duct tape, Mac showed no other signs of external damage, and any concerns about psychological damage disappeared when the girl said, "Geez, Dad, you look terrible."

Cooper laughed. He was relieved to see that in spite of the reddish bruise covering his daughter's cheek, the swelling on the side of her face had gone down. He whispered a thankful prayer for this improvement and for his own subsequent escape from Kelsey's displeasure.

The morning's phone conversation with Mac's doctor indicated that she had suffered a slight concussion, but there had been no respiratory damage from the near-drowning.

***

Sheriff Thompson sat at his desk, refreshed from four hours of sleep.

He had phoned Philomena Grayson last night and conveyed the news of Duffy's death. Unlike the devastating emotional breakdown that had followed the notice of Shawnee's passing, Philomena handled the news of Duffy's demise like a war bride who had long ago reconciled with the possibility of her husband being killed in action.

Thompson found her stoicism to be even more disconcerting than the purge of grief that had come with the news of Shawnee's drowning. His own interpretation of the contrasting reactions was simple; Shawnee was her only child—and Duffy Grayson would have been a hard man to love.

***

When Sheriff Thompson arrived at the hospital, he was pleased that the Cooper girl was recovering. He knew the concussion was a blessing in disguise; it had protected her from the horror of a fully conscious kidnapping.

Cooper introduced Kelsey. Hayes shook her hand and asked if she and Cooper could join him in the hallway for a minute.

"I know this should only be a time for rejoicing about Mac's safety, but I'm obligated to get a statement from everyone involved in yesterday's situation. I need to visit with your daughter and I. . ."

"I'm taking her home as soon as possible, Sheriff," Kelsey interrupted. "To Oregon. We're leaving the minute her doctor releases her."

"I understand, ma'am. I only need to talk to her for a few minutes. You and Mr. Cooper can stay in the room. It's strictly routine. We know the details. I just need a minute."

"Is it really necessary, Sheriff? We want Mac to forget this whole thing ever happened."

"Just one or two questions, folks. I need to make sure that we do this by the book."

Kelsey looked at Cooper.

"Okay," said Cooper. "One or two questions."

Thompson only needed one question.

"What happened yesterday, Mac? Can you tell me what happened?"

Mac looked the sheriff in the eyes. "A bad man took me. He threw me in the river."

Then she added, "I think I hooked a big fish. That's the last thing I remember before I was in the water."

***

Later that day, the sheriff questioned the other witnesses about what had taken place on the day of the kidnapping and shooting.

The recovery of the severed deer's head by his deputies and statements from Wing Redmond and the girls confirmed his belief that the details of the abduction were accurate and truthful. It was Duffy's actual death that remained uncomfortable for him. The bullet-riddled corpse was upsetting, and the question of whether Duffy's death was self-defense—or revenge—could not be ignored.

For both Whiskey Creek tragedies, it was the motive at the time of death that remained unclear.

When Thompson returned to his office late in the afternoon, the usual daytime calm of a small-town jail had risen to exceed the chaotic level of a bad Saturday night after the last call at the local bars.

The reception area was jammed with media people awaiting his arrival. There were television crews and newspaper reporters representing every city in western Montana from Bozeman to Great Falls. Everyone was talking. Some were trying to collect information from their peers; some had cell phones attached to their ears. All were shouting to be heard over the din.

Two loggers with ZZ Top-looking beards sat on a corner bench, their wrists handcuffed, watching with mild curiosity as the room full of media representatives swirled around them.

When the sheriff entered the office, the news people rushed for a position, swarming around Thompson as they shoved microphones in his face and shouted questions about the killing of the kidnapper. Thompson pushed his way through the group toward his office. "Give me a few minutes here, folks. I'll make a statement for everyone as soon as I get organized."

Closing the door to his office, he shook his head. Apparently, a kidnapping and the violent death of the victim's abductor were more exciting news than the unfortunate drowning of a mixed-blood teenage girl.

The sheriff's secretary, Bev Bradley, was not impressed with the crowd milling about in the reception area. She slipped into Thompson's office, delivering an armload of missed calls, memos, and other messages.

"Hayes, get these jackasses out of my hair before I start shooting them myself. We can't get anything done, and I've never seen so many rude people in my life. You want me to do it?"

Thompson laughed at his feisty receptionist and took the files and documents from her to set them on his desk. "Relax, Bev, I think I can handle it." He tapped the pile of manila folders. "Anything interesting here?"

"Maybe. The coroner's report from the shooting is there. Just the preliminary stuff, not including the state's analysis. The doctor rushed it through and delivered it himself. He scheduled a full-blown autopsy for tomorrow morning in Kalispell and said to have you call him if you wanted to meet and discuss it. He had to sneak it past the clowns out there."

"They're just doing their job, Bev. Just like us. Ask them to circle up in the atrium, and I'll talk to them now. I've got so much to do that I can't take too much time anyway. And Bev? Try to be civil, will you please?"

The press conference was a challenge. The sheriff volunteered few details of the killing and was forced to respond to most questions with a noncommittal, "That's currently under investigation." Mostly, he summarized the basics of the killing without speculating about things like motives or consequences.

He knew the media spin would make a hero of Clayton Cooper, the man who killed the villain who had kidnapped his daughter. In Montana, the killing would be seen as the epitome of heroism and validation of the passionate defense of the Second Amendment. The press would embrace the popular theory that this was why the right to bear arms was sacrosanct and this was why the state of Montana was a bastion of reason in a world gone soft and faint of heart.

44
CHAPTER

Thompson returned to the scene of Duffy Grayson's death the following day.

It was bow-hunting season in the valley, and he knew the little campground on the river was a favorite of hunting archers, who were drawn to the no-fee site at the mouth of Whiskey Creek.

For now, though, the campground was off-limits to the public, wrapped in yellow crime tape, with signage posted warning curiosity-seekers not to trespass on the site. He also knew that word of the killing would attract visitors, so he scheduled his deputies to drive up the Yaak River road to check the scene on every rotating shift.

The peculiar circumstances surrounding the deaths of two family members in the same location continued to bother Thompson, and he was determined to bring both situations to their rightful conclusion. He intended to re-examine each incident and confirm the accuracy of every detail. It was imperative to ascertain that Cooper killed Duffy Grayson in self-defense and not to avenge past hostilities or as punishment for killing the pet deer or kidnapping his daughter.

Hayes Thompson trusted his instincts above all else. And his instincts remained in limbo about this new hero with a troubled past.

***

Thompson sat in his patrol car behind the yellow tape that secured the camping spot. He marveled at the contrast of the ugly crime scene materials in such a beautiful setting.

Beyond the garish boundary tape, the aspen trees were turning yellow, their branches and white-skinned bark silhouetted against the evergreens on the mountainside. On the river bank, the autumn's orange and gold underbrush was a palette of color next to the black waters of the river.

Thompson was not fooled by the beauty. He knew that nature involved death and violence on a daily basis. This was the savage reality of existence in a food-chain ecosystem. His philosophical reverie was interrupted when a white SUV with green trim and lettering pulled into the campground and parked behind him. A uniformed officer stepped out of the US Border Patrol vehicle and strode to the window of Thompson's cruiser.

Border Agent Lloyd Beam had arrived in response to Thompson's request for assistance in recreating the crime scene. Agent Beam was a tall, weathered-looking man who had spent his entire life in the Montana outdoors. As a result, his face was lined and crinkly, which, combined with his prematurely gray hair, made him appear much older than his forty-three years.

The men were friends who shared the common goal of providing law enforcement to a remote area, frequently working together to resolve criminal cases. The vast distances and sparse population of the state encouraged law enforcement agencies to develop cohesive relationships—unlike the sometimes hostile interactions of city law enforcement agencies.

"Hey, Lloyd. Thanks for coming. I'm having a hell of a time getting comfortable with what actually happened here. Like I said, this is a strange one, since this is the exact location where the kidnapper's stepdaughter drowned five months ago. The first death was determined to be accidental, and the second looks like self-defense. To be honest, right now I'm not certain what really happened with either one. I thought maybe an expert tracker could help re-construct."

Starting with Shawnee's death, the sheriff pointed out where her car had been parked, and the logjam where her body had been recovered. The drowning had taken place months ago, and both officers understood the futility of the effort, but Thompson considered the background information critical in his quest to accurately resolve both deaths.

Thompson moved quickly to the current crime scene, giving the Border Patrol Agent an overview of the suspected sequence of events.

"I don't know what I can do here, Hayes. I assume your guys combed the area. We can look, but you can work a crime scene a lot better than I can."

Thompson grunted, "Maybe. My guys say Grayson was carrying the little girl when he came out of the woods across the river." He pointed to the narrow beach where Duffy had been standing. "Cooper's buddy had him in his sights with a .30-.30. When the guy threw the girl in the river, Redmond shot him in the neck. The shot dropped him and Redmond ran to save the girl."

Beam nodded and Thompson continued.

"Grayson was wounded but bulled across the river after Cooper, who was standing right there, by that rock. Everything ended right over here. Pretty grim, huh?"

Beam squatted down to examine the blood-stained ground. He said, "Let's get some boots and check out the other side."

He went to his rig and returned with two pairs of loose-fitting chest waders. They donned the boots and waded to the narrow rocky beach on the other side. Beam found splotches of blood on a river rock and a number of scuff marks pressed into the sand around the stones.

"This must be where he fell when he was shot the first time. He was lying down. You can tell because the blood pooled, rather than dripping."

They worked their way back into the woods, easily following the smashed bushes and broken branches from Duffy's mad charge through the underbrush. As they neared the salt lick, it grew more difficult, the groundcover heavy and the earth dry and hard. Only the occasional heel print allowed them to track back to Duffy's hiding place behind the salt block. Thompson's men had covered the site earlier and secured the evidence from Duffy's basecamp. All that remained was the pile of larch needles that Duffy had used for a bed.

"Looks like the father's explanation was pretty accurate," Beam said to Thompson.

"Yeah. Cooper told us about this spot and some other stuff around the house itself. My deputies checked most of it out yesterday. Things got pretty strange the day before the abduction, Lloyd. The kidnapper killed one of Cooper's pet deer, cut its head off, and staked it up on a stick across from the house."

Beam grimaced. "Sick."

"Yeah. And it could have gotten a lot sicker."

***

Back-tracking through the woods to the Whiskey Creek location, they began crossing the river to return to the parking area.

Halfway across, Beam said, "You know, Hayes, this river can be ten to twelve feet deeper during runoff. I've been thinking about your early spring drowning. Why don't we wade down toward the logjam? The river's so low that now it'll be like looking at a snowfield after the snow has melted and gone away."

"Good idea. We never could search the river. Too much water. We think she waded in from just below her car, underestimated the power of the current, and lost her balance. There was still plenty of ice on the edges of the river. She wouldn't have lasted long once she went down."

The water was vodka clear, every rock and pebble visible in the streambed. Beam walked downstream in the knee-deep riffle, watching the rocks carefully and trying to imagine how easily a young girl could lose her balance and succumb to the cold waters in the raging runoff. Thompson moved to the border agent's side in order to cover more of the river.

Thirty yards from the logjam, which was now an innocent jumble of dry-docked tree trunks resting on the shore of a deep pool, Beam stopped and looked at the river bottom. Something shiny had caught his eye. Without thought, he reached down and dislodged the object that was trapped between two stones. Even before it cleared the surface of the water, he knew it was a wristwatch.

Handing the timepiece to Thompson, Beam said, "Here you go, Hayes. This might be interesting."

CHAPTER

The watch sat on Hayes Thompson's desk, atop the evidence bag from which he had just removed it. The watch bothered the sheriff. It was stainless steel, with a tight, mesh metal band. He examined the clasp that held the two mesh straps together and was not impressed with the construction of the holding mechanism. There were no actual numbers on the face, no digital readouts, nothing to indicate it was waterproof. Made in Denmark, it was obviously for fashion, not function. The hands of the watch were locked in place, a permanent stoppage of time. They read twenty-five minutes past twelve.

The size of the face suggested it was a men's model, but with the thin profile and simplicity favored by some jewelry designers, who knew? *What was the silly wording his wife used, unisex?* In his opinion, it was not worth owning.

It was, however, an interesting discovery.

He didn't think the watch belonged to a rafter or a fisherman. The Whiskey Creek Campground was for takeout, not launch. No one went below the takeout because the logjam was blocking the entrance of sheer walls of rock at the head of a steep canyon.

Thompson knew Shawnee had been close to the location where Lloyd Beam found the watch. There was a good chance that the piece of jewelry might have belonged to the troubled girl.

The sheriff had spoken to Shawnee's mother the day of Duffy Grayson's death. She was going to leave at once to take care of the details concerning the transfer of Duffy's body back to his native Oregon.

Now, three days later, Philomena had still not shown up, and Thompson's efforts to contact her had all been in vain. Hayes was beginning to worry about her failure to arrive as planned. The discovery of the watch made her appearance critical. Shawnee's mother would know if the watch had belonged to her daughter.

If the watch did not belong to Shawnee, it was important that he discover its owner. And he would start with Clayton Kennedy Cooper. Cooper, with his fancy clothes, terrycloth bathrobe, and trendy five o'clock shadow, was the only Yaak Valley male Thompson could think of who might choose a watch based on fashion over function.

***

The next day, Philomena Grayson walked into the Lincoln County Sheriff's Department.

Mrs. Bradley led Philomena to Thompson's desk. Hayes stood when she entered and said, "Mrs. Grayson. I'm sorry about your husband's tragic death. I don't think I've ever had a case where one family experienced two terrible tragedies so close to one another. My heart goes out to you."

Philomena shrugged. The lawman suspected she was either near comatose with prescription drugs or high on illegal drugs and alcohol. He was sympathetic. He had witnessed the pain of devastated wives and mothers far too many times to take offense.

"Are you all right, Mrs. Grayson? Can I help in any way?"

"I'm fine," Philomena answered, "My brothers are going to meet me here. Coming down from Lethbridge. And they'll go back to Oregon on the train with me and Duffy."

She stopped, looking at Thompson, "Don't worry. Neither one of them drink, Sheriff. They'll take care of me."

Thompson nodded and then explained the details of transferring Duffy's body.

When he finished, he said, "Mrs. Grayson, I need to ask you one very important question. Not about your husband. About Shawnee."

When Philomena heard her daughter's name, a look of despair crossed her face, and the eyes buried in her swollen cheeks filled with tears. "What? What do you need to know about my daughter that we haven't already talked about? I can't go there, Sheriff. I'm not ready yet."

"I know. I know how hard it is. Just one question. Did Shawnee own a wristwatch? With a silver band? Like this one?" He lifted the watch off his desk and showed it to the agitated mother.

Philomena looked at the watch as if it were contagious. She shook her head. "No, Shawnee didn't have a watch like that. It's the kind of thing she would have wanted though. A white girl's watch. She couldn't afford a watch like that one." She snorted, half laugh, half sob. "The rest of her family doesn't pay much attention to time. But Shawnee was different. She would have loved a watch like that to make sure she wasn't late. Now, it doesn't matter."

"Are you sure she didn't have one that she hid from you and Duffy?"

"No way. It wouldn't have been worth the abuse she'd have to put up with if Duffy ever saw the thing."

"Thank you. That's all I needed to know. Can I take you to your motel? Is there anything I can do to help with the transfer of your husband's body? They've completed the autopsy now, so you should be able to leave in a day or so, once the coroner's office releases the body. There's a lot of red tape in a shooting death, I'm sorry to say."

"Is there, Sheriff? Even when it's an Indian that dies? An Indian kidnapper? It doesn't seem like it should be any big deal."

"That's not true, Mrs. Grayson. I promise you that I will find out exactly how Duffy died and maybe Shawnee too. I don't care what race people are—if its murder, someone will be accountable."

The look on Philomena's face made him more determined than ever to get to the truth.

Thompson knew he could send the watch to the regional crime lab for forensic analysis. DNA technology was advancing so rapidly that a genetic match might be possible. He knew that Cooper's DNA was in the database. But the process was always lengthy, and he wasn't sure how helpful it would be if a watch had spent five months in the river.

The alternative was the old-fashioned way. The veteran law officer could read people like billboards, and he was not above bluffing his way for information if he suspected someone had committed the crime.

When a quick internet search of the manufacturer's website listed the watch as a man's model, he decided to try figuring things out his way before sending the timepiece off for weeks or even months of testing.

Two days later, there was a message from the sheriff's department on Cooper's answering machine. Apologizing for the poor timing, Sheriff Thompson asked if Cooper could contact him as soon as possible. The sheriff needed to visit with him to tie up some "loose ends."

Cooper groaned.

He punched in the number that the sheriff had left on the machine, and the extension took him straight to Hayes Thompson's desk.

"Sheriff Thompson? It's Clayton Cooper returning your call. What can I do for you?"

"Hello, Mr. Cooper. Would you mind bringing Ms. Hailstone with you and stopping by the office for a few minutes tomorrow?

I've got some paperwork to complete here, and I thought if you and she were able to come together, we could wrap things up in a hurry and let you get on with your lives. Say tomorrow at eleven?"

"Sheriff, nothing would make me happier than being able to get on with my life. But I'm still trying to get myself together. Besides, Ang has been filling in at the camera store, and I know she's working for someone tomorrow. Can we make it the following day? Same time? Hopefully, you'll get much more coherent answers from both of us."

"I understand. Let me check my schedule."

Cooper listened to the rustle of papers and the turning of calendar pages. He heard the sheriff mumbling to himself.

"I can make a change or two and free up an hour on Friday. That'll work for me. Will you contact Ms. Hailstone and ask her to join us? Let me know if she can't come along."

"I'll do that. If you don't hear from me, we'll be there at 11 o'clock.

***

Cooper was feeling much better by early Thursday morning. Five days of sleeping-pill-induced rest had provided the necessary escape from consciousness. Constant ice packs had reduced the swelling and discoloration in his face, and a local doctor had reset the broken nose to closely resemble the original.

He still thought about Mac and her evil abductor every waking minute.

He and Angelina were trying to cope. She called him each night, and they had easy conversations about the weather, fly fishing, and photography. Neither mentioned Duffy or Shawnee unless it was related to their discussions about Cooper's family.

Cooper had spent the week mostly reading and napping. The literature was light and easy, non-threatening entertainment without mayhem or bloodshed. "Therapeutic reading" Cooper called it when Angie asked about his days. At least twice a day, he took a short walk to fill his lungs with mountain air.

The two of them were planning to spend a few days together in Glacier National Park. They would meet with Hayes Thompson first and then drive back to Whitefish for lunch. They would bring day packs and then head to the park to stay at one of the lodges where they could go hiking. The outing would allow Cooper to show Angelina the places he took his photo class students where they could soak in the spectacular autumn scenery.

It was the best way they could think of to begin the healing process.

***

As Cooper and Angie walked into the office the following morning, Bev Bradley said hello and asked them to wait at the front desk while she let the sheriff know they had arrived.

Minutes later, Hayes Thompson greeted the two of them and thanked them for coming.

"This won't take long. Ms. Hailstone, would you mind waiting out here while I visit with Mr. Cooper? It should only be a few minutes, and then I'll ask you to switch places."

Angie and Cooper exchanged a glance.

Cooper shrugged. "Whatever you say."

Thompson led the way into his office. Angie looked around the reception area and sat down on one of the benches.

In his office, Thompson nodded at Cooper to sit in the chair in front of his desk.

"Mr. Cooper, I'm going to get right to the point of this little meeting. When we were investigating the scene of Duffy Grayson's death, we came across something that might help us close the door on Shawnee McAllister's drowning."

296

Cooper said, "I thought the door was already closed on that. Her drowning was an accident. You know that."

"I know. But something's turned up." He slid the center drawer of his desk open and lifted out the watch, framing it with his hand as he showed it to Cooper. He watched his visitor's face intently, looking for his reaction, his senses entirely focused on the other man's response.

Cooper stared at the piece of jewelry. His face was blank, unchanged in any way unless it was a hint of confusion in his eyes.

As the silence hanging between them began to grow uncomfortable, Thompson sensed a change in Cooper's confusion, as if a spark of understanding had finally forced itself through the fog of his physical and emotional exhaustion.

The reaction puzzled the sheriff. It was obviously not Cooper's wristwatch. But maybe, in the pause that allowed each of them to assess what was happening, Cooper had some subconscious recognition that it might be familiar.

"Do you recognize this watch, Mr. Cooper? Have you seen it before?"

"No," Cooper answered. "I don't recognize the watch."

Thompson said nothing, looking at Cooper and waiting. Cooper did not respond. Once again, the silence grew uncomfortable.

"I don't recognize it, Sheriff. What do you want me to say? It could have belonged to Shawnee. It looks pretty beat up. Has it been in the water?"

"Yes. We found it in the river. I hope you're telling me the truth. Is it Shawnee's watch, Mr. Cooper? I'm going to send it to the lab in Missoula. We'll figure it out. If you recognize it, you better tell me now. I don't think another failure to provide information would work out too well for you."

"I'm not a liar, Sheriff. I've never seen that watch. It could be Shawnee's. There were lots of things I didn't know about her." He hesitated, "You misled me, Sheriff. I thought this was going to be about Duffy. Shawnee's drowning was an accident."

"I'm sorry if you misunderstood, Mr. Cooper. I've got a job to do. I take it seriously. I'm just doing my job."

"Yeah, right. Can we go now?"

"Not yet. I need to visit with Ms. Hailstone for a minute or two. Bev has taken her to another office. You can wait in the front."

"Why, Sheriff? Angie was nowhere near the shooting."

"I know. This is just routine follow-up. I'm sure you'll be on your way to the mountains in a few minutes. Meanwhile, like I said, I've got a job to do."

Cooper wished he could have spoken to Angie before her meeting, to make sure their background stories were the same. Who knew what Thompson might trick her into saying? If she admitted that they had lied about her spending the night with Cooper, his alibi was shot.

He didn't want Duffy's death to bring Shawnee's drowning out of the closet.

***

"Sorry to keep you waiting, Ms. Hailstone. Thank you for your patience."

"No problem, Sheriff. I know you're a busy man."

"Busy," he answered, "but not always productive."

Angie smiled to show that she knew the feeling and waited for him to continue.

"Just a few questions, and we'll get you on your way. I understand you're going out of town for a few days?"

Angie nodded her answer, and Thompson asked some questions about the timing of events on the day of the kidnapping that Angie had answered earlier. After several minutes of probing about Duffy Grayson's death, she began to wonder about the line of questioning.

"Sheriff, I've answered all these questions before, for both you and your deputies. Is it really necessary for us to go through the same thing again and again?"

"Sometimes witnesses leave out important details. Repetition is the only way to confirm that we have all the facts. It's standard procedure when we're trying to reconstruct what took place at a crime scene."

Thompson had been studying the girl, and somewhere in his subconscious, an idea began to form. Loose threads, fragments of thoughts, and intuitions came together, and a quick hunch blossomed into an idea. Before he knew he was going to do it, the sheriff decided to take a chance.

"What I can't figure out, Ms. Hailstone, is how something that belongs to you. . ." he reached into the unbuttoned breast pocket of his uniform shirt and held the watch in front of Angie's face, "could have ended up in the river when you and Tasha never left the Whiskey Bend Ranch until the entire kidnapping was over."

Angie stared at the suspended watch. The color drained from her face, and her eyes took on the panicked look of a cornered animal. For a long moment, she was unable to speak, struggling to overcome her constricting throat.

Sheriff Thompson was taken aback by her reaction to his unplanned ruse. Even so, he remained silent. He held the watch like a hypnotist, his face impassive, as he waited for the woman to respond. His mind was churning, clicking half-formed thoughts into their proper order and trying to process Angie's reaction into the equation. Suddenly, the pieces came together. And he knew.

Angie croaked out, "That's not my watch. There must be some mistake."

"There's no mistake, Ms. Hailstone. And we both know it. In fact, I have proof that it's your watch," the sheriff lied, "and the sooner you admit it, the easier this will be on you. Trying to hide something only gets you in more trouble. It only makes everything worse. How did your watch get into the river?"

Angie dropped her face into her hands, covering her eyes and nose. The room was silent. Hayes Thompson waited.

"You're right. It is my watch. I have no idea how it got into the river. It's been missing for a long time. Maybe someone stole it. Maybe Shawnee stole it that night at Cooper's house."

"Angelina," the sheriff said softly. "Nobody stole it. But you're right; you have been missing it for a long time. Since the night Shawnee drowned. You lost it that night, didn't you? You were there when she drowned, weren't you, Angie? Did you kill Shawnee McAllister?"

Angie dissolved into tears, sobbing with great gasps, wracking for air. She put her face in her hands again, shaking her head in denial.

"Sheriff, you've got to believe me," she sobbed. "I didn't mean to. It was an accident. I wanted to stop her; I really did. It was an accident. She wanted to die. She WANTED to die!"

"Here," Thompson handed her a box of tissues, "use this." He pulled a small tape recorder from the desk drawer. "I'm going to tape you so there are no mistakes here. I'm going to read you your rights first, okay?"

Angie nodded.

After he read the Miranda Rights, he said, "Okay. Take a deep breath and settle down. I believe you. She wanted to die. I believe everything you say. Why don't you walk me through what happened that night? Slow and easy. It's going to be all right now. Just tell me everything that happened. Everything's going to be okay."

Angie drew several shuddering breaths as she tried to gain control. She blew her nose with one tissue and dabbed at her eyes with another.

When she began to talk she spoke in gasping fragments, a desperate effort to exorcize five months of repressed emotional torment. "I left Coop's house. It was really awkward. Shawnee was. . . crazy. She. . . went berserk, scratched Clayton's face, just went crazy."

As the story unfolded, Angie began to settle down, and her words developed into a less chaotic pattern.

"I told Coop I couldn't stay. The situation was so bizarre. We were having such a nice time together. Everything was perfect. Out of nowhere, this crazy girl showed up. I was in the bedroom when she came into the house. When she saw me, she just freaked out. I didn't know what was going on. Coop never told me there was a girl stalking him.

"Anyway, she saw me and freaked. She attacked Cooper like a crazy person. Scratching and clawing. It took forever to settle her down. Finally, she just lost consciousness. I had to leave.

"It was snowing when I left the ranch. The girl was still passed out. I drove out of the valley, just thinking about everything. About how weird it was. About how much I liked Cooper. I must have driven for at least a half-hour, maybe more. Just thinking. Finally, I realized that I didn't want him to be alone with that girl. It was the first time I knew that I was in love with the guy. I started to think about her staying at his house.

"I turned around, drove back to the ranch. The snow was falling. The roads were empty, and it was just so beautiful."

She took another deep breath.

"When I got back to Cooper's, I saw Shawnee's car parked just outside the entry gate to the house. She was inside the car, just sitting behind the steering wheel. I slowed way down, and we made eye contact. I pulled my truck into the entryway to Coop's, and she sped off down the road.

"I didn't know what to do. It was so strange. So I flipped a U-turn and followed her taillights. She only went a short distance and then pulled into the driveway by the bridge. I parked on the side of the road and waited a few minutes wondering what to do. Then, I walked down into the campground, thinking she and I needed to talk. When I got near the river, I saw her car. She was sitting on the hood with her back leaning against the windshield, staring at the river.

"I called her name so that I wouldn't surprise her. She looked back at me, didn't answer. It was like she made up her mind when she saw me, and she slid off the hood of the car and waded into the river. Just after she got to the water, she looked over her shoulder and flipped me off.

"I screamed at her to stop and waded in after her. It was so cold. So cold. She stopped when it was waist deep. I got to her and grabbed her arm. We wrestled for a second in the freezing cold water. That must have been when I lost the watch.

"We were both screaming and crying. I don't know what I was saying, I don't know what she was saying. She pushed me away, and I lost my balance, slipping on the rocks. She waded into the middle of the river where the current was the strongest and had taken out the ice."

Angie paused, gulping the lump out of her throat. "I let her go. I was too cold to stop her, too scared to try to save her. I was cold. She just. . . sank down and disappeared in the river."

The tears came again. "It was my fault. I should have tried to save her. But I let her go, and she drowned. She drowned!"

Angie sobbed, unable to continue. Thompson let her cry for a while, as he sat in silence, thinking about her story. When she regained control, he asked gently, "What happened then, Angie? What did you do next?"

"I waded out of the river. I could barely walk; I was so cold. I'm sure I was hypothermic. I got to my truck and took my clothes off, wrapped my legs in my sleeping bag, and found a dry top in my backpack. I turned the heater on full blast and just sat there at the side of the road crying, trying to get my head together and warm up. I thought about going back to Cooper and climbing in bed with him to get warm. It sounded so good. But I was afraid to tell him about Shawnee, afraid of what might happen to us.

"So I just drove home. I knew no one would know that I was there. I knew that Shawnee was gone. I. . . just drove home."

Thompson let her rest for a minute. When she seemed capable of responding again, he asked, "So you lied about spending the night with Cooper. Why did you do that?"

"Because he asked me to. And because it protected both of us for the night of the drowning."

"Does Cooper know anything about this?"

"No! Nothing. He has no idea that I went back. No idea that I saw Shawnee again that night."

Now it was Thompson's turn to rub his temples. *What a mess he thought, what do I do now?*

"Sheriff Thompson? What's going to happen to me? Will I be blamed for Shawnee? Will I go to jail?"

"I don't know, Angie. I've got to talk with the prosecutor's office to see how we should handle things. If what you say is true, I don't know about them filing murder charges. On the other hand, there may be some accountability for not trying to prevent Shawnee's death. We'll just have to wait and see."

"Are you going to arrest me now? Should I get a lawyer?"

"I'm not going to arrest you right now. But yes, you probably should get a lawyer as soon as possible. And I'm going to ask you not to leave town. You and Mr. Cooper will have to cancel your trip. And don't be surprised if you see patrol cars around your place every once in a while. We'll need to keep an eye on you until this whole thing is resolved.

"Let's end this for today. I think we've been here long enough." Thompson stood to indicate the interview was over. Angie Hailstone continued to sit at the chair before the desk.

"Sheriff Thompson? What am I going to tell Cooper?"

The sheriff looked at her with an even gaze. "Tell him the truth. I'm sure it's been hard to live a lie."

***

Minutes later, Angie repeated the startling confession to her lover. As she told her story, he desperately tried to comprehend her sobbing monologue.

The confession rocked Cooper. Never, under any circumstances, had this scenario entered his mind. The unexpected turn of events astonished him.

And yet, somewhere deep within his soul, he felt something akin to relief. Cooper's perception of Shawnee's death had weighed heavy on his own conscious ever since Duffy Grayson's accusation that he had caused her drowning. Now he knew it wasn't his fault.

"Honey, you didn't kill her. No one could have stopped her from doing what she was going to do. She was sick. She was mentally unbalanced. Why didn't you tell me about this before? I could have helped. We could have figured out something to cover everything up. We could have handled everything."

"I was scared. I've never been so scared. I just wanted it to go away. And it did. I wouldn't have let them blame you, sweetheart. I swear, if they would have blamed you, I would have told them. Once you suggested that we tell them that we were together all night, I knew everything was going to be okay. We were each other's protection, and saying we were together connected us in so many ways."

Angie was talking faster now, not wanting her courage to fail her before she could finish.

"Don't you see? It gave us both an alibi. It made us partners. We actually needed each other."

"But. . . you seemed so uncomfortable about lying."

"I was! I am. I couldn't lie to Thompson when he showed me the watch. That's what ruined everything."

Cooper had forgotten all about the watch with the bombshell of Angie's revelation.

"The watch. That's how Thompson figured this out. It was yours! I thought I had seen it before. When he showed it to me, I thought it was Shawnee's. If you'd have told me, sweetie, we could have put together a story. There's no way that watch in the river makes you a murderer."

"I didn't know. I didn't know when I lost the watch. I only wore it when I wasn't on the mountain working. Besides, it wouldn't have worked. They would have found out, and then we'd both be in trouble."

"Angie, we need to get you an attorney as soon as possible. There's no way in hell this is your fault. I don't even think your confession is valid without a lawyer present."

"He taped it. He has it all word-for-word."

"I know. But this wasn't a crime. We need a lawyer. Right now," he said as they pulled into the parking lot of Angie's apartment complex.

Then he repeated, "Right now."

They went into the apartment and began to search the Northwest Montana phonebook for an attorney.

DESTINY'S ARROW

46
CHAPTER

Alexander Bondy, Attorney at Law, was the first Kalispell lawyer to list Criminal Defense as a specialty in the Northwest Montana phonebook. Cooper made the call to Bondy's office and was surprised when the attorney answered the phone himself.

Cooper identified himself, said he was with Angelina and was speaking on her behalf. Two minutes into a rambling description of her dilemma, Bondy cut him off in mid-sentence.

"Excuse me, Mr. Cooper, but is she with you now? Can she talk?"

"I beg your pardon?"

"Talk. Can she speak? Is she a mute?"

"No. Not at all, I. . ."

"Good. Put her on the phone, please. Let me speak to her directly."

"Uhhh. . . okay. One second."

Cooper covered the phone with his hand and, looking at Angie, rolled his eyes.

"He wants to talk to you," he said.

Angie took the phone.

"Are you the young lady Mr. Cooper was speaking for?"

"Yes."

"I take it this whole thing is related to the recent kidnapping that has been in all the newspapers?"

"Yes."

"And there is a connection between this kidnapper killing and the young girl that drowned up in the Arrow several months ago?"

"Yes."

"And, if I understood your talkative friend correctly, your need for hiring an attorney is related to the drowning only?"

"Yes, sir."

"Did you drown that girl?"

Angie gasped at the lawyer's blunt question, struggling to respond.

"Ms. Hailstone, if you want me to help you, I have to know exactly what happened. I know my questions can be difficult. But you must get control of yourself so that we can assess the situation. Your answers are critical because this conversation is a two-way interview. When we are finished, you may not want me to represent you, and just as importantly, I may decide not to accept you as a client.

"Now," he continued. "Drowning someone is not an easy task. I'm sure you can recall whether or not you held this girl under the water until she stopped breathing. I must know what happened before I can help. Did you drown that girl?"

"Well, I didn't hold her head underwater. But I didn't *not* drown her either. I knew she was going to be in real trouble. I'm a trained lifeguard, and I couldn't stop her. I watched her go under, watched her disappear, and I couldn't help her. I was freezing and exhausted and scared. . . but I think the sheriff believes I killed her."

"Young lady, not risking your own life to save someone from drowning is not a crime. Hardly admirable, of course, and incomprehensible to a man like Hayes Thompson, but certainly not murder.

"I think I can help you. If you want to bring your friend and come down to my office, we can discuss this situation, and you can decide whether or not you wish to hire me on your behalf. I'm on the second floor of the Chandler Building, above the hardware store. I should be done with my afternoon walk by 2:30. Why don't we meet here at 3 P.M.? I'm looking forward to meeting both of you. Good day."

The line went dead.

***

Alexander Bondy was the only lawyer in northwestern Montana who wore a bowtie to work every day of the week. It was a habit he had acquired years before when he had a small private practice outside of Boston, in Danvers, Massachusetts. He considered the bowtie an identity piece in a world full of mass-produced attorneys.

Even without the bowtie, Bondy had always been different. His body was a confusion of assorted parts. He was a few inches over five feet tall, with bony shoulders, a narrow chest, and a tidy potbelly. His torso appeared to be elongated and was attached to a pair of short, exceedingly bowed legs. The resulting visual impression was that of a mutant dwarf.

Now in his late sixties, he was mostly bald with a fringe of course, gray hair bristling in a semi-circle around his head. A matching mustache had been around for at least as long as the bowties.

Cooper and Angie met Mr. Bondy that afternoon. The meeting left little doubt as to the lawyer's unique approach to the law.

"Young lady, if what you're telling me is true, I can assure you that there is no lengthy prison sentence in your future. As far as I'm concerned, there is no conclusive evidence to prove that you committed a crime. A piece of your jewelry found in the Yaak River does not make you a murderer. Any competent defense attorney could destroy that insinuation in a heartbeat. The only thing that Hayes Thompson—who, by the way, is a very good man—has going for him, is his sometimes overzealous commitment to the moral elements of the law. That and a questionably legal confession extorted from you this morning."

310

"But I let her drown. I'm a lifeguard, and I didn't try to save her."

"No. Trying to save her would probably have killed you both. You had to make a choice, and you made it. In a court of law, I'm willing to bet that you did not kill her. Period. Now, in God's court, it may be a different story. But that's between you and God. In a Montana court of law, I think we can get you off."

Rising from his desk, he said, "If you're telling me the truth, I can assure you that Shawnee McAllister's death was not your fault. I suggest that you accept that and believe it. If you do, there is no jury in the state that will convict you of murder."

Encouraged by the attorney's perspective regarding the drowning, Angie left the meeting allowing herself to wonder if the feisty lawyer might be able to exorcize the guilt that had haunted her since Shawnee's death.

Cooper's reaction to Alexander Bondy was not nearly as positive.

"What a dick. Can you believe that guy?" Cooper asked as they walked down the stairs away from Bondy's second-floor office.

Angie answered, "What do you mean? I thought he was great. I feel better than I have in months."

"You feel better because you finally got all that crap off your mind. If you'd told me the truth from the beginning, you'd have been just fine."

"Cooper, you know that's bullshit. Don't forget that you're the one who asked me to lie to Sheriff Thompson about spending the night together. How can you fault me for not wanting to tell you what really happened?"

"You're not going to hire that guy, are you?"

"Yes, I am. For the first time since that night, I feel like there might be a chance to make things right."

Cooper hesitated a second and then said, "You're right, honey. Everything is going to be okay. But you've got to admit—he's an ornery old bastard."

"Maybe. I thought he was great." She glanced at her lover. "No bullshit is kind of refreshing."

"Umm," Cooper grunted. "Sometimes a little bullshit is okay. That guy is beyond blunt."

"Maybe. But I like him."

***

Bondy leaned back in his chair, reflecting on his conversation with Angelina. He thought the girl was telling him the truth. He wondered what Sheriff Thompson's reaction to his potential client would be. Hayes had been around as long as Alexander, and many Lincoln County residents hired Kalispell attorneys, so they knew each other well. They had locked horns a time or two but never with the animosity that marked many law enforcement and defense attorney relationships.

Alexander knew one thing was certain—if Hayes Thompson really thought Angelina had killed that girl, he would do everything in his power to prove it.

CHAPTER

It was almost midnight, and Thompson was tired. He sat at his desk and stared at the manila file lying before him. He had just completed reading it for the third time that day. The file was thick with documents and notes. He had rubber-banded Shawnee McAllister's case file with Duffy Grayson's kidnapping and shooting file, based on what he believed was the common thread that connected them: Clayton Cooper.

Thompson believed the girl. Although he considered her actions that night deplorable, he wasn't certain that she had committed a punishable crime. Especially in Montana, when the deceased was a mentally disturbed teenager whose stepfather was a convicted felon, and now a confirmed kidnapper and an attempted murderer.

He picked up the file and thumbed through until he came across his notes from the morgue following Duffy Grayson's identification of Shawnee's body.

He scanned the page until he came to the paragraph he wanted to read again. It was a quote from Duffy. It read, "He killed her. Maybe he didn't throw her in the water, but he killed her just the same."

Hayes tapped his pencil on the desktop. He smiled to himself, bemused at the irony of the tough outlaw's moral observation. *You know what, Duffy*, he thought. *Maybe. Or. . . maybe not.*

***

Cooper and Angie lay in the warm bed, Angie snuggled against him in her usual spoon position.

Cooper's eyes were open, and his quiet body camouflaged his churning mind as he tried not to awaken the woman attached to his backside. *This isn't working,* he thought. *How can I really love a girl who could let someone drown?*

The girl behind him stirred, her hands sliding down his chest to his midsection. Then lower. He closed his eyes, forcing out the clutter in his head and thought about the joys of a needy young lover. As he felt his body responding to her gentle caresses, he rolled to face his partner, smiling to himself.

***

The resolution of Duffy Grayson's death was far less complicated than the reopening of Shawnee's drowning. Both the prosecutor's and the public's reaction to Cooper saving his daughter—and his own self-defense—were overwhelmingly supportive. The editorial pages of newspapers throughout the northwest were inundated with letters supporting Cooper's actions. Most letters included what the writer would have done to any kidnapper foolish enough to threaten his own family.

Cooper was a hero among the residents of the Yaak. Once the butt of subtle "LL Beaner" jokes and comments, he was now lauded for having the courage to protect his family. Montana rednecks and tree huggers alike agreed that they would choose the same route as Clayton Cooper if they ever found themselves in similar circumstances.

Meanwhile, the Lincoln County Prosecutor's Office was able to keep Angie's situation out of the public eye. It was an internal investigation, and Hayes Thompson continued to wrestle with his decision regarding the criminal intent of Angie's involvement in Shawnee McAllister's drowning.

Thompson's role in the decision-making process was critical. Hayes was one of the most respected figures in local law enforcement, and the county attorney, a soon-to-retire politician of less hardy stock, usually deferred decisions on controversial criminal cases to the sheriff.

***

A day after agreeing to represent Angelina Hailstone, Bondy set up a meeting with Sheriff Thompson. The two veterans of the northwest Montana legal community met at the Huckleberry Restaurant in downtown Whitefish.

"Hello, Hayes. Long time no see."

Thompson smiled, "Yeah. No offense, Alexander, but for me, that's usually a good thing."

Bondy chuckled. "Thanks for meeting with me. I want to talk to you about my client, Angelina Hailstone."

Hayes raised his eyebrows in surprise. Bondy's practice the past few years involved mostly low profile driving-under-the-influence cases or disputed misdemeanors. Once in a while, a desperate—and thick-skinned—felon would persuade him to take on a case.

Thompson also knew that the very fact that Alexander Bondy was representing Ms. Hailstone could have an influence on whether or not the prosecutor's office decided to file charges against Bondy's client.

"You're representing her, Alexander? Why?"

"Because I don't think she broke the law. This is why I am a defense attorney. It is one of those rare opportunities to defend an innocent client. If what she tells me is true, and I think it is, she failed a test of courage. Such an act may not be admirable—not everyone is as brave as you are Hayes—but I don't think it makes her a criminal either."

"She let a girl drown, Alexander. She stated in her confession that she knew exactly what was happening."

"So she tells me. But I think the trauma of witnessing such a death, and a guilty conscience regarding her failure to do what she feels she should have done, have clouded her perception of innocence or guilt. And, by the way, that confession that you

315

extracted is of questionable value. You took advantage of her, Sheriff. That's not like you."

"It's exactly like me. My job is to find the bad guy. If I can prove that she was responsible for that girl's death, I'll get her."

"If she's responsible, you should get her. Meanwhile, as an old friend, let me just tell you, there's no way a jury will convict her of murder with this much ambiguity around the death. I can get her off. Do you know what I mean?"

"I understand your big words. You don't have to walk me through."

Thompson finished his cup of coffee and looked at his friend. Standing, he dropped several crumpled bills on the tabletop. "Alexander, you're her attorney, and you're a damn good one. But you're not the judge and jury. You can't decide whether she's guilty or innocent. Think about that. Meanwhile, I'll do the same."

Sheriff Thompson drove back to the office, lost in thought.

He knew that Alexander Bondy was probably right. Convicting Angie of murdering Shawnee McAllister with what he had right now was a long shot. He had some ideas about a vague motive, but his dilemma remained—was the failure to save Shawnee intentional? Or unavoidable?

Thompson had lived in Montana his entire life. He understood the mindset of his neighbors. Those neighbors, who felt so strongly about Clayton Cooper's brave rescue of his abducted daughter, would not convict the local hero's girlfriend unless the prosecution had a slam-dunk case against her.

***

It was late September, and Angie's status as a potential murder defendant was still yet to be determined.

For Cooper's lover, the tension grew on a daily basis. The short-lived relief that Angelina had experienced when she unlocked the secret burden of her conscience was replaced by the fear of the

316

consequences of that very act. Further exacerbating Angie's stress level, she began to sense a subtle change in her relationship with Cooper.

The frequent phone calls were shorter now, and they lacked the easy intimacy that had developed between them. Cooper had suddenly immersed himself in his photography and was making fewer trips to town. He still came on weekends, but he arrived on Saturday rather than his Friday night arrivals that once marked the beginning of their long weekend together.

Even in bed, she sensed a change.

When she asked him about it, he brushed off her concerns. "Honey, we're still dealing with all the emotional trauma of everything we've been through in the last six months. That and waiting for the prosecutor's office to make a decision has been hard on both of us. Nothing has changed between us. I'm just really busy right now, trying to get some good pictures, and getting ready for my class. Don't make everything more difficult by making a big deal out of something that doesn't exist."

But it did exist, and Angie knew it.

***

Cooper was looking forward to teaching another semester at the community college. He had remained in touch with several of his students from his earlier classes, including Gun-Marie Ericksen and Zoey Belford. Both had re-enrolled in his fall semester class to take advantage of the photo opportunities in Glacier National Park during the autumn leaf season.

Several times during the summer, he had taken the two girls on day trips into the backcountry to work with them on their nature photography. The three of them spent hours hiking the park's trails and talking. Cooper enjoyed the girls' company, and they played along with his innocent banter. It was fun for all of them, and Cooper was proud of their photographs, mostly landscapes that were nearly as good as his own.

Cooper used the trips to work on his portrait photography. Both of the girls were flattered by his insistence that they serve as models as well as apprentice photographers. Gun-Marie was the most photogenic, and Zoey deferred to her as the primary model whenever possible.

"Come on, Zo, you need to get in some of these, too. I need a dark-haired beauty to contrast with the Scandinavian Mountain Queen."

"No way. I'm not going to even try to compete with that."

But with a little persuasion from Cooper and Gun-Marie, Zoey would reluctantly agree to pose for a photo or two, and Cooper began to build a small portfolio of his two models with the spectacular Montana mountain ranges as background. They were both flattered by the attention and secretly pleased with the process, expecting that Cooper's black and white portraits would be more glamorous than the mountain landscapes that they themselves had produced.

Occasionally, the girls would try to get Cooper to pose for them, but he always refused. "You guys know I'm a control freak," he joked. "I have to be behind the camera."

After the field trips, Cooper would drive the girls back to town, usually stopping for coffee or burgers along the way. The three of them enjoyed the camaraderie.

When Angie asked Cooper about the summer field trips, Cooper never mentioned that only two students were involved. Nor did he show Angie the black and white portfolio he was working on, telling himself that he would share his work with her when he had completed the project.

Once the new semester began, the days flew by. Angie kept busy with her job and the occasional Sunday visit to the Yaak. She phoned her attorney often to check on the status of the pending charges against her.

***

Bondy was beside himself with frustration. The intricacy of the moral dilemma surrounding his client's case continued to delay decisions about possible charges. Hayes Thompson had requested more time to process evidence and revisit the drowning case. Finally, the lawyer snapped, and it was with typical Bondyesque fury. Descending on the prosecutor's office, he demanded a meeting with the lame-duck county prosecutor.

"Mr. Prosecutor, if you don't make a decision immediately concerning the status of my client, I'm going to petition the court to dismiss this case. This is ridiculous. Weeks of stalling while Hayes Thompson tries to drum up a charge is unconscionable. Due process has been ignored. No, violated! Violated. By God, you make a decision, or I swear I'll petition the court to wipe the slate clean!"

"Alexander, be reasonable. This is an unusual situation. We have moral issues to resolve, ethical dilemmas to consider. Hayes is just trying to find a definitive solution."

"Definitive, my ass. You've either got a case or you don't. You know if you try to prosecute my client for murder, you won't have a chance in hell. She's not a murderer. Not first degree, not second degree, not any degree. And Hayes knows it. He's stalling, hoping for my client to break or have a mental meltdown. Well, it's not going to happen. We will never confess to any aspect of foul play." Bondy's face and bald head had turned bright red. "This is ridiculous! It's harassment. I won't let my client be tortured like this."

"Calm down, Alexander. Maybe we can plea bargain this thing. You must admit that letting someone take her own life represents a certain degree of culpability. We are still trying to determine how accountable Angelina Hailstone should be."

"Well, you better make that determination right now. Because if you don't, I'm going to send her back east. You cannot destroy my client's life this way."

319

"Okay, okay. I get your point." He took a deep breath. "Plead your client guilty of manslaughter, and we'll have her out of prison in two years. Maybe less if she behaves herself. You get her back on the street quickly, and I get Hayes off my ass. Maybe."

"Manslaughter? You must be joking. She didn't kill anyone. I won't let her plead that she did just to get Hayes out of your hair. Right now, you've got me on your ass. And that's a damn sight worse than Hayes Thompson, who we both know is a nice guy. I, on the other hand, am a surly, aggravating son-of-a-bitch. And if this goes on any longer than it already has, you'll need new words to describe the extent of my orneriness."

The prosecutor sighed. "I'm sure that's true, Alexander, but I cannot fail to file charges against a potential criminal just because of the excessive unpleasantness that you can bring to the table. We are all servants of justice here, committed to resolving issues in an equitable manner. I know you understand that."

Bondy softened his words, "My friend, you've been around long enough to know that I am not sympathetic to criminals. I'll represent them to the best of my ability if I must. I took an oath swearing to do so. But I prefer to make a more positive contribution to society. If I think a client is innocent, I'll fight to the death. But who are we to judge how accountable she is under these circumstances? I don't know that her inability to prevent this death is as reprehensible as she herself seems to think it is. It might be. But I do know that the McAllister girl's drowning is not in any way a murder. I think it was exactly as you determined prior to Hayes extracting illegal information from my client. An accident. That's my honest feeling about all of this."

The County Attorney, tapping his pen on the desk pad, looked at the old man seated across the desk and considered his options. Although he feared Hayes Thompson's wrath, he feared Alexander Bondy's even more.

Leaning toward the attorney, he said, "Reckless endangerment, Alexander. Ninety days in jail, here in the local facility. One year of probation. No other charges or issues, unless Thompson finds irrefutable evidence that your client premeditated the drowning."

Bondy didn't hesitate. "Forty-five days. Six months' probation. It's more than she deserves."

"You are a son of a bitch, Alexander," he sighed. "Okay. Done."

Alexander Bondy reached a bony hand across the desk, to seal the deal. "It's the right thing, Mr. Prosecutor. A pleasure doing business with you."

"Yeah, right. I feel like I just fought fifteen rounds with Muhammad Ali."

Bondy chuckled. "I saw Ali fight Joe Frasier in Madison Square Garden. You'd never have lasted that long with him."

***

Angie accepted the plea bargain with stoic indifference.

Alexander Bondy negotiated a brief internment delay, allowing her to help the camera store find a temporary replacement, and she began serving her sentence in the Flathead Correction Center in October.

In a matter of days, it was apparent that her incarceration would be more like a rehab visit than a jail sentence. And the stressed-out Angelina Hailstone embraced the system that wanted to help her cope.

CHAPTER

48

The penal system administrator responsible for female prisoners and their mental health was Dr. Karen Alton, who was eager to work with the new inmate. Angelina's rehabilitation program began with an intensive background interview and a psychological evaluation.

Dr. Alton was tall and angular, so slender that she appeared to be borderline anorexic. In her early forties, she would have been attractive except for the angular lines on her face. She had a narrow, pointed nose above a narrow, pointed chin. Her short-cropped brown hair framed her face to just below her chin line. Cut shorter in the back than the front, the result was two more sharp points where the hair stopped below her ears.

Dr. Alton's mind was as sharp as her body, and throughout her career within the Montana penal system, her probing nature had uncovered so many dark secrets that she had come to expect some form of dysfunctional mistreatment in every female prisoner's background.

The two women had been together most of the morning, filling out forms and getting to know one another. Dr. Alton worked slowly, trying to build trust with her patient. Up to this point, most of their conversations had centered on Shawnee's drowning and Duffy Grayson's violent death. The doctor began to suspect deeper issues in her new patient.

"Angelina, tell me about your father. What was he like? What kind of relationship did you have with him?"

"My father was wonderful. He was handsome and charming and loved both of us kids. He worked for the State Department as a U.S.

diplomat. I was raised in South Africa. He always wanted to spend more time with my brother and me, but he was too good at what he did to find a job that would allow him more free time."

"Do you see him often?"

"No. He died when I was eleven. It was the worst thing that ever happened to me. My mother couldn't handle his passing. She started drinking and never seemed to recover. Most days, she was drunk when we got home from school. She was great when she was sober. But as we grew up, she wasn't sober very often. She's still alive, but I haven't seen her for a while now. She still drinks vodka on the rocks because she thinks people will believe its ice water. She's in her early fifties now, but she looks like she's seventy. She's hard to talk to. You have to catch her early in the morning."

"Does she come to visit?"

"No. She's never been to Montana. She doesn't even know about my situation. After my daddy died, we were never very close."

The doctor was curious. Angie had mentioned her affairs with the college professor and Clayton Cooper, and the doctor sensed that there might be a psychological reason for her attraction to older men.

"So you loved your father a lot?"

"He was the most special person in my life. The only person I have ever trusted completely."

"What about your brother?"

"Jonathan? He's five years older than I am. When my daddy died and mom turned into an alcoholic, Jonathan became my caretaker by default. I think he resented the responsibility; he didn't like the restrictions taking care of me had on his social life."

"You mean he was like a surrogate father to you?"

"Oh, no. More like a reluctant babysitter. He was sixteen when my father passed, and my mom was gone a lot trying to drown her sorrow. I think having to take care of me cramped his style. He was always complaining that having to babysit me was keeping him from sports and girls. Stuff like that."

"Did your brother ever abuse you in any way?"

The question caught Angie completely off guard.

"No, of course not. He's my brother. He loves me."

"I see. Do you see him often?"

"No, he still lives on the east coast. New York. He's working on a Ph.D. at NYU. In English literature. He's going to teach at the college level."

"When did you last see him?"

"When I left for Montana. Almost two years ago. We talk once in a while. It's. . . awkward."

"Awkward? Why?"

"Oh, you know. We lead different lives. We have totally different lifestyles."

"I see. Are you certain there isn't something you want to tell me? Something about your relationship with your brother?"

"Of course I'm sure. He's just my brother."

"Angie, your history has some of the classic red flags of an abusive sibling relationship. Your brother is five years older. He was an adolescent. The two of you were often together alone. You were vulnerable. It happens. And it might explain a lot about your life. The guilt trips, the attraction to older men, the counterculture lifestyle. Maybe even the scars on your wrist that you try to hide under that fancy tattoo."

"I. . . got those scars from falling into a pile of fluorescent light tubes in a dark warehouse near where we lived in New

York. Dr. Alton, my brother never touched me. Can we talk about something else?"

"Certainly. I'm sorry if I've upset you. Your background has some red flags. I had to ask."

"Well, nothing happened. So let's talk about something else."

"I'm glad. Why don't we just stop for the day, and we'll visit again tomorrow?"

"Good idea. There's nothing else to talk about on this subject."

***

At the beginning of Angie's jail term, Cooper visited almost every day. He brought her flowers and small gifts: magazines, her favorite gourmet licorice, and some extraordinary photographs of a herd of elk in a high valley in the Yaak. On the back of the picture, he wrote: "We'll ski here this winter." Angie taped the black and white photo on the wall behind her cot.

As the days passed, Cooper began cutting down his visits to only the afternoons of the two nights a week that he was teaching at the community college. He would drive in from the ranch, visit the county facility until the early evening, and then head for the college where he would meet Gun-Marie and Zoey for coffee before class.

When Angie asked about his decreased visits, Cooper explained that he had to winterize the place in the fall, and it was difficult to get away. He assured her that she was always in his thoughts and that he was already researching photography expeditions for the two of them as he scouted field trip sites for his class.

"We need to head into the mountains as soon as this is over, honey. I've found some places that are so beautiful they'll take your breath away. You'll forget you ever stayed in this hellhole."

"It's not that bad. Everyone here has been really nice to me. I'm feeling better about myself every day."

"What do you mean? Do you actually think this crap is justified? These people are brainwashing you. It's just one more example of how much the system sucks."

"You're wrong, Coop. I'm going to be a better person when I leave."

"You're crazy. You shouldn't even be near this place. This whole thing is bogus."

"It's not. Everything is going to be okay."

She didn't mention the long sessions with Dr. Alton, nor the profound impact those meetings were having on her mental health and her plans for the future.

***

Halfway through her jail sentence, Sheriff Thompson paid her a visit.

Angelina had just concluded a session with Dr. Alton when the sheriff came to Angie's cell.

"Can I talk with you for a moment, Ms. Hailstone?"

Angie nodded her assent, and Hayes signaled the jailer to open the cell door and led her to the interrogation room, where they could talk in private.

"I hear good things about you, Angie."

Angie shrugged, waiting to see what the lawman had in mind.

"You know," he continued, "being a sheriff is not all it's cracked up to be. Sometimes we have to deal with unpleasant situations when the law dictates our actions.

"I just want you to know that this entire case has been an ordeal. I hope you understand that my stance was not personal. People think that I was unhappy with your plea bargain. I wasn't. At least,

I'm not now. My job is to protect people. I try to do that to the best of my ability."

"I know."

"You know? That must be difficult for you to say." He went on, "Angie, we didn't find any evidence of foul play after you admitted your involvement. You should know that your honest acceptance of accountability is most unusual in my business. I respect the fact that you have accepted your punishment with grace and dignity. I just wanted you to know that you should be able to look in a mirror and see someone who has done the right thing. You are an unusual woman. And Clay Cooper is a lucky man."

Angie gave the sheriff a rueful smile.

"Thank you for your thoughtfulness, Sheriff. I appreciate it. But I'm not so sure that Clayton Cooper considers himself a lucky man."

CHAPTER

44

It was Tuesday afternoon, and Cooper was running late for his regular visit to the Flathead Correction Center.

"Clayton. You're late."

"I know. Sorry about that. I had some trouble with the pump system. I couldn't get out on time. I think I fixed it though. What's up, baby? Everything going okay?"

"Not too bad," she paused, "I'm getting a little claustrophobic is all. I had no idea that forty-five days could be so long."

"You're almost there. In another ten we'll be in the mountains somewhere, sleeping in a snow cave. Unless my girls are here. I'm trying to get the court to make Kelsey grant me my original custody rights. So far, she still won't let them come after. . . after the 'accident.' If she won't let them come, I might have to go back to Oregon."

Angie looked at him but said nothing.

"What? This isn't something I have any control over. These are my children we're talking about. Don't lay a guilt trip on me for wanting to see my kids."

"I don't do guilt trips, Cooper. So don't lay one on me for looking at you the wrong way."

"Hey, let's not fight okay? I'm glad to see you, sweetheart. Where should we go when you get out of here?"

"Somewhere. Anywhere. The mountains. The ocean. I don't care, just someplace without walls. Someplace open and free. Can you imagine what it must be like for people who spend their lives in prison? I couldn't do it. This has been easy for me. But under different circumstances, it would be a nightmare."

"I know," Cooper said. "I've thought about that myself. A lot. I agree with you. For people like us, any length of imprisonment would be unbearable. Thank God you'll be out soon. We'll go. . . somewhere."

"Will we? I wonder."

"We will," he looked at his cell phone. "Listen, I'm sorry, but I've got to run. I need to do some prep work for tonight's class and that damn water system threw me way off schedule. I promise I'll stay the whole time on Thursday, okay? You'll be two days closer to D-Day."

***

The girls were waiting for Cooper at the Ajax Cafe, a funky little eatery in downtown Kalispell where Zoey was now a part-time waitress. They were seated in a booth at the back of the room.

Cooper had finger-combed his hair on the way over and changed his shirt after he parked the truck. He pushed his glasses up on his head before he sauntered into the restaurant with a large manila envelope tucked under his arm.

Both girls wore designer jeans and tops with scooped necklines. Cooper thought they looked more like twenty-somethings than seniors in high school.

Gun-Marie Erickson's white-blonde hair and light blue eyes were accented by the glow of her perfect complexion. Her body was lean and sinewy, with small breasts and a hard, flat stomach. Had she been three inches taller, she could have been a runway fashion model.

Zoey, on the other hand, had a more wholesome persona. She was an inch shorter than her friend, and she wore her dark hair in a cropped style that was as thick as the fur on one of Laura

Ballantine's Karelian Bear Dog puppies. Her body was softer than Gun-Marie's, and she worked hard to keep her weight under control. Cooper suspected that she envied her friend's waif-like body.

Today was the day that he had promised to show them his photos from their field trips. Cooper spread the black and white photos across the top of the table. Most of the pictures were landscape photos of the spectacular Rocky Mountain scenery, Cooper's attempt to emulate Ansel Adams. He saved the small portrait portfolio of the two girls for last and teased them by unveiling it with deliberate slowness. The girls were anxious to see what they looked like and examined the photos carefully, less interested in artistic interpretation than in critiquing their own poses.

"Coop, you know this is my bad side," Gun-Marie complained about a profile shot that Cooper thought was one of the more artistic photos.

"Are you kidding? If that's your bad side, you better contact a modeling agency."

"You know I'm too short," Gun-Marie said. "They only want tall, skinny girls with big boobs."

"Well, you're halfway there. Just get a little taller."

The girls giggled.

"Here's my favorite shot."

He pulled the last photo from the manila envelope. It was a picture taken in Glacier National Park of Zoey resting on a rocky shelf-like ledge, cantilevered over a bottomless valley vista. Cooper had taken the candid shot with a long telephoto lens. Zoey's knees were tucked under her chin, and she was dreamily lost in the grandeur of the scenery, silhouetted in front of a snowy Glacier peak. A single beam of sunshine shone on her like a spotlight. The long lens had tightened the image, and the mountain appeared to be towering behind her, the perfect background for the rock ledge and the girl perched like a seated snow angel on top of it.

Both girls studied the picture in silence. The sunbeam made it a once in a lifetime shot, and Cooper knew it was only by sheer chance that he had taken it. Gun-Marie begrudgingly sniffed in acknowledgment of its uniqueness, jealous that Cooper had captured her friend's image for the portfolio's signature piece. Zoey was stunned. Cooper had chosen her photo as his favorite. Hers. It was the first time anyone had made that choice.

They helped him gather up the pictures, returning them to the portfolio. Cooper joked about making them famous if he could publish some of the photos. They complimented his work and predicted that the series would be well received.

"Will you show them to the rest of the class tonight?"

"No," Cooper answered. "In fact, I'd appreciate it if you didn't mention the portrait series to anyone. Some of the older students might not understand."

The girls were surprised and disappointed.

"Just be patient, ladies, until we see what happens," he paused. "I don't want anyone to misinterpret what we're doing here, okay? Someday I might put your pictures in a book. We'll see."

After class that evening, Cooper begged off from their usual meeting. He was tired and had a long drive home. He hugged both girls at the door to the classroom, promising to make it up to them on Thursday.

CHAPTER

Angelina finished her jail time late in October. As she waited for Cooper to pick her up on the Saturday morning of her release, she reflected on what a surreal experience it had been.

Dr. Alton had coaxed the story of her childhood from her, and she was now working on a recovery program that the doctor had prepared. Her acceptance of her past and its consequences were key to understanding herself in a way that she had never dreamed possible. Dr. Alton's treatment was designed to help her begin a healing process that focused on releasing the deep-seated guilt associated with her suppressed sibling trauma.

Even the burdens connected with Shawnee's death were beginning to slowly ebb. Her stay at the correction facility, coupled with the attendant therapy treatment, had soothed her conscience and begun to ease her pain. Dr. Alton's tenacity had paid off in many ways, and Angie was grateful for the doctor's role in her redemption and the effort she had made to initiate the healing process.

***

When Cooper arrived, Angie was sitting in a chair across from the front desk, chatting with the officer on duty. When she saw him, she hurried into his arms, and he held her in a gentle hug.

"Hey, baby. Let's go home."

"Yes. Let's do."

Cooper grabbed the small bag containing Angie's personal effects and, taking her arm above the elbow, guided her out of the door of the sheriff's department.

"Thank God that's over," he said as they approached the truck parked across the street. "What a pit."

Angie knew that Cooper would never understand the impact that her brief imprisonment would have on her life. *Odd,* she thought, *that it's almost like he was the one in jail, not me.* She knew she was feeling too emotional to talk about it now, and she knew it would only start an argument. So as they drove to her apartment, they chatted about the weather and how they would celebrate her freedom. It was almost winter, and northern Montana was still awaiting the onslaught of snow that had yet to arrive. There was only a skiff of snow in the area, and the ski resort was beginning to get nervous as the holiday season approached without a decent snow pack.

Angie was not concerned about the weather. She only wanted some time alone in her apartment, time to think and adjust to the real world before she got on with her life.

Cooper made a half-hearted suggestion to celebrate her release in bed.

"I can't, Coop. Not yet. I'm not ready. My mind is still reeling."

"I understand, honey. We'll save it for a better time. You just get some rest."

He hurried to get her situated and comfortable, and she teased him about his efforts.

"Jeez, Cooper, you'd think I was coming back from the hospital or something. I don't remember you ever working this hard to get me into bed. Especially without you."

"I know, baby. You look tired. I'm just watching out for you; that's all."

"Uh huh. How sweet."

"No, really. I understand. You just finished a traumatic experience. It's got to be emotionally draining. Let's fix the sofa with a pillow and blanket, and you can rest in here."

He moved toward the window to shut the blinds.

"Can you leave the blinds open, please? I need to see some open spaces. I can rest in the daylight."

"Sure. What can I get you? Something to drink? A magazine? Anything?"

"No. Thank you," she took a deep breath. "I'm fine. I want to just think and do a little writing. I'll be fine. Why don't you go back to the Yaak and do a hike without me? It'll be good for both of us."

"Are you sure? I was planning on spending the day with you."

"I'm sure. Just call me tonight."

"Okay. But this is your idea. I was planning on being with you."

He pecked her on the cheek and headed for the door.

"Love you, baby. I'll call you tonight."

***

Cooper didn't go home immediately. He went to the Ajax Cafe where Zoey was working the weekend brunch shift. She smiled when he came in the door, laying a hand on his shoulder as she filled his coffee cup.

Cooper visited with her about photography projects and equipment. He looked into her eyes and teased her about ways to elicit more tips from the tourists and soon-to-arrive skiers who frequented the restaurant, suggesting a mini-skirt and a see-through top. Zoey blushed dark pink and told him she'd have to check with the restaurant's management.

"I just might do it though, if you think it would work," she said.

"Oh, it would work. You probably need to pass inspection first though," he smiled. "Just kidding, Zo. You don't need to do anything to get more tips."

"I don't know. You might be right."

***

Cooper was halfway back to the Yaak when he saw the rotating lights of a patrol car in his rearview mirror. He checked his speedometer and pulled over to the side of the road.

He waited in the truck and watched in his rearview mirror as the uniformed officer approached. Opening the window, he was surprised to find himself staring into the familiar face of Hayes Thompson.

"Hey, Sheriff. Was I doing something wrong?"

"No, Mr. Cooper. I recognized your truck and thought we might have a little chat. I expected that you'd be with Ms. Hailstone today. Guess not, huh?"

"No. You pulled me over to talk about Angie?"

"Not just about Angie, Mr. Cooper."

The sheriff paused, then said, "This may not be the proper place to have this conversation, but it seems like it might be the right time. . . you know, with Ms. Hailstone being released today and all.

"Let me get right to the point. I just wanted to let you know that I hope nobody else gets hurt around here. I don't want any other accidents or self-defense situations to deal with. Do you understand what I'm saying?"

"Do you mean that you think people got hurt because of me? That's not fair."

"Maybe. Maybe not. Two people are dead, not hurt. I'm saying two deaths are enough. Angie is a nice girl. I wouldn't want anything to happen to her. Or to anyone else. I just thought someone should make that perfectly clear to you, Mr. Cooper. Is it clear?"

"It's clearly police harassment. This is unbelievable. I'm going to report it to the authorities as soon as I get home. You can't treat me like this."

"Oh, but I can. We're just visiting here. You're in Montana, Cooper. My part of Montana. Your credibility is somewhat suspect right at the moment. Mine is not. You probably should take this visit in the spirit it's meant."

Cooper shook his head.

"Are we through here? I understand what you're saying. I think it's way out of line that you said it, but I'm learning how you rednecks think."

"That's good, Mr. Cooper. As long as you're learning, I'll assume you understand."

He touched the bill of his hat. "Have a nice day."

***

When Cooper got home, he opened a beer and settled in on the deck, reveling in the beauty of his cherished valley. The black waters of the river were growing cooler by the day. Each morning, fracture lines of thin ice appeared at the river's edge. Despite the decreased autumn water volume, the river continued its timeless flow past the old saloon, and Cooper was still mesmerized by its journey.

The conversation with Sheriff Thompson had shaken Cooper. Reflecting on what the sheriff said, he realized that aside from his two daughters, he'd had very few relationships with women that had not ended in some degree of disaster.

The sheriff's warning alarmed him, and he knew that the two deaths had taken an emotional toll. He loved the Yaak more than anything, but his intimate connection to the dark wilderness had begun to haunt him. The image of Wing Redmond carrying Shawnee's lifeless body from the river was forever etched in his mind. He could not look across the water to the salt block without reliving the gruesome slaughter that foreshadowed the kidnapping and the subsequent killing of Duffy Grayson.

He decided that he would call Uncle Stanley and tell him that he was going to return to his family in Skyler. Even if Kelsey rejected his efforts to resurrect their marriage, and he knew that she might, he would still be closer to his daughters and his old friends. Duffy Grayson was dead. Hayes Thompson would be out of his life, and by severing that cord, the fear of being pursued by the system would be eliminated. The unspeakable horrors overshadowing his love of the valley would gradually fade away.

In addition, leaving would provide a convenient way to end his deteriorating relationship with Angelina Hailstone.

He knew he would have to stay until he completed his obligation with the college, which meant that he would be in Montana until at least the end of the semester. The timeframe would allow him to deal with some personal issues before he left.

He opened another beer and watched the afternoon light fade to dusk while he sat on the porch and gathered his thoughts. When he went back inside, he placed two phone calls.

The first call was to Angelina. When there was no answer, he left a short message.

The second call was to Zoey Belford.

***

When Angie woke, it was dark in the apartment. It took her a moment to remember where she was. The red glow of the numbers on the clock across the room read 10:14. She was astonished that she slept for so long, and as she lay on the couch, she began to realize that the emotional impact of her stay in the county jail had been even greater than she thought. She was still exhausted.

Her eyes adjusted to the darkness and began filling with tears as she looked around the cozy apartment, savoring the joy of homecoming while whispering a prayer of gratitude. She was thankful for the comfort of her home, the gift of a cleansed spirit, and the opportunity to appreciate all the small things in life that she had once taken for granted.

In the morning, she thought, *I will begin my new life.*

I am going to move home and try to reassemble the pieces of my broken family. I will forgive my mother and my brother. Together, maybe we can become a real family again. I will erase my past. All of my past. No more guilt. No more fear.

No more Clayton Kennedy Cooper.

* * *

Zoey was waiting in their usual booth at the Ajax Cafe. She was wearing a white tee-shirt that accentuated the reddish brown of her fading summer tan and loose drawstring pants that rode low on her hips.

She greeted Cooper with a nervous grin.

"Hey," she said, "Whazzup?"

"Hey, Zo. Thanks for coming. I wasn't sure you'd be around on a Saturday night."

"No problem. I wanted to. You sounded so mysterious."

"Yeah, I know. I just. . . wanted to see you. I'm dealing with some issues right now, and I need a shoulder to cry on."

Zoey could hardly believe what he was saying. Her heart had jumped when he told her that he wanted to see her.

"You know you can cry on my shoulder, Coop. I mean, what are friends for?"

"Thanks, honey. I knew you'd understand."

The word "honey" coursed through her body like an electric shock.

"I do understand," she said.

"Can we go for a ride or something? Somewhere where we can talk privately? It looks like the restaurant's getting busy."

"Sure. Do you want to drive up to The Burn? Sometimes we go up there to drink beer. There's never anyone there this time of the year."

"Is there someplace there where no one would see us? I don't want anyone to get the wrong idea if they see us together."

"Oh, yeah. There are lots of clear-cut pull-offs and logging roads."

"It's not snowed in yet?"

"It wasn't last night. Gunny and I drank some wine up there. It's right above town. There's just a skiff of snow."

"Are you okay with that? I mean, we could just drive around town, I guess."

"No, I'm great with that. It's a great place to talk and stuff."

Cooper answered, "That's perfect. Can we take your car?"

They left in her father's Volvo and drove out of town toward Blue Grouse Mountain. Cooper kept the conversation light on the drive, rattling on about his photography class and the various older students that he and the two girls often made the butt of their jokes.

The Burn was just outside the city limits, near an old homesteader's family cemetery on the mini-mountain closest to the city. Zoey drove up the main access road and then pointed out one of the spur roads that networked the mountain, the result of thirty-year-old logging operations. There was no snow. It was dark and quiet when she parked the car on a pull-off that looked over the city and its galaxy of manmade light. The stars of Montana's Big Sky were above them, and the city sparkled just below.

They sat without speaking, looking at the view, each thinking their own thoughts.

"Well. I want you to know how much I appreciate your kindness, Zo. I'm going through some tough times right now, and I really need someone I can talk to. I love having you for a friend."

"Hey, I'm here for you. What's up?"

Cooper sighed and rubbed his eyes and forehead.

"It's the kidnapping situation again. It just never goes away."

Zoey was confused. Like so many Montanans, she admired Cooper's heroics and considered his actions not only brave but exceedingly noble.

"What do you mean? Are you struggling with the mental part? I know you've told us how hard that's been for you."

"Yeah, I am. But there's more to it than that."

He leaned closer to her on the seat and looked into her eyes.

"For some reason, they're out to get me. The sheriff pulled me over today and threatened me. I think I'm going to have to move away. I don't trust him, and I don't trust the system."

He took a deep breath. "I haven't told you guys about it, but I got screwed by the school district I worked for before I came to Montana."

"What do you mean? How?"

"False accusations, administrative jealousies, things like that. That's why I decided to leave Oregon."

"That's bullshit. How could they do that?"

"I don't know, but they did." They were both quiet, thinking about Cooper's revelation.

Finally, he looked into her eyes again and gently took her hand in his own, pulling her into his arms. He nuzzled her neck and inhaled the fresh scent of her skin. As his lips moved up to her ear, he whispered, "I need you, Zo. You know I love you, don't you?"

THE END

Rob Sorensen is a longtime bibliophile and collector of modern first edition books. He is passionate about a good story and the background required to achieve it. Having lived in Washington, Idaho, and Montana, Sorensen has a keen sense of place, and he appreciates nature's beauty and the inspiration it provides. He has worked as a businessman, a newspaper journalist, and the director of Entrepreneurial Development at Peninsula College in Port Angeles, Washington. He is currently writing full time.

CPSIA information can be obtained
at www.ICGtesting.com
Printed in the USA
BVHW041109091221
623625BV00011B/158/J